Andrew Holmes's first novel *Sleb* was published in 2002 to critical acclaim and was shortlisted for the WHSmith New Talent Award. His second, *All Fur Coat*, followed to equal acclaim in 2004. He also works as a freelance journalist and lives near London with his wife and son.

'Holmes manages to perfectly capture the wider world and private despair which binds the characters together, as well as providing more darkly comic moments than the reader has any right to expect.'
Irish Independent

'Holmes builds an effortlessly exciting story, with characters who will take up long-term lodgings in the reader's imagination.'
Morning Star

'A black comedy worthy of Elmore Leonard, with spot-on dialogue . . . Holmes puts the pieces together in a satisfying, intensely readable story that will have readers biting their fingernails'
Toronto Sun

'Holmes has a cheeky, sarcastic and distinctive prose style . . . There are times, reading *64 Clarke*, when you think "if Martin Amis was less concerned with style and more interested in fashioning a story – like he was circa *London Fields* – he would write like this" . . . *64 Clarke* is a corker.'
Bookmunch

'A cross between Ian McEwan's *A Child in Time* and Elmore Leonard. It takes every parent's biggest nightmare as a starting point and uses it for a thriller that will terrify and delight in equal measure.'
Matt Thorne

ALSO BY ANDREW HOLMES

Sleb

All Fur Coat

ANDREW HOLMES

64 Clarke

F/ 2033507

SCEPTRE

First published in Great Britain in 2005 by Hodder and Stoughton
A division of Hodder Headline

A Sceptre Paperback

1

A CIP catalogue record for this title is available from the British Library

ISBN 0 340 83299 1

Typest in Sabon by
Palimpsest Book Production Limited, Polmont, Stirlingshire

Printed and bound by
Mackays of Chatham Ltd, Chatham, Kent

Hodder and Stoughton Ltd
A division of Hodder Headline
338 Euston Road
London NW1 3BH

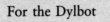
For the Dylbot

Ben Snape was separated from his father on the platform of Finsbury Park tube station on the afternoon of Saturday, 22 February. That was the day Little Ben disappeared.

Ben, six years old; Patrick, his father, thirty-six. They were on a day trip to London, where they visited the Arsenal club shop adjacent to Finsbury Park tube, and were then planning to attend the match at Highbury. The Gunners were due to play Spurs in what was set to be a hotly contested local derby – always is. They still played the game, even though Ben was missing. Arsenal won 3–2.

Ben was wearing blue jeans, a navy blue Puffa-style anorak and a newly purchased red woollen hat bearing the logo of Arsenal Football Club. He wore black woollen gloves and was carrying a Panini-type football sticker album.

His last known movements were captured by CCTV cameras in jumpy footage that has since burned itself into the public memory, the way stop-start images do – because the moment, the truth, stutters.

Ben and his father were first recorded by a CCTV camera on the main concourse at Finsbury Park station, the ticket-machine area. One of six covering the concourse, two of which were inoperative on the day, the camera picked up Ben and Patrick at two-second intervals as they entered the station, pausing at a ticket machine then making their way to the main tunnel. With their backs to the camera they walked hand in hand, appearing relaxed and happy, looking forward to the game. As it was close to kick-off, the concourse was busy with Arsenal fans, all reds and whites, all stop-starting their way towards the tunnel.

Ben and Patrick were next seen by one of the two cameras in the main tunnel, walking towards, and then beneath it. As before they seemed happy and at ease. Ben – Little Ben – appeared to be showing his father something in that Panini-type football sticker album.

His father glanced at his watch. He was fretting a bit about the time now, factoring in a pit-stop for Ben to go to the toilet, as well as a burger for the two of them, perhaps share one, no point in spoiling his appetite. The burger might have to wait until half-time if they didn't get a move on, he thought, watch-glancing again, and in that case *definitely* half each or Ben wouldn't want his tea.

A second camera, facing in the opposite direction to the first, showed their backs as they walked the final length of the tunnel, in more of a hurry here, turning to descend the steps to the Piccadilly line for the one-stop journey to Arsenal tube station, formerly known as Gillespie Road.

Now cut to the first camera again, the one on the main concourse. This showed a group of ten youths entering the station. They had recently left the Twelve Pins pub across the road, having been drinking since midday, and were in high spirits. They stop-started their way quickly into the tunnel. Also mindful of the kick-off time, they were hurrying, factoring in their own pit-stop: toilet – they'd be bursting by the time they reached the ground – plus a final round of beers before the game began. (You can buy them in the stadium, but beer may not be taken to the seats and is only available before the game, not during or afterwards.) The ten youths, dressed mainly in Arsenal replica football shirts and baseball caps, swiftly made their way past the tunnel cameras. Several had their arms held out like aeroplane wings; their mouths were all wide open, chanting something that resonated in the tunnel, as if there were hundreds of them, not just ten.

Cut to the platform. Here there were numerous cameras, but only two with the relevant field of vision, one of which was inoperative. The other picked up Ben and Patrick as they made their way on to the platform, which was already half full, and particularly congested around the entrance area.

Ben was maybe more nervous here, the crowds thicker. Bustled by the legs of unmindful, eager supporters he squeezed his father's hand. Patrick felt the little gloved hand tighten in his and squeezed it back. Not to worry, said his squeeze, just stay with me, we'll be okay.

Still holding hands they could be seen making their way to a less crowded part of the platform. Patrick glanced at his watch, wanting to get Ben free of the pillocks who stood in the entrance like zombies. It took some doing, a bit of strategic shoving here and there, but at last they stopped at a point that was marginally less congested, with room enough to breathe at least. Here they were closer to the camera, and appeared slightly to the left at the bottom of the picture. 'Train Approaching,' said the platform indicator, and Patrick edged them forward, ready to board the oncoming train.

Beside them was a group of four girls, aged between fifteen and seventeen. Little Ben stared up at them; they were all in hysterics at something one of them had said. What it was, she'd got NASA confused with Ikea, and it had cracked them all up. She was always getting things wrong – thought they put real dogs in hot dogs; thought Cary Grant was a woman. That kind of thing.

Ben stared and they saw and made a fuss of him for a moment or so. Them doing that made Ben feel nice in a way he didn't quite understand. Them doing that made Patrick feel nice in a way he understood perfectly – whoever had decreed pride was a sin had never felt like Patrick in that moment.

Now the same camera showed the ten high-spirited youths entering the platform at the top of the picture, arriving at a speed that seemed to startle those gathered at the entrance. The youths began jostling their way further down the platform, towards where Ben and Patrick stood, the train now pulling into the station. Patrick appeared to be bending down, speaking to Ben.

'We'll have to push our way on to this one I think,' he said, 'so as soon as the doors open, be quick, but don't let go of my hand.'

Now the high-spirited youths were close to the pair, their progress arrested by the sight of the four girls, with whom they began a little good-natured banter ('Tits. Out,' that kind of thing), simultaneously pushing forward to reach the doors of the train as it arrived. The train pulled in and the waiting fans – perhaps four deep from the platform's edge – shifted in the direction of the doors, the crowd seeming to tighten, as if tensing.

The doors opened, each with a closing fist of supporters around it, jostling and straining forward. From inside, passengers wanting to disembark shouldered their way out as fans began pouring on to the train. 'Please move right down the carriages,' said the station announcer. 'Make use of all available space.'

Now it can be seen that a minor altercation appears to have occurred between Patrick Snape and one of the youths. Angry at being shoved, and seeing Ben's little body disappear momentarily into a forest of legs, Patrick turned to admonish a youth. A fit man, a member of a Sunday football team and a regular visitor to the gym, he was not to be intimidated by youths in baseball caps. 'Hey. Watch it,' is what he commanded.

'Oh, fack off,' was the reply.

And maybe the person who decreed the old sin-pride thing had been right after all, because Patrick failed to register his son tugging on his arm, his son not mindful of the kick-off and toilet breaks, but of the open doors and his father saying, 'We'll have to push our way on to this one. Be quick,' and of that only. Patrick, outraged at having been told to fack off by a youth half his age (not quite, of course, the youth was nineteen), was not to be left wanting the last word.

'Just stop pushing and mind your language,' he warned, and used what crowded physicality he could to turn slightly and straighten, seeming to rise above the supporters flowing thickly into the train. No sign of Ben in the picture, obscured by bodies pressing towards the doors.

'All right, all right,' conceded the youth, his arms up the way players do when disowning a foul. He turned to shuffle off behind his mates at another door, elbowing himself aboard, the doors closing, then opening again, the last people squeezing on, the doors closing again, and Patrick frowning because they'd have to wait for the next one now, and Patrick slowly becoming aware that he was no longer holding his son's hand.

Because the CCTV footage had shown – just – Ben move away from his father: a tiny blur. A movement that, when it was magnified, was little more than one newsprint-coloured cloud passing another. But it was Ben, and when the movement was ringed for television transmission you could just see him stepping on to the train. And experts scrutinised the tape for any sign of coercion, wanting and not wanting to see the blurred white of an indistinct hand on his navy Puffa-style anorak, but there was none. It appeared that Ben, excited Little Ben, had let go of his father's hand and boarded the train of his own volition, turning, 'Dad. Quick!' watching through the bodies as Dad ended his remonstrations with the youth and looked about, searching for his son but not seeing him; the train doors closing on Ben even as his father's head swung one way then the other, the stop-start camera catching not the points in between but the hard left and right of his head, his expression barely visible but somehow horrifyingly clear: where is Ben?

Part One

SPEAKERS' CORNER

1

Max wasn't old. He was thirty-eight, which, unless you're twelve or a Premiership footballer, isn't old at all. All the same he felt old. He felt like a thirty-eight that had been taken round the back and beaten up by two twenty-sevens. Felt tired, too, exhausted in fact, the wind chafing cheeks vacuum-packed around the butt of a cigarette, trying to draw the cancer from the stick. He smoked as though cigarettes were no longer benign, smouldering commas in the day – instead they were morbid little suicide attempts; a half-arsed shuffle to the edge at Beachy Head, craning over and deciding maybe not today, tomorrow instead.

In his pocket was a letter questioning his value to the world, and he thought the answer wouldn't be worth the paper it was printed on. In his other pocket was a knife, Stanley knife. And he could run that knife across a vein somewhere, open it and watch the courage of his convictions paint the wall.

He passed a kid who was busy emptying the contents of his pockets on to the pavement. A fat kid, his fleshy, stupid forehead creased as though the act of littering was costing him much in the way of mental beans. Max supposed he could or should say something but chose not to because the kid would probably tell him to fuck off. And that was if he didn't have a knife, or a gang of mates who would find out where Max lived and start a brand-new hobby called Make That Guy's Life a Misery. So he said nothing, just walked on past as tube tickets, chewing-gum wrappers, and an empty B&H packet showered to the pavement around his feet.

At Manor House he boarded a tube train and mentally finished a game of noughts and crosses that someone – two people, probably – had scored on to the shell of the carriage. Noughts had it, even allowing for the difficulty of scoring a circle into whatever material the carriage was made of: fibreglass, something like that. Across from him a girl with the most beautiful skin he had ever seen until the next time he saw a girl with beautiful skin sat engrossed in her personal stereo. If she'd been less beautiful Max would have minded the *tish-ptsh* sound her leaky headphones made. But she was beautiful, so he didn't, and knew it and felt guilty but also, for a moment, marginally less old and less threadbare and less like taking the next step over his own personal Beachy Head. She smiled, but not at him, at something she read above his head.

The next stop was his, and when he stood and turned to see what had made her smile he expected it to be a poem or a quote selling a book, something like that – profound and beautiful, the kind of thing that would make a perfect-skin girl smile. But it wasn't. It was sexual innuendo selling lager. So his heart was flecked with disappointment as he stepped on to the platform at Wood Green, and he felt like an old man again. Don't know why they call it Wood Green, he thought, going up to ground level. Nothing green about it. He reached into his pockets for his cigarettes and set off in the direction of his sister's house.

'Oh. Max.'

Verity's hands were frozen mid-wipe across her pinny (white, clean, embroidered with the *Good Housekeeping* logo). She stood looking blankly at him, as though she was trying to compute. 'You're . . . early,' she said at last. Testy.

'Sorry, Ver.'

She looked exasperated. 'But . . . why? I mean, I don't want to be rude, but I'm not sure where I can put you until dinner. I mean, it's not that I don't want to . . .' She clawed for the right thing to say and Max stood watching her, his hands thrust into the pockets of his overcoat. In there he could feel the Stanley knife, a packet of cigarettes, his lighter, the keys to his flat, the letter. He stood and watched while she failed to find the right words to convey how unorthodox this was, him turning up some three hours ahead of the agreed time.

'I'm sorry, Ver. Can I come in?'

'You could have called . . .' she was saying and, yes, why hadn't he phoned? He stepped into his sister's house and was immediately aware of the shift in the weather gauge he brought with him. His coat smelt of old dogs who smoked; his shoes had seen better days; his jeans were the black kind that men his age wore – the sort that weren't supposed to show the dirt.

She held the door like he'd come to deliver coal and he wandered through the hall and into the kitchen, pulling a wooden chair across the flagstones and sitting down.

Verity came into the room and stood looking down at him. His eyes were tired, she saw – dark circles and bags beyond the reach of any teabag or cucumber slice. She reached for his head and leant to kiss his forehead. Feeling his face adjust as though seeking the warmth, she brought his head to her pinny and clasped it there for a moment.

'Max,' she said, releasing him. He came away and settled back into the chair. He wiped an eye. 'Max, why are you so early?'

'I'm . . . It's . . . I'm sorry, but I can't make it for dinner later,' he replied, looking away. 'I've got to work tonight. I'm sorry.'

She made some noises that might have been the advance party of a sentence before settling on, 'I don't believe it. Now, come on, I don't believe it. What work? What are you talking about?'

'It's valuation work. It came up really quickly.' He ran a hand through his hair.

'But . . .' Her eyes looked the kitchen over, all that pre-dinner stuff – hearty, earthenware bowls sprouting wooden spoons; an orderly row of spice jars; recipe book on a heavy iron stand. 'What sort of valuation work? You haven't done anything like that for months. And what sort of valuation work do you do *at night*? I've gone to all this effort—' Her voice was rising.

'It's a house clearance,' he interrupted. 'Rush job on Green Lanes. They need prices on a whole bunch of stuff. Someone else couldn't do it at short notice so they called me.' As he spoke her mouth tightened. 'It could be good for me, Ver,' he insisted.

'Green Lanes?'

'Yes.'

'But . . . I've gone to all this effort. I can't—' She seemed to soften. 'Why didn't you call, for God's sake?'

'I wanted to see you anyway.'

'Well, fine, sure, yes, but why didn't you call me when you found out? I wouldn't have gone to all this—'

'I'm sorry, Ver.' He wasn't looking at her; he was looking at the oven, which glowed like home and hummed like it, too.

'It's not like I can just dish yours up now.'

'I'm sorry.'

'I'm not sure that sorry's good enough.'

A wave of guilt as he saw her woes and deliberately increased them. 'Ver, I've had another letter.'

She'd been standing hands on hips. Now she moved forward as if to hold Max again, but stopped herself. 'Oh, no,' she said. 'Really? From her?' Her being the girl's mother: Mrs Larkin's daughter.

'Unless anybody else has decided to join in. Like it's a chain hatemail thing.'

She ignored him. 'This time, you go to the police with it. Once, okay, a rush of silly, deluded anger, but twice . . .' No trace of the flustered Verity now. In its place a kind of middle-England kitchen anger, wiping its hands furiously on a tea-towel.

'No, Verity.' He shook his head sadly.

'I'm telling you— What did it say?'

'The same stuff.'

'Yes, but what exactly?'

'Look, I don't want to go into the gory details.'

'What have you done with it? You need to take it to the police.'

'Well, I can't. I've destroyed it.'

She let out a huff. 'No, Max – I'm sorry – you should go to the police. And you tell them you're being harassed by this woman, because that's what it is, it's out-and-out harassment.' Her cheeks had blossomed angry. 'Not only that.' She made an Italian-mamma-style gesture with her hands. 'But you're not even *guilty* of anything, for God's sake. It was her *bloody* daughter

12

making it all up, that *silly* little cow.' She put a hand to the worktop, shoulders dropping.

'She obviously thinks I did something.'

'Yes, because she's being fed a pack of lies. And you sitting there meekly taking the abuse no doubt makes her think she's dead right. And this is exactly why you've got to report it.'

She talked about it as though it was a playground disagreement, one where the mums had got involved and it had caused a bit of bad blood between the families. Nothing more serious than that. Not an accusation that had sent Max to jail – sent him to jail and worse. It's not just a nasty bout of the flu, he wanted to say. It's not a case of getting over it and moving on, as if there isn't a blackness squatting in my mind, pushing down, harder and harder each day. He shook off the thought. 'I don't want to go to the police,' he said at last. 'I can't.'

She turned to face him again. 'Why not?' Her eyes seemed to burn into his, even as he looked away, refusing to answer the question.

She pulled out a chair opposite him and sat down, leaning forward to look him in the eye. 'You're innocent, Max, and the reason you need to go to the police is because a guilty person wouldn't go. But you have to,' her eyes were soft and imploring, 'because you're innocent. You get that into your head. Because you know what you're doing at the moment? You're ruining your life because of some misguided notion of guilt. It's as stupid and selfish and self-destructive as anything Mum did. You're breaking yourself up over something you *didn't even do*.'

Suddenly the front door was banging open and closed, and Verity just had time to look denied as Roger bustled into the kitchen. 'I've forgotten the bloody quiz questions,' he was saying, dumping his briefcase on a worktop before clocking Max at the table. 'Oh.'

Max sat and smiled thinly at him. Roger stood and smiled thinly back.

'Hello, Max,' said Roger, voice stretched. 'Didn't bank on seeing you here. I thought we were expecting you later.' He looked accusingly at Verity for confirmation. She flicked her eyes at the ceiling in response. Like, Don't ask me.

'Well, who wants to be predictable?' replied Max, still smiling. 'Certainly not you.'

'Exactly. We can leave that sort of stuff up to you.'

Roger turned back to his wife. 'Well, predictably I've left the bloody quiz questions at home.' Then, to Max, 'Verity no doubt told you that I'm not around tonight. My turn to host the pop quiz. Clean forgot. Sorry.'

Max didn't blink. He felt Verity's eyes on him.

'Are you sure you can't make it later, Max?' she said softly. 'All this effort . . .'

'I'm sorry, Ver,' he said. 'I've got to do this work.'

'Work?' said Roger. 'Well, then, you must go. By the way, Verity tells me you've got problems with the upstairs neighbours. Being noisy, keeping you awake and stuff.'

'That's right.' Max hated saying it.

'It's always such a risk when you've got people above you, isn't it? Now where are those bloody questions?' and he left the room.

Verity remained where she was. Her eyes flicked to the doorway. Through a gap Max could see Roger standing there, beckoning her silently and furiously from the room. Her eyes went back to Max. 'Are you *sure*?' she said.

'Yes, I'm sure.'

Standing, frustrated, outside the kitchen Roger made a pathetic attempt at throwing his voice, as though he was supposed to be in another part of the house. 'Veri*tee*, I don't suppose you know where the questions are?' Max could see him clearly through the gap, turned away and with one hand cupped to his mouth. 'I don't suppose you could lend me a hand . . .' He let the last word tail off.

'You'd best go, Ver,' said Max, staring pointedly at the door.

Verity sighed. 'You haven't even had a cup of tea,' she said. 'Why don't you make yourself one while I go and help Roger?'

She left the room and Max looked again at the door where Roger no longer stood. He imagined the two of them in another room; him giving her the third degree. *What's the jailbird doing here?* Being reminded of how fortunate she was; how tolerant he'd been.

Max stood and went over to the kettle, which was silver and shiny and sat steaming gently on its base, not long boiled. There were mugs on hooks and he took one, took a teabag from glass jar with a cork top and poured, next a dollop of milk from the fridge. He cast around for a spoon, opened a drawer full of kitchen bumf and was about to close it again when something caught his eye. A plastic document folder. The kind of thing someone like Roger would use to keep his quiz questions in crisp condition. Headed 'Mariner Quiz Night' with the date. Max glanced towards the kitchen door, brought out the folder, swiftly rolled and stuffed it into his coat pocket.

There was a noise on the stairs. He shut the drawer and returned to his chair holding his tea, settled as Roger and Verity returned. Roger was saying theatrically, 'Of course, the kitchen drawer,' and yanked it open to discover the questions were no longer there – they'd been magicked away.

'Oh.' He turned to Verity. 'They're not here. Have you moved them?'

'No,' she said. She threw a look towards Max. Her eyes found the cup of tea at his fingertips. 'Are you sure that's where you left them?' she said.

'Well . . . after I remembered that's where they were, I must say I thought they were there for definite, yes.' He, too, threw a look at Max, who sat there like butter wouldn't melt.

'More questions about REM, were they, Roger?' said Max, who would never let Roger forget the time he'd thought REM stood for Rapid Ear Movement.

'No questions about REM tonight,' replied Roger, tightly. 'Right. Well, I'll have to print off another set then, won't I?' And he left again, running up the stairs towards his office where he would angrily switch on his computer and rabbit to himself, think dark thoughts about Max as he waited for it to boot up.

There was a time when a truce had existed between the two

men. Max never was Roger's sort, that was the truth of it. Roger was the settling-down-getting-married-and-buying-an-insurance-policy sort. Max wasn't. He was a man who ran his own business, but to Roger he was some kind of beatnik. When Max had given Verity away, her new husband had used his groom's speech to ask any eligible ladies in the house to make an honest man of Max. 'Take him off his sister's hands,' (affectionate look at Verity), 'I'm afraid she'll have them full looking after me,' (pause for laughter).

'Your father would have been very happy today,' their mother had said later that day, thickly. No, thought Max then. No, he wouldn't. He would have done his best, but no – he would have sat looking at Roger, thinking, Tosspot. Mother must have thought so herself; must have done. She hadn't drunk herself to death to avoid family gatherings with Roger but, hey, every cloud . . .

Even so, at some level Roger must have believed Max was a better class of feckless, irresponsible citizen, so made an effort. Likewise Max. These days, of course, just the skeleton of civility remained. Max knew there was only one reason he was tolerated in his sister's house – because he'd proved Roger right about him. 'Look what your brother got himself into. Your mother may have been on her last legs but something like that can't have helped.' And Max being around meant Roger could be proved right all the time. Max had become a stick he used to beat Verity. He was her shame.

'So, how is Roger?' asked Max, with what he hoped was the right amount of acidity.

'As you can see, he's fine,' answered Verity.

'Work all right?'

'Don't bother, Max. And don't try changing the subject either.' With Roger away she wanted to resume her talk – the letters. 'It's harassment, Max, that's what it is. And that's why you should report it. She's harassing you. Please.' She tried a different tack. 'Please just report her, don't let her get away with it. Because you know, don't you, that the longer it goes on – the longer you do nothing – the more vindicated she'll feel? She'll think she's right. And she's not, is she?'

'No.'

'So . . . then?'

'I'm not going to the police.'

She threw up her hands in frustration. 'Well, then you're punishing yourself for no reason. I can't help you, I'm afraid. You can live in your own private hell, if that's what you want. Don't expect me to join you. You just carry on beating yourself up.'

He got up. 'I'd better go,' he said. 'Should be there in plenty of time.'

'You can still stay for dinner,' she said.

'I've got to work. It's you who's always telling me I should get on with my life. *Pick yourself up. Get the furniture going again.* Well, that's what I'm trying to do.'

'As long as you are,' she said, but her lips were tight and disbelieving as she walked him to the door. They stood there for a moment or so, her looking searchingly into his eyes, both of them heartbroken.

'Good luck, then,' she said at last. 'On Blackstock Road.'

'Thanks,' he said, and the door was closing behind him before he remembered the house clearance was on Green Lanes.

2

'Being black is not the same as being orange, man. It's a whole different thing.' Warren stopped the van to say this. He was unplugging his seatbelt at the same time, deep creases etched into an angry forehead. 'You can't fucking compare it, man.'

'Hey, listen,' said Dash, quickly, because if he wasn't very much mistaken Warren was – yes, he was getting *out* of the van. 'I wasn't saying . . . What you doing? Warren?' He was sliding over the seats to call out now. Warren was on the pavement, taking off.

'Fuck this, man,' snapped Warren, over his shoulder. 'I'm out of this shit, I'm telling you.' He threw up his hands as if to shrug off this shit for ever. And then he was gone. Exit one angry driver.

Barely a day went by when Dash didn't regret hitting the kid who had Tourette's. All those years ago, in the playground, that time. With the TV cameras watching as well. No more so than now, watching Warren disappear, with his mouth wide as a Berwick Street market trader, feeling slightly, vaguely, confused. Because he certainly hadn't meant to be racist: he was just defending his girlfriend's honour, that was all.

'Warren!' he shouted uselessly, and realised that his hand was on the seat where Warren had been sitting, and the seat was still warm, so he took it away.

Dash could see through people, that was his special talent, and he knew Warren had been looking for a fight – for some kind of excuse to slam out of the van and away. He was just taking his temper out for air because he was the kind of person who thrived on malcontent. Nothing else was real. He could drive, though. He was very good at that. And even though Dash *could* drive (as in he had the licence and was perfectly capable of manoeuvring the van around north London) he needed a driver so he could concentrate on the sales side of things. The sales side of things needed a great deal of concentration.

Under pressure, Dash's hands inevitably reached for his hair. He had middle-parted, Madchester-length hair that should have neatly curtained his face, but when he was flustered it lost its parting and milled aimlessly around his forehead, like rookie soldiers on parade. He pulled it out of his eyes, knowing and dreading. Now he would have to call Chick.

He should never have hit the kid with Tourette's. That was when it all started to go wrong.

An hour later he walked into the Flat Cap on Stoke Newington high street, where Chick sat looking like scum, which was what he was.

When Dash arrived there was great hilarity at the bar. Besides Chick there were only two customers and they were old women, already drunk and apparently fascinated by the landlord, who you could tell was the landlord because of his Foreigner T-shirt. He was using a box-cutter in an unusual manner – to cut a box – and it was this that was somehow the cause of the Flat Cap's wretchedly cheery atmosphere.

Dash approached the table as Chick pointedly drained the last of a pint of stout and banged it down. He wore his usual base-ball cap, the peak savagely arched. Below it ballooned his big, pink, round face, like a condom full of piss. His bottom lip jutted as always, red and wet, and he wiped stout foam from his mouth and burped. 'Just in time,' he rasped, voice like a concrete mixer. 'I'll have another. Guinness, no fucking shamrock.'

Dash turned back to the bar as Chick reached for his mobile phone. The two old women looked at him as he approached: worn, cackling, coven-like women – their withered faces like skulls. They watched the landlord intently as he finished cutting open the box then began to write something on a blackboard: 'Why not . . .' it said. He stopped to serve Dash, who

19

emphasised the no-fucking-shamrock element of his order before returning with the two drinks: Guinness for Chick, cooking lager for him.

Chick was on the phone. A veteran of the Oxford Street perfume rackets, he habitually held his hand over his mouth when he spoke on the phone. It was what the street dealers did so the Met's lip-readers couldn't work out what they were saying. He held it there now, whispering harshly as Dash sat down, then finished up and tossed his mobile on to the table. 'All right, Dashus,' he said. 'Got any vouchers for me?'

Chick, wielding his power in mysterious ways, demanded that Dash collect supermarket vouchers for him to pass on to his son. Computers for schools, something like that.

Dash cursed inwardly but smiled a matey, loadsa-things-going-on smile. 'No,' he said. 'No, sorry.'

Chick's face darkened. 'Well, then,' he said, 'you'll have brought my money instead, won'cha?'

Dash smiled, a little more ruefully this time. 'Not quite, mate, no.'

Chick looked confused, as though he'd just been asked a difficult square root. 'What you mean "not quite"?' He was already reaching into his denim jacket for a pad containing details of how much Dash owed.

'I've got a bit of a problem, that's all,' said Dash.

Chick looked up. 'Problem? What sort of problem?'

The pub smelt of old blankets, antique smoke and something less human. As if to check for listeners, Dash looked behind him. 'It's Warren,' he said, swivelling back. 'He's got the hump and gone off. I need a new driver.' He spread his hands. 'I can't do it alone.'

Chick looked displeased. 'You're having a giraffe, aren't ya? I hooked you up with Warren, what more d'you want? I'm not a fuckin' job agency.'

'I know, mate, I just thought . . .' said Dash, thinking back to the Chick he had first met. A Chick who'd bought the drinks and offered him, if he needed a bit of ready cash, like, some regular work. Thanks to a sudden increase in the cost of living he did need some ready cash, like, so he'd accepted, and Uncle Chick had insisted he stick around for some more drinks so he had, until pretty soon there was a group of them, Chick and Chick's mates, most with fear or need in their eyes; the really scary ones – the inner circle – with scorn in theirs. Dash had stood there with his bollocks tingling. The danger, the thrill of being in a gang. Every time Chick slapped him on the back – and Chick slapped him on the back a lot – he felt more like he belonged. Stumbling forward, his hair flopping, pint spilling, but feeling pissed and protected and part of things.

Mrs Chick had arrived. Her hair was blonde, the colour of cornflakes, and dyed the middle-aged way with the roots showing. She chewed gum. Below hard eyes were shelves of flesh as though she had once been in a fight from which her face had never properly healed. To Dash she looked like she had returned battle-scarred and defeated from the love wars of her youth and he marvelled at her, at women like her. How at some point Mrs Chick had fancied Leonardo DiCaprio, or his contemporary, whoever he had been when she was growing up. She'd imagined herself as Kate Winslet on the prow of the boat, maybe Demi Moore at the potter's wheel in *Ghost*, or Julia Roberts taking a bath in *Pretty Woman*. Yet at some point the urge to meet, mate and procreate had become so overwhelming that she had allowed her dreams of Richard Gere and Patrick Swayze to become the nightmare of Chick, a man who openly scratched his testicles, then sniffed his fingers (base notes of tobacco, heady top notes of bollock sweat); a man who, that night and despite her protestations, had insisted she show the boys her birthday present. 'Come on, darling,' he said, 'come on now, I din't spend all that money for nothing. Show the lads what you got for yer birthday.' And insisted, and insisted ('Or wait till later,' his eyes had seemed to say) until at last she had no choice.

Turned out her birthday present was a boob job. 'At least it wasn't a hysterectomy,' someone whispered, as Mrs Chick sighed and flashed her boobs, following it with her own wait-till-later look at Chick, who was too busy talking the lads through the procedure. 'Not that I was there or anything, was I, love? Too busy earning the cash to pay for them.' Wink.

Then, Chick had seemed full of danger but somehow benign. At least, Dash had thought, benign when it came to Dash himself. Things change. Now Chick leant forward with an Embassy No. 6 smoking between his fingers.

'Look,' he said, and Dash saw he was hung-over. Red-veined eyes. 'I ent into you calling me "mate". If you want to call me something, call me Chick. Or "boss".'

'Okay, sorry, Chick,' said Dash, feeling as though he was watching a big dog wake up.

'*Or boss.*'

'Boss, then.' Dash looked behind him so he could turn away from his shame.

And now Chick was leafing through the pages of his note-book. Pages and pages of numbers, Dash could see: the empire of Chick. His domain.

'You owe me a fair bit, Dashus. Wanna see?' He held out the notebook, open like a warrant card. 'Figure at the bottom is what you're into me for, mate.'

Dash knew what the numbers were but glanced at them anyway, then took a healthy gulp of beer. Chick lowered his book.

'But this is what I'm saying . . .' Dash couldn't bring himself to repeat it; couldn't say 'boss'. 'This is what I'm saying. I can't. Warren's got the hump. He's gone off.' He knew as well – he knew he shouldn't have come to see Chick.

'Warren's a black geezer. Black geezers have always got the hump about something. It's their natural state. They like aggro – why you think they're always shooting each other?' Incisive social comment there, from Chick.

'Yeah, okay, but without Warren I can't sell. I need a driver,' said Dash.

Chick sat back and blew through his lips. 'Ent you got a mate who can do it for you?'

'No, not really, I haven't.'

'What about your missus? Can she drive?' Big joke from Chick.

'She works,' said Dash, the words coming out in a whine.

Chick's lip curled. 'All right,' he said at last. 'Go and get me another pint in and I'll make a call.'

Off Dash went to the bar again. The barman had finished with his sign. 'Why not take our amazing pork scratchings taste test challenge?' The crones were wetting the bar seats as he approached and ordered Chick's pint – Guinness, no fucking shamrock.

'Fancy a go?' said the barman, indicating the blackboard. 'Quid a go. Fiver if you can tell the difference.'

'It's free if yer Jewish,' piped up one of the crones.

'Not for me,' said Dash, when the laughter faded. 'I hate the things.' All three looked crestfallen. 'What's the catch, then?' he added.

'What catch?'

Dash sighed. 'There's always a catch, mate.'

The barman winked at the crones. 'Shall we tell him?' They wheezed in response. 'All the pork scratchings are the same. There ain't a difference. It's just a bit of a laugh – we got delivered an extra box by mistake. All proceeds to charity, of course.' Another wink.

'Send 'em back.' Dash shrugged.

'No point, it's a supplier's mistake, innit?'

'Just says one box on the docket, does it?'

'That's right.'

Dash laughed, even though it wasn't funny. Not to anyone but him. 'Might as well keep them then,' he said, and paid for the drink.

Chick was still on the phone. 'Hang on,' he muttered, as Dash returned with the pint. Then, 'What's your address?' to Dash. 'Clarke Street, innit? What number?'

Dash told him and Chick relayed the information, finishing the call, meeting Dash's expectant gaze.

'Have you found someone?' Chick looked hard at him. 'I mean, have you found someone, *boss*?'

Chick ignored the question. 'Here,' he said, 'you wanna come to the bogs for a line?'

Dash didn't, but felt it would be impolite to refuse. 'Yeah, cool,' he said, and followed Chick, already off in the direction of the gents'.

Inside, Chick didn't bother with the cubicle, just turned his back to Dash so he could rack up on a shelf below the mirror. 'Yeah, I've fixed you up with someone,' he said, to the chop-chop of his Blockbuster membership card. 'A lad I know.' Swish-swish, chop-chop.

A framed poster on the wall warned against the dangers of drink-driving. Except, Dash realised, as he looked closer, it didn't really: it was advertising an edgy videogame. 'Really?' he said.

'Yeah, really. You'll have to watch him – and don't even think about getting him to talk to punters – but he can drive.'

'Who is he?' said Dash.

'Geezer's called Lightweight. He's called Lightweight because he's a crack addict. He's off it now, recovering like, so I wouldn't go mentioning it. But he can drive, and as long as he's not on whatever he'll be a useful bloke to have around. A knifer. Used to work at the Kwik Save. He's going to call for you tomorrow morning. "Is Dash coming out to play?" – something like that.'

'Great,' said Dash, hoping Chick wouldn't notice the tremor in his voice.

'Thought you'd be pleased. Right . . .' He turned, finished with the swishing and chopping, and took Dash by the shoulders.

For a second – maybe less, half a second, perhaps – Dash thought Chick might be about to impart some fatherly nugget of wisdom; or was simply holding him in a spirit of friendship, because that's what mates do before snorting coke in the pub bogs. Instead, Chick's knee crashed into his groin. Unprotected, unsuspecting. Soft and vulnerable.

'Bowf!' said Dash. He dropped down with his hands already at his jeans and Chick stood over him, watching. Dash writhed, vaguely aware (at some level not concerned with the pain between his legs) that he was lying on tiles soaked in the urine of every Flat Cap patron with a penis. And, lying there, he thought that it wasn't too many years ago that he'd been on holidays to the coast, to Suffolk it was. Taken there by parents who put sea shells to his ear, 'Hear that, Darren? That's the sound of the sea.' Who probably imagined a bright future for their son. Dash wondered why that bright future had become the piss-stinking floor of the Flat Cap and, as always, he thought of the kid who had had Tourette's.

Chick stood and admired the effect of his knee on Dash. 'Next time make sure you bring my money,' he said, and turned to snort the single line of coke he'd racked up.

3

For an evil second Max imagined placing the quiz questions beneath the wiper of Roger's Saab at the kerb, residents' parking permit smug in the window. But he restrained himself and instead pulled them from his pocket, leafing through them as he walked. 'Question 24. Name the lead singer of Dexy's Midnight Runners (Clue: Rat).'

'Name the cunt married to my sister,' said Max, and threw the questions into a bin. 'Clue: twat.'

He travelled the one stop to Manor House and walked home. He let himself in and stood in the hallway for a moment or so, craning his head in the direction of the stairs, listening for sounds from the flat above. None. He felt his shoulders ratchet out, suddenly aware of the dread he'd felt – coming home, expecting noise. Locking the front door behind him – so it was on the Yale *and* the Chubb – he opened the door to the flat.

Inside, the sofa pulled him into its embrace. It was the kind of sofa you might normally expect to see on the pavement, or in next door's front yard, or round the back of the railway station – it suited him. He reached for the television remote and lit a cigarette, muted the TV, then stared at the ceiling, listening. Nothing. He restored the sound but kept it low – low so he could hear any noises from above. He thought he heard something and muted the TV again. His head dropped back to the sofa and he stared up, listening hard. He gazed at the ceiling and wished he could see right through it, past all the stuff there – the plaster, the joists, two-be-fours, coins, bits of paper and dust – and into the flat above, where the men had come to remove Mrs Larkin's carpet and replace it with laminated floorboards. He wanted to see past the laminated floorboards and into the flat of the noisy new couple, just to check there was nobody home. Just to know. Because only then would he relax.

The noisy couple's flat was owned by Mr Frewin-Poffley, who had bought it from Mrs Larkin. Max didn't need to check the property pages to know that it would have been a dirt-cheap-quick-sale arrangement – Frewin-Poffley must have rubbed his hands raw with glee.

For-sale signs had gone up. Not one, lots. Mrs Larkin Junior gave every estate agent in the postcode a shot at selling her mother's flat, and soon there was a nest of signs out the front. Estate agents. He'd hear the key being waggled in the lock. Duplicate keys they'd made from Mrs Larkin's master. Bad duplicates that never worked but agents waggled them endlessly anyway. His door buzzer would sound. 'Sorry, the front door lock doesn't seem to be working and we're due to show the flat upstairs.' Several sets of feet tramping past his door and up the stairs. The key waggling in Mrs Larkin's door. He'd stare at the ceiling and hear them chatter and clomp their way round the flat. He'd hear the twang of the bathroom light. On. Off. Maybe even on and off again. And then the feet thumping down the stairs (pause to talk loudly in the hallway outside his flat, don't mind me), goodbyes on the doorstep. And when they left they never double-locked the front door, so it was on the Yale *and* the Chubb. So after they'd gone he trooped to the front door and double-locked it behind them. Like the door monitor. Like a caretaker.

Next a sold sign went up, and whoever put it there made sure to take down his rivals' boards and dump them in Max's front garden. A fortnight later, a letter arrived for a Mr Frewin-Poffley. It could have come to the wrong address, but Max had placed it carefully in the hall, and later some people had arrived. Three, maybe four men who spent an hour up there, the empty space lending their voices extra volume. In the flat below Max knew changes were coming, and the men were wearing hobnailed boots. When they'd left, the letter had gone.

He heard every knock and curse as they tore out Mrs Larkin's kitchen and installed a new one. They replaced the sink and bath and fitted a shower, and something happened to Max's water pressure as a result, but he didn't say anything. And when the kitchen and bathroom were new, they made good the walls; they decorated and, lastly, without considering the effect on Max downstairs, they ripped out the carpet and laid laminated floor-boards, because the kind of tenants Mr Frewin-Poffley wanted to attract were clearly going to be the sort who appreciated the finer things in life. Like pretend-wooden flooring. A media couple, maybe.

Sophie and Darren it was, the noisy couple. A day or so after they moved in, a card arrived addressed to 'Darren and Sophie'. A moving-in card, he guessed, leaving it neatly for them to collect. Welcome to your new home, that sort of thing. Perhaps he should take them a bottle of wine. Get to know them. Explain about the door, the rubbish, how there wasn't much in the way of insulation in these Victorian conversions. How loud compli-cated trainers sound when they meet laminated flooring at speed. How the house rattles my bones when you slam the door. My tired, tired bones . . .

Max awoke from a nightmare of fire to the sound of bass from upstairs. A music channel. Darren and Sophie had installed their satellite dish as though it was a life-support system, and Max had seen the TV being carried up the stairs. Like the Queen's flag at Buckingham Palace, when the TV was on Darren and Sophie were home.

He brought the balls of his hands to his eyes and rubbed, then looked over to the clock on his ancient video and feared he might be late – he hadn't planned on falling asleep. But he'd only dozed a couple of hours, plenty of time. He stood to put on his coat before realising he was already wearing it. Check the pockets: cigarettes, lighter, Stanley knife and the letter, which he pulled from his pocket and was about to leave on the side before deciding against and pushing it back. He didn't know why. One last thing.

He found a piece of paper, a map: 'One of them Internet maps,' he'd been told. The house number and road had been added in biro, an arrow pointing to the spot on the grid. He folded it up and put it into his coat pocket.

And then he left the flat, closing the door quietly behind him. Because it could shake the house to its foundations, that door, if you slammed it. He knew.

At St Pancras he bought a ticket and hung around for the last train, which he was surprised to find half full, even at this time of night. Men in suits were monopolising double seats, sitting on the outside to discourage potential neighbours. They smelt of booze and pubs and a hard day's work persuading people to part with their money. They slouched, snoozing, reading papers or talking on phones. An atmosphere of resentful silence was broken only by the peep of mobiles; low, disembodied one-way conversations; someone clearing their throat. Max imagined coffins had more life.

He found a double seat and (when in Rome) sat on the outside, pulling his knees up to the seat in front and slouching into his coat. He felt wrong here, then wondered when he had last felt right. As the whistle went and the doors closed on London, he settled in for the long trip to Kettering. Expected time of arrival: 11.59.

'No taxis,' he'd been told, as if he could afford one anyway. 'You'll have to walk. It's not far, look.' Fat finger pointing out station, then travelling down the map to where the biro stopped at Cowley Close. 'Don't ask directions, you got me? Don't speak to a living soul unless you have to. Take the map – go on, then, have it – and you'll be fine.'

He had been right. It took Max an hour but he found Cowley Close, a small, concentrated circle of starter homes ballooning off a main road; once a petrol station, or furniture warehouse – something similar. The main road was quiet, just a few cars passing, and Max kept his head low against a cool wind, dragging on a cigarette with his other hand deep in a pocket, the letter at his fingertips, the Stanley knife there, too.

Turning into Cowley Close was like stepping into an empty film-set. Pristine houses stared disapprovingly at him, shiny cars parked in the driveways and along the pavement. It was as if there was nothing behind the house fronts, like they were held up by wooden supports. He stood for a moment or so, taking in the silence, staring at the houses, looking for number six. Two were empty, the agents' signs like oversized golf flags in the front gardens. Nude front gardens, not yet planted. Some of the downstairs lights were still on; most had a light on in a bedroom, one going dark as he watched. He spotted alarms and security lights, the kind that flicked on if you walked beneath them, but what he didn't see was rubbish. More to the point he didn't see black bin-liners.

It wasn't going to be as easy as he'd hoped; not as easy as he'd been told it would be. 'Just as you normally would, no difference. Only at this particular address. Just don't come back empty-handed, all right?'

Number six. There it was, snug between five and seven. No security light – that might be a bonus. Living-room light on, nothing upstairs. These were the kind of people who kept their rubbish hidden, so Max looked for a back entrance and saw an alley at the side of the house, a gate with a handle. It was the kind of heavy, garden-centre handle that made a loud CHOK, and a loud CHOK would sound like Hiroshima on Cowley Close. He frowned, hoped nobody had seen him standing looking, then turned and left, seeking another way in.

At the rear of the houses it was no better; worse, in fact. When he saw it was a playing-field he rejoiced, only to find that the rear gardens of Cowley Close had been fenced off with Colditz efficiency. He found the back of number six, checked for dog-walkers, drinkers, gangs of kids in baseball caps, and, satisfied he was alone, put his eye to a hole in the wood. Through it he saw french windows, the living room, curtains closed and light still on. And at the back of the alley, a sight that made his heart sink. A wheelie-bin. No black bin-liners. He sighed. Might as well have left the Stanley knife at home.

He straightened and stepped away from the fence. If he had been younger and fitter and maybe two feet taller – or, better still, a Ninja – he could have chanced climbing over it but, studying it balefully, he thought no. Instead he found a climbing-frame with regulation surface newly placed around the base – not the flesh-searing concrete he'd known as a kid – and climbed up to discover that he could see number six from where he was, the downstairs light still on. He glanced around but it was too late even for gangs of baseball caps, just him and number six still clinging to the day. He pulled his coat round him, made himself as comfortable as possible, and settled in to wait.

When the light went out he almost cheered. He'd been there for what seemed like hours, and for most of that he'd been winding himself up to go anyway, light or no light. How did he know what they did with their lights at number six? Maybe nobody was awake at all, not even in. Maybe they always left the downstairs light on as a precaution. Maybe someone had gone to bed and left it on.

But then it went out. And next what he assumed was a bathroom light went on, and he imagined whoever was in there cleaning their teeth and getting toothpaste on their pyjama sleeve. He pictured them baring their clean teeth at the mirror and – click – out went the bathroom light. And then whoever was in there was padding to the bedroom and slipping beneath a cool duvet (or maybe a warm one if it had another person under it), and he imagined them falling asleep safe in the knowledge that nobody was going to come in late and slam the door, or watch MTV Base above their heads.

He waited another hour before he slid off the climbing-frame and returned to the front of Cowley Close. He was barely able to restrain himself from creeping in on tiptoe as he entered, trying to look as if he belonged there. Walking around to number six he made as if he was about to pass it, then, with a final look around – one so swift as to be virtually useless – he darted to the side of the house. Thank God for no security light. Pressed against the side of the house he looked out into the close, to windows, searching out a sign that he'd been spotted. Nothing. Cowley Close slumbered on, unaware of him in its midst.

Now he slid towards the gate, getting the measure of his new enemy. It smelt of fresh creosote, and the huge, shiny black hoop handle looked as if it might drag his fist into another dimension. Max stood on tiptoe and peeped over the top. A bolt. He slid both hands over and used one to help the other as he silently worked it free. Then he took hold of the hoop handle, pulled the gate a fraction towards him, gripped it, held it steady at the top. And, using his whole body, lifted.

CHOK. It wasn't loud but it still sounded like a detonation. He held his breath, kept the handle in the up position, waited, listened. Then he slipped through the gate and soundlessly pushed it to. In front of him the wheelie-bin, greenly challenging his authority to enter the garden. Standing there he took stock, looking around and finding no windows in view. Nobody could see him unless they were bending to that hole in the fence. The garden was still. Nothing old and loose was disturbed by the breeze, no trees rustled, no early-morning birds sang. Just the sound of a plane, five miles above. He took hold of the wheelie-bin lid and lifted.

What he was looking for was printed matter. The kind of stuff he was after nightly, when he'd walk the streets of north London, Stanley knife in pocket, an eye open for bin-liners left in front yards. Not just any old bin-liners, but those with the right kind of flat, rectangular bulge at their bellies. And when he saw one? Easy. Stoop, slice the bag, fish around, extract a moist, stinking handful of papers, and be on his way. Five seconds. A five-second job and a clutch of moist paper. The sort of documents that collect on coffee-tables, in magazine racks and in kitchen drawers full of bumf. The kind of things that get sorted and thrown away together, not a thought that the name and address printed on the Barbican's Dear Member letter can be sold to use in an identity theft. Max stooped for five seconds and someone's life got rerouted to a new address – a begging letter from the NSPCC was all it took. Email addresses were rare, but if you got one it could be used in an Internet 'phishing' scam, no problem if you had some kind of support information. Anything to corroborate identity was good, maybe for a bogus passport application. Utilities were great, bank statements like striking gold, anything with an account number, anything with a card number; receipts were enough. People collected receipts; they kept them in little piles on coffee-tables, in magazine racks and kitchen drawers, and they said, 'You're not going to bother taking that jumper back now, are you? No, didn't think so,' and threw them away and Max stooped, fished and extracted, and had enough for a card-not-present fraud.

This sort of thing was what he was looking for as he raised the lid on the wheelie-bin and peered inside.

What he saw was envelopes.

The bin was full of them, hundreds it looked like, all with the stamp assiduously removed as you would if you were sent dozens and dozens of stamped letters, because there's always an appeal going on somewhere; Max thought of the supermarket vouchers he collected himself.

Some were white, some brown, some coloured odd, even Day-Glo colours. He reached into the bin, tombola-like, and brought one out, angling it into the meagre light from the moon.

'To the parents of Ben Snape,' it said.

He brought out another: 'To Little Ben's mummy and dad.'

Another: 'Patrick and Deborah Snape.'

'Mr and Mrs Snape.'

'Ben's mum and dad.'

'The parents of Ben Snape.'

'Ben Snape.'

'Little Ben.'

All with the top right-hand corner missing, the stamp torn out.

4

The next day a young man named Barnaby Horton held up his bong to the light, studying it with a frown. The water was murky, the colour of a sweater ordered from a catalogue in 1974, and in it floated . . . matter – stuff that should have sunk to the bottom, yet, noted Barnaby, was suspended, hanging there as though he was making bong-flavoured jelly that he'd decided to liven up with a handful of grime. Truly one of nature's most disgusting sights. Not that it worried Barnaby, who removed a pinch of weed from a small plastic bag – the kind of bag he had only ever seen used to store weed or spare buttons for dresses sold in department stores. He crumbled the weed into the bong, lifted the glass pipe to his lips and fired her up with his Clipper.

The weed glowed proud red. Smoke travelled through the smeggy bong water, cooled, collected in the chamber and Barnaby sucked it up. Now the smoke crowded his lungs and Barnaby brought the pipe smartly away from his mouth, placing a finger to his lips and holding his breath. He held it for perhaps thirty seconds. He removed his finger, exhaled and repeated the process. Repeated it until all the weed was black and gone.

Now he had maybe five minutes' grace before his brain turned to happy mush and, skilled in the bong arts, he put the time to good use. He checked that the back door of his flat was locked; he checked that the iron was off, the freezer door sealed and no bong evidence lying around. Then he shouldered his bag, switched off his Denon stereo having transferred the disc that had been playing to his Walkman, put on his headphones and left for work. As he set off he caught sight of yesterday's paper lying on the coffee-table, the headline, 'Footballer Bailed After Date Rape Quiz'.

I bet he did, thought Barnaby, and laughed at himself. It had started. He was now running on bong time.

It was a long walk to work, all the way from Finsbury Park to Stoke Newington Church Street, but that was the point. Let his stoned mind play word-association football as he ambled along, happy at play in Barnaby World, just strange, random thoughts and the Wu Tang Clan for company.

Loud it was, the Wu. So loud he barely noticed the dirty white van draw up to the kerb beside him. Not until the window had been wound down and he saw – but did not hear – a black man leaning from it and saying something to him, his lips moving like this: 'Wargh, wargh, wargh, wargh . . .'

Barnaby took off his headphones. 'Sorry?' The wargh-wargh became words: 'You got a moment, boss?' said the black man.

Like most white boys who routinely get stoned and listen to hip-hop, Barnaby had an unarticulated desire to be on level terms with big tough black men. He was, therefore, ridiculously pleased that these two big tough black men considered him cool enough to stop and ask him directions. On the other hand, he was listening to the Wu, and in Wu World bad things happen with Glocks. So he approached the van with fear and desire in a 50:50 ratio. 'Yeah,' he said.

'What it is, boss . . . ,' said the passenger. He was holding a piece of paper in one hand. '. . . what it is – it's a bit of a mad one, actually . . .' Barnaby took a step closer to the filthy van. Being stoned, he became suddenly aware of his face, his mouth in particular. Fixed into a grin he tried to unlock it while listening to what the big tough black man had to say.

'Thing is, it sounds weird, but me and my mate,' he indicated the driver, who smiled and at the same time pulled an encouraging face, 'we were doing a delivery this morning, right? Two sets of speakers to a studio over in Hackney – Jesus, man, you should have seen this place, sweet kit they had, state-of-the-art. Anyway, what it is, when we've delivered the speakers it turns out they only ordered one set, yeah? So we look at the docket . . .' he brandished the piece of paper he was holding '. . . and check it out, man.'

Barnaby took it from him, not quite getting the gist. The speech had been delivered fast, and now he was being shown a piece of paper supposed to prove the provenance of a pair of speakers, but he wasn't sure why.

'See?' said the passenger.

'No,' replied Barnaby slowly, as though drawing the word out gave him more time to comprehend. 'What am I supposed to be looking at?'

'Only one set of speakers, man, see?' smiled the black guy. 'They made a mistake at the warehouse.'

'Cool,' said Barnaby, fighting to tether the conversation. The guy went on. Thing is, he was saying, they could just take these speakers back to the warehouse, but any way you look at it they're a surplus pair of speakers and most likely the foreman'll have them away. Fact is, they might as well sell them for a bit of extra cash.

At which point it dawned on Barnaby that he was being sold a set of speakers, which he didn't need, owing to the perfectly good set wired up to his Denon system at home, still cooling in his wake.

'Ah,' he said. 'Ah, thanks, mate, but even if I was up for it, to be honest I don't have any money on me.'

On me – his second mistake. First mistake: stopping. Second mistake: not ending his sentence at the word 'money'.

'Don't worry about that,' said the speakerman. 'We'll run you round to the cash machine.'

Barnaby did a mental gulp. At Poly some friends had been escorted to a cash machine by a group of black men. They took them on the bus and chatted happily on the journey before clearing out their accounts at the other end.

'That's very kind of you,' he said, 'but really, um, thanks, but I'm on my way to work and I'm already late and I can't carry a couple of speakers.'

The speakerman seemed to consider. 'Well, where you got to be?'

'Work.'

'Yeah, man. Where's work?'

'Church Street.'

'Stoke Newington?'

'Yeah.'

'Well, look, you live not far from here, yeah?' Barnaby nodded, as if drained of every last drop of guile. 'We'll drop you round yours so you can get the speakers safe home, then we'll run you round to Church Street. You don't mind doing that, do you?' He said this last bit to his mate, who made a theatrical tsk-if-I-must face in reply.

Barnaby felt as though he was in quicksand. As if he'd had all the time in the world to drag himself out but for some reason had left it too late.

'To be honest,' he said, 'it's not like I need speakers. I've got a set at home.'

The speakerman looked exasperated. Like, Jesus, this kid. 'Yeah,' he said, 'of course you have, but you've heard of Auridial, right?'

Barnaby hadn't. 'Yeah,' he said.

'Well, this is an Auridial pro set, top of the range. What sort of music you into?'

'Hip-hop.'

'Well, these are some of the best speakers for hip-hop, innit? They got superior bass response. Ain't that right?' This to his mate. A yeah-God-yeah-the-best-mad-to-miss-out face in reply. 'Have a look at this.' The speakerman produced a small colour brochure, about the size and print standard of a bad takeaway menu. Well thumbed. This was exhibit B, evidence of how really great these speakers were.

From it Barnaby gleaned that they normally retailed at a thousand pounds, and there was lots of technical spec that he didn't think it polite to spend time reading – and wouldn't have understood anyway. The quicksand burped as more of Barnaby disappeared into its maw. Next, the speakerman was out of the van, even bigger, tougher and blacker on the outside of his shell. He directed Barnaby to the back of the van, where, inevitably, it had 'also available in white' written in dirt on the rear doors, and it was these doors the speakerman flung open to reveal the speakers inside.

Admittedly, thought Barnaby, despite himself, they are impressive beasts.

They stood at the back wall of the van, strapped in. Matt black and huge: imposing, monolithic black towers of sound. Beneath the covers – covers like the stretched silk of a stocking – Barnaby could see the twin silver discs of the woofer and tweeter nestled into a diaphragm the colour of a policeman's hat. One smaller planet orbiting a larger one. These two soundpieces would throb, he thought. They'd pulse with bass. The sound of the urban landscape.

The quicksand burped one last time.

The trip to the cash machine was quite exciting. The speakermen played the sort of music he liked – music that reminded him of how stoned he was – and they played it so loudly that passers-by looked their way when they passed, and what those passers-by saw was three blokes in a van, two black, one white, a team of three. Which suited Barnaby just fine. He felt like, for the first time, he was experiencing hip-hop in its natural environment. He noticed how they seemed to find the lyrics hilarious (when he only ever found them deadly serious – interesting); and he noted the way they bobbed their heads minutely in time to the beats, almost imperceptibly, and he filed that movement away for later use.

It was so exciting, the journey, that he was almost disappointed when they reached the cash machine. And, yes, okay, it was a bit weird, sort of disquieting, when the speakerman accompanied him to the hole in the wall. He was big, and tough, and black, and Barnaby fancied that was why the homeless guy at their feet didn't bother asking for spare change. It was also why, when the speakerman asked (friendly and everything, but . . .) for 'a bit of beer money on top, yeah? Come on, we're doing you a favour here,' he withdrew some extra cash and handed over the whole wedge with a smile marked 'obsequious'.

'Nice one, man. Sweet,' said the speakerman, pocketing the cash, and he was scooting back to the van with Barnaby at his heels, climbing in, Barnaby no longer in the middle as they raced over to his flat.

'They're not fake or anything, are they?' he asked redundantly.

'The Auridial? No way, boss. These is genuine Auridial,' and the pair of them sniggered in a manner that Barnaby didn't quite care for. Then, as he directed them home, over some traffic calming, a left here, a right there, a left at the offy, he felt the impatience in the van; felt it blooming. 'Is it far, boss? We ain't got all day, yunah.'

But at least they were true to their word. They drove him to the front door of his flat and helped him unload the speakers, which turned out to be disconcertingly light, actually, considering their size, and . . . Oh. They weren't true to their word.

'Sorry, boss. Gotta shoot. Enjoy the speakers, yeah?' And Barnaby felt himself smiling like he'd known this was the plan all along, no fooling him. Smiling as the van, 'also available in white', sped away, stranding him on his doorstep.

He turned to look at his two monoliths; considered wiring them up straight away. Maybe not, he thought. No time. (And some instinct told him to save that disappointment for later anyway.)

Now Barnaby was going to be late for work. No longer stoned, he locked up his flat with the speakers inside. His was a good walk spoiled by speakermen, so he took the tube from Finsbury Park to Manor House, then out of the tube and walking quickly along Green Lanes in the direction of Clissold Park, then to Church Street, bound for Threshers where he worked, and thank God for those late opening times. Thank God for licensing laws.

And he was about two hundred yards away from the shop when a van drew up to the kerb beside him and a bloke – a white bloke this time – was leaning from the window, his lips moving, like this: 'Wargh, wargh, wargh, wargh.'

5

Sophie was taking part in the Gigantic Fake Tan Test.

She was only a work-experience girl, too, which made her achievement even more noteworthy – the way she'd outlasted the usual week-long placements by one, two, *three* whole weeks. So aside from the usual jobs, like making tea and sorting the post and talking about Ibiza, she had been entrusted with other, marginally less menial, tasks, like sorting invoices, updating files and even looking after other work-experience placements (the raw recruits, short-timers), making sure they knew the ropes when it came to collecting coffee and sourcing the right bagels for the picture desk, and maybe, say, if they arrived at work looking prettier than her, giving them a little friendly advice on how to appear the following day.

So she had her feet under the table. Her own table. People had started referring to the place where she sat as 'Sophie's desk', and as if that wasn't awesome enough she'd been asked to assess fake-tan lotions for a five-page feature going in the – God, they worked so far ahead – June issue. The Gigantic Fake Tan Test.

Naturally she hadn't been asked to do any of the really expensive courses or treatments – they'd gone to editors and commissioning editors; neither had she been asked to rate any of the top-name creams or lotions – they'd gone to staff writers and freelancers. The ones she'd been allocated were of the less pricey, Newcastle-lass-on-the-pull variety, and were likely to appear in the 'You Know When You've Been Tangoed' section of the feature. Which maybe explained that while everybody else involved had been given just one product to use, she'd been asked to do four. A whole four lots of different skin-staining lotions, which – not that she minded – had begun to turn her flesh the colour of brick.

She didn't mind because you know how you can never be too rich or too thin? As far as Sophie was concerned you couldn't be too tanned either. In addition, her gradual transformation had given her something of an office profile, chipping away at her anonymity. It meant people noticed her, and for the ambitious work-experience person being noticed is the first battle won.

As well as her skin tone there was something else she was semi-famous for: her boyfriend, Dash. Even before 'Sophie's Orange-O-Meter' there had been 'Dodgy Dash'. When Gabrielle, the editor, had interviewed Sophie for work experience, she'd been eating breakfast, a slice of cheese, which rested on a plate more stylish than Sophie had ever seen. When she huffed foul breath over Sophie she apologised, saying she was on the Atkins diet and Sophie gave up carbohydrates on the spot. Several times their conversation had been interrupted as staff members approached the sofas where they sat. They came with dazzling questions for Gabrielle. Questions about a shoot in Mauritius, the weather there; questions like, 'Are we using a new sex expert this month?' Did she have that number for Kate Winslet's friend, because Kate's people are being, like, *vile*? And do we say we tested the anal vibrator or not? ('Well, did we?' asked Gabrielle. 'Sian did, yes,' came the reply. 'Er, okay, say we didn't, then. Be coy. Go "not tested, thanks" exclamation mark – and Sian knows she can keep it, right?').

The girls who steamed over with questions were posh and hassled; their eyes slid over Sophie and quickly away, as though they were reading offensive graffiti. But Gabrielle wasn't hassled or posh and when she looked at Sophie her eyes were warm, and Sophie fancied that Gabrielle saw something of herself there in the sofa opposite.

Easy, then, when Gabrielle asked about her boyfriend: 'What does he do?' Easy because most of the girls had boyfriends who worked on other magazines, or did something equally glamorous and cool, and even the other work-experience girls had boyfriends who *wanted* to work on other magazines or do something glamorous and cool. Easy to say, 'Dash? He sells things out the back of his van,' in her very best council voice. Sure enough, Dash became Dodgy Dash, Gabrielle liking the idea of him, and the rest of the office liking it, too. When they were not watching Sophie turn orange they'd go, 'He's a little bit whooh,' at the sound of Dash's name, and throw up their arms like Girl Guides at the top of a rollercoaster. Up and down went the arms. 'He's a little bit whaey!' Up and down again. Before she ever started turning orange, she'd had Dash. He was her passport to recognition.

There was a flipside – there always is. Passports are used to flash briefly, gain entry, then packed away. The photograph is good for a quick laugh with mates, an icebreaker on holiday, but it's never the face you want to present to the world. It's a reminder of another time, the past.

'When are we going to meet this Dodgy Dash, then?' said Gabrielle, whose boyfriend was a famously northern and gorgeous editor of a men's style magazine. The answer, Sophie began to realise, was never.

Now she was in the bathroom, smearing herself with a self-tan towelette and realising with horror that she had to leave – God – *twenty minutes* for it to dry.

Dash knocked on the bathroom door. Banged on it actually. 'How long you going to be in there, Soph?' he bawled.

'A bit,' she bawled back, looking again at the instructions on the side of the crumpled towelette wrapper. 'Say about ten minutes.'

'I need a piss, babe,' yelled Dash. 'I'm desperate.'

'You've been!' The memory was still fresh.

'I need to go again.' Too much coffee.

'Can't you wait?'

'You've been in there ages. I've *been* waiting.'

She sighed. 'Well, you're going to have to wait some more. I'm in the middle of something.' Her words echoed in the tiny bathroom, hardly more than a cubicle, really.

'Can't I just come in and have a slash?'

'No,' she said, indignant. 'I'm in the middle of something. How come every time I'm in the bathroom you need a piss?'

'How come every time I need a piss you're in the bathroom?'

'Tough. You'll have to wait.'

She stood there, arms and legs apart, like a mannequin, hearing Dash curse and stalk off to the kitchen. 'And don't go in the kitchen sink,' she called. There was no reply. 'And I'll have a cup of tea if you're making one,' she added, flapping her arms slightly.

Dash needed a piss so badly he ended up going in the kitchen sink, running a tap at the same time. That meant he'd have to pretend to go for a piss once Sophie was out of the bathroom, otherwise she'd guess, and she had a thing about pissing in the sink. He was forced to do it often, and each time he thought of the same joke. The one about this guy, and he pulls a bird at the club one night and they end up going back to her place. 'You'll have to be quiet,' she says, as they get settled on the sofa. 'My mum and dad are asleep upstairs.' So they get down to a bit of heavy petting – a bit of foreplay – when he apologises and says he's dying for the toilet. 'Well, you can't go upstairs,' she says, 'you'll wake Mum and Dad. You'll have to use the kitchen sink.' So off he goes into the kitchen and he's gone a while before she hears him calling through the kitchen door and goes to see what he wants. 'Everything all right in there?' she says from the other side of the door. 'Yeah, fine,' he says, 'but where's your toilet paper?'

See, Soph, thought Dash, finishing and shaking, slooshing the final drops of wee down the plughole. See – there are worse things you can do in a kitchen sink.

And then, as if on cue, he heard someone shouting from the street below, followed by an insistent buzzing of the doorbell. He went through and lifted the intercom handset. 'Yeah,' he said, deliberately adding a forbidding bass note to his voice.

''S Lightweight,' rasped the comeback. 'Chick sent me.'

Were there three more unsettling words in the lexicon? *Chick sent me.* Inside, Dash sighed. 'Right, yeah. Wait there.' And Dash wished Mr Frewin-Poffley had fixed the door latch so he could buzz Lightweight in, but Mr Frewin-Poffley appeared with the frequency of a solar eclipse, so Dash pounded down the stairs, past the downstairs flat, and opened the front door to reveal Lightweight on the doorstep.

Immediately he wished he hadn't hit the kid who had Tourette's. He could see right through the kid, that was the thing. He was putting it on. And when Darren's fist connected with the Tourette kid's silly, proud face, Darren died and Dash was born.

It was the same here. He could see right through Lightweight. Literally, almost. The humanity withered to grasping desperation.

Lightweight was thin. Very. He was black but only nominally. His skin had begun to turn the colour of escalator metal. He wore filthy black jogging bottoms and a denim jacket, which despite the bright day he held closed at his neck with a trembling hand. Above nasty milky eyes and a pinched mouth accustomed to pleading, his hair was unkempt, antique and coloured like someone had tipped an ashtray into it. Perhaps they had. As he stepped across the threshold he brought with him an overwhelming stench of cigarettes that even Dash, no stranger to the joys of smoking, found revolting.

'All right, mate?' said Dash.

'Yeah.' He spoke with tortured vocal cords. 'It's just early, innit.'

Dash hadn't been referring to his new mate's *tremens* but there you go. 'You're the driver, then.' This guy didn't look capable of driving a shopping trolley, let alone the van.

''S what Chick said. A driving job.'

'Chick said you're good with a box-cutter.' Dash could hear himself trying to sound tough.

'He din't say nothing about no trouble.'

'We're not expecting trouble. I was just saying. By way of conversation, you know?'

Lightweight sniffed. 'Yeah, well, I used to work at the Kwik Save, din't I?'

'Course.'

Lightweight coughed fit to die, like he might deposit his lungs right there on the hall carpet, slap-bang outside the old guy's flat. Dash waited for him to finish. 'Sounds healthy.'

Lightweight looked at him. 'It ent.'

'Right. Well, wait here. I'll get the keys. First stop the depot. I'll explain everything on the way.'

A look of great darkness and confusion descended over Lightweight. 'Chick said it was just driving.'

'Yeah, well, there's a bit more to it than that.'

'He said it was just driving, man.' His mouth set, his head tilted warningly.

'Yeah, all right,' said Dash, holding out peacemaker hands. 'Just wait there a minute, I'll be down in a sec and we'll talk on the way to the depot.'

He left Lightweight leaning against the downstairs-flat door and thundered back up the stairs. Sophie was out of the bathroom with her dressing-gown on, glowing like she was radioactive. Dash loved his girlfriend too much to tell her she was turning into an oompah-loompah, but still – he wondered how much longer he'd be able to look at her without needing sunglasses. Between her and Lightweight he was beginning to wonder if he was the only one still wearing the skin he was born with.

'Did you get me a tea?' she asked, settling herself into the sofa and unzipping a makeup bag.

'No,' he said. 'I'm going to work.'

'Oh. Is Warren here?'

'No, babe. Warren pissed off on me yesterday. I've got a new driver.' Searching for his jacket on the hook. Sophie's jacket, Sophie's jacket, Sophie's jacket. 'Where's my jacket?'

'I dunno. Where you left it. Who is he, then, your new mate?'

'His name's Lightweight. Look, you're sitting on my jacket.'

'Oh, yeah. Here, have it. It's what – his name?'

'Lightweight.'

'Well, where is he?'

'Down in the hall. Look, have you seen my keys?'

Sophie put down the bottle of nail polish she held – put it on the cardboard box in front of her – and went to peer round the flat door. At the bottom of the stairs Lightweight stood leaning against the downstairs-flat door, smoking. He glanced up and she withdrew.

'Jesus,' she said, in a whisper. 'He looks like a skull and cross-bones. What's up with him?'

'He's a crackhead,' replied Dash, absurdly proud.

'Really?' She looked again. (*'He brought some crackhead round this morning.' 'A little bit whooh! A little bit whaey!'*)

'Yeah, really.' He shouldered on his jacket and squeezed the pocket – so that was where the keys were. 'A real live crackhead. Listen, we're off down the depot. You going to be here when I get back?'

'Not likely. Going to work.'

'Okay.' He paused in the doorway, looked to where Sophie now sat, engrossed with her nail stuff, and his eyes went to her cleavage. 'You're not wearing your new necklace,' he said.

She cringed. 'Wore it yesterday,' she replied. She bit her lip without knowing she did so. 'Don't want to overdo it, do I?'

'Only I haven't seen it on you yet.'

'You'll see it,' she said. 'Just not today, that's all.'

'All right, doll,' he said, and made a kissy sound. 'See you later, then.'

'Hey, I thought you were desperate for a piss.'

But the door had already slammed shut behind him. Please don't call me doll, she thought, but didn't say, as he crashed down the stairs, him and his new mate slamming the door behind them.

'That your woman?' said Lightweight, with the menace of a midnight prowler. Still he held his denim jacket closed as they walked to the van.

The van was white, and dirty, and in the dirt Warren had written 'try slapping the top of this fucker' because he had a thing about people slapping the tops of vehicles when they got out. Dash found himself staring almost wistfully at the words as they approached. 'Yeah, that was her,' he replied.

'Funny colour,' sneered Lightweight.

You can talk, thought Dash, but didn't say as they clambered into the van and set off for the depot.

6

At least Lightweight could drive, thought Dash. After a fashion. His hands shook on the steering-wheel, and when he rested his left on the gear-stick Dash feared he might simply tremble the van into another gear. Still, at least he could drive. There was that.

Over on his side of the van Dash regarded his new mate as though he belonged to a different species, which, in a way, he did. *Homo crackheadus*. To Dash, crack was so far out of his orbit of weed, the occasional pill and line of coke as to be in another star system. 'Even his monkey had a monkey,' Chick had told him darkly. Dash had never had a monkey, nor did he ever want one, but despite himself he was fascinated by Lightweight's. Don't ask him about it, Chick had warned. So . . .

'So,' began Dash, 'what you been up to lately?'

Lightweight shook the van down a gear. He missed and the gears crunched. Dash winced; Lightweight was blank. 'This and that,' he croaked. 'Just been around.'

'You been ill?' asked Dash, a bit impertinently, he thought, given that Lightweight was clearly a vicious thug and had probably hurt people in pursuit of his addiction (*and* once worked at the Kwik Save).

Lightweight greeted the enquiry with a long, steady stare across the seats. So long that Dash worried they might veer off the road. 'Nah, man,' said Lightweight at last. 'Nah, I ent been ill.'

'Oh, okay, sorry. I just wondered.' Dash pushed his curtain hair out of his eyes and let silence salve the rift, until after what seemed like a decent interval he reached into a side pocket of the van and pulled out an Auridial brochure. 'This is what we're selling,' he said, holding it up for Lightweight to see.

'You're selling, man. I'm just driving.'

Dash sighed. This was going to be hard work. 'Yeah, yeah, course you're driving, man . . .' Nervously his eyes twitched to see if Lightweight thought he was taking the piss – saying 'man' like that. It hadn't sounded right in his voice, like trying on clothes that nearly fitted but not quite. No reaction, though. '. . . but we're kind of a team. You have to back me up a bit. What did Chick tell you?'

'Said it was a driving job.'

'It's not *just* driving. You have to say certain things to help me out.'

'Like what?'

That first night in the pub, just before Mrs Chick had arrived to show off her double Ds, Chick had told Dash what you did to be a speakerman, and one of the things he'd said then was 'Get your driver to back you up, all right?'

Dash, half pissed, thrilled and nervous, had asked if the speakers were any cop.

'Any cop? I wouldn't give them to the wife. But the beauty thing about this is that the speakers look the business. You'll see them. They'll get any geezer's juices flowing. But forget them a minute, you want to learn or what?'

Dash did.

'Right,' said Chick. 'You got your hit, your pitch, your show, your close. Say that back to me.' Chick, pissed and enjoying playing teacher.

'You got your hit, your pitch, your close, your show.'

'Wrong way round, son, but it don't matter. Start with your hit. That's finding someone to sell to, and once you get that right you'll be minted. Obviously, forget about women. We got perfume to flog to women, know what I mean?' He winked. 'Speakers is for the men. And forget about old geezers as well. We can pretend to be reading the meter when we need a bit of "old money", know what I mean?' Dash felt a mild twinge of unease. 'Nah, what you want is young blokes, anything between eighteen and thirty-five. Get them alone is the first thing, or with a girlfriend.

Sometimes with a girlfriend works, cuz they want to impress their bird. Sometimes the bird drags them off by the ear. That's how you'll have to play it – by ear.' He laughed at his own joke. The laugh became a cough, which became a hack and a clearing of the lungs, a throaty bringing of mucus into the mouth, where it stayed, Chick rolling it around his mouth as though it were chewing-gum.

'Alone is best,' he continued, poking his tongue into the green like he was about to blow a bubble with it. 'You can usually tell the way they're dressed whether they're going to be interested. If they're wearing headphones you got a sale. And students. If they're students you got a sale. Shame for you is that the Holloway Road patch is already gone. Holloway Road is packed with students gagging to impress a couple of guys in a van by buying dodgy speakers off them. Like I say, though, that patch is gone, and you better not get any thoughts about trying to pinch sales off it cuz you'll get your head kicked in and there won't be a thing I can do to help you. Got that?'

Dash had, the extra element of danger thrilling him further.

'Still,' continued Chick, 'there's a fair few students round here. White geezers are the best. Black geezers be careful of, know what I mean? They're smarter than the average bear when it comes to street deals. Little Pakis are also good, especially if they're walking with that attitude they've learnt off the black geezers.' He took a sip of beer and Dash knew that he was mixing the Guinness with the matter in his mouth and creating a Guinness-mucus taste sensation. The thought made him feel sick.

'The most important thing, though, whoever it is, they got to feel, like, *flattered* that you've stopped and asked them. Like you think they're a cool cat, they got the street smarts, they're the kind of geezer who's going to appreciate the wicked speakers you've got to sell them, the kind who knows a good deal when he sees one. You straight so far?' Dash nodded. 'Good, cuz then you got your pitch – what's up?'

'Sorry,' said Dash. 'I need a piss.' He was beginning to think that matching Chick pint for pint was a mistake.

'Well, hurry up, I ent got all night.'

When he returned (one piss, a half-hearted shove of the fingers down the throat – nothing doing), Chick took him through the pitch: the Docket Approach – as developed and refined over years of use on the likes of Barnaby Horton. He went on to explain trips to the cash machine, and how you should keep the mark talking – talking about anything other than speakers – so he won't be able to think about the cash he's about to waste; how his missus is going to kill him when she gets in.

Then Dash asked where he got his van from, and Chick told him the depot, same place you picked up the speakers.

'One thing, though,' he added, as if it was nothing. 'This is like a video-club deal. You have to pick up at least two sets a day, which you'll have to sell to pay me my cut of twenty-five quid per set.' He smiled and wrinkled his nose, like, hey, just a minor catch. Nothing.

'What I don't understand . . .' started Dash. The pints had begun to mount up. His world had gone Willy Wonka on him. 'What I don't understand, right, if I need to pay you twenty-five quid per set of speakers sold, and I've got to sell at least two pairs of speakers a day, that means I owe you fifty quid a day.'

Chick agreed that, yes, that was what he meant, as it was Chick who'd set him up with the job, and a driver, and a couple of hundred start-up cash, and that made him '*ergo* your employer, and as your employer I get a cut – fifty quid a day. But you don't have to give it me every day, we're both busy men – or you will be anyway – you just give it me in weekly instalments. It comes to two hundred and fifty a week – I don't expect you to work weekends.' Nice, benevolent Chick tipped Dash another friendly wink.

'Yeah,' slurred Dash. 'Yeah, okay, got that, right. But why do I still *have* to collect two sets of speakers from the depot each day?'

'Cuz you'll need to sell two a day to give me my cut.'

'Yeah, but what I mean is, right, what if I *don't* sell two a day?'

'Well, you better had, cuz I want my full cut.' Chick smiled.

'Yeah, yeah, no, I understand that. But what I mean is, you're going to get your cut anyway, so why do you care how many speakers I collect each day?'

'Oh, sorry, mate. I got you. Well, thing is, the guy at the depot's a mate. And every set of speakers he sells to you he gives me a cut, on the basis that I guarantee him a certain amount of speakers sold each day. See? That's all it is.'

'Oh.' Dash thought about this for a moment, found he didn't understand it and went back to his original concern. 'Yeah,' he said, 'but then I might not be able to pay your cut because I might not have sold two a day, and then I'll still have to pay the depot.'

Chick leant forward and smacked Dash on the arm, friendly, but held it there, his trotter-like hand squeezing. 'That's it.' He laughed. 'You got it. And listen, don't worry about selling them speakers. You'll sell 'em, no problem. Ah, just in time. Here's the missus . . .'

He should have known.

'Hey, Dashus,' called Chick, last thing, as Dash staggered out of the pub. He turned. 'Don't forget work tomorrow. Bright and early. I'll let them know you're coming. I got your address if there are any problems. All right, mate?'

The next day Dash caught the train to Walthamstow, bound for the depot. His hangover perched on his shoulder like a morbidly obese woodpecker, wearily hammering at his skull. But even from beneath his headache he was able to recognise the potential pitfalls of Chick's plan. Pitfalls for him, that is. He had to buy the speakers each morning. A hundred quid per set. He had to sell them, pay the driver a percentage, pay Chick. If he could sell the speakers, cool. If he couldn't, come on, Chick would understand. Which is what he'd told himself. Maybe even believed it at the time.

He was beginning to wonder. Like, maybe Chick was from the fuck-you-pay-me school of economics.

And now he felt the resident fear in his stomach shift,

Lightweight sitting next to him, clearly uninterested in helping to sell speakers that Dash *really* needed to sell, because, fact was, business wasn't so good.

First time out, him and his driver, Warren, getting acclimatised, only sold one set, out of thirty people stopped. What a learning curve, though. Next day they sold four. Had to make a trip back to the depot. They ended the week on a roll, trousering a major profit, and Dash duly took Chick his cut, plus the startup loan, and Chick snatched it, grunted thanks and Dash left. That week, perfect. Next week, not so. They managed two a day except on Tuesday (traditionally, he soon found, a day when people don't buy stereo equipment) when they only sold one and though they were down on profit they were still in the black – Chick got paid, grunted. The following Monday they sold three, shifting the leftover from the previous week, but the next day, bloody Tuesday again, they didn't sell any. They sold two a day for the rest of the week and went into the weekend still in the black – Chick got paid, grunted – but with two boxes of Auridial speakers in Dash's flat.

These days Dash tended to think, Just two Auridial boxes? Luxury. Because now there were far more than two – he'd stopped counting. Now he was averaging less than one sale a day, but still picking up two sets of speakers every morning. He'd had weeks when he'd not sold a single set, and even going out at the weekends and in the evenings was hardly denting the backlog. Each day they went to fetch two more sets of speakers from the depot. Each day they deposited one at Dash's flat and ferried the other round their patch. It was a small area, he'd soon discovered. Or maybe, as areas go, he'd been given a lemon. The same faces kept popping up. The young men of the parish either knew and hated them, or knew someone who knew and hated them. Once again, he should have known. 'Young Dash is taking over the speaker run in this area,' Chick had told his mates, and Dash had thought he saw a comic grimace pass between them.

The next morning, when Dash and his woodpecker rolled up to introduce themselves, Phil the depot manager said, 'You got the Stoke Newington beat, eh?' Sharp intake of breath, face like he was passing a kidney stone.

Even Warren, his driver, his *so-called* partner: 'Fuckin' Stokey, man. It's all vegans, yoga teachers, Jews and Turkish, innit? We ent gonna sell no speakers round there.'

He had been right. The only time they seemed to make a sale was when they tested the boundaries of their area, across in Dalston, down to Seven Sisters and Tottenham; or, better, sneaking past Finsbury Park and into Holloway, where there were *students*. Dash was all for poaching on a daily basis, urging, 'Come on, Warren, weekends at least,' but Warren was reluctant. Like, he was *attached* to his legs, all right? So each day they went out, collected two, deposited one and tried and usually failed to sell the other, and the depot got its money, so the manager was happy, and Chick got paid, grunted, and Dash found himself fretting more, a constant tang of Dash-sweat in the cab of the van. Until, last week, when he'd been a hundred short for Chick.

'You'd better make it up next week, then,' said Chick, happily, and Dash had gone away not discouraged by the experience. After yesterday he knew Chick was happy the way a bull terrier is before it eats. His bollocks throbbed glumly at the thought.

In the end it was no wonder Warren had walked. Most days his cut was zero. He was sick of driving weekends. His girlfriend had started nagging him. The argument he'd had into the bargain with Dash was just the excuse he'd been looking for – Dash saw through him.

One good thing about his desertion, though: Warren gone meant no resident 'fraidy cat to stop them visiting Studentsville. And Lightweight? Well, Mr Grey Skin looked like he could handle himself: he lacked the bulk of Warren, but there was that crack-veteran stare to make up for it. Plus he used to work at the Kwik Save. What was more, Dash had another cunning plan . . .

They drove past the dog track and Dash tried to engage Lightweight in conversation. 'Saw Vinnie Jones in there once,' he said, indicating the track. If he was hoping for some reciprocal tale of star-spotting he was disappointed. Lightweight coughed in reply. Probably spent the last year lying zonked-out on the floor of a crackhouse, thought Dash, before pointing to an entrance and saying, 'Turn here. This is the depot.'

In the yard, white-van fumes seemed to hang, layered in the air, like empty hammocks. Theirs was not the only van making the pilgrimage. As always the yard was heaving, the roller doors open and Phil at the entrance, directing teams of speakermen, ticking off items on a clipboard. Everywhere, it seemed, men were hauling boxes with the industry of worker bees, sometimes two at a time. Over the way, Dash jealously noted a team loading one, two, three, *four* Auridial boxes into the back of their van – tick and a wave from Phil.

'Best back it up,' said Dash, cringing inwardly. Sure enough, the worker bees stopped their carrying to watch Lightweight perform a seven-point turn in the courtyard. Gears crunching to cheers and handclaps, the van finally rattling back to the depot doors.

'Stop,' called Dash, his eyes on the wing mirror. 'Jesus, you almost killed a geezer there.'

Lightweight looked mildly abashed. 'I ent driven a van this big before.'

Dash felt weary and dragged damp hair off his forehead. 'Yeah, well,' he said, 'better wait there,' and he climbed from the van.

The smell in the depot reminded Dash of Scalextric sets he'd been bought as a kid. It comforted him, kind of. So, too, did the other speakermen. Kind of. He half hated them because they all had better areas than he did and most wore designer sportswear and could afford good trainers and probably, though he couldn't say for certain, didn't have a Chick-type figure lurking in their background, slowly squeezing them. But there was a kind of conviviality, and he had certain status at the depot. As a joke, for sure. The poor twat with the Stoke Newington beat. But still.

'Oi, Stoke,' said one, 'got a new driver?' Those in the vicinity laughed. Dash did too, hoping Lightweight hadn't heard – and wasn't now leaping from the cab of the van, brandishing his fabled box-cutter, ready to take on any motherfucker who dissed him, cough all over them . . .

'What happened to Warren, then?' He had a big grin, this one. Had a right to it. As far as Dash knew he worked somewhere in west London – itinerant population, lots of trustafarians, hundreds of young lads into their music.

'We fell out.'

'His missus giving him grief?'

'That too.'

Phil ambled over. 'Dash, my man, how's things?'

'Could be better, Phil,' said Dash, assuming a hangdog expression.

'Tell me about it. Two sets, is it?' His pen hovered over the clipboard.

'Er, no, I think I'll just take the one today, thanks.'

Phil's pen continued to hover, only he looked up at Dash with that same painful-kidney-stone expression on his face. 'One?' he said, as though Dash had just told him how many hours that kidney stone gave him to live.

'If that's all right.'

'Chick say you could take just one?'

'Do we have to tell Chick?'

'You've just answered a question with a question, Dash. "Do we have to tell Chick?" What do you think?'

'I think we don't have to tell him, no.'

'But he'll find out, won't he?'

Dash looked around. He leant in closer to Phil. 'Look,' he said, 'it would really help me out if . . . You know, business is slow, Phil.'

'Too right it is, which is why I need you to take your quota.'

'But there isn't anybody buying speakers in Stokey.'

'If you don't take two I can't rightly pay Chick, and Chick ain't going to be happy. I'll put you down for two. It's a nice day, you'll be fine.'

'No, no, wait.' Dash put his hand over the clipboard just in

time for Phil to draw a biro line over it. He sort of did it deliberately – thought it was funny.

'Now look what you made me do.'

'Wait up. Look, help me out here? What if . . . what if I gave
you Chick's cut to give to him? Then you can still pay him.'

'Yeah, I could do that.'

'Right.'

'And Chick would get his cut, so Chick would be happy.'

'Right . . . But what would I get out of the deal?'

'You . . . get to help out a geezer in a tight spot?'

Wearily, Dash loaded two sets of speakers into the back of
the van and climbed in beside Lightweight, who sat smoking.

'All right,' said Dash brightly. *(Two sets of speakers. Another
two sets of speakers in the back of the van. Why, Lord, why?)*
'We're all set. Let's get going. We'll need to stop at B&Q on the
way back to the flat.'

Lightweight threw his fag out of the window and let go of
the collar of his denim jacket to start the van. Gears crunching,
he eased it to the courtyard entrance as another van turned in.

'It's the Holloway Road boys,' said Dash, and the vans drew
level, stopping, one arriving, the other departing. Lightweight
and Dash looked across and the Holloway Road boys looked
back. The Holloway Road pair looked especially at Lightweight,
who looked especially back, all their lips seeming to curl. Dash
felt like, Okay, but leave me out of this, as he watched the three
men size each other up. And then the moment was gone.

'Do you know them?' said Dash, as the van pulled out into
the road. He tended to think that all black people knew each
other. They did where he lived anyway. Down his street the betting-
shop doorway was always flanked by a group of black guys
drinking out of cans, waving at cars that beeped as they drove
past. Then there was that fist-banging handshake. Dash envied
them their solidarity. But he was wrong. Certainly as far as
Lightweight and the Holloway Road team were concerned.

'Nah, man,' replied Lightweight. 'I dun't know 'em.'

They drove on with their precious cargo. Dash's thoughts

returned to selling speakers and he cranked open his window. As if Lightweight's stench wasn't enough, he'd broken out in a sweat himself. A nervous sweat. He'd read once, in that magazine Sophie worked for, that sweat didn't smell if it was your common-or-garden working-hard sweat. It only smelt if it was nervous, shit-dude-you-just-lost-a-million-on-the-stock-exchange sweat. That was how the magazine pitched it anyway. They didn't say anything about flogging speakers to yoga teachers.

At B&Q Dash got down and left Lightweight in the van while he scoured the aisles for packing tape, found it, bought it and rejoined his grey mate.

'All set,' said Dash, jeans meeting van seat, and they rattled off, back on the road, until presently he said, 'Here. Stop here.' Then, as he climbed down, 'Keep an eye out, okay?' Lightweight stared down at him, as though he was about to say, 'Chick din't say nothin about looking.'

'Jesus,' said Dash. 'Listen, please, just keep a look-out for a second, okay? I'm going to nick these bricks.'

He hated getting his hands dirty. The bricks, they'd be dirty. He picked up four. Then, conscious Lightweight would be looking, picked up two more, scooted back across the road and dumped them in the back of the van.

He clambered inside. 'Thanks for keeping an eye out,' he said sarcastically. He looked across at Lightweight, expecting him to ask about the bricks, but he didn't, just stared blankly ahead as he pulled off once more. Which was a shame, because Dash had been planning to tap the side of his nose and go, 'Ah. All will be revealed.'

Instead they drove in near silence to Dash's house, where they (actually, Dash) unloaded the two speaker sets, the bricks and packing tape, and yomped them up to the flat.

Inside, Lightweight lit a cigarette and leant by the door. 'You got a lot of speakers in here,' he said, in danger of breaking into a smile.

True. Dash had a lot of speakers in his flat. Much of the available floor space was taken up with cardboard boxes bearing the

Auridial logo. On their side and piled three high. Upright and piled two high. Dash and Sophie had no coffee-table: they used an Auridial box. On it sat the morning's cereal bowls, an ashtray and Sophie's nail polish. Over the way a potted plant sat atop an Auridial box next to the television. A stack of Sophie's magazines on another. In another corner an Auridial box made an interesting place to put the phone. And, ironically, Auridial boxes made excellent speaker stands for Dash's stereo. He surveyed his home balefully in the light of his new driver's remark.

'Yeah,' he said sadly. 'Yeah, I got a lot of speakers in here. But . . .' and he gave Lightweight an encouraging mates-together grin '. . . not for much longer, eh? Watch this.'

Deftly he removed the first of today's speakers from its box, fetched a screwdriver from the kitchen. Not that he needed it. He hadn't studied the rear of the speakers before, but the back panel clipped out with embarrassing ease. Oops.

For a moment or so he marvelled at the inside of the Auridial. Talk about beauty only being skin deep and all that. On the outside these speakers were behemoths of the music world, steroid-pumped stereo pumps. On the inside? A near-empty cabinet yawned derisively at him. A couple of spindly bits of wire, components like afterthoughts. No wonder they were so light.

Easily remedied. He cuddled two bricks together, wrapped them in packing tape and stuck them into the cabinet, replacing the panel to produce – hey, presto – the same speaker, *but heavier*. He repeated the process with the second and returned both to their box. Lightweight stood watching him, sometimes glancing down the hall like he wouldn't mind taking a look down there. But mostly just watching and smoking.

'A new sales technique,' explained Dash, although Lightweight hadn't asked. 'Gonna get the customers to have a lift of this thing so they know what a shit-kicking bit of kit they're buying.'

They loaded the newly heavy speakers into the van and drove off. Dash: not optimistic, not exactly. More . . . hopeful. Or hoping, at least. Okay, praying. But he spotted their first mark on Stamford Hill, early doors, could be a good sign. Or so he told Lightweight, who duly tortured the gears slowing and stopping.

Jesus, thought Dash, we're supposed to be deliverymen. Deliverymen can drive, for God's sake. At least they had the kid's attention. Dash grinned and cranked down the window as the kid went to walk past, eyeing them, knowing they were about to ask him something. Dash already had his docket in his hand. Always have your docket in your hand, he'd learnt. That way they thought you were about to ask for directions. Everyone liked being asked for directions.

'All right, mate?' he said to the kid. A white kid, in his teens, white polo shirt with the collar up, baseball cap and pimples. Ooh, thought Dash, as the kid came reluctantly closer, *bad* pimples. 'This is going to sound a bit mad, mate,' he said.

'What is?' said the kid.

Dash faltered. 'What I'm about to tell you,' he said.

The kid's eyes weren't looking at Dash. They were taking in the strange grey ghoul sitting next to him, who now sat in his customary pose of fag in one hand, collar of his denim jacket in the other.

'Thing is,' said Dash, all at once forced to fight a great tsunami of tiredness that threatened to engulf him, 'we've just made a delivery of speakers to one of the big clubs in town. Anyway, we've gone to the depot and picked up the order, which says two pairs on the docket, right, and then we get to the place and it turns out they only wanted one set . . .'

The kid's eyes ping-ponged between him and Lightweight, who broke out into a coughing fit, the noise like two dogs fighting.

'Sorry, mate,' the kid said, his eyes widening, backing away at the same time. 'Don't think I can help you. I'm not from round here.'

'No. You don't get it . . .' said Dash, but the kid was already turning away, off up the street with a final 'Sorry,' and a last nervous glance at Lightweight.

Dash turned to his new mate. 'You know, it might help if

you . . .' and Lightweight did a stare so his sentence never got to 'could try looking less like a dying junkie'. 'Oh, come on,' he said. 'Let's try down in the high street.'

They drove. Dash spotted another likely mark and they stopped, but this kid turned out to be wearing an ultra-discreet hearing-aid, and Dash, who hardly rated his salesman skills anyway, settled for asking him if he knew the way to Church Street.

'Kid with a hearing-aid,' chuckled Lightweight, as they drew away once again.

'You do realise,' said Dash, 'if I sell a set of speakers you get a percentage? But if I don't sell any speakers at all, you get nothing.'

'Best sell some speakers, then,' warned Lightweight.

'Best help me to, then.'

They drove on, until at last Dash pointed. 'There. Kid with headphones. We'll have a bit of that.'

They stopped. 'Hey, mate,' said Dash, 'this is going to sound like a bit of a mad one . . .'

The kid took off his headphones. 'Sorry?' he said.

'I said, this is going to sound a bit crazy, but—'

'Look,' said Barnaby Horton, 'if you're trying to sell me speakers, I've just bought a pair.'

7

'I think I'm going to leave him,' she said.

'Oh, Sophie, because he bought you that ghastly necklace?' asked Peter, and tipped lunchtime wine into an evil smile.

She cringed. 'No. You don't finish with someone because they bought you a pikey necklace.'

'Maybe *you* don't,' he said archly. 'Seems to me it's as good a reason as any . . .'

'It's not because of the necklace. It's because we're going in different directions.' She sounded as if she was quoting from the mag but she believed it. 'It's like, oh, I dunno, it's like, I feel as though – without sounding funny or anything – like I'm leaving him behind. Like I'm growing out of him. I mean, I'd die if he met you, or any of the girls at work, or Gabrielle. And that's not right, is it?'

She'd met Peter at work. In the toilets to be precise. She'd been in a complete daze, exciting day and all that. She'd been asked to wade through models' cards by Sacha on the picture desk, entrusted with the job of finding the right 'look' for a shoot they were doing on how to train your man like a puppy. This meant sorting through hundreds, and by the end of the day probably thousands, of pictures of male models, every single one of them staring from their cards with pleading eyes: 'Pick me, Sophie. I'm perfect to illustrate a feature on how to train your man like a puppy.' She was assiduously sorting them into piles of 'no' and 'maybe' (but by the end of the day she would be sick to the back teeth of staring at muscles and pouts and stubble, something she never would have thought possible, and would be tossing the cards on to piles with little or no deliberation) and dizzy with the thrill of it all, which was perhaps why what happened happened. Because she walked into the girls' toilets and came toe-to-toe with someone leaving. A bloke.

'God!' he said, and his hand went to his mouth. 'I'm *really* sorry. I'm in the wrong bog.'

'Oh,' she said, surprised.

'God, look, sorry,' he repeated, and went to hurry past her, dying of embarrassment, then stopped suddenly. 'Wait a minute,' he said. 'If I'm in the wrong toilet, what are *those* doing there?' And she looked to where he pointed, at a row of urinals against the wall, each adorned with a yellow go-faster stripe of ingrained piss down its centre, and she realised that it wasn't him who was in the wrong toilets – all those male models, she had men on the brain – it was her.

Now it was her turn to say, 'Oh, God', and 'Sorry', and be about to walk out but he was already doubled up laughing, stopping her, telling her, 'Christ, love, honest mistake, anyone can do it. I've done it meself only the other way round,' and she knew three things about him. One, he was from Liverpool. Two, he was gay. Three, he was going to be her friend whether he liked it or not. Because Sophie had always fantasised about having a gay male friend. And Liverpudlian gays were clearly the best sort. He would have an outrageous, irreverent sense of humour; he would have questionable dress sense himself but an almost inhuman ability to pick out the best outfits for her; he would have a disastrous, or pretty much non-existent love life; he would occasionally cry when he got drunk and talk about his parents, revealing a deeply wounded person beneath the professionally gay exterior; sometimes he would hurt her with unfeeling acerbic, waspish comments; he would change her life.

His name was Peter, and in the two weeks since that meeting they had indeed become friends, and although she'd never seen him in tears he ticked most of the other boxes. He worked on another floor, another magazine, where he entertained colleagues with his outrageous, irreverent sense of humour, and he'd taken to her immediately, treating her as a mix of best friend and exciting anthropological find.

So yesterday, when she'd worn her brand-new Tiffany necklace, it was Peter she'd been looking forward to seeing for the first of their many daily fag breaks so she could show off her new bit of bling.

Because it hadn't been easy. Like, she'd had to virtually bully Dash into buying it for her.

Sitting in the van now Dash found his thoughts revisiting the moment – like a man compelled to lift a bloodsoaked dressing and gaze at the ghastly mess below. In his mind he saw Sophie's finger, a carrot with a glossy oval pearl at its tip. It pointed into the display case and his gaze travelled past her pampered, ornately decorated nail through the glass of the case to land on a necklace. Not a ring, he thought, his feelings balanced somewhere between relief and disappointment, but a necklace. A heart pendant on a chunky chain: the Tiffany heart. And as tiny turquoise bags were passed to and fro around him, he realised he had not been persuaded up to level one of the Bond Street store for a look-and-that's-all. No, he'd been brought there for a more fundamental reason. Sophie's mouth was moving and her eyebrows knitted in such a way that he knew she was explaining how much she'd like a Tiffany heart, but he heard nothing. Around him other customers, mainly his age, bellowed into mobile phones. The staff were overworked, serving the Saturday crowd, dishing out Tiffany hearts as if they were Big Macs. Customers crowded the counter like it was a bar and they were dying for a pint with last orders seconds away. The air was heavy with smell-me scent and bristling with look-at-me attitude. A sea of bobbing baseball caps, already tooled-up with enough jewellery to feed a department-store Christmas tree. Later they'd do doughnuts round Asda car park, but not now: now they were making sure that no collarbone went naked. Now they were buying Tiffany hearts.

'I'm not sure, Soph,' said Dash, weakly, sickly, thinking only of Chick and the flat chock-full of Auridial boxes. Speaker's Corner, that was what Warren was calling it then. 'I just don't think I can afford it, babe.'

Sophie wasn't listening. All she could see were the girls around her, receiving their turquoise takeaways, already dialling to tell friends. All she could think about was Monday morning and the girls at work, Gabrielle, and Peter. She couldn't afford her own Tiffany heart, not on the tiny goodwill weekly money they paid her at the magazine – and, anyway, she shouldn't *have* to buy her own Tiffany heart. Her world-view was shaped and warped by MTV, where lyrics had been replaced by shopping lists. She didn't want no scrub. She wanted a man who could pay her bills. She wanted a Tiffany heart and she wanted Dash to buy it for her.

And she got it. Unaware that as she travelled to work on the Monday, with the heart proudly displayed round her neck, Dash was facing a crisis – Warren walking out; unaware that as she met Peter for the first cigarette of the day and raised her chin so her gay best friend could see her new bit of bling, Dash was being invited into the toilets by Chick for a phantom line of coke he didn't want anyway. 'Dash bought it for me,' she said proudly, as Peter took a closer look.

'Oh, God, you poor thing.' He recoiled. 'How common. And you're wearing it? Can't you pretend to lose it or something?'

Unaware that as she removed the necklace, feeling sick and wrong and stupid and cheated, Dash lay on the piss-stinking floor, crying tears of agony.

'And it's all those boxes,' she said, sipping her drink, which in direct contravention of the Atkins diet was also wine, watching Peter light a cigarette. 'And the people he brings round. This morning we had some crackhead at the door – you should have seen the state of him,' making out she wasn't secretly proud of Dash's crackhead.

'And the ghastly necklace.'

She sighed and pursed her lips at him. 'If I do, could I stay at yours?'

'Course you can, doll,' he said.

Somehow, when Peter called her 'doll', it almost sounded cool.

8

The television flickered silently. It had been flickering that way since about 6.30 a.m. when his journey had finally delivered him into the arms of the sofa, near-crying with relief to be home (such as it was). He'd lit a cigarette and smoked as financial news unfolded on the screen, trying to block out the memory of number six Cowley Close and failing – just as he'd failed on the journey home, the milk train they'd called it when he was younger, the first train to leave. Maybe once he would have shared it with bottles of milk (although, come to think of it, he couldn't recall ever seeing any milk on those trains, all those mornings, him and his mates piling drunk and wired on to the first train home). Now he shared it with half-awake men in suits, half-awake men in overalls, and two girls who wore black and had lots of piercings, and who were not half awake because they slept all the way, their heads leaning together. He watched them most of the way to London and envied them their youth, and that whatever weight they carried was almost certainly dwarfed by his own. But most of all he envied them rest.

So he'd arrived home and sat, bleached of sleep, while the fluctuations of the Tokyo market meant something to somebody somewhere; and then, as he felt himself at last drifting off, Darren and Sophie had woken up. With a thump. Which was probably one of them getting up . . . Yes. He imagined feet swinging from beneath a duvet and meeting ersatz wooden flooring, a bony heel making contact before steps began their odyssey to the bathroom and the light came on with a twang. Their clip-clop-thudding was almost comforting, as though there weren't many things in the world that could be relied upon, but Sophie and Darren, with their footsteps and bathroom light that went twang, were two of them. Above him he heard the rain of piss on porcelain and he took deep breaths rather than scream as the bathroom light twanged off (You didn't flush, thought Max. Wouldn't want to be in your shoes when Sophie twigs) and he followed the bony heels as they made their way along the hallway, jumped the three small steps there and entered the lounge.

Now, like a conductor, Max held trembling fingers in the air, counting Darren in as he hunted for the remote, found it, pointed it blearily at the TV, scratched his testicles and – ta-da – on came MTV. The day's curtain raised, Max followed Darren's footsteps into the kitchen where they came to rest, hiss of the cold-water tap, the kettle being filled. He reached for his cigarettes and lit one – Max, not Darren, who, upstairs, put the kettle on and stared out over Clarke Street, checking the van in the road below, a yawn that became a sigh that became a hand reaching into his hair.

'Darren. *Dar-ren*,' it came. Like a dog being told, 'Down.'

Both men heard it, their ears perking up.

Dash instantly recalled not flushing the toilet and assumed he'd failed to put the seat down into the bargain. And that second 'Dar-ren'? It probably meant drops of orange-coloured wee on the Armitage Shanks. A three-in-one deal. For a second he considered throwing up the sash window and taking a step outside. Maybe the fall would kill him. Knowing his luck, probably not.

'Darren, come and sort this toilet out!'

Below, Max rubbed a stubbly cheek and laid his head back to hear better. In front of him his TV continued to flicker silently. Two presenters sitting on a couch were laughing at something a guest had said.

He didn't need to turn up the volume on his television, he was tuned into *The Darren and Sophie Show*. No . . .

'Dar-ren.' MTV Base in the background.

'Yes, babe.' *Thump-thump-thump.*

It was *Darren & Sophie: The Musical*. Or simply *Darren & Sophie!* And it really got going in the morning, started off with one of its most bracing numbers. Got a bit quieter come nine-ish, when Sophie was off for most of the second act, but Darren kept the action going, thanks to a habit he had of leaving for work in his van then returning, hefting huge boxes with another man. These huge boxes were taken upstairs (*dub-a-dub-a-dum*) where they made a scraping-sliding sound on the not-wood floor (*fsh-k-fsh-k-fsh-k*), like a tuxedo-bloke at the back of the orchestra going mental with one of those drums you play with a brush. And then in the third act anything could happen. Sophie might come home and put her music on or – as she had been doing recently, Max had noticed – she'd arrive home late, clearly drunk, and stage a rousing late-night encore, a symphony of boozy uncoordination to the strains of MTV.

Max listened to the show – he barely even moved – until he heard a banging on the front door and Darren rushing to answer it. Someone in the hall leant against his door as Darren ran back upstairs. Whoever it was lit a cigarette that Max could smell.

Darren left, and some time later Sophie followed. Their flat fell quiet and, still without moving, his head thrown back and hands thrust deep into the pockets of his overcoat, Max gave himself up to sleep.

He woke shortly; sleep given to him, then rudely snatched away. Pushing palms into eyes that felt glued shut, he heard voices outside his door – Darren and friend. Up they went into the flat above, presumably hefting boxes. Max groaned.

From upstairs he heard the sound of box (or plural, numbers unknown) being dragged across the floor. Then, after some minutes, the upstairs flat door banging shut and one set of trainers taking the stairs two at a time, landing outside his door, another set moving more slowly. They'd been in the house – how long? – fifteen minutes? Ten? Enough, whatever – enough to wake him.

And then, to make himself feel worse, he shifted a hip and rooted in his coat pocket for the letter, which he unfolded and placed on the coffee-table in front of him. 'Dear Pervert,' it said. 'Why don't you do the world a favour and kill yourself?'

She got straight to the point, did Mrs Larkin's daughter.

He left the letter on the table and pushed his hands back into his coat pockets. A cold shiver, that just-woken-up chill. From the other pocket he pulled another envelope, different from the first in that its corner was missing and whatever it once contained had been removed. 'To the mum and dad of Little Ben,' it said, in felt-tip pen – sombre navy, a respectful colour. He replaced it in his pocket. In there were other envelopes, the same but different, a handful pulled from the wheelie-bin of number six Cowley Close.

Then, for the first time since the early hours, Max stood up, patted his pockets and left the flat. It was silent, too; he could have slept, but suddenly there was something he wanted to do.

'Oh. Max.'

Verity looked surprised, but not quite like the full drama of last night.

'You didn't expect to see me?' he offered, with a smile. 'And coming unannounced is not allowed, is strictly *verboten, ja?*'

'You could have called,' she said simply. 'Like you could have called last night.'

The wounds were still fresh, he thought. 'But if I'd called ahead I wouldn't have got to see you flustered and I like it when you get flustered. It gives the rest of us hope.'

She folded her arms, pursed her lips. 'What do you want? If you'd called ahead I might have been able to tell you that I've got to go out.'

'Well, have you?' He hoped to God she was saying it to make a point: his soul lurched at the idea of having to turn back.

'No.' There was a ghost of a smile at her lips. 'But that doesn't mean I've got time for you.' The lips tightened again. 'I had time for you *last night.*'

From behind his back he produced a bunch of flowers and presented them to her on the doorstep. A small bunch – all he could afford. Even so, she softened at the sight of them, saying, 'Oh, Max,' as he held them out towards her.

'I'm sorry, Ver,' he said, from behind crinkly plastic. 'But I had to work. Come on, take the flowers. Let's go inside.'

She ignored him for a moment, wanting to make a point. 'Oh, yes. Where was it you had to work? On Blackstock Road?'

'Green Lanes.'

'You sure? Not Balls Pond Road?'

'Green Lanes.'

'You're certain?'

'Can I go fifty-fifty? Ask the audience?'

She smiled in full then. First with him, then at him. But when Verity looked into her brother's face she saw he was going through the motions, doing the same brother-and-sister stuff they had always done. But not feeling it, doing it by rote. His own smile failed to dent his eyes, which had sunk, as though his eyelids bore invisible weights. Grey-black stubble seasoned his face and that same grubby coat hung off him. She looked up the street and realised – at some level she once hoped she'd never sink to – that she was looking out for neighbours: worried they might see Max on the doorstep; worried about what they might think if they did.

'I'd better take those,' she said, reaching for the bouquet. 'And you'd better come in. People will think I've got myself a fancy man.' She stepped aside to allow Max through. 'I can spare you the time for a cup of tea at least.'

He passed her the flowers and walked in, assaulted by the smell of a plug-in air-freshener, and made his way to the kitchen, pulled out a chair and sat down. The kitchen was pristine, all the countrified earthenware just where it should be; colder, thanks to an open window, and brighter than last night. He glanced around, not really looking for anything, as if verifying that the kitchen was empty.

She moved to the side and took up the silver kettle, clicked it on and turned to face Max, who sat brushing a hand over the table's surface: soft, moist, almost bouncy. She watched him do it; saw the look, like complete contentment, that came over him as he ran his hand across the wood. He'd restored it in the back room of his shop, then presented it to them as an anniversary present. Late, of course – he had an image to maintain.

'How did it go, then, "the job"?' she said, arranging the flowers in a vase.

'Oh, you know,' said Max. He stood and went to the mugs on hooks, took two down and passed them to Verity, who accepted them with thanks.

'Will it lead to anything else?'

'Hopefully. Maybe.'

'And did you have any more thoughts about what we discussed yesterday?' she said, reaching for the cork-topped teabag jar.

He looked at her and frowned. 'Where are your spoons?' he asked, pointedly ignoring her.

'Please don't avoid the question,' she said, found a spoon herself and stirred the tea. They returned to the table, mugs in hands.

'Okay, then, the answer is, no, I haven't had any more thoughts about what we discussed last night.'

She shook her head and stared hard at him. He avoided her eye and the silence between them ticked on, each of them sipping tea and thinking private thoughts.

'How did Roger's quiz go last night?' he asked, after a time.

'There was a bit of trouble. Some homeless bloke turned up and won. Apparently he'd found the answers in a bin.' She looked at Max, frowning but pleased that the silence was over.

Max brazened it out. 'That reminds me,' he said. 'I was wondering, could I use his computer?'

She snorted. 'Roger's computer? Don't be ridiculous. What on earth would you want with his computer?'

'The Internet, that's all. I won't be a couple of minutes.'

'And what on earth do you want on the Internet?'

'There's a site, apparently, jobs in the furniture trade.' He attempted to smile.

'And you know how to use it?' she said, then thought how patronising that was – that, anyway, she was pretty sure Max could use the Internet. Before he could answer: 'Well, you can't use Roger's computer. Not even I can use it – which is why I have my own. You can use that.'

Minutes later he sat in her dressing room in front of the

computer and she leant over him to type a password and double-click the Internet icon. 'I can do it,' he said. 'Thanks, but I'll be fine. You go and do whatever you've got to do.'

'Can't I see this site?' She looked down at him.

'Are you really interested in a load of jobs to do with furniture? Just leave me to it. I don't like to be watched – nobody does.' He gave her a light shove towards the door.

'All right,' she said, leaving the room. 'Give me a shout when you're done.'

He watched her go and turned to the screen. It was a long time since he'd used the Internet; he wondered if he'd remember. He aimed the little pointer and clicked, half expecting sirens to go off, thought about it a second and typed the Google address.

The new page was familiar and he felt it all coming back to him, old dogs never forgetting how to ride bikes and all that. He stole a look at the door, then clicked on the Google subject box. He typed 'Ben Snape' and clicked Search.

He'd known the name, of course, as soon as he saw it, a fistful of envelopes in his hand. He'd known about Ben Snape and how the little boy had gone missing on the Underground – just down the road from him, as it happened.

As it happened? Yes, maybe, yes – because these things had a habit of going on, especially in London. You turned on the telly and there was a national news event in your front garden, streets you knew like the back of your hand suddenly in telly size, so you had to look twice, make sure your eyes weren't deceiving you. But that was it. That was as far as your relationship with it went.

Except yesterday he'd been told to forget doing the bags in his area that night, needed elsewhere for a special one-off, this address in Kettering. And it had turned out to belong to Patrick and Deborah Snape.

He clicked for news stories, sifting through what he found, searching out the details, looking for something although he wasn't sure what.

Ben, he read, six years old. Patrick Snape, thirty-six. The family lived in Kettering, Northamptonshire. (Number six Cowley Close, to be precise, thought Max.) The mother's name Deborah, thirty-five. Ben had disappeared on the afternoon of Saturday, 22 February, when father and son had been due to attend a football match, Arsenal v. Tottenham Hotspur. Ben had become separated from his father following an altercation with some youths on Finsbury Park tube station, leaving Patrick Snape on the platform and his son on the train, ferrying him onwards alone and, presumably, frightened. Of those passengers on the train who came forward, several had seen Ben Snape in the carriage, but none, they said, was aware that the boy was alone. He did not seem in any particular distress: the carriage was bulging with supporters; they themselves had been concerned about reaching the game in time. No witnesses reported seeing Ben leave the train at Arsenal station, but that was because he hadn't. The next sighting of Ben was taken from CCTV cameras on Holloway Road station, one station along the Piccadilly Line. At some point between boarding the train at Finsbury Park and leaving it at Holloway Road Ben had been approached by another party, because indistinct security pictures showed him leaving Holloway Road station in the company of what looked like an adult female. This woman was described as being anywhere between about seventeen and forty, white female, androgynous sports clothes. Head down, all that marked her out as female was cleavage pushed into a scoop-necked T-shirt top and a ponytail pulled through the back of her baseball cap, this bearing some kind of logo – probably of Arsenal Football Club. Her features were not visible: she kept her head lowered, possibly aware of the camera. One hand held Ben's. The other was in front of her, perhaps covering her face. Ben and his companion were briefly captured by a camera located at a Peugeot dealership on Holloway Road. It was the last known sighting of either of them. Police were keen to speak to the woman seen with Ben, in order to eliminate her from their enquiries. As far as Max could make out, they had not been able to do so.

The officer in charge of the case had made appeals. 'I am

talking now to the woman who took Ben Snape. You are in our thoughts. We can help you,' he said, the first time; on the second occasion he was appealing not to the woman who had taken Ben but to her friends and family, anybody who might suspect something strange. 'We think Ben is alive and being cared for somewhere,' said the detective chief inspector. 'And probably being cared for very well. But wherever he is, whoever has him and however much they love him, Ben belongs with his mummy and daddy. If you suspect anything, whatever it is, however insignificant you think it might be, please, please, get in touch. Please help us find him.'

9

'What's your name?' he'd said to her once.

She turned her head away before she answered him. 'You can call me Auntie, darling. Just call me Auntie.'

She did that, he noticed, when he asked her questions. Like when he asked her: 'Auntie, when am I going home?'

Turn of the head. 'Soon, darlin'.' And her voice went high on the word 'soon'.

Then there was: 'Are you sure this medicine works, Auntie?'

Turn of the head. 'Of course it does, darlin'. Of course it does.'

The first time she'd given him the Coke he drank it all the way down the way she wanted him to. Even though it had some kind of grit in it, and he didn't really want to, it seemed rude not to drink as she'd asked. He looked at her over the lip of the beaker. She was making a drink-up face at him, gesturing with her hands, so obediently he gulped it down. When he left some at the bottom, bits of stuff floating in it, she took the beaker from him and gave it a swish, handed it back to him and made the same drink-up face until he'd swallowed it all.

'When am I going home?' he'd asked. (He'd been asking the same question for hours: it was Daniel Marshall's birthday party the next day.)

'Soon, love,' the woman replied. She looked like the sort of woman you see in the supermarket, shouting at kids who blinked and looked sideways at Ben, tightening their mouths, scaring him a bit. 'Soon,' she added. 'But I've called your mummy and daddy and they're a bit too busy to come and get you at the moment so they've asked me to take care of you until they can. I said, "That's fine, I'd love to take care of the little chap," but I'd have to put him in the spare room, which ent been decorated yet, and they said, "That won't worry Ben, he can sleep anywhere because he's such a good little boy and he always does what a grown-up tells him." And it's the same with the toilet, darlin'. We're having, uh, work done on it at the moment so we're having to make do, all of us, so for you I've got . . .' Apologetically, she indicated a large bucket in the corner of the room, roll of toilet paper beside it. 'Look.' She went over to it and showed him how he could cover the bucket with a square of what looked like kitchen worktop 'to stop the smells'. She demonstrated the procedure like it was some mod con to be proud of.

There was something about the way she spoke to him. She seemed not-right-somehow. Like his mum when she'd had to stop and ask directions that time and the first person she spoke to wasn't very helpful so she'd got a bit snappy with him. This woman was like that. As though she was a bit scared of something. It made him even more nervous, and he already felt unhappy because he'd missed the match (his first football match ever and he'd missed it!), and it was Daniel Marshall's birthday tomorrow, and he'd been promised Chicken McNuggets for tea. And because he really, really wanted to be at home.

But he was being brave, like the lady said. She said if he was brave then Mummy and Daddy were going to make it up to him, and what was the thing he most wanted? He'd thought about it and said that he wanted a club shirt, and lots more stickers for his album and a new Mario game, if there was one out. She'd said, well, funnily enough that was exactly what they were planning to treat him with if he was brave. And what was his favourite food? She'd make sure she brought him some to eat – as a present for being good.

Not long after that she'd tucked him up in bed, and she'd flicked off the light and closed the door behind her, and he immediately wanted to switch the light back on but suddenly felt very sleepy and the bed – even though it wasn't his own and, looking at it, should have been the most uncomfortable thing he'd ever slept in, including the one he had to sleep in when he went to

Nanny Snape's – suddenly felt really, really comfy. And as he began to doze off he thought of Christmas Eve, when it was so hard to get off to sleep, and how annoying that was, because the sooner you went to sleep the sooner it was Christmas morning. This was different. It was easy to sleep, and when he woke up it would be the next morning and he'd be going home, and to Daniel Marshall's birthday party . . .

Only he didn't, of course. When he awoke next he was still in the room, which was cold and dark – grey-dark. He lay there feeling drowsy and scared until the door opened and a hand slid through and flicked the light switch. He sat up, rubbing his eyes, which hurt with the glare. A moment later the woman came into the room. She slid through the door the same way she had done the day before (at least, he thought it was the day before, but had no way of knowing for sure. And did that mean he'd missed – or was *actually missing* the party? Was it going on without him?)

'Hello, darling,' she said, sitting on the side of his bed. She'd brought him some food, his favourite Chicken McNuggets, which she let him eat from the box – something he wasn't allowed to do at home. Had he heard anything? she asked him. There were no noises disturbing him, were there? No, he'd told her, truthfully – he'd been sleeping. She said that was good, and smiled. And the smile and the McNuggets cheered him up slightly, but when he asked about going home she told him that he'd be going home soon – just 'soon' – and she gave him another gritty beaker of Coke to drink. Just like before.

'It's got bits in it,' he said that time, not worried about being polite, just not wanting to drink another gritty Coke.

'I know, sweetheart.' She stroked his hair. 'But this is special Coke, with a special flavour.'

'Can't I have the Coke that came with the Chicken McNuggets?' he asked.

She thought about this, then said, 'You can't have that Coke, you've got to have this special Coke. See, you're a bit ill at the moment. It's the sort of ill you can't feel, but you are. And drinking this will make you feel better, and you can't go home till you're properly better, can you?'

So he drank the Coke – all of it: she swished it around to make sure – and she made him lie down and tucked him up, collected up the empty McDonald's boxes and left the room, switching off the light, then closing the door.

He lay in the dark room and stared up at the window. He began to cry, which he knew he shouldn't because crying only made it worse; but then again, sometimes it was good to get it all out. In the end he just let himself cry until he felt a bit better, and he started to sing 'Yellow Submarine', and even though he wished he could be singing it with his dad, the way he normally did, the words cheered him up a bit. So he sang it over and over until he realised he felt really drowsy again, and the bed felt really comfy. And he fell asleep.

And the grit wasn't just in the Coke.

'What other food do you like, darlin'?' she asked early on, stroking his hair, which he half liked, and half didn't (when she was doing it, he wanted her to stop, but when she stopped he wished she hadn't). 'It can't be just Chicken McNuggets, now, can it? Must be something else you like. Little lads that I know love their baked beans . . .'

Up until then he'd forgotten, but the words 'baked beans' lit up in his head like the Hollywood sign. 'Baked beans,' he said, 'and sausages!'

'Aha,' she said, pleased with him.

'But only the Heinz ones,' he remembered. 'Not the other makes.'

So then – and this, he thought, was a massive change from the usual routine – he was given baked beans and sausages, but . . . for breakfast. They came in a flask. The first time she did it he was a bit disgusted the way the beans and sausages slopped out of the Thermos. She poured them into a bowl, like a cereal bowl – about the only breakfasty thing about his morning meal – and handed them to him with a spoon. Still, though, they were baked beans and sausages and they were the Heinz type (you could tell: the sausages were like mini hot-dog ones) and the flask had certainly kept them warm. They were steaming, and they smelled up the room. They reminded him of the kitchen at home.

'I didn't know if you'd want bits of bread with them,' she said. 'If you'd prefer to have baked beans on toast I can do you some toast, no bother, like.'

'This is lovely, thank you,' he said politely, but thinking that, actually, bits of toast with melted butter (like at home) would be perfect.

'Good lad.' She ruffled his hair. 'Now, let's see if you can be a big boy and eat them all up.'

It was one of her worst habits. She talked to him like he was *four* or something. Come on, he was six. That's six, not stupid. Still, he ate the beans and sausages and what should he find on almost the first spoonful out of the bowl? Those very same bits of white grit. The white grit she insisted he drink out of his Coke when she came to visit later in the day.

'Sorry, darlin',' she frowned sympathetically at him, 'but you got to have your medicine, ent'cha? What would your mum say to me if she thought I wasn't helping you get better? She'd have my guts for washing-line, she would.'

Ben wasn't entirely sure whether the lady's guts would make good washing-line. They had a rotary in the garden at Kettering. What she meant was that Ben's mum would be angry, and she'd probably be the kind of angry that made Ben's dad look at Ben and do a cartoon 'erk' face. 'Shall we run and hide, Ben? Sounds like your mother's on the warpath.'

'And you two can stop looking like butter wouldn't melt as well,' she'd say, always. They drew pretend halos over their heads.

Not long ago, before the day of the match, Ben had learnt a lesson. Getting off the school bus he'd joined a throng, a million kids like him, all making their way up the path to school, and all wearing more or less the same clothes, with more or less the same rucksacks on their backs. They all talked about more or less the same things: last night's TV – the daily who-stayed-up-latest-last-night contest – and football, which they measured not by their team's results but the merchandise they owned, and sticker albums, and Nintendo, and what they planned to do that day, which they talked about like they'd only just discovered the first-person, which they had: 'And then, later, *I* am going to go swimming, and *I* am going to have Ben & Jerry's, and *I* am going to watch a *Spider-Man* film on dee-vee-dee . . .'

Walking up the path with another six-year-old boy's day ahead of him – of constant oneupmanship and the fat weight of learning they were supposed to bear each day – something hit him. It jolted him. It bashed into him like a punch that was surprising more than painful. It was the love he felt for his mother. He was shocked to suddenly find himself fighting back tears; shocked to find the word 'love' that he heard in his house often, and that had existed as just that, really, a word, was something more than that. It was a feeling, and a scary one. And it wasn't necessarily something you could rely on . . .

10

Standing on the pavement, Dash doing the wargh-wargh thing at him, Barnaby Horton looked pissed off – and with good reason. 'If you're trying to sell me speakers, I've just bought a pair,' he said, and added, 'from two blokes in a white van, as it happens.'

'What did they look like?' said Dash.

'About this high.'

'Not the speakers. The guys you bought them off.'

'I dunno.' Barnaby frowned at the memory. 'Two big black geezers.' His eyes shifted to Lightweight, smoking.

'White van, you say?'

'Just like this one.' He began to walk away.

'Did it have "also available in white" written on the back?' called Dash.

'Don't they all?' said Barnaby, over his shoulder, and he was gone, into the offy, where outside a homeless man with a huge cobweb tattoo on his face sat watching the world go by.

Beside him Lightweight chuckled. 'Already bought speakers,' he said to himself, chuckling some more. 'He don't want no more speakers.'

'Yeah, but you know what this means?' said Dash, turning, his eyes bright with plans. 'You know what this means?'

'Yeah, man, it means you ent selling no fuckin' speakers and I'm wasting my time with you.'

Yes, well, my off-colour friend, thought Dash, now we're going to sell some speakers at last, and *you* are going to start helping. But he said, 'No, it means the Holloway Road boys are out of their area. They're round here. And if they're round here, we can be round *there*.'

'Why would they be round here?' Lightweight's eyes narrowed.

Dash should have thought, Yeah, actually, what would they be doing round here? But his logic centre was impaired by excitement. Instead: 'Who cares? Let's get down there.'

Lightweight shrugged, released the collar of his denim jacket and pulled away from the kerb. This is more like it, thought Dash. None of Warren's moaning. Now he had Lightweight and whether he was indifferent or simply unafraid made no odds to Dash. They were on their way to Holloway Road. Dash found his breath catching as they rattled down to Finsbury Park. He didn't need to consult his map to know they'd betrayed the black marker-pen outline of his area. He thought of the speakers in the back, weighed down now with his innovation.

'Go round here,' he said to Lightweight, who crunched the gears but obeyed, and at last they nosed on to Holloway Road, just north of the country's most infamous women's prison, landmarked by a huge Odeon cinema in the art-deco style, where local kids let each other in through the fire escapes; base for thousands of north London students, college buildings lining its imposing length almost up to Archway, where it then joined Highgate and next filtered motorists to the A1 and M1, which led to places like Kettering.

And it was home to the *al fresco* salesman. Here on Holloway Road the pavements were miserly lanes between street stalls. You could buy six lighters for a pound; batteries that looked a lot like Duracell, but weren't, and wouldn't last two minutes; cigarettes that really did look a *lot* like Marlboro Lights, but would shred your lungs soon as you set fire to one; and perfume, ditto the perfume. All sold by streetwise entrepreneurs one rung above the kids who raced across the road soaping unwilling windscreens with smeggy water; another rung above the homeless people who sat with dogs panting at their feet. If you've got something to sell, come to Holloway Road. And if you've got something to sell to students, come to sunny Holloway Road.

'Stop here a sec,' said Dash, his mouth watering. Lightweight drew to a halt outside one of the college buildings and the pair of them drank in the sight. Or Dash drank in the sight. Like the beer in *Ice Cold in Alex*, he gulped it down. Students were mounting the steps carrying folders. Others were coming out and groups sat smoking, gabbing away, enjoying the bright, fresh day. All of them young, desperate to spend their grants, or loans, or whatever it was they were given to waste these days. Desperate to buy speakers. To Dash it was like arriving at the Promised Land and finding all the rumours were true. Like the drought was finally over.

'Tell you what,' said Dash, 'go about fifty yards up the road so we're not right in front of the building.'

''S a bus lane,' pointed out Lightweight, drawing forward and stopping.

'Yeah, well, keep a lookout,' said Dash, grabbing his docket and the Auridial brochure and diving out of the van before Lightweight could say the inevitable.

New approach. Got to get the customer feeling the weight of these beauties. He threw open the van doors and pulled the speakers forward, rubbing his hands and stepping out, waiting for the first customer and feeling like P.T. Barnum. He didn't have to wait long. Strolling past was a kid who looked like he'd been born to buy speakers, ambling along in the sunshine, titchy little personal-stereo headphones and a look on his face like someone off to market in a nursery rhyme.

'Hey, mate,' said Dash, with a smile. He stood by the doors. Behind him his speakers guarded the interior to the van, impressive-looking sentinels. The kid was like, *'Me?'* He looked as though he'd just discovered hair gel, his fringe moulded up into a fierce barricade.

'Yeah,' said Dash, still smiling as warmly as he could manage. He judged that a smile was key in this sale. 'Yeah, look, got something you might be interested in here . . .'

The kid was flattered. That was the idea. He was flattered that Dash thought him a cool enough cat to want a boss set of speakers, so he took a step closer. If the Auridial was equipped with a tractor beam, effective only on young men, it was now switched on.

When Dash was a child his dad had taken him on fishing trips. The young Darren liked buying floats best. In fishing terms, the more floats you had, the better fisherman you were – or that was how he had seen it. You'd attach your float to your line, then bait your hook, either with maggots, which Darren's mum disapproved of ('There's no way you're storing those in my fridge, young man'), or with bread, which they squished up and mixed with custard powder. The fish liked custard powder, for some reason. And what you did – you cast your line and then you'd sit and watch your float navigate the undulations of the canal until it bobbed. Just a little bob at first. It meant a fish was showing interest. 'Not too soon, Darren,' advised Dash's dad, because if you struck too soon you'd lose the fish. So you left it until the float really started bobbing, and when it got super fast, you'd know it was ready to go . . . under. Then you struck. And Darren usually lost the fish because he was too quick, or too slow, and it was always with a slight sense of relief, because he was a bit squeamish about getting the hooks out of their mouths, to tell the truth. He was quite a sensitive youngster.

Now he looked at the kid and he felt the float begin to bob, just a little. Like the kid was having a wee nibble.

'Feel the weight of that.' He motioned to the kid to heft a speaker, and as he looked suitably impressed Dash went into his spiel about the delivery, introducing the detail (a clever one, he thought) that the pair he'd just delivered had been for the students' union. He explained that taking them back just meant a gift for the depot foreman. He fished out the docket, continuing the pitch. 'So, might as well flog them. You know, make a bit of beer money . . .'

'How much you looking for, then?' said the kid.

'Four hundred quid!' shouted Dash, waving the money like a quiz-show host.

He'd done the sale and clambered into the van with the kid, making sure his customer sat on the outside, as far away from

Lightweight as possible. All the time he was thinking, *Four hundred quid.*

They'd gone to the kid's bank where Dash had overseen the withdrawal of *four hundred quid*, then driven the kid to Kentish Town and the dump where he lived to help him offload the speakers. Then they kindly gave him a lift back up to Holloway Road, where he stepped out with a grateful wave and a nervous glance at Lightweight, and now – at last – Dash shouted, 'Four hundred quid!'

In return Lightweight looked unknowable and malevolent, like running feet in the dead of night.

'Four hundred quid, come on,' said Dash, his smile fading. 'I've just earned four hundred quid.'

'You did good,' said Lightweight.

Praise indeed. Damn straight I did good, thought Dash. I did better than good.

They were on the Seven Sisters Road. Headed back through Finsbury Park and ultimately to *chez* Dash. New consignment of speakers. Second visit to Holloway Road – he'd already decided.

'But thing is,' said Lightweight, his voice low, 'how much of that four hundred quid is for me?'

Dash instantly regretted his boasting. He thought quickly but not hard. 'How much did Chick say?'

'He din't.'

'Well, you get fifty pounds a day for driving. That's all.' *Oh, Jesus, that was such a bad lie.*

And it didn't wash with Lightweight. 'He din't say how much, he said a percentage that I had to negotiate with you.'

'Right,' said Dash, thinking, *Negotiate?* 'What about five per cent?' Warren had been on ten per cent.

Lightweight's face crowded in on itself as he attempted to do the maths. 'Twenny pound?' he said at last.

'Yeah.'

Lightweight pulled over to the side of the road.

'Hey,' said Dash. A medley of car horns greeted their sudden arrest. 'Don't stop it here.' Customers at a packed hairdresser's looked round uninterestedly at the noise. Pedestrians gazed at the white van for a moment, then away. Behind them cars beeped and were forced to pull into the next lane, a consecutive reach for the indicator arm.

'Twenny quid ent gonna do it, bro,' said Lightweight, evenly.

I'm a 'bro' all of a sudden, thought Dash, but replied, 'Twenny quid is five per cent.'

'Then five per cent's a bullshit number. Chick din't say nothin' about you not selling no fuckin' speakers.'

'What do you mean? I just have.'

'One sale, man. Thass like fuck-all. I want a hundred off that one.'

At their backs cars went on honking, and Lightweight looked at Dash as if to say: I used to work at the Kwik Save, and Dash shook his head, thinking, For fuck's sake. 'All right,' he said, in a sigh. 'All right, I'll give you a hundred but only because it was an okay sale. There's no way I'm giving you a hundred for every pair we sell.'

'I'll tek it now, if it's all the same to you.' Lightweight held out one grey, trembling palm, and Dash reluctantly crossed it with paper money. The recovering crackhead stuffed the lot into a top pocket of his denim jacket. 'Nice doing business with you,' he said nastily, and didn't really bother checking his wing mirror before he pulled back into the traffic flow.

It hadn't always been like this, thought Dash, ruefully. The early days, him and Warren, they'd rocked it. Not for long, granted, but they'd rocked it all the same. And for a brief time Dash had dared believe that things might turn out okay: that he might be able to meet the sudden hike in rent forced upon him by his girlfriend, who threatened, 'I want to live somewhere *nice*. It's got to be something *modern* and *trendy*,' and who nearly swooned when she saw the wooden flooring. And as for paying for it, well, she did what she could, which mainly, it seemed to him, was sit around complaining about the speakers, which he needed to sell to afford the nice, modern, trendy flat. Only it wasn't so nice, modern and trendy when it was filled with speakers. There are only so many games of hide and seek you can suggest.

The early days, though. Things had looked rosy, they really had. It felt like the sun was always shining on them as they sped around Stokey in their white van, like two gods. Dash had felt seven feet tall. Ask him about the kid with Tourette's and he would have said, Who? He'd sold a pair of speakers to a bird who drove a Merc, who had long, delicious legs, and who was *definitely* coming on to him, no question. If it hadn't been for Sophie – if he wasn't, like, one hundred per cent faithful or your money back – who knows what might have happened? Who knows?

Things change, though, he thought. And things had really changed. But why did they have to change so quickly? Why couldn't he have enjoyed the sun-and-god feeling a bit longer?

Lightweight never checked his wing mirrors. And those wing mirrors – they were fine for admiring the Eiffel Tower if you happened to be driving away from Paris, but they were too tall and thin for motoring around north London, especially if you were supposed to be keeping an eye out for a rival team. So they were useless, and Lightweight never bothered checking them anyway, which was why he didn't see the van behind. Neither of them did.

Time had stood still since Dash's last visit to the Flat Cap. There at the bar were the three crones, cackling. Polluting the atmosphere was the smell like old blankets, with maybe just a hint – now he thought about it – just a hint of damp second-hand novels; there was the blackboard – 'Why not take our amazing pork scratchings taste test?' – and the landlord in, no, not a Foreigner T-shirt this time: he had switched allegiance to Van Halen. Apart from that, everything the same, including Chick, raising mock-surprised eyebrows as Dash approached, almost forgetting to down the last of a pint of Guinness. Almost.

'Dashus,' said Chick, wiping foam from his vile mouth. 'Wasn't expecting to see you so early. Knocked off for the day, is it?'

'Well, yeah, kind of,' replied Dash, wondering if maybe he should have waited. Yes, on second thoughts he should have waited. Stupid Dash. 'But I got you your money.' He reached into his jeans for the wad.

Chick sniffed as Dash produced it and handed it across the table with a glance at Van Halen – too busy entertaining the crones; besides, Chick didn't seem to care either way.

'How much you got?' said Chick. 'Tell you what, I'll count it while you get a round in.'

Dash had just handed over all the money he had on him. 'Actually . . . boss, I'm a bit brassic at the minute,' he said. 'I need to get to a bank.'

'Don't sweat it. There's a Lloyds over the road. I'll see you in a minute. And don't fart around. I'm gasping here.'

Dash went out into the high street and across the road to the Lloyds, where a homeless man sat by the cash machine. He wore dirty tracksuit bottoms and an old coat like a bookie's cast-off. He looked up as Dash pushed his card into the machine, dreading the ATM's answer. 'Spare change?'

'I'm sorry, mate,' Dash said, tapping Sophie's birthday into the keypad. 'No spare change on me.'

'I'll take a tenner.'

'Like I say, mate, sorry. Nothing spare.' Dash had bigger things to worry about. The fact that the cash machine was refusing his request for forty pounds, for example; refused it when he down-sized it to thirty, then acquiesced at twenty.

'Jesus, don't do that to me,' scolded Dash, snatching the money and not bothering to wait for his receipt. He cringed at the memory of Tiffany's, handing over his card, wondering if it would get rejected and almost disappointed when it wasn't. Another thought – *next month's rent* – hovered like a vampire bat.

Now he scooted back over the road and into the the Flat Cap where he waved at Chick, who didn't acknowledge him, went to the bar, ordered a Guinness and a half-pint of your weakest and cheapest lager, landlord, then returned to the table having avoided once again the amazing pork scratchings taste test challenge.

Chick looked down at his pint like it was HIV positive. 'What the fuck is this?' he said.

'Guinness,' ventured Dash, remembering too late. 'Oh, no, look, I'm sorry.' For a mad moment his hand hovered over the creamy head on Chick's Guinness, as if he was about to try to wipe off the offending shamrock. He resisted a look behind at Van Halen, imagining the treacherous landlord laughing spitefully at his back. 'Do you want me to go and . . .'

But in reply Chick lifted his Guinness, took a deep breath, puffed out his cheeks and blew the top off his pint as hard as he could.

Dash took it like a money shot, straight in the face. He closed his eyes for a second and felt foam stream down his cheeks. Behind him Van Halen and the old crones guffawed. At him, he assumed. He didn't bother looking round to check.

'Come on,' said Chick. 'We're going to the bogs for a line.'

'Oh, no, please,' said Dash. 'Look, boss, I'm sorry. I just . . .'

Chick leant across, snarling, 'Listen, you grovelling little poof, get your arse into the bogs now,' and Dash had no choice. No choice but to stand and follow as Chick led the all-too-familiar way to the gents', Dash the condemned man. They'd barely stepped inside when Chick turned and began chopping up on the shelf below the mirror, his Blockbuster card going swish-swish, chop-chop. 'I ent happy.' He stated the obvious.

'It won't happen again,' said Dash, desperate not to grovel, thinking only of how to avoid the inevitable knee in the bollocks. He'd heard that Sumo wrestlers had a way of tucking their soft and vulnerable sexual organs up and into their bodies to prevent injury in that area; found himself wishing he'd paid more attention – maybe there were instructions as to how they did it. On the Internet, perhaps.

'It better not. But I ent talking about the pint. I'm talking about the money.'

'But it's there, what I owe you.'

Swish-swish, chop-chop. 'It ent. Only some of it's there. You're a hundred notes short. And you turn up here, early doors, like you've taken the afternoon off,' swish-swish, chop-chop, 'and give it me light. What do you think I am? Some sort of fucking bank?'

Swish-swish. Chop-chop.

'No. No, of course not. I thought – I honestly thought – it was the whole whack.' And he had, he honestly had. But what he hadn't done was taken into account the interest Chick had added for late payment, because even though Chick didn't like being taken for a bank he was going to act like one. It was all there in the notebook Chick had shown Dash only yesterday, except Dash hadn't given it a close look.

'Well, it wasn't the whole whack,' said Chick. Swish-swish, chop-chop. Not bothering to explain about the interest, the notebook. It was all there in black and white. Fucked if he could be bothered to explain it to the little poof if he couldn't be arsed to read it. 'Like I say, you were a hundred short, and that's before we even talk about what you owe me for this week, which is almost due by my reckoning.' He finished swishing and chopping, turned to face Dash.

Dash who stood now, like it or not with his hands hovering at his groin, as though waiting for a free kick.

'Oh, behave.' Chick took a tenner from Dash's wad, rolled it up and handed it over. 'Get your hands away from your bollocks and hoover that up,' he commanded, indicating the shelf. For the first time Dash noticed that two lines of coke were laid out. He began daring to believe that his punishment would be . . . not cancelled but delayed. Put on hold.

'Are you sure?' he said.

'It's there, innit?' said Chick, stepping aside.

Dash took the rolled-up note and leant in to snort up the line. His hand shook. For a mad second, as his trembling hand seemed to spread half his line across the shelf, he wondered how Lightweight managed, being a junkie. Did you need a steady hand to smoke crack?

'Look at that,' said Chick, using his video card to append his own line with Dash's wastage, 'you missed half of it,' and he, too, bent his head to the shelf.

Immediately Dash felt better. The coke seemed to widen his eyes, wake him up, shrug off some of his fears.

Then: 'It's an anaesthetic, did you know?' said Chick.

'Sorry?'

'Yeah, it's an anaesthetic,' said Chick. 'They used to use it for medical purposes, and still do, for cancer patients and that. So you can't feel pain, innit?'

'Really?' said Dash, his head nodding despite himself, as though on a spring.

'Yeah, really,' and Chick smiled. Suddenly Dash understood and his hands went back to his groin ('Come on, boss, no, come on'), wishing he knew how to do that Sumo thing, or that he'd fitted a cricket box before he came, or had come later, or better yet not at all. Wishing that in all the bars in all of Stoke Newington he hadn't stepped into the Flat Cap the day he met Chick.

Wishing that cocaine was, in fact, a general anaesthetic, not a local one . . .

'Hands away,' said Chick.

Dash danced in front of him, his nose running suddenly, his head, which just a second ago had been nodding madly, now shaking just as madly, his hands at his groin.

'Hands away,' commanded Chick, steadying him at the shoulders. 'Come on, hands away.'

'Boss, no, I'll bring it tomorrow. All of it.'

Chick let go. 'You sure about that?'

'Yes,' said Dash, nodding again. 'Please, yes, I promise.'

He gestured for emphasis and Chick used the opportunity to knee him in the bollocks. 'Best make sure you do, mate,' he said, as Dash writhed on the Flat Cap toilet floor. 'And don't think I've forgotten you owe me some vouchers into the bargain.'

That night, Dash would lie lay awake in his bed, his eyes wide and wet, his hands deep between his legs. He'd lie awake that way hearing the front door go – late, very late – and listen as a drunken Sophie kicked off her shoes and put on the television; keep listening as it went off some time later and Sophie tottered first to the bathroom, where she threw up, and then to bed. Later, he would pull himself from the bed and begin to dress.

11

Max lit a cigarette and dug the ball of his thumb into his eye, sanding away the tear that lurked there. In his head was a picture of a little boy who might have been Ben, or even Max at that age, when it had felt to him like life would never change. How it would always be smiles and glasses of orange squash on a sunny day – gloves if it was cold.

He composed himself as he took the tube, then began the walk to Neesmith House, a new, heartbreakingly familiar feeling at the thought of it – fear, with a side-order of self-disgust.

A kid and his passenger were tearing around the courtyard of Neesmith House on a moped, engine noise bouncing back twice as loud from the flats. Max made for a stairwell guarded by a group of teenagers, some standing astride their BMX-style bikes, others lounging on the steps. He recognised the smell of spliff. It hung intimidatingly over the group, who passed round a joint and squinted so-what through the smoke at him as he approached. Perhaps because they were stoned, or too busy swearing and spitting and watching their mates on the moped, they left Max alone as he took the stairs, restricting any punishment to a simple, silent refusal to make way, forcing him to clamber gingerly over their legs. Behind him one of them spat, but Max didn't think it was aimed at him. All the same when he turned a corner on the steps he ran a hand up and down the back of his coat, just in case.

The steps smelt how steps in council flats always smell, like it's part of the architecture; and there was graffiti, of course, tags, because if you can't afford the car or the clothes, and you don't fancy stabbing somebody, then leaving your spray-can spoor is a way to get noticed. Max thought he could understand that. He reckoned that if he lived like this then he . . . What was he thinking? *How do you live, Max?* he thought. *Like this? Or worse?*

He reached the landing and walked to his left, past flats made of red brick gone brown, the doors protected by steel shutters and iron gates; some of the windows boarded up. His shoes crunched on the concrete, and when he looked over the balcony he could see the kids below, three of them still circling the court-yard on the noisy moped. At the far end of the landing two women stood talking and smoking, one with a baby. From some-where came the thump-thump of music and a Pavlovian instinct made him wince at the sound of it. He reached the door, pulled his hand from his coat and knocked.

Inside the flat there was a minor riot. A kid shouted; an internal door slammed shut; then the front door flew open. There stood a thirteen-year-old, his chest bare aside from two chunky gold-rope chains. He wore a pair of large gold signet rings on one hand; on the other (Max was drawn to check), yes, he wore three on that one. His ears were pierced – gold earrings doing the honours there; around his wrist chunky gold identifi-cation bracelets. The kid looked as if he'd run through the jewellery cabinet at Argos without stopping, then clear through to Boots where he'd come to rest in a display of super wet-look hair gel.

He took one look at Max on the doorstep. A little wave of hatred passed between them. Neither quite understood it, but there it was.

'Dad,' shouted the kid, turning away, 'it's only Paedo.'

She dropped the charges, thought Max.

There was a curse from behind a door at the end of passage, then, 'Paedo, the price is right, come on down.' The kid had disappeared, jangling off down the hall, so Max stepped in and pushed the door closed behind him. The thought came to him, not for the first time, that this was the only flat on the landing without an extra door, a gate or shutters – that second level of security. He was inside the only flat on the block that nobody dared break into, and perhaps that should have been a comforting thought – should have been.

It smelt of old cooking, and cheap carpets rank with nicotine, fried food and bad relationships. Even Max could smell it; his soul shrank at the odour. He took a deep breath and walked to the end of the passage where a sliding door was shut, the kitchen on the other side. From the lounge he heard the sound of the television and recognised an advert, one where a famous television presenter urges you to take out a loan for holidays and weddings and special occasions and all the nice things life has to offer – all the nice things you may not be able to afford unless you take out the loan.

Also from the lounge he could hear the kid, Carl. He fancied himself as a rapper. He liked making up rhymes, insulting ones – battle rhymes, he called them. Whom he was battling, Max never knew. All he saw was the kid spouting abuse with his dad egging him on, as if rhyming 'motherfucker' with 'cocksucker' made him some kind of rap genius. He could hear him now in the lounge, working on his rhymes: 'I was just about. To wear my Speedos. I changed my mind. When up turned Paedo.'

Max suppressed a shiver, slid open the kitchen door and went through.

'Well, if it ent the Kettering Kid. All right, Paedo?'

Chick sat eating his dinner from a tired, greasy cardboard box courtesy of Perfect Fried Chicken. His smiling lips glistened, smeared with animal fat. He held a bone in his hand, a strip of meat hanging off like it was making a break for freedom rather than disappear into Chick's hungry maw. Too late. Chick held the bone as though it was a bunch of grapes in Roman times and the rest of the meat went in. 'Siddown, then,' he said, through chewed chicken, threw the bone to the box, picked out another victim.

Max took a seat at the kitchen table. He could have told Chick that this kind of kitchen table was really quite hip so long as you didn't mind covering the surface with something ironic and chintzy. It was the sort of thing he'd have sold in the shop to earnest young trendsetters who would've put it in the corner, maybe topped it with an antique typewriter and a bronze ashtray, an unsmoked Gauloise resting on it for decoration. Sure, thought Max, seventy quid at least. And he thought of mentioning it to Chick just as a conversation opener; a way of going, 'Hey, Chick, I had a life before' – when he caught sight of Chick's wife.

She stood by the kitchen sink with her arms folded and studied him with more watchfulness than usual. Which was a lot of watchfulness. She looked awful. Hair in need of a wash. Complexion in pain. Shoulders pointing at the floor. Beneath her eyes, half closed and resting on dark, puffy pillows, Max could make out tiny road-map veins on her cheeks. Still, though, those eyes. They watched Max, and there was something going on in there, but it was impossible to read.

And he thought of an indistinct picture of a woman at Holloway Road tube station . . .

'Trish.' Chick had seen Max looking over at her. 'Trish,' he barked, when she did not respond. 'Are you going or staying? Either way, pretend like you're awake, yeah? Snap out of it. Ent you got washing-up to do?'

She had. She snapped out of it. 'Yeah, sorry,' the words barely existing in the room. She turned away to the sink, her eyes ripping slowly from Max as she did so.

Chick sniffed. 'What you got for me, then?' He waved a drum-stick at Max.

On the other side of the table Max told himself to sort it out, play it cool. He reached for an inside pocket of his coat, his hand shaking, pulled out a wad of vouchers. 'These,' he said, placing them on the table.

'Good lad, good lad.' Then, 'Carl! Get yourself in here.'

MC Carl slouched in.

'Paedo's got you some computers-for-schools vouchers, mate,' said Chick indicating the wad, which Carl snatched up and fanned out like it was pimp money. Despite himself, Max thought, What do you say? Carl turned to go.

'Oi.'

He turned back.

'Give us a battle rhyme before you go, eh?'

Carl composed himself, grabbed the crotch of his jeans, addressed Max and went, 'Thanks, Paedo. You're the king bee. Best not hang. You'll try to rape me.' He pressed his non-crotch-grabbing hand to his chest and beamed at his own mic skills before turning and slouching off. Chick roared.

Max's eyes went to the table surface. 'It was a girl,' he said wearily. 'And she dropped the charges.'

'He knows that,' bellowed Chick. 'You wouldn't be here other-wise. He's just getting a rise out of you, that's all. You ought to rap back.' He chortled. 'What you *really* got for me, then?' he said.

Max shifted in his seat to reach into his coat pocket, dragged out a handful of envelopes and let them drop to the table. He watched Chick's eyes range over the small pyre – rectangles, all with the corners removed.

Chick reached to the envelopes and swished them about with his finger, dispassionately looking them over.

Now he looked up and Max saw rage there; he swallowed at the fury in the other man's face.

'What's this?' said Chick, controlled at least.

'There were no bags,' began Max, 'just a wheelie-bin.' He indicated the pile. 'It was full of those.'

'Oh, no, it weren't,' said Chick, with a tiny shake of the head. 'It weren't *just* full of these. It had other stuff in it, too, din't it? The stuff I wanted you to get.' Elbow to the table, chicken-shined finger pointing at Max. 'But you din't bring it.'

'Look . . .'

'Are you trying to make some kind of point with me, Paedo?'

'I recognised the name,' said Max.

Chick laughed drily. 'Yeah? And?'

'It's that boy.' Glance towards Trish. Did the shoulders slump a fraction?

Chick waved him back with his finger. 'Yeah? *And?*'

'Chick,' said Max pleadingly. *'It's that boy.'*

Chick sniffed and folded his arms – chubby forearms, tattoos like blurred Rorschach tests. 'This ent gonna cut it, mate. I need more than this, you know full-fucking-well I do. You're going back.'

'No.'

'Don't you say no to me, Paedo, you're going back.'

'Do you know where he is?' The words flew out of Max before he had time to stop them, and he knew there were only two reactions a man like Chick had to a question like that – and one of them was to fly across the table at him . . .

And the other was to laugh (but his eyes flicked to Trish). 'Nah, course I don't know where he is. What do I want with a little kid? It's a scam, that's all it is. A scam, innit? We need to find out what this geezer's worth.' He paused. 'And that means you're going back.'

Max's world had shifted so far on its axis that, for a second, he felt almost grateful. Like, thank heavens – that's all it is, a harmless scheme to extort money from a man whose son has been kidnapped. Oh, how silly of me to jump to conclusions, I'll catch the first train back . . .

'I can't,' he said, as much to himself as to Chick.

'You're going back.'

'Get someone else.'

'Can't, Paedo. Got to be you.'

'Max. My name's Max.'

'Once it was, yeah. Paedo now, innit?'

Max took a deep breath. His head had sunk low, his words came out urgent and pleading. Shame stabbed at his soul. 'Listen, please, Chick. The other stuff is fine. I'm grateful, thank you, for the money. But, please, I can't get involved in this. You must realise I'm not the right person.'

'Talking about? You're exactly the right person. I can trust you.'

'Can you?' said Max, appalled.

'Yeah, mate, I can.' And now he reached to grab Max.

Thrusting himself forward to snatch Max's arm, he simultaneously pulled away his coat sleeve, then twisted.

Against his will Max offered up his wrist for inspection. The scar shone in the room; time had barely dimmed its lividity. Not a slash – not the warm-bath whisper of a razor – but a churned-up accrual of traumatised flesh: a dark-red reminder living on his skin of men who picked him up, who called him Paedo, pervert, nonce, and worse than even Chick's son could invent.

Max tried to pull back his arm, which Chick refused to release, triggering a sudden memory of Chick taking his arm that way before, when it had been bandaged, and Chick had been sitting at the side of his bed, elliptical, insinuating. 'You don't want me thinking you're ungrateful, do you, mate? Like, I might decide to let the community know who's living in their midst. You hear terrible things that mobs do to paedos.' He squeezed his own crotch and made a painful face. 'What happened in prison is going to look like a lucky escape, innit?'

'She's dropped the charges,' pleaded Max from his hospital bed.

Chick sniffed. 'Mud sticks . . .'

It certainly did.

'This is why I can trust you,' said Chick, and he pulled his finger across the scar, bunching the dead tissue, leaving a smear of chicken grease behind.

Part Two

COCK-KNOCKER

1

The car teetered on the lip of the swimming-pool for about two seconds before it fell in. In that time, Detective Inspector Clive Merle imagined himself turning to his wife and saying something that would incorporate the following two elements. One: that, yes, he had accidentally placed the car in a forward gear, and that had he not been driving recklessly (i.e. angrily attempting to turn the car round before driving it angrily to Pollença for an evening meal spent in angry silence), then perhaps the force of the forward propulsion wouldn't have been so great; perhaps the hired Peugeot 206 would not have cast off the gravel chains of their villa's driveway and leapt through the screening shrubs like some returning explorer, to land with its rear tyres on land, its front ones quaking over their swimming-pool.

And two: at least it didn't go in.

But as he imagined this the front wheels dipped and gently kissed the surface. He saw shimmering black ripples illuminated by the underwater lighting. Pretty, he thought. The car rose again, just a fraction, hanging there as if it was calculating the weight distribution. Then, it tipped forward into the shallow end.

She still had her hands over her face. She had placed them there prior to the accident. They'd gone up there so she could say, 'I can't take any more of this!' her standard argument-closer, and they'd stayed there as her husband had driven their car into the pool. If she'd just listened, he reflected, as the water slurped at the bonnet, he wasn't saying they *never* went to his choice of restaurant, just that *this holiday* they never went to his choice of restaurant.

It took her some time to remove her hands from her face, as though she was waiting for something else to happen. 'I *don't* believe you,' she said. 'I *really don't* believe you.'

She went to let herself out and Merle dived across to stop her, thinking that you shouldn't open the door until the car is full of water, then remembered that the rule only applied if the car was submerged, and swimming-pool shallow ends didn't count.

'Leave me!' she said, thinking he was reaching to hug her and he pulled back, briefly admiring the two arcs of underwater light created by the car headlights. She got out, her dress billowing up round her waist. With her handbag held high, she waded to the swimming-pool steps. As a policeman, Merle had seen many strange things, but nothing quite as surreal as his wife at that moment – he found himself reminded of Katherine Hepburn in *The African Queen*.

'I'll be in in a second,' he called to her.

She turned angrily in the water. 'Why not just stay there, Clive? Perhaps you could try driving to the earth's core.'

'Idiot,' he told himself, reaching for the door.

Standing in her dressing-gown making a sandwich (for one person only, he noted ruefully), Karen insisted he ring the holiday rep that very minute.

'There's nothing they can do until morning,' he argued weakly.

'We need to tell somebody straight away,' she insisted, turning and pointing with her knife. 'And you'd better hope they don't come along and breathalyse you.'

The thought had crossed his mind. 'Why on earth would the police get involved?' he said.

'You don't know.' She turned back to her sandwich.

'I do know. I'm a policeman.'

'Not in Majorca, you're not. How do you know they don't attend all minor accidents?'

'Well, then, all the more reason why we shouldn't report it until morning.'

'Oh, no. Oh, no. We're reporting it now. And you'd better hope the police don't come and breathalyse you.'

'You said. But if on the million-to-one chance they do come, we'd have to say that you were—'

'Oh, no. Oh, no.' She wheeled around, waggling the knife again. '*You* were driving. I don't drive cars into swimming-pools, Clive, that's your speciality.'

'Oh, I see. This is a punishment, is it? You're actually *hoping* the police will come. And what if I was done on a DUI?'

'I think they have different acronym for it in Majorca, Clive. And it would serve you right.'

'So let me get this straight. You sit there glugging wine all day and I'm supposed to—'

'I can't take any more of this!'

So he did as she said: he rang the rep, who was clearly disturbed in the middle of her evening meal, and not nearly as accommodating, friendly and helpful as she had appeared at the beginning of their week, when she'd called in to welcome them to Las Olbas. Four days later and the end was in sight. Now, more than ever, he couldn't wait for it to be over.

'What do you mean the car's "gone into" the pool?' she asked, after he'd tried to explain the problem in as non-culpable terms as he could manage.

'I mean, there's been an accident. I think the clutch must have—' *Stuck? Slipped?* 'Stuck. And it, er, the car sort of shot forward off the driveway and into the pool.'

'You crashed it into the pool?'

'Kind of.'

'I see. Is anybody hurt? Do you need medical treatment?'

'Only for a case of acute embarrassment.'

'And it's safe, is it, the car? It's not going to – er, no, I don't suppose it's going to explode.'

'No, nothing like that. It's just kind of leaning in the pool at the moment. It'll be fine until morning.'

'Just hold on a minute.' She went off the phone and he heard her say, 'Chap from Las Olbas has driven his car into the pool . . . Don't think so . . .' She came back on. 'You're a policeman, aren't you?' she said. Yes, he told her. 'No, he's a policeman.' Then back to Merle: 'My colleague wanted to know if you were a rock star. He says to please not throw your television out of the window.'

Karen shot him a very specific look when he got off the phone saying people would come in the morning: *you don't deserve the luck.*

Hardly luck, though, he thought, as they spent the following morning in total silence. She helped herself to cereal and he followed her out to the patio with his own bowl. On the driveway two skidmarks led to a car-sized gap in the shrubs. He could just see one tyre and part of the axle, hoisted in the air. 'Wow,' he said. 'Hot one today.'

She ignored him. He attempted to make further conversation by pointing out a lizard on the whitewashed wall.

'I'm not interested. And it's not a lizard,' she said. Pitiless sunglasses, mouth thin.

'Well, no, it'll be a gecko. That's what I meant. But it's sort of a lizard – it's part of the same species.'

'You're part of the human-being species, Clive, but that doesn't make you a human being.' She swept her bowl from the table and disappeared back into the villa.

Later, the pool man arrived, got out of his car and went round to the pool area before they had a chance to stop him. They arrived to find him admiring the pool-car arrangement, staring with the googly-eyed fascination of someone who'd never seen a car in a swimming-pool before – not in real life anyway. Merle had been thinking about his wife's comment, how harsh it had been. Accidentally crashing the car – and pool or no pool, a *little* prang was all it was – was hardly an act of inhumanity. But now he wondered, as the pool man looked from the car to him, studying him as though Merle really did belong to an alien species.

The pool man moved from being astonished to amused.

Oblivious to the tension between the couple he made what he thought was a brilliant joke, pretending to scoop the car out of the pool with his net. Merle felt duty-bound to laugh but, still, he was hardly surprised when Karen turned on her heel and marched once more to the kitchen. Her husband laughing: not what she wanted to hear.

And that was where she stayed, even when a pick-up truck arrived, depositing two men who did astonished and amused before going into consulation with the pool man – presumably over the best way to remove the car. Excluded for a moment, Karen safely out of the picture – probably preparing a single cup of tea – he removed his mobile from his pocket and tapped out a text message to Detective Sergeant Simon Cyston, another officer involved in the investigation – one who wasn't on bleeding holiday. 'Cy,' it said. 'Can you give me a call?'

His finger hovered over Send.

DI Merle thought of himself as a misanthrope. He wore his misanthropy as if it was a badge on his lapel that he had to keep adjusting. And if he ever had cause to doubt it, all he had to do was go on holiday.

At Gatwick he'd stared in horrified wonder at those who shared his airport space. These people – the salt of the earth – retired football hooligans and loud Cockneys, even louder wives, brassy and damaged, abusing enough Lycra to persuade its inventor to put a gun to his head. Everything upside down. Men with tits, women with tattoos, babies with earrings hanging off taut earlobes. The lot of them squawking into mobile phones, stuffing burgers into their mouths like there was a world cow shortage.

He loathed them at Gatwick, then he loathed them when they got to Palma airport, lighting fags in No Smoking, waiting on their cases and swearing at their children. He guided Karen to the rep; no, that was wrong – Karen guided *him* to the rep, who took them to the car that should have been their shuttle to freedom, and maybe, if he wasn't such a fuckwit, would have been. He loathed them not because he was a snob, although Karen thought so, but because all they cared about was projection. About swearing at the world until it noticed them, all the time their mouths flapping like their stomachs. These were the people who sat around in offices, pubs and factories, saying how they couldn't believe nobody saw that little boy – that Little Ben – get taken, someone must've seen. But they were the same people who supported Arsenal, who supported Tottenham Hotspur, who took the tube. And their mouths would have been flapping, and they had no room to register a lost little boy standing at their feet. They had been there – that was the thing. They always were.

And now he was stuck in a Majorcan hell. He hated the sunshine, the quiet, the boredom, having to smoke half the cigarettes and drink half the amount he'd like to, and finding, predictably, that even half was too much for Karen. He hated having to drive everywhere, because she refused to; he hated being forced to cook half the meals they ate in the villa because 'It's my holiday too, you know'; but most of all he hated the fact that he'd driven his car into the pool and these three men, twinkling happily beneath the sun, acclimatised and brown, were punctuating their conversation with regular gestures at the cornflour-skinned chump staring morosely at his mobile phone. They smiled at Merle and he smiled back – the smile of a man eating his first eel. He pressed Send.

Leaving the Spaniards to it he dragged his shame to the villa where Karen sat on the veranda with a coffee – not far wrong on that score, then – reading a novel. He settled into a chair; she looked up briefly and back at her book.

Come on, Cy, he thought, trying psychically to influence the sergeant. Come on.

'Shouldn't you be out there?' she said at last.

'No, not really. Not much I can do. I'd only be in the way.'

'Yes, but shouldn't you be out there *anyway*?'

His phone rang in his pocket. *Thank you, thank you.* He pulled it out and started as he read the window. 'It's Cy. God, what does he want? Nothing big, I hope.'

Karen was looking at him, chewing the inside of her cheek as he answered. 'Cy. This had better be good.' He stood up, turning away from Karen.

'What had better be good, sir?'

'Come on, you know I'm on holiday.'

'You texted me, sir.'

'I see. Well, fire away.'

'Fire away with what? Sorry – are we talking for the benefit of somebody else here? Your wife, perhaps?' Cy postdated Karen's time on the force. Although she had once been well known, popular and highly competent, to Cy she was only ever going to be Merle's missus.

'Quite right, Cy. Wait a second.' He placed a hand over the phone. 'Kaz? I'm going to take this inside. Something's cropped up.'

She nodded a curt but understanding okay and Merle felt a twinge of guilt as he walked into the villa then through to the bedroom, as far away from his wife as possible. 'Cy,' he said into the phone, 'what's the difference between a holiday in Majorca and having your eyes pulled out with fish hooks, the barbed kind?'

'Don't know, sir.'

'No? Neither do I.'

'Oh. I see. Like that, is it?'

'Yes, it's like that. And, to add insult to injury, Karen's driven the car into the swimming-pool, so now I've got to sort that out on top of avoiding mosquitoes and smearing myself in gunk so I don't get burnt to a crisp.'

'Drove your car into the swimming-pool, did she? Very rock 'n' roll.'

'Right. She'll be chucking our TV out the window next.'

Cy snorted with laughter at the other end and Merle felt guilty about nicking the rep's joke although, strangely, not for lying about the architect of the pool-car catastrophe.

'You have my sympathies, sir, but I'm not sure there's a lot I can do about it from here,' said Cy, speaking from cool, probably raining London.

'Of course there is. You can tell me something so bloody important that I've got to fly back at once. So bloody big and important that I don't get a peep out of Karen about it either.'

'Jesus, that's pretty important. Like, what kind of thing are you thinking?'

'Oh, God, I don't know.' Merle tilted his head and stared up at the bedroom ceiling. On top of the wardrobes he noticed some folded blankets for the first time – for when it got cold, no doubt (and if only it would, for one second, get cold, he might not be so bloody miserable). And as he did this he thought, Yes, what? Exactly what kind of thing am I thinking? 'Nothing on Snape, then?' he heard himself say.

At the other end of the line, Cy paused in a way that said no for him. 'Just the usual.'

From outside Merle heard the sound of a motor. Maybe his car being lifted out of the pool.

'What? Like what?' he said.

'Well, there is one thing,' said Cy. 'Maybe something, most likely nothing. We're keeping an open mind.'

Merle had been standing but now he sat and looked at his feet where his flip-flops had left a white V, mocking him. From outside came the sound of machinery in crisis. A motor straining, high-pitched. He heard raised voices; even though he didn't speak a word of Spanish he knew they were saying, 'Shut off the fucking winch – quick.' His hand went to his forehead. 'What is it, then?'

'It's a couple of things from Patrick Snape. He rang asking for you. First he reckons someone was going through his rubbish the night before last. He can't be sure but he heard the wheelie-bin lid go, kind of put it out of his head as nothing but then he heard the side gate banging – reckons someone had been in round the back.'

'No way of saying whether anything was taken?'

'Nah.'

'Press?'

'I mean, who knows, eh? Press was my first thought.'

'But?'

'Yeah, yeah, but. Because last night something else happened.'

There was a splash. The noise a Peugeot makes when a winch has failed to remove it from a swimming-pool.

'What happened last night?'

2

He'd been right, Chick – he'd been bang on: Max would go back to Kettering.

The carriage had yesterday's air of weary futility and alcohol. He sat and pulled up his legs in front of him, hoping, like his companions, not to have to share his seat, never meeting an eye just in case. Luck was on his side: the carriage stayed fairly empty, the odd straggler arriving, hoisting briefcases up to the parcel shelf, unbuttoning jackets ready to travel.

And then Max saw him.

He wasn't sure at first. Remembering the moment later, he realised he'd immediately assumed it was his mind playing tricks, conjuring an image of the boy's father in front of him, getting on to the train, taking a seat, now sitting with his back to him.

Max sat up in his seat; his thinking cleared. It was Patrick Snape, he was sure of it. No, no, not sure – it looked like him, though, like the pictures he'd seen on the Internet. He stood up to get a better view, but all he saw was the back of what might be Patrick Snape's head. The maybe-Pat sat still, not opening a paper or arranging himself. He'd done the decent thing, moving to the inside of his two-seater, thoughtful. Outside on the platform a whistle blew and the doors bleeped to close as Max made his way down the carriage, past the guy who might be Pat, resisting a look behind him until he came to the opposite end, then turning and looking.

It was him, and in the end it wasn't the features that made him certain, although they definitely were the features of Patrick Snape. It was the look, the stare. He recognised it from the pictures. It was the look of a man who had just lost everything – lost everything, but not fully accepted the fact.

'Sorry,' said Max, the sort of unnecessary sorry the situation called for, smiling as he sat down next to Patrick Snape, seeing himself do it and thinking, What am I doing? Not sure of the answer. Pat smiled don't-worry in return, regarded him a moment, then turned to look out of the window. In the seats opposite a young bloke sat sprawled, reading a magazine and wearing a pair of giant headphones. Like everybody else in the noiseless carriage, in his own little world.

'Sorry,' said Max again.

'I'm sorry?' Pat seemed pulled from his thoughts.

'I said I was sorry, for taking this seat.' The words were tripping from him and he could hear how ridiculous they sounded. 'It's almost like you got picked on because you chose the window-seat.'

He could see Pat studying him carefully, doing all but putting his nose to him and sniffing for alcohol fumes before he replied. 'You must excuse me. I'm not quite with you.'

Max felt himself wanting to reach out and touch Pat, as though doing that might conduct some of the other man's pain. 'Most people, they sit on this side – to discourage others, I suppose.' His voice was hushed. It was all he could hear in the carriage and to him it sounded impossibly loud.

'That's all right,' said Pat, evenly, politely. 'It's not a problem. I mean, I'll swap if that's what you'd prefer.'

'No, no, I just meant . . . I'm sorry, I'm babbling. You're the little boy's father, aren't you?'

'Yes.' Like it was the most natural question in the world. Like a film star being asked, 'You're in that film, aren't you?'

'I recognised you.'

'Yes.' Pat was looking at Max. His feelings were unreadable. His mouth had opened and closed to deposit the word but his eyes betrayed nothing.

'I'm so, so sorry about Ben.'

'Thank you.'

'There's no news?' Max virtually whispered.

Pat sighed. 'No, I'm sorry, no, there isn't.'

You're sorry, thought Max, then thought of the people who must approach Pat every day, the same kind of approach he'd just made. Like him, wanting somehow to help with his pain. 'You must get this all the time.'

'It's okay. I don't get it all the time, hardly ever. If I do, though? I wish I could say that, yes, there's news, but there never is.'

'Still no closer, then? To knowing, I mean – who it was, the woman in the pictures.'

'No, I'm afraid not,' replied Pat.

There was a silence Max found himself desperate to break. 'I live round there, you see, so I gave them a good look.' He shouldn't have said that, he thought. In one self-justifying moment he'd told Patrick Snape he lived near where his son was kidnapped. 'I mean, not in the area, sort of roundabouts.'

Pat looked at him. 'You didn't recognise her, then,' he said.

'No. Sorry.' Max felt his soul shift.

'You wouldn't, not from the pictures. There was a psychologist who didn't want them publicised. Not good enough quality, he said, but she'd recognise herself and she'd maybe panic, end up doing something . . .'

The ghastly thought trailed into silence.

'I see,' said Max, wanting now to keep Pat talking. 'They keep you involved, then? In the investigation?'

'Oh, not really, no. Only if they need to give me to the press in exchange for a favour.' Max looked shocked. 'But it's all right,' added Pat. 'We get looked after.' He smiled a thin smile. He had this way about him, Max saw. As though he'd simply shouldered the burden of public sympathy and carried on, as if it was no big thing. Or as if in comparison it was no big thing. 'They've been great, the police,' he finished. 'Really great.'

'That's good. And what about you? How are you coping?' Max could hear himself sounding like the agony aunt on break-fast TV, the words ringing false.

But Pat heard nothing except sincerity, and all he could do was nod for a moment or so. 'I'm coping,' he said at last. 'You have to.'

Max sat tiny in the shadow of what Pat had suffered. 'I'm sorry,' he said, after a pause. 'But I don't know – what is it you do? For a living.'

'When I'm not on compassionate leave I work for the highways. I go round making sure the roads are built properly.'

'I see. A lot of responsibility.'

'Well, you know, if a road's wrong it can play havoc. You get problems.'

Max didn't know how to follow up that one, didn't know whether he should even; perhaps just pretend the next station was his, slip away, with that – whatever it was – that *urge* to speak to Patrick Snape somehow satisfied. In the end it was Pat who spoke: 'I'm sorry, you know my name but . . .'

'It's Sam.'

'And what is it you do?'

'I'm a chef, a commis chef – although I voted Tory at the last election.'

Pat laughed and looked at Max. There was a silence between them, the sound of somebody on their mobile a few seats back, standard-issue *tsh-tsh-tsh* from another passenger's headphones.

Then, Max said, 'What's he like – Ben?'

Pat took the question in his stride. It was as though he'd been waiting for it to be asked, because he was, regularly, by people wanting to know what Ben was like, as if wanting to identify symptoms, reassure themselves their own children were safe.

'What's he like? I suppose he's like every other six-year-old boy – except he's a unique six-year-old boy, because he's Ben. He worships his father. He thinks his dad walks on water and he feels an emotional pull towards his mother that he can't explain and will probably never be able to, and together the two of us make up a huge percentage of his life and we savour it but it's still sort of sad because we're already mourning its passing. So he still supports the team I do, but I've only got a couple more years, I reckon, before he'll choose his own, probably Man U knowing my luck.' He stopped. That 'knowing my luck' hung in the air – if only his son switching teams to the old enemy was as bad as it got. And then he continued: 'Apart from us and Arsenal there's his Game Boy – he loves Mario – and his favourite song is "Yellow Submarine", and he loves his sticker album, which I don't think he fully gets, really, I don't think he sees identities as such, it's like a jigsaw puzzle to him. You know, they've all got them, the kids, these albums. Ben would be some kind of social outcast if he turned up at school without his sticker album in his hand. It's hilarious, Deborah says. All these little kids at the bus stop, one hand holding the sticker album, all of them with these huge outsize rucksacks they wear. And they get so excited to see each other, they're swarming round comparing albums, and it's like the way they start their working day, like me checking my voicemail. It's how they check in, how they reaffirm their world. Like the way when they're born you always want to touch them. Even when they're sleeping and you know you shouldn't you still want to. You want to check that they're still there, that they're real, not an illusion, that they're breathing and they're alive and they'll still be there when you next look. And apart from being a little mini-version of a grown-up, and Mario, oh, and Chicken McNuggets, *of course* – because even when the nuggets aren't strictly speaking Chicken *Mc*Nuggets they're always Chicken McNuggets.' He tapped the side of his nose and, as he did so, Max noticed his eyes were bright with happy-thought tears. 'It's like the big parent conspiracy. All nuggets are Chicken McNuggets. We guard it as closely as the one about Santa Claus, just waiting for the inevitable question, the observation one day that gives the whole game away. And apart from Chicken Mc-bloody-Nuggets, and looking cute but bashful when women smile at him in the queue at the supermarket, and his sticker album and Mario, he's got his little friends. That's what Deborah calls them. "His little friends". And she's right, because they are – all – so *little*, and not just small either, but like tiny versions of people, little versions of friends. They're just beginning to develop rivalries and compe-titions. The sticker album's one of the main culprits – they all want to have the special metallic stickers, and these tiny jealousies are occurring and you watch them happening and you mourn that, too, because it's another little incremental stage of their awakening to a world you'd rather they never saw . . .' He stopped himself and looked across at Max. 'As I say, really – just like any other six-year-old.'

All Max could do was nod. Pat let him, watching him before asking, 'So, where are you off to tonight?'

'Kettering, actually.'

'Oh? Really? Why Kettering? Work?'

'No. No, I'm off to see my sister.'

'Have you got a lift the other end?'

'Yes, thank you. She should be there waiting for me.'

'And what? Snape thinks this guy's the same guy going through his bins?'

'That's about the size of it.'

'Okay,' Merle said slowly. 'What makes him think that?'

'He checked the gate again this morning, not been latched properly. And this guy, there was something about him that Snape . . . well, what he said was that this guy didn't have the ring of truth about him. And he didn't smell right, apparently, not like someone who works in a kitchen, whatever that smells like – chip fat, maybe. But the clincher, as far as Snape's concerned, is that this Sam had no overnight bag, nothing. Just the clothes he stood up in. Factor in this morning's gate business and the alarm bells were going like Notre Dame, so he called you.'

'He's a good lad.'

'Ayuh.'

'What does the DCI think?'

'Doesn't fit with anything we're looking at. DCI thinks he's probably a ghoul, or press. We're checking the bin for prints, anyway, and requisitioning any CCTV. Snape's going to keep a lookout.'

'Sounds about right,' said Merle. He was thinking about bins. Then, 'Had he been to see us?'

'Who, sir?' said Cy.

'Snape. When he met this Sam? Was he on his way back from seeing us?'

'No, sir, not as far as I know.'

'Okay, fine. Look, just to let you know, I'm going to give him a call. Nothing operational, I just want to check in, that's all, find out how he's doing.'

He clicked off the call and thought for a moment or so before dialling Pat.

Sam, he thought. Sam. As in Samaritan.

3

Kettering. It's not what you'd call commuter belt, unless you were describing a particularly fat commuter. But plenty of people made the daily trip on the Midland Mainline to St Pancras. Patrick Snape included.

He was in the shower at home on an estate of similar houses, all built by a company called David Wilson Homes, which builds houses for people like Pat: part-time Arsenal fans who take their sons to the occasional match; who lived in the capital once, perhaps, but moved away to find better lives, and so what if the shops are always shut? At least there wasn't so much dirt and noise. At least people looked out for each other. The kids were safe.

To Pat, David Wilson had bequeathed a shower cubicle with a sliding door. It was frosted with nice, tactile knobbly bits that he used to run his fingers along, back in the old days when there were such things as simple pleasures. Now he turned his face to the spray and plucked his soap from the soap-dish. He had taken showers in here with Deborah, before. And once the cubicle had seemed cluttered with her products. Shower gel, hanging off a big shower-friendly plastic loop. Shampoo. Conditioner. Shampoo and conditioner. You could tell the difference only if you looked at the bottles really closely. He used to stand beneath the spray not knowing which to use (she would have said, 'Buy your own!'), squinting to see, and wondering why so much of it was written in French.

But that was before. Deborah didn't do the shopping any more: he did it. For soap he bought Simple because why make your life more complicated? Anyway, that was the brand she seemed to prefer. But for shampoo and conditioner he didn't know which she liked. The bathroom's rotation had confused him enough before he had to buy the products. So he settled for whatever, and whatever seemed fine by Deborah, but he wished it wasn't.

He got out of the shower, slid the door shut quietly as he always did, so as not to disturb Deborah, who got up late and went to bed early, and sometimes didn't get out of bed at all.

He towelled and watched himself in the mirror as he did so. A thirty-six-year-old man, hair slightly thinning and a little grey around the ears. And thin. Very. Deborah used to joke that the only way they'd ever lose weight would be to split up. Neither of them worried about losing weight now. And he looked old; felt it, too. He felt as though someone had taken the story of his perfect life and torn out the middle section.

Because Ben's disappearance had thrown their lives into a ghastly time-warp, fast-forwarding their life as if their child had grown up and left home, ageing them to the status of a couple in their autumn years – although, of course, they were denied even that. For them it was winter, always. 'You've got to look after each other,' they'd been told by parents, friends and counsellors. But they hadn't, he supposed. It was as though each lived in a permanent state of resentment at the other, impeding their ability to grieve. 'You've got to look after each other.' But they hadn't, because . . .

Because 'It was you. You lost our son,' was the most egregious thing she'd never said to him, but it was always there – odourless, colourless, poisonous gas in the air.

He finished drying, dressed in T-shirt and jeans, and went across the landing to their bedroom. Inside it was dark, the curtains drawn – always drawn. And the room was dusty and smelt of the bed. He kept the house tidy, he did his best, but cleaning and dusting were more problematic: they fell below his radar, and now he noticed a thin layer of dust on all the bedroom surfaces. On the bedside tables, and on her dressing-table, which she barely used.

Their bed was placed in a corner of the room. Shortly after

Ben disappeared she had changed sides. Before, she had slept on the outside, because it was her who usually got up when Ben was crying. These days she stayed on the wall side, and she lay there now, in her usual position, with her hands against the wall, as if preventing it moving in and crushing her; as if needing to feel it there, solid beside her.

'Deb,' he said softly. The mound beneath the duvet stayed still. The back of her head, hair in untidy knots; nails, once her proud 'talons', now bitten to the quick. 'Deb, I was going to make something to eat. Will you have something?' Not sure if she was asleep. For a long time he only knew she was asleep if she wasn't crying. She didn't cry as much any more. Often she just lay like this, her hands touching the wall in her dusty David Wilson bedroom.

There was no answer. He tried again, 'Deb?' and with no reply he turned to leave, about to close the bedroom door behind him, when she said, 'Pat?'

'Yes, babe?' She hadn't turned or moved, and her voice had been muffled by the cover. It was still their winter duvet, he thought vaguely. He should change it for one with a lower – what did you call it? – a lower *tog*.

'Did you go to London today?' Her voice, he realised, had that sleepy, sedated quality that he knew to be Valium.

'I did, yes. You said it was okay.'

'And did you have a shower just now?'

'Yes, I did.'

'Will you check, then? Because I thought when you were in the shower I heard the phone go.'

He closed his eyes because the phantom phone ring appeared most days. Not a Casper the friendly ghost, no, a damaging, deceitful poltergeist. 'I'll check,' he said. Then, 'I'm making something to eat. Will you have something with me? Perhaps we could sit at the table. You could help me, if you like,' the words began to tumble out of him, 'or you could just sit in the lounge while I make it. Or we could watch a film if you want – we could go and rent one, even. Or I could tell you about my day. Or we could just watch telly. But it'd be good, wouldn't it, to eat together?'

'That's nice, Pat.' She sighed. 'Maybe tomorrow night. Sleepy now, though. Had a sandwich earlier, when you were in London.'

'Okay,' he said, knowing they would not cook or rent a video tomorrow, and that she hadn't had a sandwich earlier. 'You get some rest. Maybe tomorrow.' He closed the door behind him.

There was Ben's bedroom, over the way. He went to the door, opened it and looked in as if Ben might be there, all tucked up like a Night Nurse commercial. Sleeping innocent, peaceful sleep. There was a thought Pat had sometimes. A vicious thought. It ended with him in Ben's bedroom, on his knees with his son's pillow pressed to his nose, sobbing as if he'd never be able to stop.

He checked the phone anyway, expecting the dialling tone but getting instead the siren note of a message left. She was right. Maybe that was a good sign. 'Hello,' it said. 'It's a message for Pat. It's . . . Clive, DI Merle.' Pat felt his hand grip the receiver, his chest tightening; he was already beginning to tremble. 'Please,' said the message. 'Please don't get . . . I'm sorry, I don't have any news. I was just calling, well, I was hoping to have a chat, really. Nothing urgent, but if you'd call me back when you've got a moment I'd appreciate that, thanks. Hope to speak to you soon. Oh, sorry, my number is . . .' and he left his mobile number, which Pat jotted down on the pad he always left by the phone, then called him straight back.

Merle had been thinking about this holiday he was on when he first met Patrick Snape. That day he'd visited a burglary where the guy had left an eighty-year-old woman blind in one eye after he'd refused to believe she had nothing of value in the house. That day, also, Merle had helped to exercise a warrant on a murder suspect, nearly been attacked by a dangerous dog and failed to persuade a bruised and bleeding woman that she hadn't fallen down the stairs. He'd have happily repeated the day just to avoid discussing holiday plans with Karen, but that was what he'd been doing when the call came through. At least it gave him an excuse to ring off.

The British Transport Police had handed Snape to the Met and he was brought to Stoke Newington, where he sat, agitated, in an interview suite. Merle was the first to speak to him, the only officer on the investigating team except the superintendent and the DCI to witness the magnitude of Snape's suffering at first hand. Hot blasts of it pulsing off him as his hands wrestled with a plastic coffee cup, wanting to crush it. You witnessed the pain, and however much you didn't want to, however much you were trained not to – and as a cub constable he had been warned not to by superior officers relaxing grimly in the pub after hours – you couldn't help it. You couldn't help but absorb a little of it. And that made you different on the investigation. And although nobody ever said so, or acknowledged it, and it didn't mean you could cancel your leave for it, it made you different. It meant you had a special kind of lurgy that operated just below procedural level. And you had to shoulder that particular burden alone, because nobody else wanted the lurgy. They wanted to do their jobs, not care.

But they always turn up, that was the thing: eighty-nine per cent of missing children turn up in the first twenty-four hours; ten per cent within a week. So he could feel his horror mounting when the footage came through, the woman leading Ben away. Then, nothing.

The phone in his hand rang and he brought it to his ear. 'Hello, Pat,' he said.

'Hello, Clive.'

There was silence. Insanely, Merle thought of estranged lovers speaking to each other for the first time in long-lost years. 'You're whispering,' he said.

'Deborah's upstairs in bed. She may not be asleep and I don't want her to know you've called. She'll think – well, she'll think what I thought when I got your message.'

'I'm sorry.'

'She heard the phone go.'

'I'm sorry. I should have called your mobile.'

'It's okay.' There was a pause. Merle heard a rustle and remembered that Pat had a strangely crinkly sofa, like it was filled with bits of polythene. He imagined him there now. Merle had only been in the house twice. It was a strange investigation like that, the parents living so far from the operation. For the first week they'd stayed in London, and it was Merle who had suggested they return home, closer to family; his real motivation was to stop them contaminating the investigation. First week, you wheel out the family quick, get them in the public eye, put faces to the anguish. Use emotion. When that doesn't work, concentrate on getting the facts out there. Make the facts the case, not the faces. Back home in Kettering he'd visited them twice in the second week, both update visits. Sitting there, cup of tea, female liaison officer with her arm round Deborah, Pat carbon-frozen. Sorry, there's nothing to report, but we believe it's only a matter of time before someone comes forward. The forensic psychologist is certain he's being looked after. Merle was the man the liaison officer had called when the couple wanted to see an investigative face. The third week, of course, he'd come on a week's holiday.

'You said you wanted to talk,' whispered Pat, at the other end. 'About Sam, was it?'

'Sort of about Sam, yes,' said Merle. 'Although no, not really about Sam. I mean, on that subject. Is everything . . . Are you happy about everything?'

'They say to wait and see if he contacts me again.'

'Yeah, that's pretty much it, Pat. I know it sounds obvious, but don't get your hopes up. There's any number of explanations, not least of which he's some tabloid reporter, a freelance, someone off the leash. Or maybe he's just a sicko . . .'

There was a sigh and a crunch of person on sofa. 'I won't get my hopes up then,' he said drily.

'It's best not to. Let us check it out.'

'I didn't think you were on the case. I called and got a Detective Sergeant Cyston. The number you left . . .'

Merle sighed. 'Yeah, I'm on leave, that's all. I know that's not what you want to hear, but I have to take it after a certain amount of time. It's, you know, a law. An officer comes in to take my place on the investigation, so there are the same amount of bodies on the case, don't worry about that, but you can still call me if you want to talk. Anything operational, go to Cyston, but if you just want to let off steam give me a call. I'm back in a few days anyway.'

'Okay, thank you. Enjoy the rest of your holiday.'

Merle sifted that sentence for meaning but found none. He took a deep breath. 'There's something else, Pat, actually. Can I ask . . . um, what were you doing on that train?'

'I beg your pardon?'

'I mean. I don't mean it like that. What . . . Just, how come you were on that train, is all I mean. I know you had no business with us that day and it was a late train, wasn't it?'

'Yes.'

'So . . . how come you were on it?'

'Sorry, Clive, is that your business?' Snape sounding brittle.

'You tell me.' And Merle meeting it head-on.

There was a pause. 'I was working.'

'Really? You're not back at work, though, surely?'

'A meeting I wanted to attend to try to take my mind off things.'

Merle could smell it from here. 'Ah.'

Again silence came between the two and Merle wondered how to break the deadlock.

He didn't have to: Pat decided to tell the truth.

'It wasn't a meeting,' he said finally.

'Ah.'

'I've been going into London. I've been going every day.'

'I see. Why is that?'

'Why do you think?'

'Okay. How long for?'

'A week, not long.'

'Since you moved back?'

'Yes.'

'And did you talk it over with your counsellor? Family liaison?'

'No. I haven't seen anyone lately.'

'Is that a good idea? See, Pat, I'm sure they would have advised you against going to London every day.'

'Well, then, it's a good job I haven't seen them, isn't it?' Pat, whispering, sounded urgent and besieged.

Merle sighed. 'If you had they would have told you that what you're doing isn't . . .'

'Isn't what? Healthy?'

'Probably not.'

'Constructive?'

'Probably not, Pat. After all, what do you think you can turn up? And, to be honest, I don't want the media getting hold of it. We've asked them to leave you alone, and they've been all right about it but something like this they're going to want to go with.'

It was Pat's moment to sigh. 'Oh, look, what would you do if you were me, Clive? Would you go back to work? Would you stay at home? If your child went missing – okay, so you don't have one,' Merle winced at his end, 'but if you did and your child went missing, what would you do? Of course, if it was your child you'd be part of the investigation. You'd put yourself in charge, wouldn't you? You'd be out there hunting day and night, because there's no way, is there, you'd ever sit this one out? But I'm not you. I'm not a policeman. I'm me. So tell me, please, honestly, what would you do if you were me?'

'I'd like to think I'd stay at home with my wife,' lied Merle. 'What about Deborah? She needs you – you need her.'

'Deborah needs me, that's right,' he said at last. 'But I'm Ben's father and a boy relies on his father not to sit at home. Wherever Ben is, if he's . . . if he's alive, then the one thing he'll know is that his dad will be looking for him. Every belief he has in the world being a nice place full of people who look out for little kids like him is failing him right now. The one certainty he has left is that, any minute now, his dad's going to take him home – and I can't let him down on that one.'

4

Last night Dash had waited patiently in bed, listening to the solo Sophie show, buffeted by the mattress as he pretended to be asleep while she fought with her clothes. At last she stopped. Some inside bit of her, previously determined to remove every last scrap, finally held up its hands and admitted defeat. She lay back, grunted once, did a sort of shiver – then fell asleep.

Dash turned over, recoiling from the smell of her breath – a devastating cocktail of vomit, Atkins diet, fags and alcohol. Her skin seemed to glow like orange neon in the darkness, her chest rose and fell, bra half on and half off. There was no Tiffany heart on that chest, he noted, seeing also the makeup that had shifted on her face, a mask on the melt. One regretful morning she'd groaned, 'Please, Dash, if you ever see me falling asleep in my makeup again, no matter how far gone I am, promise to wake me up and make me take it off. Like, remind me of me saying this. Get a tape of it or something and play it to me because . . .' A flourish of a hand-mirror and a yuck-face finished her sentence for her.

So the next time she'd been drunk he'd done exactly that, but she'd told him to fuck off, and to fuck whatever she'd said before, she just wanted to sleep and what was he anyway, some kind of fucking *makeup monitor*? Next time she'd been drunk it was the same thing. He gave up after that.

God, that breath. It seemed to settle round his face like fly-spray, and thinking that took him back to the Flat Cap and the sudden slap of Guinness foam, the sharp smell of hops, the crones laughing it up behind him. The thought spurred him on. He waited just a minute or so more to make sure her ladyship slumbered dead to the world, then left the bed and dressed, fingers trembling as he buttoned his jeans. When he left the house he pulled the door closed quietly behind him, almost tiptoeing, so as not to disturb anybody.

There were only two tills open at the twenty-four-hour Tesco's but a sizeable queue at both. Dash had always wanted to know what kind of people did their shopping in the witching hours, but the truth was less exotic than he'd imagined. The customers belonged in a bad stand-up routine: insomniacs, shift-workers, cab drivers, clubbers, the odd couple trying it out for dinner-party conversation, smiling at other customers like it was some kind of kooky adventure. They wouldn't be back, thought Dash. Twenty-four-hour shopping wasn't a convenient alternative, or cool or funky: it just meant you'd failed in life. He should know, he mused, as he located the little section they had for barbecues. There he grabbed himself two squeezy bottles of lighter fuel and a bag of briquettes and headed for the checkout.

The briquettes were for show – he didn't really need them but thought two bottles of lighter fuel alone might get staff looking at him narrow-eyed. As it was, the checkout operator didn't even glance at the goods, dragging the bag across the bleeper and staring over the top of Dash's head, sweeping the plastic bottles without so much as a first, never mind second glance. If Dash was worried about arousing suspicion he needn't have been – this guy would have scanned a turd if it had a barcode on it.

'Do you want the vouchers, mate?' drawled the assistant, squinting up at him with sleep-starved eyes.

'Yeah, thanks,' said Dash, taking them. 'Better had.'

He chucked the briquettes into the rear of the van but kept the squeezy bottles close at hand. Standing in the car park (near-deserted, one or two mystery cars parked at its fringes), he regarded the van and wondered about – what? – disguising it or something, perhaps getting a handful of mud and wiping it over the licence plate. But there was a film he'd seen. The guys are pulling a bank job or something similar and they have to steal a car – 'boost' it. The boss guy tells them to make sure all the tail-lights are working and keep within the speed limit cos they don't want any five-oh sniffing around. Mud over the licence plate was the kind of thing that would catch a cop's eye. Thinking about it, he checked the plate was clean, then verified that all the lights were working. He took a look round the car park, checking self-consciously to see if anyone was watching. Then he clambered into the van and set off for the depot.

Quite when it had occurred to him to burn down the depot he wasn't sure. Maybe with the cold slap of hoppy Guinness froth; or maybe with the knee thumping into his bollocks for the second time, doubled up in the toilets fighting tears of pain and rage. Either way, it was an idea that had been waiting for its name to be called. 'If you could just let me clear the backlog,' he'd once pleaded with Phil. He couldn't increase demand, but he could stop supply. He could do it with barbecue lighter fuel and a box of matches, and providing he wasn't seen all he had to do was turn up the next day with Lightweight and act shocked, restrain himself from dancing in the ashes, make out he was just as gutted as the next man. And if Phil turned to him all suspicious, like, 'Where were you last night, Dash? You had good reason to see this place burn,' then, 'Christ, no, Phil, we had a great day yesterday, didn't we, Lightweight? And anyway I'm Dash, the likeable-but-doomed sad-sack with the Stoke Newington patch. I don't burn down depots. I'd just as likely set fire to myself.'

He could get away with it.

As long as he wasn't seen.

And as long as he didn't, really, set fire to himself.

He pulled up, switched off. The van cleared its throat and went silent. On one side a metal fence bordered a no man's land, railway line beyond. It was plastered with posters and graffiti but any B-boys with spray cans were absent now. As far as he could see it was deserted. Lining the road were a skip, a huge mound of rubbish next door, a lorry, a couple of random mystery cars. His white van looked at home in the sub-industrial mess. And there, up ahead and on the right, was the entrance to the depot yard. He took deep breaths, stared at the entrance. Willing himself to move . . .

If only he hadn't hit the kid who had Tourette's, he thought. That was where it had all gone wrong. Thing was with this kid, it started with his name: *Corvin*. It was deliberately different, American-sounding. And then there was his Tourette's.

'Arse-jack. Bum-come.' The sweary kind of Tourette's: the one that makes good TV.

'Corvin is not very well,' they'd been told. They were gathered into a classroom and the teacher sat perched on the edge of the desk, oh-so-casual and treating them like young adults. The girls all wore the same self-righteous look of resolving to do good. The boys were laughing but thinking, Hey, maybe Corvin's got things worked out here.

'He's not very well,' they were told. 'He has something that makes his brain sneeze, and when his brain sneezes he says things he doesn't mean, and what you must remember is that even when he says something rude or hurtful, he doesn't mean it because he can't control it.'

Yes, he can, thought Darren then, but at some subsonic level – knowing it, not thinking it. *Yes, he can.* And when he grew up and thought about Corvin with an adult mind he realised that what he had wanted to know was how, if Corvin's brain was sneezing, did it know to sneeze out only rude words and insults? How come they weren't simply random words, like 'jam' or 'lorry'? How come they were always directed at the people least likely to land one on him? And how come these sneezes always seemed to happen at the right time, once or twice a class, say, just when the shockwaves of the last were a memory, or when the teacher had been paying a little too much attention to a non-Corvin pupil. It was as if Corvin couldn't have that. Up he'd pipe: 'Your crack's cracked. Your minge mings.'

The boys were still laughing but thinking, Hey, maybe Corvin's got things worked out here, because he sure got a lot of attention. From teachers he got attention, from the girls he got attention. He was like the most exotic person they knew.

'He called me a sad haggy slag bag,' they'd share gravely with one another, like mini-Florence Nightingales.

'Really? He called me rich scum, and I'm not rich at all, just well-off, Mum and Dad say.'

It was close to the end of school when the cameras arrived. Darren's year was terrified about moving on to the upper school where it was legendary that all first-years had their brand-new uniforms ripped, muddied and their shoes stolen, or were bundled into bogs for beatings by fifth-years who spent their time smoking and torturing first-years. Toilets were used and heads flushed down them. Whole tins of Ralgex were sprayed on testicles. Anything of sentimental value, anything new, anything bought with good heart by Mum, Dad or well-wishing grandparents was stolen, ridiculed and destroyed by older kids, the ones who'd already learnt that you had to deface your own stuff before someone else did it for you.

So they were scared stiff back at primary, and into this hothouse of dread came the camera crew, three of them, there for Corvin, who wasn't going to the upper school, oh, no. None of that abuse for Corvin, he was going (of course) to a 'special' school, the transition to be filmed by a documentary crew keen to record his every expletive; Corvin happy to provide. Was Darren the only one who knew, deep down, that Corvin's illness became inexplicably worse when the crew was present? It felt like it. Perhaps everybody else thought so too, but nobody ever said, all of them abiding by an unwritten conspiracy of tolerance and understanding. For perhaps two weeks the crew followed Corvin around – him sneezing for England – and the rest of the kids followed the camera crew, crowded together and right behind, as if connected by a bungee cord. 'Back, kids, back. Just take three steps back,' the film guy would say. 'We need to get a shot of Corvin.' They'd shuffle in reverse, wait a moment, then move forward again. The film guy would turn back, repeat till fade.

Thinking about it later, with everything behind him, Dash wondered if Corvin intuitively knew that his story needed some end-of-act drama so that he deliberately brain-sneezed in Darren's direction because he wanted to wind someone up, actually *wanted* them to lamp him with the cameras rolling.

The way it played in his mind, he was sitting on a bench with the bench between his legs, facing another boy, name long forgotten. They'd been playing with some kind of collectable cards, doing swapsies, whatever, when suddenly Darren felt a presence and in that same moment Corvin bellowed, 'COCK-KNOCKER!' into his ear. Darren lurched sideways on the bench, like his horse's saddle wasn't properly fixed, and he had this image of Corvin, the camera crew, the other kids, all laughing; although, later, when he saw the incident on the documentary, it was clear that nobody was laughing, certainly not the crew or even the other kids. The faces were shocked. Only Corvin wore a non-shocked look, his expression almost beatific in the half-second between screaming 'COCK-KNOCKER,' Darren falling, then springing up and hitting him with all the suppressed anger of months of imagined inequality and the pure, white-hot hurt of the moment.

One summer holiday later, Darren was in the upper school where, even though the TV people blurred his face out, everybody knew he had hit Corvin, and where, suddenly, they were less respectful of Corvin's brain-sneezing. Where Corvin was the spastic, the flid, and Darren was the hip kid who hit the flid, and as a result missed out on all the bog-flushing and Ralgex-spraying; indeed, he soon joined the ranks of the flushers and sprayers. Not in any kind of flushing or spraying capacity, nothing physical, but as chief wiseass, provider of quips, the big gob who hung around with the tough lads. There was no way he could escape his notoriety so instead he embraced it. He metamorphosed. Only instead of caterpillar to butterfly he kind of went the other way. Mum and Dad were mystified as to why their previously well-behaved little boy was never at school or disrupting lessons when he was, stinking of cigarettes and swearing all the time – friends with the kids who had run-ins with the police. Everybody thought he was a good kid; nobody could understand why he behaved that way – a bit like the way

Darren couldn't understand why Corvin couldn't control his brain-sneezing.

These days, Dash realised something he never had at the time: his heart had never been in it. Being bad, it had never really been 'him': he'd just got caught up in its tow . . .

Now he stared over the top of the steering-wheel, trying to put himself outside the cab – outside and walking towards the depot entrance with the two bottles of barbecue lighter fuel stuffed up his sweatshirt. Not too slow now, not too quick, wouldn't want to attract the attention of anyone happening by. Slip into the depot yard. Do they have one of those lights that comes on when it senses movement? Doesn't matter: who's going to see it? Up to the office door, not the big roller doors, the other one, because you can either trip the Yale lock easy, or there's a letterbox. A letterbox perfect for squirting barbecue lighter fuel through. Squirt it all, get the carpet good and damp inside, drop a match in and get moving. Want to be sure the fire spreads? He had a bank card. Push the card into the lock and he could get inside the office, which had one of those fabric-covered partitions that looked as if it'd go up a treat. It had box files and old newspapers spread on every surface. It had a corridor and a standard wooden door that led through to the warehouse where there were pallets full of boxes gagging to burn. Christ, even if the whole place didn't get razed to the ground the damage ought to be enough to put them out of action for – what? – a week? Two? More time to try to clear the backlog, clandestine visits to Holloway Road. And if it did burn, and the place was gutted, hurrah. Maybe the whole thing would fold. He'd finally prise himself free of Chick. 'Because otherwise he'll keep squeezing, won't he?' said an inner voice. 'He'll squeeze until you're dry and keep on squeezing just for the crack.' Because Chick had never been cast unwittingly in the role of bog-flusher and Ralgex-sprayer: Chick was the real deal. He'd been born flushing.

All this, if he could get out of the van. Still Dash stared up the road, kidding himself he was looking out for possible witnesses but knowing, really, that he was trying to grow a set of *cojones*. From behind, the sound of a car broke into his thoughts. His wing mirrors lit up and instinctively he pulled himself low into the seat, waiting as it passed. He stayed that way, watching the car, which, instead of continuing up the road, slowed and pulled to the side ahead of him, lights going off with the engine. Breath held, he slid further down, thanking God for no streetlighting here. Maybe someone just stopping to look at a map — a courting couple, perhaps. Jesus, was he going to be invaded by gangs of doggers, suddenly appearing from behind the corrugated fence like feral children?

There were no doggers and, as far as he could make out, the car contained only one occupant, who now opened the door. It was a Saab, Dash saw, a good one. From it stepped a man who looked up the road and then down towards Dash, who cringed back in his seat, not visible anyway.

The Saab, it had one of those internal lights that stay on for a moment or so once the engine's stopped. The car was lit up from inside, illuminating its owner as he stared down the road, not seeing Dash, then making off in the direction of the depot entrance, a supermarket carrier-bag swinging at his leg. He didn't see Dash, but Dash saw him, and had to restrain himself from rubbing his eyes cartoon-style, because it couldn't be, not here, not now. Couldn't be Chick.

But there he was, like a malignant growth, making for the depot and then out of sight. Dash felt the breath escape him and pushed away a what-if image that saw him held down and doused in his own barbecue fuel by a vengeful Chick. He was near tears as he turned the engine over and, with one eye on the entrance, reversed slowly away until he felt safe to three-point the van round and head for home. The tears never came, but if they had, would they have been of frustration or relief? He couldn't say.

5

Waking up the following morning Dash had one of those blissful moments when he thought he might have dreamt last night. But then he shifted in bed and felt his bollocks ache. Not a deep, dull, just-kicked sickness, more a kind of weary protest, like 'Whoah there, ace. Remember us?' And it was followed by an image of the architect of that very bollock-ache at the depot delivering another – this time metaphorical – kick in the balls. Sorry, son. Not a dream.

Beside him, Sophie lay sleeping. Drunk-sleep. Her hair was stuck sweatily to her forehead and despite himself Dash reached to remove some strands from her eyes, and did so not caring whether she looked elegant or stylish, or if she had a beach-bunny body or whether she had a hair-do or a hair-don't, just thinking of the piss-take he'd put her through when she was feeling better, and how he was going to milk this – the number of times it had been him coming home late and drunk, her going postal the next morning. Oh, yes, he'd be milking this one.

He walked through to the lounge and switched on the television, which came on with a boom – Sophie last night. Thinking of sleeping Sophie now, but oblivious to the effect it had downstairs (where Max groped sleepily in his bed for foam earplugs that had caterpillared out during the night, trembling hands patting the bed like a blind man's), Dash killed the volume, went to make tea. Five minutes later he sat on the edge of a box in Speakers' Corner, cradling a cup and wearing his grungy dressing-gown, the source of countless arguments. In the red corner, Sophie, forever whisking sixty-quid dressing-gowns across his vision whenever they came across a shop selling them: 'What about this? Try it on. At least try it on. I'd really *fancy* you in this.' Like giving up the grungy gown and embracing a Persil-white robe would turn him into some kind of Sunday-morning Brad Pitt. While in the brown, threadbare and, if he was honest, slightly smelly corner, Dash, who just liked his dressing-gown and didn't want another. Maybe if he could somehow get himself out of this mess, he thought, he'd buy a new dressing-gown, since it seemed to mean so much to her.

Some minutes later Dash entered their bedroom bearing a cup of tea and set it on the floor by the side of the bed. 'Soph,' he said gently. 'Babe?' She stirred and passed a hand over her eyes as if to shut out the cruel sunlight interrupting her sleep. 'Soph,' he said again. 'I've brought you a cup of tea.' Her eyes opened and he wasn't looking at her, so he didn't see what was unmistakably guilt in them. The kind of guilt you might feel if somebody whose life you were planning to demolish brought you a cup of tea, welcoming you softly back to the land of the living, you nursing a hangover from the night before when you had spent the evening in excited conversation with your gay best friend, talking about the laughs you were going to have living together, the parties you were going to hold, the ice-cream you were going to eat watching DVDs of *Sex and the City* and *Moulin Rouge*, the makeovers and shopping trips.

Last night, after ostentatious goblets of wine, several Marlboro Lights and much talk of dinner parties, makeovers and nights out, with Peter promising her the best bars and wildest gay nights, he'd asked, 'So, when are you going to finish with him?'

'You don't have to say it with such, you know, such *glee*, like you're getting a big gay thrill out of it or something. I can't just turn round and dump him, not just like that.'

They each lit another Marlboro Light. 'You've got to be cruel to be kind,' Peter advised.

She ignored him. 'I want to let him down gently.'

'No, no, no.' He shook his head. 'That way you'll give him false hope. You've got to make a clean break. Don't give him a chance to talk you out of it or you'll stare into those puppy-dog eyes and before you know it he'll be whisking you back to Tiffany's and this time he'll be picking out an *engagement ring*.' He held shock-horror hands to his face.

'Stop it.' Guilt gave her insides a Chinese burn at the mention of Tiffany's. But he was right. She dreaded the final conversation, the platitudes: 'I need a little time to think. A trial separation. Might not be the end.' She imagined his baleful look – dark, sad eyes peeping at her from inside his fringe. There was a time when she'd have found that look, or versions of it, heart-squeezingly cute. Now she thought it was borderline sad. As in pitiable. As in 'get a life'.

'How, then?'

'Oh, I dunno. Email?'

'Peter . . .'

'Letter, then. Write him a letter, pack your stuff and leg it when he's not there. As long as you make it soon.'

'Like when?'

'Soon. Sooner the better.'

Soon. She pushed her nose into her armpit and had a sniff, snuggling deeper into her pillow. They'd spent the remainder of the evening draining their ostentatious goblets and making plans. She'd tottered to the tube and then home, needing a wee so badly on the walk back from Manor House that she'd had to go through the kissing gate and crouch in a hedge (and that would make an *outrageous* story to tell Peter). Getting home she celebrated her impending freedom by dancing in front of MTV (and hurting her foot on one of the boxes), before the *vin rouge* repeated on her and she found herself on her knees, face in the toilet bowl.

'Babe,' said Dash now. 'Dirty stop-out. Where were you last night, then?'

He said it smiling. She reacted as though he'd grabbed her by the throat.

'Oh, God. Here we go.' She swung her legs out of bed and reaching for her dressing-gown.

'I'm not having a go,' he said, back-pedalling, 'It's just . . . I just . . .'

'I was *out*, that's all. It wasn't a big night.'

'Er, okay.' Dash marshalling his wits here. 'But it must have been *quite* a big night. You were back pretty late.'

'How late? Not that late.'

'You don't remember? It was past one.'

'Oh, hardly *late*. It's not like I was out clubbing or anything.' (Although Peter had been trying to drag her somewhere, she remembered now.)

'What do you mean "clubbing"? Since when do you go clubbing on a weekday?'

'God, people *do* go clubbing on a weekday, you know. It's not unknown.'

'Who goes clubbing on a weekday? *Peter*, I suppose.'

She'd reached the bathroom and locked herself in. 'Peter does, yes, sometimes.'

'And I suppose it was Peter you were out with last night?'

'And a couple of the other girls from work.' She sat on the toilet and put her head in her hands. *Carry on, Dash. This only makes it easier.*

'You know what I think?' he said, from the other side of the door.

'No, funnily enough, I don't. I suppose you're going to tell me whether I like it or not.'

'I think this gay friend of yours has got the hots for you.'

'Oh, God, don't be so typical. That's just the most ridiculous thing I've ever heard.'

He thought about it and decided it *was* fairly ignorant.

Inside the bathroom she gave the concept a bit of thought herself, wriggling a little on the toilet.

'Okay, I'm sorry,' he said. 'It's just that we haven't seen much of each other lately.' There was a wheedling tone to his voice he didn't like. The moral high ground wasn't what it was cracked up to be.

In the bathroom she bit her lip. 'God, we see each other all the time. We see too much of each other, that's our problem.'

'What problem?'

'Look, let's not talk about it now, Dash, we've both been busy, that's all. That's the thing with busy people. You've both got jobs and social lives so you don't see so much of each other. Gabrielle and her boyfriend have to make appointments with each other just to have dinner.'

'Well, I've got a window tonight.'

'A what?'

'I mean, let's make an appointment. Come on, we'll go for a Chinese.'

Inside the bathroom she curled a lip, trying to think, then thought a restaurant might be the perfect venue – like that film where they sack Tom Cruise in a public place so he can't make a scene. 'All right,' she said. 'That sounds fine.'

'Tonight it is.' He beamed.

A moment or so passed.

'Don't stand outside the bathroom, please,' she called.

'Okay, okay. I'm sorry.' He steeled himself. With one hand he picked at a piece of wallpaper by the side of the door. 'Look, Soph, sorry to ask, but I was wondering – I don't suppose I could borrow twenty quid? I need to put some petrol in the van and I haven't got any cash on me. I'll have some in a bit but I've really got to fill the van.'

'I haven't got any money, Dash,' she said. 'Sorry.' Guiltily pragmatic, she was mindful of the fact that she'd never see her loan repaid, not after today. 'You'll just have to go to the bank.'

He stepped away from the door and thought about things for a second or so. He heard the loo seat shift as she stood up, and his eyes narrowed.

'What are you doing hanging around out there?' she called. 'Just go away, will you?'

'How long are you going to be in there, then?' he said.

'Oh, for Christ's sake, how long have you been up? How come I'm in the bathroom and suddenly you need to go? You'll just have to wait.'

He didn't really need to go. He was thinking about the fact that she was out on the piss last night, and that meant she'd have been casting money around like confetti, bits of paper floating out of her purse, unaccounted-for. She'd said she didn't have any money; perhaps she'd run out. But perhaps she'd simply told him that in the embers of their argument.

He wandered through to the bedroom and poked a trainer at a pile of her clothes on the floor, deposited there last night. There were flecks of sick, he noticed, on her blouse, and he picked it up, frowning. It smelt of booze and sick and fags and perfume and tanning lotion. But her handbag was nowhere to be seen.

Dash trod back through to the lounge and there, on the sofa, was her handbag. It had been there all the time of course, but only now did he pick it up, and whispering a near-silent, 'Sorry, Soph', he reached in and plucked out her purse, opened it and ('Sorry, Soph' again) removed a ten-pound note. He returned her purse to the bag before remembering that it hadn't been at the top like that. No, it was more . . . more at the bottom. So he pushed it down to the base of the bag – as if she'd remember anyway. But as he did so his fingers brushed against something. Something that shot messages to his brain. Dash lifted the Tiffany heart from the bottom of Sophie's handbag and held it up before his face, where it swayed slightly. There were bits of fluff sticking to the chain. The pendant had become stuck to some chewing-gum inexpertly disposed of in a wrapper. He regarded it for a moment or so before placing it back in the handbag, once again ensuring that it went right to the bottom, stuffed down there with the fluff and chewing-gum. Just as it was before. Then he walked through to the bathroom. 'Soph?'

She tutted, a tube of tanning lotion in one hand, mid-slather. 'What?'

And then the doorbell went. Lightweight. 'Oh, nothing,' said Dash. 'It's okay. It can wait.'

''S Lightweight,' said Lightweight, from down below.

Dash squeezed his eyes shut. Lurking behind them was the image of Sophie's Tiffany heart, bits of fluff sticking to it. And now to add to his misery was Lightweight. 'Okay,' he said into the intercom. 'I'll be right down.' He looked around for his jacket. 'Soph,' he called, 'I'm going out.'

The disembodied response: 'Okay.'

He shouldered on the jacket and launched himself down the stairs, the flat door slamming behind him.

Lightweight looked considerably brighter than he had the previous morning. Not that he was all smiles – he didn't greet Dash – but there was something about his overall demeanour, something that made Dash wonder what Lightweight had got up to with his share of yesterday's spoils. Is he high now? he wondered. He didn't know and didn't want to find out. First item on today's agenda was selling some speakers.

'Oi, Dash, over here.' Phil was beckoning him over with a crooked finger. 'I want a word with you.'

'All right, Phil.' Dash ambled over, the depot noisy and busy behind him. When they'd driven up he'd found himself scanning the road guiltily, as if he might somehow have left crucial evidence lying around. Chick's Saab was gone.

'No, I'm not particularly all right, mate,' said Phil. 'I've had the Holloway Road boys on my back. Do you want to know what they told me?'

'Go on.'

'That you've been on their patch. They saw you.'

'Well, so? It's not against the law to go to Holloway. I needed something from Argos.'

'Yeah? What?'

'Something for the missus. A hairdryer.' Dash smiled, hoping it didn't look too forced.

Phil looked at him closely. 'That's not what the Holloway Road lads are saying, Dash.'

'What they say, then? That it was curling tongs?'

Phil bopped Dash on the head with his clipboard. 'Smartarse. The Holloway boys saw you with a punter. You. A punter. A set of speakers in the van. By the time they'd done a U, you'd fucked off – and count yourself lucky you had.' Dash gulped. 'Yeah,

141

exactly. And they're fucking livid about it, mate. I'm getting all kinds of grief off them.'

'Well,' said Dash, bridling, 'I saw them on my patch.'

Phil bopped Dash on the head with his clipboard a second time. 'What would they want on your patch, Dash?'

'Flogging speakers to my punters, what do you think?'

Phil looked at him as if he'd just been fed the tallest story ever. 'Don't be daft,' he said.

Dash felt strangely defensive of Stoke Newington. Tree-hugging or not, it was his patch. What was so wrong with it that the Holloway Road team wouldn't want to chance their arm?

'Now listen,' said Phil, 'me and you get on famously, and I'm sorry if the good people of Stokey aren't so keen on buying speakers at the moment, but a deal is a deal, and the deal is that you stay on your patch and they stay on theirs.' He looked at Dash like a concerned headteacher. Dash nodded compliantly, pushing his hair out of his eyes. 'So you're not planning on going back?'

Dash shook his head.

'Now, how many sets of speakers you want?' asked Phil.

'One?'

Phil laughed and bopped him on the head again with the clipboard. 'I'll put you down for two, shall I?'

It was later that morning when it occurred to Dash that Lightweight couldn't read. And in a day where he already felt events clamouring at the door, zombie-hands bursting through, the thought calmed him somewhat. *He can't read.* Like, there it is: a capsule explanation for the silent malevolence sitting beside him.

What set him along this path was the business with the map at the depot. After accepting a bop on the head and a clap on the back from Phil, and loading up two sets of speakers, he'd got back to the cab and had Lightweight drive them off then stop again. 'Now,' he said, dragging the map from the glove compartment, 'let's work it out, yeah? Where we're going to start . . .'

He'd decided to try afresh with Lightweight. If he was ever going to get out of this – and if he wanted to avoid burning down the depot – he needed Lightweight on message, on song, on board. And, hey, maybe the new, possibly high Lightweight might be a bit more open to the enterprise today. After all, it was in his interests, too . . .

'Here's our area, right – the area marked. And a lot of it borders the Holloway Road area, right? Now, it's not like there's an invisible anti-student forcefield there or anything, there must be some stragglers, right? So what we'll do is . . .' Lightweight was staring at the map with an expression Dash couldn't decipher, and wouldn't until later: it was a look of angry incomprehension, of a man who can't read. '. . . stick to the borders, but really stick to the borders. As long as we're not in their area we're safe, although we'll still need to keep an eye out for them. They might want to kick off about yesterday.' Angry incomprehension from Lightweight, as if he wanted to pick a fight with the map.

'Look,' pushed Dash, rustling the map, 'what I'm saying is we'll stick to this side here.'

At last Lightweight nodded slowly, shrugging. 'Just tell me where to go and I'll go there, man,' he said.

Where it says on the fucking . . . Oh, forget it. For. Get. It. 'Okay, then,' surrendered Dash, thrusting a hand into his hair, holding it there and scratching in sheer, silent frustration. 'Let's just get a move on.' He checked the rear-view mirror.

And it struck Dash at the very second he saw them that since he'd been planning on parking up to talk tactics it would have been a good idea to get clear of the depot first.

What he saw in the mirror was the Holloway Road team turning into the depot entrance and lurching to a halt as the passenger saw Dash and Lightweight at the kerb.

'Better go now,' said Dash. 'The Holloway Road lot are behind us.'

Lightweight looked his way, then wound down his window. In the rear-view Dash saw the other team's van – Also Available in

White – half in, half out of the entrance, blocking it for anyone trying to come out. Not that the other team was fussed. The passenger door was opening now, the passenger getting out, reaching back into the cab.

'Come on, mate,' urged Dash. 'Get a move on, yeah?' Lightweight cleared his sinuses and spat from the window. Dash's eyes were still fixed on the mirror where the passenger from the van was hunting for something stowed on the floor of the cab. He wasn't moving fast, Dash saw, probably didn't realise Dash could see him, had probably identified the van, thanks to Warren's graffiti: 'try slapping the top of this fucker.' Why couldn't he have written 'also available in white', like everyone else? Better still, why hadn't Dash just wiped the fucker off? He cursed himself for being such a muppet. And the passenger was turning back now, having found what it was he was looking for.

'Fuck, he's got a baseball bat,' said Dash – screeched it, actually, embarrassing even at that moment. Lightweight looked at him and hissed in disgust, his shoulder dipping to turn the key, Batman only feet away now. He heard beeping, imagined angry speakermen piling up behind the Holloway Road van.

'Just go.'

At last Lightweight pulled away from the kerb, and the last thing Dash saw of batman was an angry swing of the club, which met thin air as he turned away, angry and spitting.

Lightweight laughed nastily. 'You know what, man?' he said.

'What?'

'You're a fuckin' bitch.'

The next thing had been the business with the card, when they'd made their way to the furthest-flung outposts of Stoke Newington and were coasting along Endymion Road when Dash had spied a possible punter, a mark, and told Lightweight to stop and Lightweight did, catching Dash's eye and rubbing his fingers together in a money way as if to remind Dash that he'd better sell some speakers because he wanted his cut. Like Dash needed reminding.

He wound down the window. 'Do I know you?' he asked.

'Because I think I can always recognise a man who knows a good deal.'

Instead of smutty lines for pulling babes in theme pubs, Dash had witty openers but, looking closer, he thought he might have made a mistake with this one; the suit was never a good sign. Up close it was shiny enough so you knew it was silk. His teeth were a bit too white and his skin the leather end of brown.

Gary Spencer, who used to be called Gaz by his mates until he insisted they call him Spence, couldn't believe the fucking neck on this kid. 'Sorry, mate?' he said. Scratch him and he bleeds East End. Even so, and despite his moment of disorientation (like, the fucking *neck* of this kid), he said it with a big smile, a big misspent-youth smile. Shit, thought Dash, it was a you-can't-kid-a-kidder smile. He was wasting his time here. This guy looked and acted like he knew every trick in the book, and a few more not in the current edition.

Dash faltered, then pressed on: 'I was just saying it might be your lucky day. Are you into music at all?'

'Because you've got some speakers to sell.' The bloke's grin was even broader, his whole face bunching up around his eyes. 'That's it, innit? You've got some speakers to sell. Am I right or am I right?'

Dash ignored Lightweight, who was making some kind of noise beside him. 'Yeah, all right, mate. Forget it, eh?' He was about to wind up the window.

'No, no,' said Silky Suit. 'Matter of fact I may well be up for some speakers. You got 'em in the back now? Let's take a look.'

Dash let himself believe the guy might really be up for buying speakers. Going through his patter as if on auto-pilot, he wrenched open the back doors and let the Auridial work their magic. Silky Suit oohed and aahed, hefting each one and looking impressed.

'All right,' he said, reaching into his suit and removing a wad of cash. 'How much do you want for them?'

Dash looked at the wad. 'Um,' he said, his mind working. 'Well, er, they normally retail for . . .'

Laughing, Silky Suit clapped a hand to his shoulder. 'Mate,' he said, 'I ain't going to buy your speakers. Sorry.'

'Oh.'

He held up the roll of cash so Dash could almost smell it. 'I don't need any speakers. See, I got Bang and Olufsen at home.'

'Oh.'

'But I do need someone to work for me, someone with a bit of this up here,' he tapped the side of his head, 'a fast talker. Interested?'

'Doing what?' said Dash, eyes on the roll of money, waving cobra-like before his eyes.

'Sales.' Silky Suit waved his hand dismissively. 'Look, don't say anything now. Think it over.' He pulled a business card from the top pocket of his jacket. 'Give me a call if you're interested, all right?' Dash took the card as Silky Suit laughed. '"Do I know you?" Good line, like it. Better luck next time, eh?'

Lightweight was rubbing money fingers together when Dash took his seat again, still staring at the card in his hand.

'Bloke out there,' he said, as much to himself, 'just gave me his card,' and he held it for Lightweight to see; he stared at it with the same look of angry incomprehension Dash had noticed earlier. At which point – at that *exact* moment – it had hit Dash.

He can't read. To me the card says 'Gary Spencer, entrepreneur'; to him it says 'billig bootsh thatfgtuh'. He. Can. Not. Read.

'You din't sell no speakers, then?' growled Lightweight.

Did Dash imagine it or was there a slight shake to his hands on the wheel all of a sudden? 'No,' he said. 'Nah, not this time. Next time, though. I feel lucky now.'

Lightweight snorted. 'Such a fuckin' bitch,' he said, under his breath for Dash to hear.

At least I can read, thought Dash.

6

'You could have rung ahead.' It was Max saying it this time.

He'd opened the door to find Verity on the step, and she was standing there with her handbag in both hands, looking stern, like a new governess sent by the agency. 'I did.' Alongside looking stern she seemed cross, with just a hint of uncomfortable. Anybody would think Wood Green was some kind of Beverly Hills Utopia, the way she looked up and down Clarke Street, expecting muggers to pounce at any second.

'Did you?' he said, thinking.

She ignored him. 'Are you going to ask me in? You're not on your way out, are you?'

'Me? No.'

'Nowhere to go?'

'Just come in, Ver. I think I saw one of our coloured brethren over the street.'

She frowned and stepped inside, wiping her feet on the mat and glancing up the stairs as she did so. Only when Max had shut the door to his flat behind her did she say, 'How are the Munsters upstairs?'

'Like having a permanent migraine.' Max sank back into the sofa, watching Verity look his flat over.

'You wouldn't say that if you'd ever had migraines. They're no joke,' she said. Then: 'You know, I *love* what you're doing with this place.'

'Thanks.'

'What is it you do? Furniture? I mean you can really tell, looking round – you've brought an educated eye to the flat.'

'*Used* to do, Ver.'

'No, no, still do. The other night, remember?'

'One night doesn't constitute a career.'

'Just one night?'

She stood over him and he regretted taking a seat. He'd done it because it was a Max thing to do – leave his big sister hanging and wait for her to complain about not being offered a cup of tea, tease her a bit. Some habits never die. But now he was in a position where she loomed over him, still in governess mode. If she'd been wearing a hat it would have been fringed with roses. 'Yeah, Ver,' he said, 'just one night.'

'Not last night?'

'No.'

'Then where were you last night?'

'Here?'

'Oh. Then why didn't you pick up the phone?'

'I was in the toilet.'

'Half a dozen times, Max.'

'I'd had a curry at lunch.'

'*Bull* . . .' she hardly ever swore '. . . *shit.*'

'Okay, look. Enough, Herr Verity. I wasn't here, that's right. Apologies for not being at your beck and call. But that valuation, I didn't tie it up in one session – I had to go back.'

She stared hard at him. 'You haven't had any more letters, have you?'

'No.'

'You're sure? Because, you know, I have the distinct feeling you're hiding something from me.'

'I haven't had any more letters, I promise.'

She looked hard at him, as if trying to catch him out, and he met her gaze.

'Are you staying, Max?' she asked, changing tack suddenly. 'I mean, make yourself at home.'

He hadn't realised he was still wearing his coat. It had been on his back since he had arrived home from Kettering on the milk train, his pockets stuffed full of documents from Patrick Snape's wheelie-bin. He'd been right, had Chick, he'd been bang on. Underneath those envelopes with their corners cut away was the same old household detritus common to every bin from Land's End to John O'Groats. A telephone bill – Max stuffed it into his pocket not with the normal feelings of grim satisfaction but with sheer self-disgust and pity. There were handwritten letters, too, and he took those, riding a ghoulish feeling that threatened to engulf him. There was other stuff: circulars, junk mail. Life going on. Silently Max had thrust it into his pockets and left as before.

Now he shouldered his way out of his coat. The paper inside seemed to crinkle incriminatingly as he did so.

'Happy now?' he asked Verity, who said that at least he looked like he was staying, and as that was the case perhaps he could pretend to be some kind of host and make her a cup of tea. Relieved that it looked as if normal service had been resumed, he led the way to the kitchen where they stood as he boiled the kettle.

'Your front yard's in a terrible state,' she said, peering through a yellowing net curtain.

'It's the Munsters,' he explained. 'They just chuck stuff out there and the bin-men don't bother picking it up. I used to go out and pick it up for them.'

'Why did you stop?'

He shrugged in response. The words 'because I've given up' seemed about to make an appearance but, thankfully, didn't.

'It smells a bit, too.'

'They smoke in the hallway,' he said in explanation.

'Well, they shouldn't, it's a communal hallway. It smells out there as badly as it smells in here.'

'Gosh, that bad, eh?'

'I'm just saying. You should have a word with them. Why don't you just *say* something? All this might stop.'

He didn't know. His silence said so.

'All part of the great Max penance?' she said.

'It's all really rather simple for you, isn't it?' he said – snapped it, actually. 'Everything's so black and white. I should just pull myself together. Is that what Roger tells you over dinner? I should stop feeling sorry for myself, something like that?'

Verity blustered a moment, failed to find the right words. 'Well,' she said, 'wouldn't that be a good idea? Can't you try to put everything behind you?'

Hollow laugh from Max.

A silence. He poured boiling water over teabags, sniffed some semi-skimmed then handed it to Verity.

She held it to her nose and nodded an admonishing 'just', then watched him pour it into the cups before she spoke.

'Mum was dying anyway,' she said gently. 'She would have died *anyway*, Max.'

The only sound in the room, the tinkling of spoon in cup.

'She said she loved me,' he said. 'At the end.' He felt tears on their way. Squeezed his eyes shut.

'You see.'

'What she actually said was that she loved me no matter what.'

'There you go.'

'"No matter what", Verity. She loved me *no matter what*. That's what she said. She died wondering about me.'

'No, she died wondering who she could borrow a fag off. For God's sake, she never for a second believed anything but your complete innocence, you know that. And this is the thing with you: you *know* all this. That you did nothing wrong. That Mum would have drunk herself dead whatever. But you won't accept it. It's as though you've decided to be guilty because being guilty stops you having to face up to life. And now . . . it's got you into trouble, hasn't it?'

He looked sharply at her. 'What do you mean?'

'I mean— Can we go through and sit down a moment, please?' She ushered them out of the kitchen and sat Max on the sofa. He could see her looking for the leather armchair he used to have but had sold. She ended up perched on the side of the coffee-table, struggling to look like Verity as she did so.

'I was using my computer after you left yesterday,' she said. 'You know, you can see what websites have been accessed.' She took a deep breath. 'It wasn't jobs, was it?' He said nothing. 'Max, why were you reading about the little boy who went missing? You said you wanted it to look for jobs but every page was about that boy. You *searched* for pages about him. I want to know why, and please – please don't tell me it's something to do with furniture.'

There was a long moment.

'I can't tell you,' said Max at last, unable to meet her eye.

Exasperated, she looked to the ceiling, as though it was Max who didn't understand this thing – how big it was. How it was bigger and more important than they were.

'No. You see, you've got to tell me the truth here, Max. Because I'm sure that whatever it is you tell me can't be as bad as some of the things I'm thinking. It wasn't far from here that he went missing.'

'Christ, Ver, you don't think—'

'You've been lying to me about phantom jobs and now this. What am I supposed to think? Please – just tell me you've got nothing to do with it.'

'I've got nothing to do with it.'

She jerked back as if an electric current had passed through the coffee-table. 'My God,' she said. 'You're lying.' Max could sense the shock, knowing that deep down (no matter what, because he was her brother) she had expected that answer – but for it to be the truth.

'Ver . . .' But Verity was standing and Max saw panic there: she actually looked towards the door as if she was checking she could leave if she needed to. 'No, please, I'm not lying.'

'You're making this worse, Max. I know you're lying, okay? And you'd better start telling the truth now or I'm leaving and who knows where I might go? Ready? One.'

'Please, Ver, I can't . . .'

'Two.'

'You don't understand.'

'Three.' She went to the door and opened it, letting in the fusty-faggy smell of the hallway.

'I'll tell you,' he said quickly. She stopped, not turning round. 'Please, Ver, come back and I'll tell you the truth.'

She returned to her perch.

Max sighed. 'When I was in hospital I had a visit. It was someone from inside – he'd finished his sentence. It was the man who saved me, Ver, who stopped the bleeding and saved my life.' Here Max showed Verity his wrists, hating himself for hijacking her pity. Light reflected from the smooth, thick layers of scar tissue. Verity looked once, then flicked away her head. 'He wanted me to work for him.'

Verity groaned, clasping a hand over her eyes. 'Oh, Max. What sort of work?'

'He saved my life, Ver – I would have bled to death. And . . .'

'And what?'

'He threatened me.'

(*'Mud sticks.'*)

'What work, Max?' said Verity now.

'Bin-raiding.'

'*What?*'

'Bin-raiding.'

'*Bin-raiding?*'

'Yes.'

'And . . . and that's where you go and raid bins, is it?' As though she expected bin-raiding to be something else – just had a misleading name.

'Yes.'

'Uh . . .' She looked around herself, as though she was on a new and confusing planet. 'Whose bins?'

'Anybody's bins.' And he told her about his Stanley knife, and the five-second stoop and scoop, and how it meant people could have their identity stolen or their online activities phished, or their cards hijacked for card-not-present fraud, or have their mail rerouted, or their identity used for false passports. And despite himself he felt a small glow of black-sheep pride as he explained it to her; him the hitherto second-hand furniture restorer. It passed, though, when he saw her face. It passed and he felt sick and wrong and ashamed.

'Oh, Max,' she said, when he'd allowed a pause for it to sink in, knowing he still had more to tell her.

'The man's name is Chick,' he continued. 'The other night he told me I had to go to an address in Kettering, a particular address. It was a special job, he said. He wanted what was in the bin there.'

'Kettering. That's where—'

'Yes. It was their house.'

'You've gone to the police. Please tell me you've gone to the police.'

'No.'

'Why?'

'Because if I do, they'll send me back to jail.'

'Will they? Okay, never mind that now – why were you sent to that house?'

'To gather information on the family, see how well-off they are.'

'Why?'

'For a ransom demand.'

'So these people you work for are the people who took the boy?'

'I don't know.'

'Max . . .'

'Really – Ver – I don't know. I think . . .'

'Think what?'

His head dropped. *What?* What did he think? Mights and maybes. That a woman took Ben. That the woman who took Ben *might* have been the same woman who, yesterday, had stood in Chick's kitchen, quietly washing the dishes, helpless; her husband, a monster, talking about Ben like he was nothing more than a payday. He imagined the woman weeping silently.

'I think so. I *think* so. But I *only* think so.'

'Then you must go to the police.'

'No. Absolutely, totally no. Don't say it again.'

'Max, this is a little boy.'

'No. I'll go back to jail.'

'Not necessarily. But, Max, whatever. It's someone's *little boy*.'

'I might be wrong.'

'Even so.'

'I'm not going back to jail, Verity.'

'You wouldn't! Well, why would you? On what charge?'

'Verity,' he insisted, 'whatever it is, I'm part of it. I've been to their house. Last night I – I spoke to the father.'

'Oh, Max.' Verity stood and whirled round, not knowing what to do with herself. One hand was on her hip, the other to her forehead. She looked for all the world as if she was standing in a car park, trying desperately to remember where she'd left the car.

'I'm sorry,' she said. All her thoughts led to pushing the doors open at the nearest police station. 'I'm sorry, you've got to take the risk. And if you don't I'm going to have to do it for you. This is— It's something you have to do. It's your *duty* to do it, and if . . . if that means going back to jail – well, you've done the right thing. That's what you've got to think. Isn't it?'

'I might be wrong.'

She shrugged. *Even so.*

'They may not have him and I could *still* go back to jail, Ver. It's still blackmail. I'm still involved.' The notion seemed to calm her. Of course. That was it. The little boy was somewhere else, in another orbit, which made perfect sense because she couldn't comprehend him being in hers. People like her, they watched the reports on TV and tutted, and said how terrible it must be for the parents and there's a Mel Gibson film on after the news, he's quite dishy. They were never involved.

'What makes you think they might have him?' she asked.

'It's more a feeling. I need to find out for certain.'

'You need to, yes. You need to know for sure one way or another, because if they've got him you *have* to go to the police.'

'I know. I know.'

She'd sat down again, arranging herself on the table, seemingly exhausted. Questions she wanted answering lined up behind her teeth, but in the end all she could say was, 'Why?'

'What do you mean?'

'Why? Just that. Why? What on earth did you think you were

doing, you . . . you . . .' She couldn't find the words. '. . . *stupid man*? You'd just come out of *prison*. A bloody funny way to make sure you don't end up going back there.'

Max looked away. 'He gave me no choice.'

'Well, you know, I hate to sound like a stuck record, but you could have *told* somebody he was blackmailing you.'

'He saved my life. I'd be dead but for him.'

'Oh, sorry. Of course. That new law they passed. He owns your soul now. You should have tried bargaining with him when he was saving your life, did you think of that? Weekends off, that kind of thing?'

'I was unconscious at the time. I think it was a whole-soul-or-nothing sort of deal.'

She pursed her lips. 'Funny? Is it?'

'No.' Dry laugh. Not funny. He sighed and felt something close to serenity in the face of Verity's hurt, as if she was using all the available agony in the room. 'I'm never going back there,' he said. 'Never.'

Later, when she had gone, he sat looking around his flat and remembering it as it once was: with the leather chair in it, which he had sold when it became a choice between that and the van, and the chair was worth more; when the air was cleaner, fresher, windows had been opened, clothes washed and Italian foods were regularly prepared.

That day the television had been on, of course (a habit he'd always had), but the sound was muted. Instead a tiny, silver-shiny hi-fi system (since sold) played a soft, jazzy hip-hop as its owner got busy in the kitchen with a bottle of wine, hoping the soft, jazzy hip-hop wasn't too loud for Mrs Larkin upstairs, knowing it wasn't, but thinking about it anyway.

It had been a slow day at the shop, his shop, Got Wood. (And that raised a smile from customers. Once. Now the name disgusted and degraded him.) It had been another slow day in a line of slow days. People were saying house prices were about to plummet (and he didn't know it then but the worth of his own investment was already falling below what he owed on it), so business was suffering as a result. The day had been saved by a couple who bought a 1950s kitchen table Max had restored in the back room, a room that had smelt musty and woody and in which there was a fine layer of sawdust everywhere. The table was the kind he'd later find himself sitting at in Chick's kitchen, and even though one single solitary kitchen table was cause more for commiseration than celebration he was going to open a bottle of wine anyway. Pop. Glug.

There was a knock at the door.

And, anyway, you didn't need a reason to open a bottle of wine, not a specific reason, like selling a table. You could just be opening it as a full stop to the day, because you're happy, content, ticking over, thanks, can't complain. Which he was. Job, good; home, good. Even a girl on the horizon, although less of a girl, a woman, really; he'd seen her twice and thought she might be the one to help him get over the woman before, whose house he'd left before he moved to 64 Clarke Street.

The knock. He darted to turn down the already barely audible jazzy hip-hop, then went to the door where he expected to see Mrs Larkin. Not with a complaint, couldn't be. Perhaps with a tiny errand she wanted running – maybe her rubbish needed bringing down the stairs. Always done up tight it was, any left-overs bagged-up inside. That way foxes and other scavengers wouldn't tear into the plastic at night.

It wasn't Mrs Larkin. It was her granddaughter. He couldn't remember her name and didn't know how old she was (and why would he? Didn't matter to him how old she was, the grand-daughter of the woman upstairs, met her in the hall once) – hovering somewhere in her mid to late teens. She stood in the doorway with a holdall in one hand, posing self-consciously, head slightly to one side and feet artfully arranged. She wore brand-new trainers, the kind he'd only just given up on after hearing something on the radio, a fashion editor who said men over thirty should never wear trainers. He'd pushed his to the back of the cupboard, invested in some shoes.

'Hello,' she said.

She'd teamed her trainers with an ankle bracelet and jeans rolled up at the leg and low at the waist so he could see a flash of midriff below the T-shirt. Her belly button was pierced.

'I've come to collect Nana's stuff,' she said brightly, hoisting up the holdall. 'She's at ours and she's going to stop over. She said to tell you she wouldn't be home tonight, just in case you got worried.'

'Oh, okay. She's all right, though, is she?'

She laughed. 'Nana? Yeah, she's fine. She's already half-way pissed.'

'Oh, right.' Max was finding it hard to square the image of old Mrs Larkin – softly spoken, slipper-shod Mrs Larkin – with the picture he suddenly had of her cackling over a half-pint of stout.

Later, of course, much later, Max would think back to the moment he had allowed Mrs Larkin's granddaughter into his flat. He had plenty of time to give it thought. Why had he? He wondered. What had he been thinking of?

And the answer was revoltingly simple. He was flattered. He was flattered by the look on the girl's face, the idea that she might find him . . . not attractive as such, not really – although it went hand in hand – but . . . cool. He interpreted the attention as (the hubris would make him want to curl up with shame) minor adulation. In that moment he kidded himself that to her he was a guy with stylish-trendy shoes and cool music playing; own business, short haircut and dancing eyes. Some kind of ideal. At the back of his mind the idea lurked that she probably didn't meet many men like him, and was impressed by him, and (the hubris again – that and the wine) why wouldn't she be?

'Can I come in a minute? Bus'll be a while yet.'

It seemed like a good enough reason to let her in so he could bask a while in that minor adulation, wittily but sensitively deflecting any flirtation.

She saw his half-full wine glass on the coffee-table and indicated it. 'I'll have some if you're asking.'

As he poured her a glass – only a small one, mind – he did not do it, as a red-faced sergeant was later to assert, to get her drunk. God, no, what a waste of wine: he only had the one bottle. He did it in a spirit of mentor-cool, because he didn't want to be the kind of stern stuffed shirt who told her she was too young to drink. And, anyway, was she? Was she too young to drink? What did eighteen look like?

When he reappeared from the kitchen, she'd already flung herself into his sofa, tossing the overnight bag to one side. 'Can I smoke?'

'I don't smoke.'

She shrugged. 'Don't suppose it's worth asking if you've got any weed, then?'

Ha! Because he did have some weed, somewhere, from long ago – probably gone to dust by now, but 'No, sorry.' He smiled. A real know-where-you're-coming-from smile.

'Why don't you smoke?'

That took him by surprise. Like, 'Why don't you hold that loaded gun to your head and see if it goes off?' She'd brought a packet of ten Marlboro Lights from her denim jacket and was playing with the Cellophane sheath.

'I could say because it's bad for you, but I smoked when I was younger. I gave up when I started my own business.' 'So I wouldn't be lying on my insurance form,' he might have added, but didn't.

'Yeah, Nana said you had your own shop. You sell furniture.'

He laughed. 'It's a bit more creative than that. I recover and restore furniture . . . and then I sell it.'

'Like what?'

'That table there. I restored that.' He pointed at the coffee-table. Her trainers dangled over it. 'This armchair,' he patted its side, 'all kinds of stuff. Anything, really, that I think I can sell.'

For some five or ten minutes, she asked him about the business and he gave her answers, perhaps exaggerating how well it was doing and how much of an artist it made him. All the time she watched him carefully, not seeming to listen to his replies, a half-smile playing about her lips. At that time he might have described the scrutiny as refreshing and cheeky. Precocious, but not predatory. He'd change his opinion on that.

'Are you rich, then?'

He laughed. 'I do all right, thanks.'

She put her hands into her hair and pulled it back – two gold hoop earrings dangled at her neck. She held it a second and dropped it, stealing a glance at Max to make sure he'd noticed. Yes, his pursed-lip smile said, very good – you have been noticed. I know what you're doing and don't think I'm not flattered but honestly, really . . .

'I'm afraid I can't remember your name,' he said.

'Feather.' She sipped the wine.

'Heather?'

'No, Feather.'

The music stopped and she seemed to notice at once, jumping up and moving over to the stereo, a small pile of CDs beside it. She picked one up and looked it over, tossed her hair and glanced behind to see if Max noticed.

'I don't think it was Feather when we were introduced before. I think I would have remembered a Feather.'

'That's why it's Feather now. People remember Feather.'

'I'm sure.' He was trying to sound urbane, but didn't carry it off. 'And you're at school . . .'

'College,' she said.

'Ah, right. Doing what?'

'Learning.'

The music began to play and she walked over to the coffee-table, picked up her wine and took a sip. She watched Max over the lip of the glass.

'Learning what?' he said, forcing a casual note.

'How to succeed in life, I s'pose.'

She held Max's gaze and he held hers. Held it because, sorry, I've played this game before and with far more cunning opponents. Try it with someone your own age. Saying, 'I've not heard of that course. Is it new?'

She didn't reply. She placed the glass on the table and moved over to him. Then, with a movement that looked copied and awkward but was still devastating, she tossed her hair to one side, climbed on to the chair and sat astride him, her knees to the arms.

And he went to smile, to say, 'Now, look, steady on, this is all very flattering. It is, it really is, and you're very, you know, and if I was ten (twenty?) years younger, then maybe, but . . .'

But her lips were suddenly close to his, and they glistened with the wine she held in her mouth and he became aware of her smell, of perfume and cigarettes, and below that of her skin, which took him back somewhere, to another time and place. Their mouths were meeting, her lips opening and he was receiving the wine, feeling it leaking down his chin. His senses stunned and reeling.

At the same time she was moving on him, in his lap, the reaction there as predictable as it was shameful.

'No.'

He was lifting her off and, God, how light she was. How easy to lift and maybe carry and, just for a second, he imagined . . .

'No,' he said again. She regained her balance and he held out his arms to block her and met a look in her eye, which he later imagined as like that of a vampire. 'I'm sorry, no.' Shaking, angry, aroused and panicking, he wiped his mouth with a hand that came away slick with wine and lipstick red.

Her look became a smile. A smile that said she'd won in a game she couldn't lose. Because as he opened the door, full of apology but you must go because, really, I don't think . . . I'm sorry, but I think you should go. Now. As he ushered her out to the front door and held it open for her, unable to meet her eye, no, he wasn't cool. He was hard, sure. But not cool.

7

Dash had never seen Lightweight smile before. Previously it was like the muscles in charge of smiling and laughing had been disabled in a stroke. But now he was going great guns, basking in Dash's agony.

'Okay, mate, we're in the Holloway Road patch now,' said Dash, edgy and exasperated.

'Here is in their patch,' mocked Lightweight, 'but not over there?'

'Yeah, that's right. There's the map.' *Not that it'll mean anything to you.*

Lightweight shook his head, smiling at what a bitch Dash was; how Dash was constrained by these bitch rules that didn't apply to him and never would. He pulled over to the side for a piss behind a phone box, using the van as cover. 'I'm pissing into their area, man. Shit, ooh, what's gonna happen?'

Technically he *was* pissing into their patch, thought Dash, casting a look into the rear-view, half expecting Also Available In White to heave into view. That bat was still a vivid memory. And as if Lightweight's new-found love of larking wasn't enough, they hadn't sold any speakers. Maybe he'd been right. Maybe there was some kind of invisible forcefield around Stoke Newington, repelling students, allowing entry only to vegans and down-and-outs. Whatever, they hadn't sold a bean. A *mung* bean, ha!

'You got some money, man?' said Lightweight, getting back into the van.

'Christ. Look . . .'

Lightweight laughed and made a sudden movement. Dash flinched. Not much, but enough to keep Lightweight in laughter.

'No, man,' he said, still chuckling and starting the engine, 'we need some petrol, thass all. I ent gonna take your money.' He let it hang a beat as the engine turned over. 'Not yet.'

Sophie was overjoyed to have the lift to herself, especially today. In this building it was virtually unknown: it was always full of a bunch of people who seemed to know each other and spoke over you while you tried to pretend you weren't there. Having it to herself, though . . . She was already turning to check her reflection as the doors closed. It was bad: she looked as hung-over as she felt – like she'd been told bad news in a wind tunnel. Her eyes wanted to close, and the effort of keeping them open gave her the look of someone peering; her cheeks had migrated a little south and even fake tan couldn't hide the corpsey colour of her skin. She'd gone tonto with the makeup but instead of hiding a multitude of sins it simply lit the path. Oh, God.

'Wait a sec.'

There was only one thing that could possibly be better than having the lift to herself, and that was sharing it with Gabrielle. Or would have been if she hadn't felt so bad. The editor got a foot between the doors, entered and brightened at the sight of Sophie. 'Hello, *Sophia*,' she said, as in Loren. 'You look like shit.' (Gabrielle was *so* forthright.) 'What's wrong?'

She hadn't given Dash a second thought. It was the drink that gave her the undead look, but she wasn't about to tell Gabrielle that and, anyway, here was a far better opportunity to bond with her idol. 'I'm splitting up with my boyfriend,' she announced, sad-proudly.

'Oh, Soph. No more Dodgy Dash? What's the problem? Are you falling or pushing?'

'We've just . . . grown apart.' She placed a dramatic hand to her face, hoping to smother any tattle-tale alcohol fumes. 'I'm moving out.'

'It happens, Soph. People do. They do grow apart.' (Gabrielle's secret history was *so* cool.) 'I'm sorry to hear that, Soph. You know, it's not like we pay you much so if you need any time to sort yourself out or get your head together just shout, okay?'

The lift arrived and they stepped out together, Sophie impossibly proud of the fact. Then, as they were about to go to their separate desks, Gabrielle stopped. 'It must have been a tough decision,' she said.

Sophie nodded sadly.

'I wonder, would you be up for doing a piece on it? You don't have to use your real name. I'm thinking a diary-style piece for the Hearts and Minds section. It doesn't matter if you've got a lot on.'

'No,' said Sophie, quickly. 'No, just the tan test. And admin.' She gave Gabrielle a look to say she didn't mind doing admin but, you know . . .

'That's great, then, I'll mention it in Conference, get Bryony to commission you later, okay?'

'Brilliant. Oh, Gabrielle . . .'

'Yes?'

'I don't mind having my name on it.' *The thought of her name on it!* 'That's okay.'

'Fine. I'll look forward to it.'

He was thinking of that business card in his pocket.

Lightweight rattled into the petrol station and Dash directed him to the correct pump. ('There. Where it says unleaded.') The two of them waited out a pointless half-minute – Dash's protest at knowing he'd end up doing the petrol-pumping.

'I'll do it, it's okay,' he called, safe on the outside of the van. 'You just sit tight, yeah? And once I've done that I'll go and pay. Is that all right with you?' He imagined Lightweight, the curled lip.

Inside, the station was supermarket-size. Dash paid and took himself off to a corner where he dragged out his mobile and called Sophie.

'Can you tell her it's her boyfriend, Dash?' he said, to the girl who answered. She came off the phone and he heard her calling to Sophie. There was some kind of loud chant in the office as the call was transferred.

'Hey,' he said. 'Sounds like a party there.'

She was laughing at something. 'Yeah, no, it's just the usual, really.'

'Look,' he said, 'I'm really sorry about this morning, Soph.'

She was quiet. Actually, she was recovering herself, the girls having done their 'little bit whoo' number. Also, she was thinking how this conversation might make it into her break-up diary.

'Come on, Soph,' said Dash. She was really making him work for this. Like, it wasn't just his fault. She had come in pissed up.

'It's not just that,' said Sophie, as gravely as she could manage.

'What do you mean?'

'I mean . . . things aren't right, are they?'

'What things? The speakers? I tell you, Soph, I'm going to get shot of them soon.'

'It's not just the speakers.'

Dash had been leaning on the microwave and now made way for a customer wielding a sausage roll. 'Well, what, then?'

'I can't talk about it now. I'm at work.' She noticed that several girls near by were listening in. 'Let's talk about it later.'

'I thought we could go out for that meal,' said Dash. 'Chinese.' Not adding, 'That you'll pay for.'

'Okay,' she said. 'I'll see you at home, okay? We'll talk.'

'Yeah, okay,' he said, puzzled. The phone had already gone down at her end. He cast a look out to the forecourt and rooted around for the business card he'd been given earlier.

'Hello?' said the voice that answered.

'Uh, hello. Is that Mr Spencer?'

'Yeah-yeah, who's this?'

'It's Da – Darren. We met this morning. The speakers? You said to give you a call, a job, maybe?'

'Yeah-yeah, I remember. Darren, yeah. Of course. You interested, then?'

'Absolutely. Depending, I mean – what it is.'

'Selling, mate, only not from a van. On the phone. You get a desk, a phone, you get to sell. You got a suit, mate?'

'Yeah,' lied Dash.

'You'll get a chance to wear it, then. Why don't you come down to the office and we'll talk about it? Say tomorrow night, early evening after work. You got a pen?'

Dash hadn't but dared not admit it. He memorised the address, repeating it over and over in his head until he got the bloke on the till to lend him a pen. A suit. The words thrilled him. (A thought was tugging at his coat, but he ignored it.) Okay, so he didn't have a suit, or an idea how to get one. But *a suit*. A suit equals money and respect, and stuff like pensions and Christmas parties and cream cakes on your birthday. Suit equals salvation. (That thought was there again. *He'll never let you go*, it whispered. *Chick. He'll never let go, not until he's squeezed you bloodless. And I don't think you're going to be able to combine the two jobs somehow. It's one job and it's flogging speakers unless you can grow a backbone some time soon, make another nighttime trip to the depot . . .*)

Chick had been there, though. What was he supposed to do? And what if he returned, only to find Chick paying another nocturnal visit? He might not be so lucky next time.

And what had Chick been doing there anyway?

8

'Hey, Mum, alert, alert. I opened the door to a dangerous pervert.' Carl grinned at himself, then darted off, leaving the door swinging.

'She dropped the charges,' said Max, to the empty corridor.

Trish came through from the kitchen, wiping her hands on a tea-towel. Denim skirt, T-shirt, gold hoop earrings.

'He's just called. He's on his way back,' she said, not looking at Max, her head angled, as if watching Carl in another room. 'You'd best come through and wait.'

He tried to meet her eye, but couldn't. 'Thanks,' he said, closing the door and following her through to the kitchen, the 1950s table. He took a seat.

'D'you want a cup of tea?'

'Thanks, yes. As it comes is fine, Trish.' Madly, he felt all old-Max and in control.

She turned and filled the kettle. The radio was on, he noticed. A travel bulletin was playing; next, the news. She would have followed it on the radio, he thought. Standing in this kitchen she would have heard all the news reports about the missing little boy. The updates and appeals. The appeal that said, 'I'm now talking to the woman who is holding Ben. I know how difficult it must be for you at this time . . .'

Had she listened and thought of some mystery woman holding Ben?

Or was it her they were appealing to? If so, every maternal instinct must have been pulling her to the phone. To take the handset from the cradle, creep through to another room and make the call. Hushed tones because *he's* next door, the man who, instead of allowing her to telephone the police, said, 'Wait a minute, Trish. Wait a minute. Let's think about this, eh? We've got the kid safe, he's in no danger. Better with us than a lot of them out there. Put the phone down, Trish, this kid could make us a bit of cash. Put the phone down. Don't make me tell you again . . .'

Was that how it had happened? He thought so. If . . .

If it was her in the pictures.

She plonked a cup of tea in front of him and turned back to the worktop. Still she hadn't met his eye.

'Trish,' he said, 'do you know anything about the little boy?'

There was no answer, a swish of dishcloth.

'Trish, please.'

'Don't say nothing.' She continued wiping.

'Do you know where he is?'

'I don't know what you're talking about.'

There was a shout from next door – Carl reacting to something he'd seen on TV.

'I think you do.'

Her head dropped.

'I think,' he continued, 'that you're the woman in the pictures.' He heard her catch her breath. 'You recognise yourself, don't you? I think you found Ben and took him away and you were about to return him to his family but Chick stopped you, didn't he?'

There was a sob, her shoulders shook.

'Trish, whatever it is, whatever you've done and whatever he's making you do now, we can work it out. I'm on your side.'

At last she spoke. 'Stop it, right? I don't know what you're going on about.'

'You do, though,' he pressed. 'Come on, Trish. It's a little boy.' He found himself picturing the emotion in Verity's eyes. 'Just a little boy. He belongs with his mum and dad.'

Imagine how you'd feel if Carl was taken, he thought of adding, but decided against it.

'Stop it.'

Max stood up and left the kitchen in two strides. There wasn't much flat for him to check: two bedrooms, a toilet, the lounge where Carl sat watching television. He pulled open a small cupboard that housed a Dyson, then returned to the kitchen. Trish stood at the worktop, her arms by her sides, dishcloth in one hand.

'Just tell me where he is, Trish. Please.'

She shook her head, looking at the floor. From his coat he pulled a letter taken from Pat's wheelie-bin: *I lost my little boy to a road traffic accident so I know the pain you must be going through now. Please stay strong and remember our thoughts are with you.*

'Look at this, Trish.' Thrusting it at her. 'Look. And this.' He felt for another. *Last night I had a dream they found Ben alive and well. Maybe my dream will come true.* Another: *Yesterday my class all said a prayer for Ben and I hope you don't mind but we also said a prayer for the lady who took him.*

'Look.' He waved it in front of her face. *I hope you don't mind but we also said a prayer for the lady who took him.*

Whether she looked at them he didn't know: her face never moved. 'Trish,' he said quietly, urgently. 'Please.'

From the front door there was the clickety-click of a key in the lock, a tell-tale hacking cough. Chick.

'Trish.' Max was beseeching.

Carl had run to the front door. 'Dad!' he called, the only person ever happy to see Chick.

'Give us a battle rhyme, son.' Chick's disembodied voice from the hallway.

Max pushed the letters into his coat pocket.

Carl, battle-rhyming: 'Seeing you home is really bitchin'. Your mate Paedo's in the kitchen.'

'Trish,' said Max one last time. Quietly, urging her.

Chick: 'Is he now?'

He walked in. Baseball cap, flammable tracksuit bottoms. He wore a T-shirt with 'it ain't gonna suck itself' printed across the front, a gold chain round his neck. He looked first at Trish, who avoided his eye, then at Max, sitting at the kitchen table, an atmosphere in the room. 'All right, Paedo?' he said. Throwing a look at Trish he pulled out a kitchen chair and sat down. 'You got me any vouchers?'

Max shook his head slowly, trying to meet Chick's gaze.

'You got me something else, though, yeah?'

The letters were in one pocket, but Max reached into another and pushed a bunch of papers across to Chick. 'I've had a look through them. There's nothing.'

'You leave that for me to decide, mate,' said Chick, collecting them up and leafing through.

'I've seen his house,' insisted Max. 'His car. He's not rich.'

'Oh, yeah? What sort of car has he got?'

'It's a small Renault. I'm telling you, please, don't do this.'

Chick looked up. 'You can leave now, Paedo,' he said firmly. 'I might need you again for something – I'll be in touch about it. Another delivery in Kettering . . .'

A ransom demand?

'I won't go again. I won't be a part of this.'

'Oh, I think you will.' He said it softly, with absolute conviction.

'I won't.'

Chick smiled. 'Well, let's not talk about it now, eh? Let's cross that bridge if we come to it.'

9

One good thing about handing over the last of your money at a petrol station: it kind of balances the books. To zero, yes. But it focuses the thinking. Nothing in his pockets, nothing in his bank account. He needed exactly £550. Of that he owed Chick £350 (at the last count anyway) and the rest he needed to pay Phil the following morning. So, he thought, folding himself back into the van, add Lightweight's share and he needed over £600 from the rest of the day. He looked over to Lightweight, who sat looking noticeably more edgy than when Dash had last seen him. Was he trembling? Dash's heart sank.

It was a lost cause right from the start.

The first failure was wearing a large pair of headphones, and his head was bobbing slightly as he walked, so Dash waved a pointy finger for Lightweight to pull over. The kid turned out to be a bit simple. No sale.

Kid Two was not a new face on the Dash radar. They'd met before. It was Barnaby Horton, who, the previous evening, had decided to test his new speakers' 'superior bass response' – and found instead of superior bass a kind of wet *pish*. The sort of dickless *pish* his girlfriend's catalogue-bought 'ghetto-blaster' made *before* she'd activated the bass-boost button. Superior bass response? As long as the response is no. Ask these speakers a question and the response is, 'Whoever sold you these speakers saw you coming, mate.'

So Barnaby Horton was not best pleased to see Try Slapping the Top of This Fucker when it drew up alongside him, Dash already leaning eagerly out of the window with his lips moving. Wargh, wargh, wargh. Not best pleased at all.

'This is going to sound a bit of a mad one,' said Dash, as

Barnaby Horton removed his headphones. Then, as he recognised Barnaby, 'Oh . . .'

It wasn't like it had been the first time it had happened. Stoke Newington was a heartbreakingly finite area, and now Barnaby Horton was going into one.

'You can tell your mates that the speakers they sold me were crap, absolutely crap,' he snapped, from the pavement.

'No mates of mine,' said Dash, shaking his head sadly, arm along the door. To Lightweight he said, 'Did you hear that?' but Lightweight ignored him. Dash reflected that, all things being equal, he preferred the earlier, more jocular version.

On the pavement Barnaby noticed that Lightweight was trembling. You could just see it, at the wrist, hand on the steering-wheel. The arm shaking a little.

Dash looked back at him. 'Round here they sold them to you, was it?'

'No,' said Barnaby. 'Further down there. Just before Finsbury Park.'

Phil had been right all along. They hadn't been trying to poach sales in his area at all. 'Ah, well,' Dash said, 'down there. Tsk. What do you expect?'

Barnaby looked at him. 'What I expect, maybe, is a pair of speakers that work properly. I'm assuming you know these guys, right? Well, maybe you could . . .'

And then Lightweight was leaning across to the window, Dash pushing himself back into his seat, as shocked as Barnaby by the sudden movement of his partner. Barnaby took a step back.

'Listen, man,' snarled Lightweight, through the window, warped face. 'You checking these speakers or not?'

Barnaby took another step away, glanced at Dash, who sat pinned to the seat and petrified, not moving and barely daring to inhale. 'No, thanks,' said Barnaby. There was a shine to Lightweight, he noticed. The man was sweating. 'No, you're all right, thanks.' He turned and walked away, steeling himself against the sound of a van door opening behind him. A sound that, thankfully, never came.

Lightweight spat from the open window, then withdrew to his side of the van. Dash sat there, absorbing what had just happened and wondering whether he had the courage to invite air into his body. At last he took a tentative breath. By his side, Lightweight had resumed his former position.

'What did you do that for?' asked Dash.

'Getting on my nerves.'

'Yeah,' said Dash carefully, 'yeah, okay, but, like, don't do that to the customers, man. Just, like, don't, okay?' Lightweight snorted. 'I mean, I know he wasn't exactly gagging to buy speakers off us, but he was a punter, you know? And you can't go scaring off punters just because you're . . .' *What? A nutjob? Drug sick? What?* '. . . losing your patience with them. I'm trying to make some money here and—'

'Then make it,' snapped Lightweight. 'Just make the fuckin' money, man.'

Dash looked at him. 'Come on, then, let's go.'

The day was about to get worse.

The next kid (a fail) passed without incident. So did the next (also no sale) as long as you define 'without incident' as having Lightweight fidgeting at your side, the movement like a snake in a sack, his impatience barely restrained.

And then there was the next kid: baseball cap, gold earring and bad teeth. This one had a cocksure look about him, fancied he could handle himself. Dash knew his type, could see right through him.

'Never heard of Auridial,' he said, after Dash had done his bit.

'Hold up, I'll show you.' Dash popped open the door and, with a look back at Lightweight (fidgeting, trembling), dropped out of the cab. 'The reason you've never heard of these is because they use them in all the clubs and studios in town and that. You know, the studios in Soho.'

'Maybe I ain't never heard of them because they ain't any good,' offered the kid, still smirking. He was enjoying himself. Dash damped down feelings of irritation and moved to the back of the van where he wrenched open the doors and threw them wide. Inside lurked the doctored pair of Auridial.

The kid squinted into the van, unimpressed. 'Don't look anything special to me,' he said. 'Looks like you're having a barbecue, though.'

Dash ignored him. 'Okay, mate, take a look at this.' He reached into his back pocket, magicked out the Auridial flyer and handed it to the kid. 'Look at those specs.'

. He took it, holding it at arm's length, not really interested. 'No, mate,' he said. 'Don't really mean anything to me.'

'No,' said Dash, 'you don't understand . . .'

But then there was a great clanging sound as the kid's head made contact with the door of the van. Thinking about the incident later, Dash realised he hadn't registered Lightweight get out, let alone walk to the back of the van, grab the smirking kid and slam his head into the nearest hard thing. In this case the door of the van. But that was what had happened.

The kid had time to shout. A cry that started loud and was almost instantly metal-smothered: 'GARGH—' He fell to his knees, a thick stripe of red, lumpy blood running from nose to chin. Dash was open-mouthed. Deep in the evil depths of Dash, where witches with familiars stirred bubbling cauldrons, he realised with glee that the smirk had been wiped off: the kid's face seemed to have shifted on its skull, slipping like a rubber fright-mask. His hands went to his face; his body crunched on to the road as he went from his knees to lying curled up. Lightweight drove a foot into his stomach. The kid grunted. Deep in the evil depths Dash thought, Kick him again. And Lightweight did. The sound of the street, of Saturday night in the suburbs, of someone who dared to complain to the kids outside Sainsbury's. The sound of trainer meeting body. Thud. Grunt. *Again*. Thud. Grunt. *Again*. Thud. Grunt—

'Stop.' He caught Lightweight by the shoulder on a backswing and pulled him away from the hurting body of the kid, whose smirk was now a distant memory. (The next day though, after the kid had been to hospital, his nose would wear a bandage, his eyes would be bruised, like panda eyes, and he'd swagger the streets of Stoke Newington pleased with the looks he attracted. And smirking.) Dash slammed the doors of the van and reached for the kid, dragging him as best he could to the pavement. The kid's feet scrabbled so Dash left him – sod him, anyway – push-dragging Lightweight back to the front of the van, then shoving him into the driver's seat. All the time Lightweight looking back to the guttered and groaning body of the kid, looking like he wanted to return and finish the job. All the time Dash was going, 'What are you doing? *What are you doing?* Jesus . . .'

He thrust home the driver's door and scampered round the front to his own side.

'Go, will you?' Dash said to Lightweight, who sat there shaking, his face blank. *Christ, go.* 'Go!' The van started and Dash looked into the wing mirror as they pulled away from the kerb – people approaching the kid already, one kneeling to help the wounded soldier, another looking in the direction of the fleeing van, maybe memorising the plate – maybe noting 'try slapping the top of this fucker' written in the dirt on the back. (And as they turned a corner, and Dash looked to Lightweight with wide, disbelieving eyes, the wounded kid sprang up from the road and threw off the arm of the Good Samaritan who had knelt to help him, shouting, 'Fuck off,' some bloodied notion of pride. And later the Good Samaritan was at a dinner party with his wife, new friends from ante-natal class, and he mentioned the incident, not as a self-contained anecdote but as part of a point he wanted to make about how, these days, you didn't stop to help. And wasn't it sad? And that was why he hadn't phoned the police, and neither had the other chap, who'd scowled, waved a fuck-you-then hand and gone on his way.)

Dash looked to Lightweight. 'What are you doing?' he screeched. 'What do you think you're fucking doing?'

The van rattled along, Lightweight saying nothing and Dash thinking that maybe it was best they got as far away as they could before they stopped to chat about his partner's sales technique. Soon enough he was directing Lightweight down this road and that, gratified that at least his psycho driver seemed to be responding to his instructions.

At last: 'Just pull over here, behind that silver car,' outside a pub with big blackboards that wasn't open, and the van pulled over and Dash was about to repeat his perennial request '*What are you doing?*' when Lightweight had him by the throat.

'Yurgh,' said Dash. Lightweight's face was in his. Dash's eyes bulged and so did Lightweight's. 'Yurgh,' he said. Inside the pub a barman moved about, white towel over his shoulder. Dash's eyes flicked to the wing mirror and somewhere up the road a woman walked pushing a buggy. Quiet street. Lightweight's fingers squeezed. Out of the windscreen a junction up ahead. Cars passed, and a bus, and a girl with a rucksack, and all were unaware that Lightweight squeezed, bulging eyes and mouth set. Dash gripped the squeezing hand. 'Yurgh,' he gurgled.

'You ordering me about, man?' said Lightweight, at last. His eyes skipped as though he was watching fireworks. 'You ordering me? I don't like being ordered about, man.'

'*Yurgh.*'

'Y'nar?'

'*Yurgh.*'

Lightweight relaxed his grip. Only a bit. Enough for Dash to take a breath. 'You know what I'm thinking?' hissed Lightweight. 'I'm thinking you better get selling them speakers and soon, because I'm losing my patience, understand, *bitch*?'

Dash nodded yes.

So, it had been a fruitless day, and there was no question of going to see Chick without the money. Not unless he fancied a toilet-visit hat-trick. He'd left his mobile off during the day, but now, at home, switched it on to check for voicemail: 'You have – no – new messages and – four – saved messages. One of these messages will be deleted in . . .'

No word from Chick; nothing from Sophie, either. A strange mix of relief and disappointment. He called Sophie, who was in a pub. Behind a quick, grabbed 'hello', as though she'd only just picked up the phone in time, was the unmistakable sound of young people enjoying themselves with fags, drinks and generally lewd banter.

'Dash!' she said loudly. Behind her in the pub he heard laughter, that chant again, and realised that he was its subject.

'Why do they do that when I call?'

'What?' She sounded as though she was moving away from the group to somewhere quieter.

'That chant. "Wooh" and "whaey" when I call. It's, like, the second time they've done it.'

'Don't be daft. It's nothing.'

Any laughter had gone out of her voice. Had he become that bad, he wondered. So wrapped up in his problems that she'd come to dread talking to him?

'Doesn't sound like nothing to me.' He tried to keep his tone casual; jolly, even.

'Look, it's nothing, okay. God, don't start . . .'

'"Start"? What do you mean, "start"? Start what?'

'Look, what do you want, Dash? I'm with a bunch of people from work.'

'Um.' He was thrown. 'Well, I thought we were going out for a meal tonight.' He felt guilty bringing it up, knowing he would have to ask her to pay, but it had been, hadn't it, a date?

'I thought we could go out tomorrow night instead.'

'Oh. Right. Were you going to tell me you'd decided this?'

'Look, it's a girl at work, her last day, so we've come out for drinks. It's just a couple of drinks. If you want we can still go out but I thought we could make it tomorrow night instead. Okay?'

'I suppose,' he said.

'Tomorrow, Dash,' said Sophie.

Dash imagined her in the pub, being beckoned back by an impatient group. 'Okay,' he said. 'Okay. I love you.'

'Okay, Dash, see you later.'

'What time?'

'Dunno, just later. 'Bye.'

''Bye.' Dash heard the line go dead. He looked at the phone in his hand and made a decision, pulling on his coat and heading out to the van.

10

Warren was having problems with his girlfriend, LaDonna.

LaDonna had not been born with an intercap – the capital D in the middle of her name: she had performed that particular piece of brand surgery herself, doodling with a biro one day in the appointments book. Born simply Ladonna, like Madonna but not, her capital D was the latest in her ongoing plan to turn herself into some kind of Stepford R&B clone. Hair extensions, braids – she had them, and she swished them extravagantly about herself whenever she had an attack of indignation, which was often. Her nails were like talons – they *were* talons – and each was intricately painted. Three were pierced, while from her lips dripped dazzlingly glossy lipstick and around her hung an atmosphere of perfume so dense it seemed to threaten rain. Next to her, Sophie's attempts at self-improvement were the work of a hapless amateur, and Sophie with her tiny Tiffany drive was a mockable rookie compared to LaDonna, who knew a lot about men. What she didn't know about men and hair and nails wasn't worth knowing, and what she knew about men, hair and nails she knew *hard*.

So it was Warren's misfortune to be going out with LaDonna, who spent her days augmenting nails in the American Nail Bar, passing on homespun man-wisdom to the grateful customers who sat opposite, hands outstretched, receiving LaDonna's grace.

And, furthermore, it was Warren's misfortune that LaDonna used to go out with Dog Years, a well-known drug-dealer. Although he was well known, Dog Years was not a particularly prosperous drug-dealer, mainly thanks to the great pains he took to look like a drug-dealer. He drove a black Mercedes and drove it the drug-dealer way, sitting low in his seat, his steering arm hoisted high and staring moodily over the top of it, like a Kilroy in a bandanna – he was always stopped at the kerb, always had impressionable acolytes with BMX bikes between their legs crowding round his window. Normal days, Warren wouldn't take a character like Dog Years too seriously: he'd have given him a wide berth for sure – the likes of Dog Years were volatile, unpredictable, usually carrying a knife, maybe even a gun – but Dog Years was just another joker in a Merc giving kids the big I Am. In five years' time he would either be dead or in prison.

Normal days, that is. But Warren was now going out with LaDonna, and not only had Dog Years kept an approving weather eye on LaDonna's latest look, but he was also not keen on sharing any kind of DNA with Warren. In a drunken rage Dog Years had announced to various acolytes that he intended to kill Warren the next time he saw him. Shoot him. Like this. And Dog Years demonstrated exactly how he intended to do it, with two fingers held at right angles to his arm. Fuck him up in the head. Fuck him up, blud. This information, shaved of its accompanying hand gestures, had reached Warren as he strode down Stoke Newington high street one day, courtesy of Shaw, a friend of his brother's.

'Maybe he's angry cos a you and LaDonna,' postulated Shaw, having delivered the news.

Warren's forehead bunched up in confusion. 'He was the one who cut her loose, man.'

Shaw shrugged. He didn't know exactly why Dog Years was on the warpath and, anyway, he'd had enough of being seen in public with Warren, who was a yellow police information board waiting to happen, as far as he was concerned. He let the back wheel of his BMX drop to the pavement and stood on the pedals. 'Take it easy, man,' he said, and off went Shaw.

Warren had immediately taken steps. The very next day, after a morning spent constantly scare-eyed, barely able to drive for keeping an eye out for Dog Years's black Mercedes, he had left his job. It wasn't like he made any money doing it anyway. (LaDonna, not a woman to whom restraint came easily, had been unstinting in her contempt for Warren's pecuniary woe. Like Sophie, she subscribed to the R&B-sponsored theory that jewellery, clothes and sundry beauty treatments should be subsidised by the person for whom they were intended. 'How'm I expected to *pay* for all this?' she'd asked, sweeping sharp, expressive hands up and down herself. 'Get a refund,' replied Warren – it wasn't a night the neighbours were likely to forget in a hurry.) Plus Dash had been on at him to go to Holloway Road, and he didn't remember danger money ever being part of the deal. So walking out seemed the simple thing to do, and he pounced on the opportunity when Dash made out that being overtanned was like being black. He'd felt guilty about leaving Dash in it like that – he knew all about the situation with Chick. But he also knew Chick, and he was fully aware that Chick wouldn't let Dash off the hook, ever – no matter whom he had driving him around. There were forces in this world. LaDonna was one of them; Chick was another. All you could do was hope you were on the right side of them.

So with Dog Years uppermost in his mind, Warren had gone into hiding. He wouldn't have chosen to describe it like that but that was what he did, rarely venturing out of doors and spending his time fielding criticism from LaDonna while simultaneously working up the courage to dump her.

She was in the kitchen and he was in the front room when the doorbell went. Warren jumped at the sound. Silence. Were these his killers, coming with smiles? He tutted the thought away, smiling at himself, but still, at some level, thinking, *Is it, though?* After all, this was LaDonna's flat: he just lived in it. Dog Years would have been here plenty; maybe even had a key.

He went to the net curtain and tweaked it, feeling a bit like the famous picture of Malcolm X and wishing he had a gun in the other hand. He needn't have worried. The figure standing at the door to his flat, moving up and down – as if he badly needed a piss – was Dash.

'All right, Woz,' he said, when the door opened.

There was no way Warren wanted to bring him in.

'Who is it?' LaDonna called from the kitchen.

'Dash,' he replied, over his shoulder. Dash stood there, bobbing. 'I'm going out for a sec,' called Warren. LaDonna shouted something he couldn't hear and he stepped out to the walkway, clicking the door on the latch behind him.

'Can't we go in?' said Dash.

Warren didn't want to be seen out of doors any more than Dash did – but the alternative was his beloved. 'Nah, we'll just be here a minute.' He felt something like a benevolent rush towards his erstwhile partner, found he was pleased to see him. The guilt he felt at leaving him in the lurch intensified.

From other flats came various sounds: music, shouting, the clinking of dishes and televisions. The night was still and warm, and windows were open. You could smell cooking and weed smoke, and it was nice and comforting. When Warren talked his voice was low, as if respecting the hubbub around him. 'What's the matter with you, man? Take a look at yourself.'

Dash had already decided to be truthful. 'It's Chick, Woz. I owe him some money. I'm like, I don't want to be outside at the moment, you know?'

'You trying to avoid Chick?' Warren chuckled deeply. 'And you came here? He lives just down there, man. One floor down. Gob down there and you'd probably hit Chick's doorstep.'

Dash scuttled away from the balcony to cower at the wall of LaDonna's flat. 'You're joking? Fuck, the van's on the pavement.'

He'd been cruising the streets, hunched over the steering-wheel, eyes ping-ponging about like he was searching for a house number – but all the while looking out for Chick, the one person he didn't want to see. All that, and the whole time he'd been making his way to Chick's flat.

Warren watched him with a bemused smile. 'How much you owe him, man?'

'Almost four hundred.' Warren screwed up a sympathetic face. 'I'm behind, and he's really on my case. He fucking kneed me in the bollocks.' There was a break in his voice as if to illustrate, and for a horrible moment Warren thought Dash might cry. 'Twice, man. I can't fuckin' face it. And the driver he's given me – he's given me Freddy fucking Krueger as a driver. This guy—'

'What's his name?'

'Lightweight.'

'Don't know him.'

'This guy, he's a crack addict and he's a knifer – so Chick says – and he fuckin' attacked me today. He wants his money.'

'Yeah?' said Warren, as if to say, And? Course he wants his money. Why do you think I walked?

'Yeah, but you didn't used to beat up the customers. Lightweight's insane, Woz, he's a fuckin' nutter. He laid into a punter – guy's probably called the police on us. He attacked him and when he'd finished mashing this guy's face into the road he started on me. He tried to strangle me.' Dash stopped himself. A smile was playing around Warren's lips.

'Just calm down, man.'

'Yeah, yeah,' Dash pulled a hold of himself, hearing in his head the ghost of Lightweight: '*Such* a bitch.' 'Sorry, sorry. I'm just a bit kind of sick with it, you know? It's just doing my head in.' He was pacing in a tiny, self-imposed prison, his words whispered and urgent.

'All right, man. All right. Just settle down, okay? Did you tell Chick that – what's his name? – Lightsocket tried to strangle you?'

'I can't, can I? Because if I go and see Chick he'll knee me in the bollocks because I don't have his money and I can't get his money because Lightsocket keeps beating up the customers.'

Warren shrugged. 'Get rid of him, man.'

'I can't. I need a driver and he wants his money. I didn't sell today – he's expecting some cash tomorrow.'

Warren spread his hands. 'I don't know what I can do about it, man. I can't come back and drive for you. It ain't possible.' He sniffed. 'I've got another job now.' Lies, lies.

'Listen, look, I'm really sorry to ask, but could you hook me up with two hundred quid to pay Phil tomorrow morning?'

Warren clapped a hand over his mouth to stop himself guffawing. 'Are you smoking crack?' he managed, in a whisper.

'Come on, Woz, you'll get it back. I wouldn't be in this mess if you hadn't walked out.'

'Ah, bullshit, we were already behind.'

'And I'm not a racist, you know I'm not. You were taking the piss out of Sophie.'

'You don't compare going disco with the self-tan to being black.' Warren still truculent about that.

Dash pulled his hands through his hair. 'I know. I know. Look, could you, though, lend me it? You know I'm good for it.'

Once again Warren was holding his mouth. 'In what universe are you good for it? You've just got through telling me how you're in to Chick for four hundred quid.'

'Please, Warren.'

'What about your girlfriend? She spent it all on tanning lotion, has she?'

'She hasn't got anything.' *That she'll lend me,* he could have added, but didn't.

'Well, I ain't got two hundred quid, and *if I did,* I'm sorry, Dash, man – like, no offence and that – but I wouldn't be lending it to you.' He shook his head sadly.

Dash was suddenly seized with a plan. 'Is Chick in now?' The thought that if he knew where Chick was, if he was in his flat, then he could have himself an Auridial barbecue.

'How should I know? I never see him. Sometimes you can see his motor.' Warren moved to the edge of the balcony, looking for Chick's Saab parked down in the bays. 'Can't see it, man. Why?'

'It doesn't matter. Doesn't matter.'

Warren moved back, looked at his ex-partner and winced at the defeat he saw in his eyes.

'Okay, if you can't lend me the cash . . .' said Dash at last. Warren shook his head, sorry, no. '. . . then have you got a suit I could borrow?'

11

Was there a piece of machinery on Majorca capable of winching a car from a swimming-pool? It didn't seem so, but of course there must be. Donkey-powered, perhaps, but there must be one. So when was it going to appear? Merle was hardly in a position to complain, and his delicately worded enquiries to the rep were met by a tone of voice that suggested as much. Karen, on the other hand, *was* in a position to complain, and nothing he did would pacify her. No amount of drinks fetched, snacks made or 'Do you need some cream rubbing on your back, sweetheart?' It was as though she'd decided she was now on holiday by herself, leaving him stranded, a comedy figure at the mercy of the maid and the pool-cleaner, who inexplicably still arrived that morning, cheerfully netting insects from the oil-slicked pool. And at the mercy, also, of his own thoughts.

He went and pretended to ring the rep, then came back, going to Karen's sun-lounger and dropping to his haunches beside her.

'Well?' she said.

'Same old story.' He sighed. 'Still trying to get hold of a truck or something.'

She made a sound, like 'Humph'. As in, 'Humph, I bet you never called her.'

He stood. 'God,' he said, for something to say. 'God, it's hot today.'

'Why don't you take a dip in the pool, Clive? Might cool you down.'

He went back to the villa, his flip-flops slow-clapping her sarcasm. In the villa he opened the fridge door and leant in, letting it cool his face. He clicked the temperature dial round to five. He was fighting a silent war with the maid, who kept clicking it back to four, but four wasn't enough to chill his beers, which were running low due to lack of transport, and one of which he took now. He opened it quietly: didn't want Karen thinking he was in any way enjoying his time in the dog-house. He went to look at his mobile phone, on the top there with his keys and wallet. But on it was just that weird service logo you get abroad: no 'missed call', no text message to read. He drank his beer, put his empty can in the rubbish and went out to the pool.

'When do you want lunch?' he asked her.

'I'll make something in about an hour,' she replied. With, he thought, the smell of burning martyr hanging heavily in the air, he went back into the villa where he unearthed a paperback thriller from their luggage. He looked at his phone and went back out to the pool with his book. The hero was a detective who sat drinking because his wife had left him. He cleared his throat and went back into the villa where he replaced the book and looked at his phone. Just the weird logo.

Only this time he gave in and picked it up. He dropped into the sofa (sandy, and smelling of sun-tan lotion), and dialled DS Cyston.

'Hello, sir. Another crisis?' Cy sounded bright.

'No, thank God. Car's still in the pool, though.'

'That's foreign for you,' laughed Cy. 'Still, wish I was there.'

'With me or instead of me?'

'Not fussed. Either's fine.'

'Busy, then?'

'Crime stops for no man, sir.'

'Very good, Cy. Well, look, I won't keep you. I just wanted to know. Well, I wondered – have you got any prints off Snape's wheelie-bin?'

Karen walked into the kitchen and to the fridge, throwing a look Merle's way as she did so.

Cy said no. There was nothing from fingerprints so far, but they did have one thing. That CCTV they requisitioned? From it they had picked up a bloke boarding the Kettering train who answered Sam's description. They'd worked back and found footage showing their man on the southbound Piccadilly Line at King's Cross station, on his way to St Pancras. Which meant he originated from somewhere north of King's Cross on that line, corroborating what he'd told Pat. Caledonian Road. Holloway Road. Arsenal. Finsbury Park. Manor House . . .

Merle went out to the pool. Karen was on her sun-lounger, reading. He took a seat beside her.

'Prints?' she said.

'Sorry?' he said.

'I heard you talking about prints. Were you talking about photographs, or were you talking to Cy?'

'I could have been talking to Cy about photographs.' He clasped his hands over his belly and stared out over the car in the water.

Beside him, Karen put down her book. 'Prints on what? Of whom? You're not working, are you?'

'No. Not really.'

'So why are you discussing prints, then?'

'Well, it's not working, is it? And I wouldn't normally be discussing anything – glad to see the back of the bloody place for once . . .' Disbelieving snort from Karen. 'It's just that this was something to do with the Snape case, and Cy thought I might want to know.' He told her about the bins, the mystery man and his conversation with Pat on the train.

'And what do they think?' she asked.

'Well, he's not the abductor, is he? So I guess the feeling is that he's just a weirdo, but it looks like he comes from our patch.'

'Could be working with the abductor?'

'It's a possibility they'll be considering, yes. But it doesn't fit.'

Didn't fit the profile of the abductor, he meant. A woman, obviously. Married or with a long-term partner, but it's a bad relationship that she's trying to save and she thinks a kid will do it. Or maybe she can't have babies. Either way, our woman somehow believes that having a kid, or an extra kid, around is going to keep the household together. Other than her immediate family she probably doesn't have a strong network of family and friends and feels quite isolated. It wasn't planned, so she's not likely to be very confident: she just did it on the spur of the moment rather than planning it. So maybe the relationship is destructive, or perhaps she's the victim of some kind of domestic abuse and she seized the opportunity to take Ben for, like, a quick fix. We're looking for a little dormouse basically, he told Karen. A homebody. She's probably spoiling the kid rotten, but obviously her possible domestic situation represents a danger factor. Plus, if she's spooked, if she suddenly feels vulnerable, she might panic.

So, not the kind of person who would be working with a male partner.

Which meant, as they knew, the mysterious Sam was more than likely a sicko, press, or a sicko working for the press. Or maybe just a bloke who wanted to speak to Patrick Snape.

Karen frowned, then looked at him. 'You know who it could be?'

'Go on.'

'Not the press, but someone who wants to sell them information he thinks he'll find in Snape's bin.'

He looked at her. 'Right,' he said slowly.

'But he'd have to know what he's looking for, wouldn't he?'

'How do you mean?'

'I mean that if that's what he's trying to do, then he's not going to try to sell the actual stolen post to the press. He's going to try to sell them information he gets off it. So he'd have to have a good idea exactly what he was looking for.'

'Right, yes,' he agreed.

'It could be something he does . . . professionally.'

'Could be.'

'And he was from our patch?'

'Yes.'

She peered at him over the top of her sunglasses. 'Well, who do we have on our patch who knows all about the kind of things you find in people's bins?'

'You could have something,' he said admiringly.

'Worth a call, I'd have thought,' she said, and went back to her book.

'You're a genius,' he said, standing.

'I know.' She sighed, turning a page. 'Aren't I blessed?'

12

'All right, Charlie,' said Merle, stretched out on the sofa in the lounge. And, come to think of it, why was the sofa sandy? There wasn't a beach around for miles.

'All right, Merlin,' said Chick, at the other end. 'Always good to hear your dolcet tones.'

'Dulcet. They're dulcet tones.'

'Well, it's always nice to hear them, whatever they are.'

Merle had known Chick since school. Well, not 'known'. More like, 'known of'. Chick, one of those kids who was always going to take the door marked 'Bad'; Merle, one of those who was always going to take the one marked 'The Rest of You This Way'. Almost twenty-five years after Merle had watched Chick bully younger kids out of their cash, and hated him for it with his whole soul, Chick worked for Merle. He was a covert human intelligence source. He was a grass. And Merle still hated him with his whole soul.

He was, Merle had thought then and still thought, a person you would have believed it impossible to like. He was a rodent without any of the redeeming features of rodents, and there aren't many of those. And yet. And yet he had ended up with Trisha Campbell, a girl from the year above with whom the younger, beneath-the-sheets Merle had been very well acquainted. He hadn't needed to pursue a career in the police force to know that there was no justice in the world.

And the worst thing was the way Chick seemed to treat the situation. He was Merle's grass, his snitch – therefore his bitch. Yet Chick consistently failed to behave as if this was the case, meaning he wasn't Merle's bitch at all. In fact, Merle was just another part of his empire, another bit of business.

Throw a few old and knackered-out lions to the Christians; get Merle to turn a blind eye to certain other businesses in return.

'What can I do you for, anyway?' said Chick, brightly.

'Bins,' said Merle.

'What about them, then?'

'You slash them.'

'Not me, Merlin. That would make me a member of the criminal classes.'

They went through this pantomime every time. 'But you are a keen observer of the criminal classes.'

'A scholar, you might say.'

'So you might be able to point me in the direction of someone who could help me with my enquiries?'

'In a spirit of reciprocated goodwill I might, yes. What you got?'

'All right, have you ever come across anyone who sells info on to the media?'

Chick thought about it. Merle heard him light a cigarette, imagined him at the Flat Cap, alone, or probably making whatever poor sod was working for him stand in another part of the pub out of earshot. 'Sells stuff on to the media,' he repeated, lungs happy. 'Can't say that I have, no. Why do you ask?'

Merle ignored him. 'What about anyone approaching you asking for stuff?'

'Me?'

'Sorry, no, the members of the criminal classes in your acquaintance.'

'That's better. But no, can't say I've heard anything.'

'Nobody's been approached and perhaps put someone on to someone else?'

Chick enjoyed a couple more noisy drags on his cigarette. 'Nah,' he said. 'Nothing like that.'

'Anybody of your acquaintance in that line of work been anywhere unusual recently?'

'How do you mean? On holiday, like?'

'Don't take the piss, Charlie. I mean have they been working elsewhere at all?'

'Listen, Merlin, this is all a bit smoke on the water, if you don't mind me saying. Is there something you want me to keep an eye out for?'

'I'm looking for a guy who might have been to Kettering, or a guy selling anything to the media.'

'Well, I'll keep my eye out. Anything else?'

Merle sighed. 'No, I suppose not, really. By the way, I saw Carl the other day, him and a bunch of other lads up to no good. Correct me if I'm wrong, but isn't he supposed to be at school?'

'No, he's off at the minute. He's been excluded for persistently swearing at the teachers. He's fuckin' awesome at it.'

'Well, I wonder where he gets that from,' said Merle, wearily. His body was lying on a cool sofa in Majorca; his brain was being thrust into a dog turd. The two sets of sensory data didn't quite gel.

'Dunno,' said Chick proudly, 'but he rhymes it, his swearing. He's like a rapper, and he's better than the black geezers – he's almost as good as Eminen.'

'And how's Trisha?' asked Merle. 'Lick me,' the Trish in his head had commanded, almost three decades ago.

'She's fine, mate. I bought her a boob job for her birthday.'

'Really?' said Merle, hearing himself croak the word, and not picturing Trisha Campbell with bigger breasts because the Trish in his head was already perfect. Instead, he found himself greeting the *idea* of Trisha Campbell having a boob job. 'That was very generous of you,' he found himself adding.

'Present to me as much as it was to her,' rejoined Chick.

'Right,' said Merle sourly.

Part Three

DIRTY PERVERT

1

Sophie woke up, still pissed, the flat silent around her. She felt euphoric, at some level believing not that her hangover had been deferred – and that later, about midday, any strength she had would leach out of her, her skin would seem to sag on her bones, she would be gripped by a darkness of the mind – but that it was non-existent. No, she had escaped the hangover, of course she had. Because there was no way she could wake up feeling this good, this lively, this certain of heart.

Today was the day her new, glamorous, exotic life began. A life with Peter, her gay best friend and now flatmate. A life of being catty and wantonly rude about people's weight, their clothes and their cellulite. The pair of them had been the last to leave the pub the previous evening. One by one the girls had left for dates, or to be up early for a glamorous interview the next day. Or home to dinner prepared by a boyfriend whom Sophie pictured as a cross between Brad Pitt and Jamie Oliver, cooking in a cool flat like you saw on TV – one without towers of boxes everywhere.

Peter sat with his legs crossed in the gay way and waved his hand with increasing flair as the red wine went down. They'd been discussing her Dash-leaving strategy, the tactics. They'd decided she would do it the following morning, first thing. She'd pack overnight bags, holdalls, everything she thought she couldn't do without – just in case Dash cut up nasty later on and wouldn't let her back to collect the remnants of her stuff.

Then she'd write a note, the contents of which they'd discussed in some depth – which she'd since forgotten.

She sat down to write it now, from scratch, an Auridial box as her desk.

Dear Darren, [The formality of that: 'Darren'. The name she only ever used to scold him about the boxes, or plead poverty when it came to paying the rent – or to give him bad news such as this.]

I am so, so sorry, but I have decided to leave you. Things have not been right between us now for so long, and I can't bear the constant falling out and arguments. [There was no such thing in their relationship as 'constant falling out and arguments' unless you counted Dash's mild dejection at the influence of Peter, her sudden interest in the pub after work, the speaker boxes. Still, though, as she wrote the words she conjured scenes, fictional ones – the two of them constantly at each other's throats, a non-existent missile thrown, never-spoken words that wounded. She convinced herself that what she wrote was the truth.] Things were so great for us in the beginning, we both used to laugh so much more then. [And they had, it was true. He'd had just the right amount of whoo and whaey to attract her; just enough of the new man not to repel her.] But it seems our lives have changed so much that we have changed as people and so has our relationship. I miss the 'us' of a year ago, I miss the best friend I ever had and a wonderful lover. [Damn. That last bit. She considered scratching it out, but then he'd wonder what she'd written and if he managed to decipher it, well, writing it then deleting it was worse than writing it in the first place. She considered the words: 'wonderful lover'. They felt wrong. They felt like sticking the knife in. But were they? What was so bad about throwing him a bone?] But the fact is that people change and so do circumstances and there comes a point when someone has to be strong enough to stand up and do what's right. Making this decision has been the hardest of my life [!], but I am certain it is the right thing to do and that it is better to be strong now than to be weak and regret it years down the line. I am so sorry because I know this will hurt you as much as it hurts me but please try to understand why I am doing what I am doing. I know this will leave you in the lurch with the rent, but it is paid up until the end of the month so at least that gives you time to find a lodger or speak to Mr F-P. Please don't hate me, please think of us as I will, with affection. I cannot say that I love you. [Damn. Those last words. Ouch. Amend? No. Can't. Why, oh, why hadn't she written this on the computer at work?] But I will always care about you and I hope that one day we can be friends. [She hated herself writing that, knowing that the last person she wanted in her life was Dash. He was lovely and she'd cared about him once – she honestly had. But he was like an old winter coat, and he had to go to Oxfam.]

Love, Sophie XX

She sat looking over the ramparts of the Auridial castle and thought about the repercussions of what she was doing; of the effect it would have on Dash. When that failed to work she imagined her mother dying in a car crash and the tears came. She shook one over the letter, making sure it created a wet-ink bubble on the paper. When it was dry she folded the paper and wrote his name on it, left it there, on the box, where it could easily be seen.

She helped herself to a glass of water and realised her self-delusion was exactly that – there was a hangover coming. She felt dark clouds arranging themselves and when she touched a hand to her forehead it came away moist with sweat. She looked out of the front window a final time, checking the street for Try Slapping the Top of This Fucker. When there was no sign of it she shouldered a holdall and took the handles of another. As she left the house she pulled the front door shut softly, almost as a mark of respect.

Only when she got to the tube station did she finally relax. She found herself meeting the glances of her fellow passengers in a new way, her head higher. It was as though . . . as though all of a sudden she'd got a whole lot cooler in this world.

Max heard her go. He'd muted the volume of his television to hear her more clearly, and when the door went he moved to the front window where he hated himself for tweaking the curtain to see Sophie leave, unable to stop himself all the same.

The sound of the telephone startled him. Once an out-of-hours business number, it used to ring off the hook, his messages always full. Now it never rang, just Verity if it did, and when he answered it was her he expected to hear.

'Max?' said the voice. Female, low, hurried: he struggled to place it.

'Who's this?' he said.

'It's Trish,' she said. 'I can't talk long. It's about the boy.'

'Go on,' he said. A lurch of the soul made him close his eyes. Knowing he was right.

2

Now when they gave him the Coke and the baked beans he kept the grit in his mouth until they'd left.

'They', because there was a man who came sometimes. Only, unlike Auntie, Ben never saw him. He spoke in a gruff voice, like he was trying to disguise it, and from outside the door he'd say, 'You awake, son? Get away from the door,' and the door would open a fraction for the man to push through the food. A flask, or the beaker of Coke and a box of McNuggets.

'I want you to be a good little lad and eat all that up,' the gruff voice said. All Ben saw of him was fat fingers. 'Knock on the door when you're done and I'll collect the empties.'

'I've done toilet,' said Ben once. The room was beginning to smell. The door stayed ajar and Ben could hear the man sniffing.

There was a pause. 'Yeah, well,' said the voice. 'Er, your auntie will have to sort that out when you next see her. She's in charge of the toilet, you see. Tell you what, wait there a sec.' The door closed and Ben did as he was told. Moments later it opened again and the fat fingers pushed something into the room: a small plastic air-freshener, the type with what looked like a shrivelled piece of plastic inside. He picked it up. 'Best I can do for the moment,' said the gruff voice. 'Like, I would come in and sort it out, but I've got this flu and we don't want you catching it, do we?' The man on the other side of the door did a cough to make his point clear. Ben had been to a Christmas panto once, him, a friend and Mum and Dad. The man's gruff voice reminded him of the villain – more funny than scary.

At least with him not entering the room it was easier not

to eat the grit. For that reason, he sometimes wished the man came more often. Usually, though, it was Auntie.

Ben had learnt to eat his food and swallow his drink using his teeth to filter out as much of the white stuff as he could and, although it made rude noises, Auntie either didn't notice or didn't mind. He'd learnt other things as well. Like whenever he asked her when he was going home she'd always – but *always* – say 'soon', the same head-turned-away pose, until the time he asked her how soon 'soon' was, and she told him not to worry, he had to get better first, but maybe tomorrow or the next day. To which he'd asked her what day it was, and how many days he'd been here, because even though he'd had Chicken McNuggets, and baked beans and sausages and glasses of Coke, and they came regularly and must have marked the passing of time as he slept, he didn't know *how much* time. Instinctively he realised how much he took for granted the simple transition of a day, the comforting signposts to the hours that were suddenly absent. In answer she laughed and stroked his hair and said what a lot of questions he had, and she hoped he didn't think there was anything wrong with the accommodation, she was trying her best, your lordship. Didn't he like the Chicken McNuggets?

He was six, not stupid, so he'd learnt that the white grit in the food wasn't medicine at all. By keeping it in his mouth then spitting it into his toilet bucket he found he didn't feel so sleepy all the time. Still, though, every time he spat it out it was always with a nagging worry: what if she was telling the truth? If she was, then every time he deceived her he risked not getting better, and that meant spending longer in the room.

But he wasn't sleeping all the time, there was that. And he felt better for it. He tried to communicate this to the woman by appearing extra-specially chirpy when she visited. Not like somebody who was ill.

'You're ever so brave,' she'd said to him once. She had misty eyes that time the way his mum looked sometimes when he did or said something grown-up.

'I'm much better,' he told her brightly. 'I think I'm ready to go home now.'

She looked sharp then. There was a time before when he'd cried and shouted at her that he wanted to go home *now*, and she'd looked that sharp way then, telling him off and threatening no McNuggets, 'You don't want that, do you?' Actually, he was getting bored of McNuggets but judged it best not to say so. 'And I'll make you clean your teeth, and you don't want that, do you?' Actually, he really wanted to clean his teeth and said so, which threw her. 'Oh. Really? You must be the only little boy who's ever wanted to clean his teeth.' The next day she handed him a toothbrush, which he looked at in obvious disgust.

'Yeah,' she said, almost bashful. 'Sorry it's not new, like, but, look, beggars can't be choosers.' Ben was no doctor, but even he thought that using somebody else's toothbrush wasn't the best way to recover from his apparent illness. 'Here.' She handed him a near-empty tube of toothpaste as an accompaniment. 'Now you can clean your teeth whenever you want. Use your water,' they left him a bottle of water, 'and spit it out in the bucket, all right?' There was another thing. She'd brought him a poster of Roy Keane.

'This'll make it a bit more like home,' she told him, and he didn't have the heart to tell her that Roy Keane was a Manchester United player, not Arsenal, and being an Arsenal fan meant he automatically hated Roy Keane.

And still he remained in the room, and no matter what he said to the woman, or how much he cried and sang 'Yellow Submarine', he was still there.

'You ever hear any noises, sweetheart?' she'd said to him before. Coke beaker in hand, about to take a swallow, he'd told her no – and was only half telling the truth. She'd said good, because he shouldn't be disturbed when he was trying to get better. But if he ever did hear any noises, then just to ignore them. He nodded, no more words now as he kept his mouth full of the Coke grit. (Although the bits had got bigger lately, like the woman wasn't being so careful when she crumbled up the 'medicine'. It made it easier to store in his cheeks, keeping it there like a hamster does.)

But he *had* heard noises. The first time he'd been sitting on the camp bed with a magazine the woman had left for him. She left it, she said, in case he ever woke up and was bored. These days, now that he slept less, he was bored most of the time, and he knew the magazine like he knew the back of his hand. It had hundreds of pictures of colourful cars and women with not much on. He knew it as well as he knew his sticker album, which was very well indeed.

When he heard the noise he realised he was terrified. Normally he was either bored or scared – or some combination of the two – all the time. He had slipped into something of a routine, and within the confines of that routine he felt relatively safe. Either the woman or the man came, the woman was nice to him (and the man was cautious), and there had been that sharpness only once. Auntie seemed to know his mum and dad, knew all about them: she knew where Ben went to school and what he liked to do. He had Chicken McNuggets and somewhere to sleep and the room wasn't that bad when you got used to it. The noise was new, though. His environment had become familiar to him, and this was unfamiliar. Without knowing why, he slid off the bed and tried to fit beneath it but found that he couldn't. Instead, he just stayed on the floor, listening, his heart hammering. A whimper was bubbling and he placed a hand over his mouth to smother it, quietly humming 'Yellow Submarine' into his fingers.

What were the noises?

Coming from far away it was the sound of men – lots of them it seemed like – talking and shouting and moving things around. The sound of engines, too. Vehicles moving here and there. Revving up.

The first time it happened he just lay that way until the noises stopped. Then he climbed back on to the bed until it began to get dark and he pretended to be asleep until the woman came, lying dead still as she busied herself emptying his toilet bucket (another thing he'd learnt: how to time his number twos just right), then shook him awake by grades. Softest, soft, bit harder, hard. He pretended to wake before she reached 'really hard'.

'You slept right through again,' she'd said.

'Yes,' he responded, knowing that by not sleeping he'd learnt something – something he wasn't supposed to know.

3

'How many speakers is it, then?' said Phil, with a smile.

Around them buzzed the usual worker-bee atmosphere: speakermen hefting boxes and not whistling exactly, but almost, buoyed by promise, the day ripe on the vine and waiting to be plucked. Looking around at them, Dash was sure they were beset by their own problems: women, booze, drugs, money, the usual. Somehow, though, he couldn't imagine it. His world-view had shrunk now. Like when he was at school and they'd put crisp packets in the oven to make tiny badge-sized versions. His mother had done it for him, collecting packets wherever she went and bequeathing them to Dash, or Darren as he was then. Shrinking packets. Something pleasing about their new size and texture.

'Just the one, Phil?' He couldn't help but make it a question. 'Dash . . .'

'Come on, Phil, look – you're going great guns this morning.' He waved a hand around at the hive-like atmosphere. 'Can't you cut me a bit of slack? Just today?'

In a way, it would have spoiled things if Phil had agreed, if he'd gone, 'Tell you what, Dash, because it's you I'm going to let you off just this once. You have a good day now, y'hear?' Because there was one thing that was pleasing about his new, shrunken crisp-packet existence. Yesterday he'd felt it too – that same sense of the day petri-dished and boiled down to its simple constituents. He'd woken up knowing only one thing. Like a junkie – like Lightweight – with a single objective: to get money, score and get high. Today he knew he wouldn't worry about bills or the rent or Sophie, or if his dad's birthday was coming up, or whether his hair needed a cut or if he'd put on a bit of weight.

All he need worry about today was selling speakers and getting the money to pay Chick. Simple.

First, of course, he had to pay for the speakers from Phil.

Last night, with shame eating at his soul, Dash had lain awake and waited for Sophie to return home for the second night in a row. So much for spending the night together; so much for a couple of drinks after work because a girl was leaving. As it was she didn't roll in until well gone midnight and he could tell from the rattle of her heels that she was as drunk as she'd been the previous night. So he lay there, waited out the MTV, the stifled giggles, the war of attrition waged on her clothes, and then he got up.

Under his breath: 'Sorry, Soph.'

Dressed and peering like a mole in the dark, not wanting to risk disturbing her with so much as a single light, he found her handbag. He brought it close to his face, like a nosebag, and rooted around within its depths, tanning lotion, cigarettes, matches, chequebook . . . until he found her purse. From it he extracted her cashcard. Also at the bottom he found the Tiffany heart, and held it up as if to verify. The sight of it tugged at him and he pushed it back to the bottom of the bag. Moments later he was closing the door silently behind him and making his way up the street in the direction of Safeway.

Her pin number was four zeros. She had it that way so she could remember it. Dash had mentioned to her that his own formed the date of her birthday but she'd said she couldn't do the same – she needed to remember it. A black cab rattled down the road and stopped at the kerb. 'I'll just be a minute, mate,' slurred the occupant, taking his place at a cash machine beside Dash, who felt criminal – found himself wanting to hide his identity. What was he thinking? He *was* criminal: he was robbing his girlfriend's bank account. And even though on a scale of one to ten that was, say, a two – while setting fire to the depot was at least a seven-and-a-half – it didn't make him feel a great deal better.

'Sorry about this, mate,' groaned Drunk Bloke beside him,

and before he had time to dance away there was the splash of urine at his feet. Drunk Bloke making the most of his pit-stop.

He stood on tiptoe to examine Sophie's balance, thinking, What's her overdraft limit? And thinking the way she complained about money she must be near it. But the figure that flashed up was £300. The bloke next door sighed with relief and stopped pissing, burped, cleared his sinuses, then spat and left. Dash stared at the figure, incredulous. *Three hundred pounds?* He could take it all, he figured. What was her limit? About five hundred. He could go up to the limit and his problems were solved. Not for-good solved, but solved as far as tomorrow was concerned: Phil paid, Chick off his back. He could go to his interview knowing that at least – then feign illness, a trip away, pretend to move . . .

And what if . . . ? She'd come home drunk – really drunk. The kind of drunk where you could easily lose your cashcard, and who's to say it wasn't picked up by someone who plugged in four zeros, thinking the dozy cow who lost it might have a simple number? *Take it all*, said Bad Dash. *She need never know.* 'I told you so,' he'd say. 'I always said you should have changed your number.' Chances are she wouldn't even discover it until lunchtime tomorrow. *Take it all.*

The machine bleeped impatiently. Decision, it said. Now. *What's it gonna be, boy, yes or no?*

Yes.

Or . . .

No. He tapped in two hundred before he could change his mind, his senses suddenly returning and smelling the urine that pooled at his feet. It seemed fitting somehow, he thought, taking the money and returning home.

As he pulled himself into bed and inched the duvet over himself he thought about Sophie's three hundred pounds; all those times she'd pleaded poverty at rent time, the Tiffany heart necklace that gathered gum at the bottom of her handbag. Of the two betrayals, his was worse. But still.

So. Now . . .

'Dash, Dash, Dash.' Phil made a face like he was breaking bad news to a relative. 'I can't, not even this once, mate. Because if I let you off they'll all be wanting them on account.'

'They won't,' insisted Dash, 'because they don't *need* them on account. They're not working Stoke Newington. Everyone in Stokey's either got speakers or they'd rather spend the cash on wind chimes or something.'

Phil sympathy-grimaced. 'Mate, look, it's feast or famine in this game. What you'll find is that all of a sudden everyone'll want new speakers at once and you'll be laughing, begging me for more. Take my word for it.'

Dash stared at Phil. As if to stare at him might force the truth from the grinning depot manager. *There's no feast, is there, in Stoke Newington? The only feast in Stoke Newington is mung bean and lentil soup. Stoke Newington is famine, always.*

'Shall I put you down for two, then, mate?'

Dash reached into his pocket for Sophie's two hundred pounds. 'Yeah,' he said. 'I'll take two.'

'We going, man?' The two of them sat in the van, still in the loading bay. Dash had hefted the two sets of speakers through the rear doors, then let himself into the passenger side. For a long moment they sat in near silence, the only sound Dash sighing.

He did the mental equivalent of clapping his hands purposefully together. 'Right. We've got to sell some speakers today.'

Lightweight manoeuvred himself out of his jacket and Dash immediately wished he hadn't: the two of them were now polluting the cab with their scent: Dash's, of fear; Lightweight's, of not bothering to wash.

He fixed Dash with a stare. 'Too right. *You* gotta sell some speakers, boss. I ain't taxi-cabbing you about for the practice, understand?'

Dash did understand. It was just one more pressure to add to those already vice-gripping his testicles. He wondered if it was too soon to crank down the window – the smell was overpowering.

Perhaps leave it a moment or so. 'What I'm saying,' he sighed, 'is that I'm going to need your help.'

Lightweight laughed, then started the engine. 'Where to, man?'

'Back to mine. Stop off at the building site on the way.' And Dash the defeated opened the window, tilted his head to the gap and breathed fresh, clean air.

With his head unnaturally angled into the flow, he watched his partner from the corner of his eye. Stripping off his jacket had revealed a black T-shirt with tidemarks under the arms, as though it had decided to quarantine the danger areas. As far as his mood went the outlook today was moderate, possible temper-loss later. Going by yesterday that about summed it up. Unless . . . unless Dash could pacify him with money.

'It's for both our sakes,' he said, like breaking the deadlock in a lovers' tiff. 'If we could work together we might be able to earn some money.'

Lightweight made a noncommittal sound. At the building site he took the opportunity to light a cigarette and lower his eyelids as Dash made a journey to the brick pile. On arriving at the flat he allowed Dash the exercise of lugging the speakers up the stairs. And as Dash closed the door behind him and made a beeline for the toilet, he lit a cigarette, then wandered over to a box in front of the sofa and picked up a piece of paper there.

It had been folded once and sat on top of the box like a place-marker. On one side was the word 'Darren'. Lightweight cast a look in the direction of the bathroom, picked it up and turned it over to read it.

Which, of course, he was perfectly capable of doing.

'Dear Darren,' he read. And next to the words was a kind of bubble in the paper, as though a speck of wet had dried. There was a second watermark on the page by the signature, two crosses for kisses. Lightweight read the letter, smiling. Then he placed it back on the box, just as it was before.

Then he put his hands on his legs, bent to the letter and blew it off the box, letting it land on the floor – hidden in the foothills of the Auridial mountain. He straightened.

Dash came back, looking perplexed. 'Weird,' he said. 'Sophie's got rid of half her stuff in the bathroom.' His eyes ranged across the lounge, as if searching for clues.

Lightweight said nothing. Behind him on the floor lay the letter addressed to Darren that fully explained the bathroom but he kept silent, a nearly-smile playing across his lips as he watched Dash's face work a picture of mild panic and confusion. 'Maybe she's just having a tidy-out, man?' he suggested.

'Yeah,' murmured Dash, his eyes still jumping from point to point in the room. 'Yeah, maybe that's it.' His mind was already repainting the picture in the bathroom. The new image was of a neater, rearranged bathroom, rather than what had really greeted him – the shelves bearing the stuff she'd never used, like the Body Shop hand lotion his mum had given her at Christmas, the perfume he'd bought her from Chick, all those weird scrubs and face-packs she'd got in the magazine product sale and never used. Must be it, he told himself. She was just having a tidy-out. That, or maybe it's show-and-tell day at the office, or she was staying at a mate's house and she'd told him but he was too preoccupied with the whole Chick situation to pay her much attention.

Must be having a tidy-out. That'll be it.

Just decided to get rid of her toothbrush at the same time, that's all.

'Okay,' he said. Lightweight was watching him with a smile Dash wasn't able to translate. 'Better get the bricks in these things.' And he set to work on the back of a set of speakers. Lightweight stood smoking, watching him. Occasionally his eyes flicked to the letter on the floor. That same cruel smile.

Not long after, they were back in the van. 'Where to, man?' said Lightweight, opening the van window. He was grinning broadly, a dare in the question.

'Look, before you start with the bitch stuff, we're not going down Holloway Road,' answered Dash. 'We'll try Dalston first.'

Lightweight cleared his sinuses and spat from the window. 'Be another team there, won't there?'

'Yeah, but they haven't threatened us with baseball bats. Yet.'

Lightweight spat again and started the engine. 'Just so you know, man, I ent scared. And just so you know, I'm getting paid today, you understand?'

Dash did understand. He knew, with tragic inevitability, that he'd end up paying Holloway Road a visit before the day was out.

4

Max had only ever been there twice. When they were building it he had had mad ideas about how it was going to turn out – that it would go at the speed of a fairground wheel; that it was going to lift up and down, almost slapping the Thames; go underwater even. When he'd finally been dragged along he was disappointed, thinking it wasn't even turning as he approached. He'd done it, though. A London sight ticked off on his mental list. Otherwise, work had kept him in north London. After prison his life had been reduced to bins, trying to sleep and, latterly, Kettering. Being here now felt like being in a different world, like appearing in a travelogue. A picture of the scene would show the Eye slowly turning, the sun glinting on its windows, the bank opposite, the crowds in the foreground, the vans selling food. And if you squinted and looked closely you could spot the odd one out in the bottom left-hand corner of the image. The odd *pair* out, in this case. Max and Trish. As far away from Chick as they could get, she'd said. She was shopping with a mate if he asked, which he wouldn't. But nowhere near home, that was the thing. Max had approached her on the bench, thinking, despite himself, of George Smiley. Like he should have been carrying a copy of the *Financial Times* and using code words.

He settled on, 'Hello, Trish.'

She looked up at him, jutted her chin – a resentful, cornered greeting. Her eyes skidded about, nervous. Even here, even far away. I'm right, he told himself, on seeing those eyes. She's terrified and I'm right. 'You wanted to see me,' he said.

They sat with their backs to the wheel and Max felt iconic, knowing that something momentous was happening. A child stopped by the bench and hoisted a leg to tie his trainer lace, a jangling rucksack coming to rest on his back. His mother appeared and she greeted Max's smile with a suspicious tightening of the lips. Through her eyes he saw two strangers on the bench, a couple of party-poopers: Trish staring straight ahead, the pair of them clearly waiting to do whatever business they'd come to do. With trainer lace secured, mother and child left, and Max turned to Trish. *Don't lose your bottle,* he urged her mentally, seeing the skittering eyes and the hands moving restlessly in her lap. She wore a hooded top zipped up and seemed to have folded her shoulders round her chest. *Don't lose your bottle now, Trish.*

'You were right,' she said, speaking to her lap.

'You know where he is?'

She nodded slowly.

Okay, thought Max, composing himself on the inside. She's admitted it. *Okay.* Then: 'Is he safe?' he asked, hardly daring to breathe.

Again she nodded, twisting her hands like a fretting heroine. *He was safe.* For a moment Max felt a great, almost ecstatic draining. Ben was safe.

A group of teenagers stopped close to their bench, swarming about as though each of them was trying to get a better view of something happening at the centre of the circle. Max held up a hand to ward off a rucksack hovering near his face. Trish went back to stare mode.

'Let's walk,' said Max. The kids were talking loudly in French.

'No,' she insisted. 'I can see here. It's safer here.'

'Okay, whatever you're happier with.' He sighed and together, silently, with bags swiping about their noses as if they didn't exist, they out-waited the group of French tourists, who sped off in the direction of the Eye, each clasping whatever it was the group leader had handed out, oblivious to anything but seeing views of London from the sky.

'What happened, Trish?'

'I was on the train when he got on. In the carriage. There were loads of fans in there – it was packed. A load of Spurs and a load of Arsenal. People were opening and closing the connecting doors and they were chanting at each other. The Arsenal were calling the Spurs fans Yids. I'm an Arsenal fan,' she looked at him to make her point clear, 'but I don't agree with that. I'm not a racist. There's no need for all that. They was all shouting. It was really noisy, and someone had lit up a fag, and that puts everyone on edge, doesn't it? And everyone's there and they're all wanting it to be good-natured, kind of half smiling the way you do, because some of the chants are quite funny, but still there's that worry it's all going to kick off and get nasty. There was an edge in the air. It was hot and smoky and noisy and in the middle of it all I saw this kid, this little boy. He was standing there, kind of looking around him, and I could see that he was – not lost, but he was in a bit of a muddle. He was looking around him, like he was searching for someone. He's got noise and people in his face, but he's such a good kid, he's such a *nice* little boy, he just stayed quiet, stayed put, didn't make a fuss. And I think, I swear, that I was the only person who even saw him there. I keep thinking now . . .' her hands went to her face and her fingertips swept angrily at her eyes '. . . I keep thinking if only someone else had seen him, someone *decent* – more decent than me, anyway—'

'Hey, hey, Trish, come on. What you're doing now, you're doing the right thing.' He wondered about putting his arm round her, decided against.

'But the poor little sod, it wasn't his day, was it?' She laughed drily. 'Gets split up from his dad and then has the bad luck to run into me. He missed the match an' all.'

'You never meant it to be like this, though, did you?'

'I wanted to see him home, safe, back to his mum and dad where he belongs. I never even thought about nothing else.'

'What did you do?'

'At Arsenal it was like everyone got off, and I had my eye on him and he kind of got off, too – had no choice, really. I seen him get off and he was standing on the platform looking around again. I couldn't just leave him.' Saying it with a plea in her voice. 'My heart went out to him. Because, like, even though you don't normally – you see things and maybe think you should do something but there's always that worry that you're reading it wrong. Like if you see a bloke and his girlfriend arguing. I was on the tube once and some poor bloke stepped in to help this girl and she ended up scratching his face, going, "Fuck off," and all he wanted to do was see if she was okay. You see stuff like that all the time and you tell yourself you can't do anything or you shouldn't do anything because it might get you in trouble, or you're busy going somewhere else. But Ben, it just seemed – it wasn't like there was anything – nothing stopping someone at least asking him if he was all right, if he needed help. What I'm saying – I did what I thought was the right thing . . .'

'It *was*,' insisted Max. 'It was the right thing.'

That hollow laugh again. 'It wasn't, though, was it? If I'd done the right thing, if I'd left well alone, the chances are that boy would be at home now. He probably wouldn't even have missed his football match.' Her voice broke with emotion.

'Come on, Trish. Who knows what might have happened? I don't know, you don't know. We don't know who he might have run into, maybe someone . . .' He was going to say 'worse' – someone 'worse' than you. Maybe Ben would disagree, wherever he was – sleeping, hopefully, not lying afraid and weeping. He might think there was nothing worse than being approached by Trish. But she had had it in her heart to do the right thing and maybe one day Ben would understand that.

'What did you do?'

'I went up to him. I said to him, "Where's your mum and dad?" and he told me his dad was back there – he meant back at Finsbury Park. I wanted to use my mobile so I said, "Hop back on the train, there's no point getting out here because it's too busy," so we got back on and went to Holloway.' She sighed. 'All I wanted was to get him somewhere safe. He was . . . spooked out, you know, really nervous, the poor little boy. He took my hand. He wanted to feel safe, and he thought I'd be helping him. All I needed to do was get a signal on my mobile. Them pictures they put on the news, they said on the telly that I had my head down to avoid being seen, but that's a lie. I was looking at my mobile.' Eyes wide, imploring. 'I was looking to see if I'd got a signal yet. You can see. He's holding my hand, he's coming along fine because I told him just as soon as I got a signal I'd ring someone who'd come and get him. I was saying I'd buy him a Coke if he was thirsty. I said to him, "Do they let you have Coke, your mum and dad?" because I didn't want to go giving him something his parents disapproved of and a lot of them do. You hear it all the time on the radio about kids and junk food, you got to be careful. Carl drinks it like water, but you can't do a thing with Carl. Ben, he was different. He was well brought up, you could tell, and I wanted to respect that.'

Max broke in, trying to slow her down: 'What happened next, Trish?'

She croaked as if she was about to burst into tears. 'He rang.' Wailing it almost, her hand at her mouth, wet with emotion. 'Charlie rang me. I'd got up the road and I was talking to Ben. I was telling him I'd call someone when the phone went in my hand and it was Charlie and I told him what was happening . . .' She ran out of breath, ending in a sticky sob, pushing the sides of her hands into her eyes.

'I told him because he wanted to know where I was, so I had to tell him, and he was calling me a stupid cunt and telling me I'd kidnapped a kid off a train and I better not bring him back home, I better get rid of him, just leave him in the street. And I couldn't do that. I was panicking, and he said to calm down and let him think, and in the end he said to keep walking, not to stop, keep my head down, don't let the kid talk. He said he'd come and pick us up and that we'd take him to the police together. I made him promise because he had that tone in his voice – there's a tone he gets – but he said it was me that got us into this, that I better shut it and let him get us out of it before I landed myself in prison. So I went along with it. And I went along with it when he said that if we were going to give him back we might as well make some money doing it.'

Max squeezed his eyes shut.

'Just a couple of days was all he said,' continued Trish. 'Just so he could find out what the mum and dad were good for. And that they'd pay, course they would, to get their little boy back – they'd pay anything, and it served them right, taught them a lesson, because if they'd taken more care of the little boy they wouldn't have lost him in the first place. But it's not right. Ben's on sleeping pills all the time, he's barely awake, it's not right for a little boy—'

'Trish.' Max stopped her. 'Can you tell me where he is?'

She nodded.

'Trish?' he prompted.

In a rush it came out: 'He's at the depot in Walthamstow, in a back office. It's open in the day, but the bit Ben's in only me and Charlie go to that end of the warehouse. There's boxes stacked right up against the window and Charlie's stranded a fork-lift there so you can't get to them. We take him food twice a day. Charlie, sometimes. Me mostly. Early in the mornings Charlie'll crunch some pills into his baked beans and sausages. We put them in a flask for him. He likes baked beans and sausages, he told me. Them and Chicken McNuggets – they're what he has in the evenings. He loves them.'

As a little boy, Max had liked baked beans and sausages, the Heinz ones. Only Heinz ever got them right. He wasn't so keen on Chicken McNuggets.

'Please tell me you don't put sleeping pills in his Chicken McNuggets,' he said.

'No, he has them in his Coke. He likes his Coke.' Trish rounded on Max. 'I've wanted to take him away, you know, but he'd kill me, Charlie would. So you can't do it on a night I go down, he'd think it was me, that I'd let him go or left the door open or something. You'll have to do it on a night he goes.'

Max went suddenly cold, shifting on the bench. 'Sorry?' he said. 'Do what?'

'Get him,' she replied.

'Get him,' he repeated, thinking, *Get him?* 'What do you mean, "get him"?'

'I mean rescue him,' she said. She swivelled on the bench and was suddenly holding his hands, the sensation strangely pleasant. 'You've got to get him out of there.'

'What?' He looked down at their joined hands as if they were nothing to do with him. 'What do you mean? I can't . . . I can't . . . We've got to go to the police.'

'No,' she urged. 'No. This way's better. You can go and nobody will ever know it was you. Not Charlie, not the police, no one. You can break into the depot. I can tell you where to go. There's no guard there or nothing and Ben'll be asleep – even he won't know it's you.'

'I can't.' He pulled his hands away, suddenly aware of his scars. 'You don't understand. I'm not . . . I'm not going to get him.' He wanted to stand, get away, but his legs wouldn't allow it. 'We'll have to tell the police.'

'No,' she almost shouted. 'If you go to the police you'll go to prison.' The word ripped at his insides. 'We'll all go to prison. They'll lock us all up.'

'They won't,' said Max, trying to believe it. 'Not all of us. Just him, Trish. Just him.'

She snorted derisively. 'I've been taking Ben food. I was the one who took him off the train. And you . . . you've been to his dad's house. You know what Charlie was saying. There'll be CCTV of you. He was talking about fingerprints on the wheelie-bin. Betcha didn't wear gloves, did you?' He shook his head and looked at his hands, the culprits. 'If Charlie goes down he'll take us both with him. We're all in it together.'

'We could just . . . anonymously . . .' said Max, his voice weak. 'We could tell the police where he is.'

'The police'll trace it back to Charlie. How many people do you think have keys for that place? They'll trace it back to Charlie and he'll take us down with him. Both of us. You too. There's no other choice.'

In his head Verity's voice was urging him to go to the police.

He felt his breathing quicken, his palms moisten. *I can't*, he said to the Verity voice, loudly enough for Trish to catch.

'You can. It's the only way. Get him out of there. Get him away from Charlie. You can drop him somewhere. Anonymously. Nobody would ever know it was you.'

He stared out into space, silent for so long that Trish had to prompt him. 'You *can* do it,' she said.

He looked over at a group of kids being corralled by a teacher. She wanted a show of hands. 'Yes,' he said finally. 'I can.'

5

Dalston was busy. The Gherkin building looked like a spaceship in the distance, like some kind of futuristic Judge Dredd Megacity where the rich lived in the skies and looked down on the hurrying Dalstonites below. Dash couldn't see a market, but it was like market day on the high street, great swarms of people, none of whom even bothered to stop when Dash tried to beckon them over. Tired of being ignored, he gave up on the main drag and directed Lightweight to the back of the supermarket where it was quieter. Two lads in baseball caps took the piss. Dash was getting desperate, discarding the lone-punters-only rule. Now he was going for any kid who looked the age and type, twos-up or not. In his head he was frantically shaking dice, Maybe I could sell two in one go – you never know, got to try everything now, all the time ignoring the voice taunting, You're wasting your time.

Now he wore a look of jerky desperation as his eyes flitted about the streets looking for marks, but not seeing much, just flitting. And the whole time he was checking the wing mirror for signs of the Dalston crew: two white guys, prove-myself types in England shirts. On the back of their van someone had written, 'If my girlfriend was this dirty I'd marry her.'

'Stop here,' he said at last. 'On the left, where it says McIntosh.'

The one tiny but glittering diamond in the day so far was giving Lightweight directions that involved having to read. So: 'Look, the guy by the *Evening Standard* sign.' Or: 'Over there, standing in front of the Cancer Research shop.' This followed by Lightweight's crunching halt in the general direction of Dash's finger, his furrowed uncomprehending brow.

Now Dash leant from his window and beckoned a black kid,

who shook his head, sneered, and walked off. Dash slapped the side of the van in frustration and told Lightweight to drive on. Then his phone rang.

It was Chick. He should have known – it would have said 'Chick' on the little window of his phone. If he'd looked. Which he hadn't. He'd wanted it so badly to be Sophie that he'd reached into his jeans, flipped open and brought the phone to his ear without looking at the display.

'Hello?' His voice eager – Sophie-wanting. Thinking, *Her toothbrush was gone.*

'Dashus,' said Chick.

Just hearing his voice made Dash want to clean out his ear. 'I'm sorry about last night,' he said quickly. 'Boss. Sorry. I just – I couldn't make it, but, uh, I can come tonight.'

Chick sniffed. 'Too right you're coming tonight, poof-boy. I want to see you with a pint of fucking Guinness, some fucking vouchers and a good reason why *I* am having to ring *you* for my five hundred quid.'

'Five hundred?' Dash scraped a hand through damp hair. 'It was . . . it was nearer four hundred . . . boss.' Beside him Lightweight scoffed with derision.

'Not no more it ent,' said Chick. 'It's just went up. It's like the bank, see. I'm charging for the phone call.'

'Boss, that's . . .' *What? Not fair?*

'Just be here tonight, Dashus. I wanna see you tonight without fail or I'll come looking for you, and I charge a lot more for that, my son.'

Dash pushed his phone back into his jeans. The high street teemed around them.

'Where to, man?' croaked Lightweight.

He took a deep breath and again dragged a hand through his hair. 'Best get on down to Holloway Road,' he said.

6

Max sat engulfed in his sofa, coat hitched up round his shoulders. His hands were thrust into his pockets and he had them there to stop them worrying at his scars. On the coffee-table in front of him was another letter from Mrs Larkin's daughter, a new arrival that morning. 'You're a dirty pervert,' it said. 'You deserve to die.'

Once again he had to salute her brevity, the knack she had of taking his soul in hand and squeezing till the tears were pushed from his eyes. And with it the feeling he couldn't chase away. Not of victim-anger, or injustice, but a sense of responsibility. The feeling that – maybe – she was right: maybe he did deserve to die. Not for what he'd done to her daughter, the guilt there confined to a kind of self-disgust, but for what he'd done to Verity, whose husband was permanently right. And for what he'd done to their mother, who died reeking but loving him 'no matter what', him in prison, charged with an act of gross indecency involving a minor, remanded in custody. 'She never believed,' insisted Verity later, 'she never *for a second* believed you were guilty of anything.' But he had been *in prison*. As though he'd been tried and found guilty. Mud sticks. At least Max had been spared Verity's trauma: at least in prison he hadn't had to watch their mother kill herself. He took his hands from his pockets and looked at the scars on his wrists. 'Just pull yourself together,' he heard himself say, and laughed at how easy it was to speak the words.

Max jumped as the front door open-closed with a thump, and a set of feet raced up the stairs, with another following more slowly. Five minutes later he was peeking from behind the curtain and watching Darren load a box into the back of his van, him and his companion rattling off with the job done.

He took his seat on the sofa, hands out of his pockets now. The scars there, winking at him.

The riot had started on a Sunday night. It was the worst prison riot since Strangeways.

He'd learnt that later. Most of what he knew about it was what he'd read after the fact, because at the time, curled up in his cell in the Vulnerable Persons Unit, all he knew was noise and running and shouting as the prison imploded. And the noise and running and shouting were getting closer . . .

Trouble had initially flared up in C Wing towards the end of the evening period when inmates were allowed out of their cells to watch television, play pool, stand around and chat – shoot the breeze. They would have been aware that there were fewer prison officers on duty than usual. A virus had been going round the staff; prisoners were affected, too. The infirmary was almost full.

One of the officers, Andy Morris, sensed an uneasiness. You didn't need to have worked at the prison as long as he had to feel it: it was in the air. Like Friday night kicking-out time in Anytown, more police vans than taxis, girls crying, night-out shirts billowing in a chill wind, there was that sense that it might not, but it could – it could kick off.

Casting an eye over the rec area, Morris saw that the inmates were jumpier, snappier than usual. They avoided his eye. The metallic clamour common to prisons was, if not absent, considerably dimmed: none of the usual below-decks hilarity or the occasional territorial dispute quelled with a look, a finger, a hand to a baton. Morris took an umpteenth look at his watch, wishing the period over, looking over the wing to locate colleagues who glanced back, also concerned. Then, for the first time, he noticed a small knot of inmates by the pool table. Two or three faces he preferred not to be in close consultation with each other, not tonight anyway. So he strolled over, dissembling his real purpose, stitching on a forced smile, an oh-so-casual amble, just to say hello. Prison officers prefer to work in pairs, especially in situations such as this where a large number of prisoners are under the supervision of a smaller number of guards. That's the ideal situation – like policemen should have back-up and soldiers should always be equipped with body armour. It's not always the reality. There were only twenty-seven officers on duty that night, making about twelve inmates to every guard. And nobody was watching Andy Morris's back.

'All right, fellas?' he said.

The three inmates smiled at him as he drew near. 'All right, Mr Morris,' said one. Only he said it with a sneer.

Another inmate, Jason Blake, aggravated assault, had peeled away from a game of pool and came up behind Andy Morris.

'Everything all right over here?' asked Morris, as cheerily as he could manage, the weapon here not a baton or harsh language but a matey demeanour.

It wasn't enough. Reports later would point to a build-up of resentment involving the usual problems of overcrowding, withdrawn privileges and a general, possibly apocryphal feeling that those in the Vulnerable Persons Unit were given more lenient treatment than others. The report would confirm that this was indeed the case, bearing in mind the fewer cases of disorder and drug possession arising in the VPU, but concluded that a problem of perception among the general prison population had not been adequately addressed. Meanwhile, at the opposite end of the ground-floor landing there were just three card-operated phones, one of which had taken early retirement, leaving just two. Always a flashpoint, even at full strength, tensions had been mounting further, with inmates impatient to use the phones: jostling, queue-jumping, barracking those whose turn it was.

Back by the pool game and table football, Morris felt it more than saw it. The only real warning was a movement, like a shadow in the far-corner of his vision – Blake's cue raised high, fat end out. A big man, Blake. He swung so hard the cue snapped as it drove into the back of Andy Morris's legs, taking them from beneath him with a crunch of shattered bone. There was a split second of death-silence. A fraction of a moment during which Morris felt the cue, and heard the snap of bone, then the sound of wood skittering over the concrete floor, but felt nothing, and was half-way to thinking, That wasn't so bad, only tapped me. I can save this situation, when delayed agony exploded up his legs like fireworks and he was hitting the floor, senses screaming, self-preservation making him reach for his baton.

His fingers found nothing. The baton was taken from him, used on him. On a landing above another officer reached for his radio but found it snatched from his fingers, blows raining down on him as he withdrew. Downstairs, two officers went to the aid of Andy Morris, but they were driven back by inmates brandishing pool cues, radioing the control room as they fled. Flailing and writhing, his own baton thumping mercilessly into his body, Morris was dragged to an empty cell. Hands reached for his keys, which were passed out to other prisoners. Inmates pulled his clothes from him, blindfolded him; still the punches and the baton continued.

The report suggested the riot might have been pre-planned. Certainly prisoners had hoarded newspapers and magazines, which were now used to start fires, pushing staff back further. Still they hoped to control the disturbance. Even as mattresses burned, as paper and toilet roll were set alight and thrown from upper landings, a small squad of officers attempted to force a lockdown while desperately trying to retrieve Andy Morris from the ground-floor cell. But as prisoners were unlocking cells to free fellow inmates they were forced to withdraw, eventually pushed as far back as the gatehouse.

Their reluctant retreat meant, said the report, that a significant portion of the prison was in the hands of the inmates.

Windows were smashed. Police called in to form a perimeter around the prison watched helplessly as faces appeared at the broken glass, framed by shards – some taunting and swearing, others calling for help. Inside, the broken phone was pulled from the wall, but an inmate who tried to prise off a working phone was punched and kicked until he withdrew; he went off to help smash a table-tennis table instead. Even as the riot raged round them, several prisoners patiently waited their turn for the phone. Of the thousands and thousands of pounds' worth of damage caused during the disturbance, the two working phones went undamaged.

As the noise, the smoke, the chaos bloomed and infected the rest of the prison, many prisoners fled terrified to their cells, using a voluntary privacy system to lock themselves in. Meanwhile, old scores were being settled. With the riot spreading to B Wing and parts of A Wing, three inmates were severely beaten; one later died. The infirmary was broken into, as was the pharmacy. Of the thirty-two inmates who required hospital treatment, most suffered self-administered drug overdoses.

The rioting spread as far as Block B, one of three blocks in the Vulnerable Persons Unit. Max thought he smelt it before he heard it, and when he did it was like a distant echo, like a football match being played miles away, but coming closer now, intensifying. There was a shout. Like one person, a forward party, running along the landing, opening doors, overriding the privacy systems. Other voices joined his. Max pushed himself to his door. The noises had reached other cells on the block, the VPs beginning to shout now, calling not for freedom but for the guards: the self-harmers hoping they wouldn't get mistaken for the paedophiles; the paedophiles hoping they could pose as self-harmers, suddenly finding it difficult to swallow, hands fretting at their necks. There wasn't a paedophile there who hadn't heard, 'You know what they do to your kind in prison, don't you?' but hoped that gob in their food and marginally more lenient treatment was as far as it went.

But the guards weren't there. Back at C Wing they were putting together a tiny riot squad with shields and protective clothing. Forming a phalanx they entered the ground-floor landing of the wing, forcing their way through the billowing smoke and patchy fires to the cell where Andy Morris lay with his liver split. Those inmates still on the landing watched them beetle to the cell and back again, giving them bemused looks, not interfering with them. There was the dull thump of an explosion – a fire extinguisher thrown on a fire. At the noise the phalanx collapsed into a pile of splayed arms and legs, Andy Morris's head making new acquaintance with the floor. In a moment the rescue squad had righted itself and carried on to safety. Seconds later a riot squad in breathing apparatus appeared on the landing, followed by a fire team who began dousing fires, the hollowed-out gush of extinguishers; moments after that the ground-floor section of C Wing was secure.

On Block B Max heard them coming, heard doors opening, shouts, people dragged bodily from their cells, and the muffled *doof* of a kicking.

The report later pointed to 'the sadly arbitrary nature' of Max's treatment: 'There were several notorious inmates in the VPU but John Riley, the deceased, and Maxwell Coleman were picked seemingly at random.'

He was being carried and, for some reason, a mad part of his brain was associating being carried with being a fun thing, and his mind could not comprehend that his body was unable to wriggle easily away. And as he was taken to where a wing spur housed toilets and a shower room, he felt phlegm on his face, a fist that repeatedly slammed into his groin until he was sick, wriggling and reaching to try and eject his vomit, coughing on it, choking. He was dropped to the floor, the kicks coming in but Max barely feeling them, doubling up to cough and spit, gasping for breath. 'Scum. Filthy scum,' he heard. Then his clothes were being pulled from him and he was wriggling and shouting, and the only thing he could manage to shout was 'No', his mind unable to produce the words he needed to tell them they were wrong – he wasn't like the others, not like the others. And dimly, through the blows, he saw the other man, the man he would later know was called John Riley, a convicted paedophile. He was naked, writhing. He was being picked up, arms and legs, and dragged to a row of metal towel hooks high on the wall, just above head height for safety. They were taking his arms and pulling them up to the hooks, as though they were prostrating him at the wall. His mouth was moving, saying, 'Please,' over and over and his body went limp, pulling down, but they hoisted him up, pressing his wrists against two hooks. With grunts that were half physical exertion, half pure hatred, they pushed and pushed, forcing his wrists on to the hooks with a wet crunch.

At that noise, at the crunch, everything in the shower room seemed to stop for a moment. There was a sound, among the rioters, like an, 'Uh, gross,' sound, like vicious kids torturing a pet and just as keen to see if the same trick would work twice. In that moment Max saw John Riley's feet scrabbling at the suddenly slick tiles, trying to take the weight. Scrabbling then finding purchase, gaining support. But then his legs were being lifted, and he screamed like he'd found a new level of pain he believed could never exist, and the final thing Max saw of John Riley was John Riley being crucified.

Meanwhile C Wing was coming under control. B and A followed, as officers moved swiftly through the prison, the riot reaching its natural end anyway, the guards meeting little resistance.

But Max was being picked up, naked, his penis small, acorned with fear, and him ridiculously ashamed of the fact, as though it provided proof of his perversion. He was being hoisted up by what felt like hundreds of arms, imprisoning him, allowing no movement. All that moved was his mouth, like John Riley screaming, Please, as he watched his hands pulled towards the hooks, which he tried to grab on to but couldn't. Then feeling a sudden agony of pressure at his wrists, pushed on to the hooks. Pushed surely as far as they could go. Then pushed some more.

He shrieked. He continued shrieking until he passed out, and what the riot officers saw when they stormed into the shower room was John Riley, the deceased, hung and draining from the hooks, the floor awash with his blood. And, near by, Maxwell

Coleman, against whom all charges were subsequently dropped, the report noted later, emphasising the random brutality of the attacks, who was in the prison having been remanded in custody by magistrates after petitioning from the Crown Prosecution Service. The accused lived in the same house as an elderly female witness for the prosecution, they had said, and there was, therefore, a greater than significant risk of interference. He lay unconscious on the shower-room floor coated with his own blood, the hooks above his head red and dripping, when the riot squad entered the room. An inmate was kneeling at his side, tearing at a shirt and wadding it to make a bandage for the left wrist, the right dressing already soaked dark red.

When Max awoke from his nightmare it was to the sound of the phone ringing. It was Trish. Same as the first call her voice was whispered and quick, guarded against Chick – or Carl, or maybe nobody. The plastic of the receiver seemed to scrunch as his hand squeezed. *Already?* screamed his mind, like he wanted more time; longer to come to terms with it. *Already?*

'Hello, Trish.'

'He's going tonight to see the boy, Charlie is. You can go after.' Max still wasn't accustomed to Chick's real name: Charlie. Cheeky Charlie. Charlie Brown. Charlie Chuck's, was it? The place you took your kids for a birthday party.

'When? What time?' Feeling like an actor, speaking his lines but it not being real.

'It'll be later.'

He said nothing.

'Do you hear me?'

'Yes . . . I hear you, yes.' He wanted there to be another way, still he wanted that. He said nothing.

'There's something else,' she said.

A feeling of dread came over him, saying, 'What? What else?'

'He's being moved,' she said blankly.

'Who?'

'Who do you think?' she snapped.

'Well, why's he being moved?' Madly, unable to think straight, he was thinking of Ben 'being transferred', like he was in some kind of institution.

'Charlie's worried the pills have stopped working. He wants to get him out – get him somewhere there's no people around. I don't know where. He's been talking,' her voice dropped, 'about *selling* him.'

Instantly Max felt sick. 'Christ,' he managed. 'When? When is he being moved?'

'Dunno, maybe tomorrow. All it means is you've got to go tonight. Get him out of there, Max, please.' Her voice, imploring.

'Okay,' he said. 'Okay, yes, I'll do it tonight.'

'I've gotta go,' she whispered, hoarse. 'I've gotta go now, but I'll ring you later when it's safe. I'll give you the address and directions. You'll be there, yeah? At home?'

Dust-mouthed. 'Yes.' Voice twisted. Curdled with defeat. 'What's he . . . Is Ben all right?'

'He's all right, nobody's done nothing. He's a bit lonely and that, and he misses his mum and dad, and between you and me he could do with a bath, but he's all right. I wouldn't let no one do anything.'

'Will he be awake?'

'No. He'll have had his Coke.'

'You said they've stopped working.'

'Don't worry – he'll be asleep. Now listen, what are you going to do with him?' she asked.

'I think . . . I'll bring him home. He'll be safe for the night. I'll take him properly home in the morning.'

'What do you mean, you "think"?'

'He'll be safe, Trish.'

'I've got to know.'

'Why? Look, he'll be safe.'

'I ent letting you take him out the frying-pan.'

'He'll be safe.'

'How do I know?'

'You have my word.'

Pause. 'That'll have to do then,' she said at last. 'I gotta go. Wait for my call.'

She was gone, and Max thought he might splinter the receiver he gripped it that hard; wanted, in fact, to break and smash it. Instead he put it down with exaggerated care and placed the phone on the coffee-table in front of him – on its own little altar.

7

He didn't want to have to burn down the depot.

He didn't want to feel the plank-slam of Chick's knee in his bollocks.

So it was the bloke in the shop who gave him the idea. And then, when he thought about it, it was 'Blue Monday' by New Order that gave it a certain glamour. That and the fact that he was getting dangerously low on choice.

He'd left Lightweight smoking and dysfunctional in the van as he jumped down with instructions to wait, and scooted into the shop. There was a back room. 'Hi-fi & electronics thru here,' said a sign, and he was about to go through when he spotted a sales assistant: young, unkempt, smelling strongly of cigarettes. Exactly the sort of kid Dash would have attempted to stop in the street.

'Excuse me, mate,' said Dash, feeling for a second like he really was trying to stop him in the street, then remembering he wasn't and thinking how nice that was.

'Yeah?'

'Do you sell speakers at all?'

'Yeah, through there. Got tons, mate.'

'No, what I mean is, do you *buy* speakers to sell?'

The sales assistant looked at Dash's feet as though expecting a set of speakers to be at his ankles. 'We do, yeah. It depends.'

'On what?'

'Condition. Make. Whatever, you know. It just depends if we think we can sell them on or not.'

Dash brightened. 'I got some that are new.' He stopped. Were they allowed to buy gear that was new? Like, it was clear that they took just about anything – new, second-hand, stolen or bought – but perhaps they couldn't *officially* take new stuff. 'More or less new,' he corrected. 'Unwanted present. Really good speakers.'

'For separates?'

'Absolutely.'

'What are they?'

'These? Auridial, mate.'

'Auridial,' said the assistant, sounding impressed. 'Really?'

'Yup,' said Dash, warming. 'Like I say, never even been used. Well, just to check they work, like, and they do.'

'Well, follow me,' said the assistant, turning and leading the way to Hi-fi and Electronics. Dash followed with a spring in his step. Then stopped short as they entered the room.

One wall of the room was devoted entirely to speakers. Every single one Auridial. Stacked up like that and out of their boxes they looked really imposing, he thought – like they were in a music video. You imagined some rock god strumming away in front of them, hair blown by their sheer, nut-shrinking mega-wattage. If only he knew a director making a rock video, he mused.

'Bought them off a couple of blokes in a van, did you?' asked the assistant, a gloating glow about him.

'Yeah, I did, as a matter of fact.'

'So did the original owners of every set of speakers there, mate. And we'll take yours off your hands but I gotta warn you, we sell 'em for fifty quid, and we buy 'em for a *lot* less than that. More like twenty.' He grimaced, still gloating, though. 'Just depends on how much you want rid of 'em really.'

At that moment Dash knew the kid was right. How much he was prepared to ask for the speakers depended on how much he wanted rid of them. Which was a lot. And he thought of 'Blue Monday', the first single by New Order after Ian Curtis had died and they changed their name from Joy Division. Their label, Factory, didn't think it would sell, so they weren't too worried when an extravagant sleeve design meant every copy sold lost the company three and a half pence. It was a great design, the record wouldn't sell anyway, it was a small price to pay. But it went on to become the best-selling twelve-inch ever, so the moral of the story is . . .

Dash was going to have to sell his speakers at a loss.

He had no choice. Because he didn't know any music-video directors, and he was having no joy selling them at a profit. All he had left was a roomful of speakers. He was going to have a sale.

'All right, mate, thanks,' he said sadly, 'I'll give it a bit of thought, maybe look around elsewhere, come to back to you, yeah?'

The assistant smiled, like, *You'll be back*. 'Suit yourself,' he said. 'See you later.'

No, Dash wasn't going to admit defeat just yet. At least, not that much defeat. Not twenty quid when he normally opened the bidding at around six hundred.

He pulled open the van door and released an atmosphere from within. *L'eau de recovering crackhead par Lightweight*. The driver gave him a sideways look as he climbed into the cab. 'You din't sell no speakers,' he said flatly.

'No.' Enthusiastic Dash now. 'No, I didn't, but I got an idea. I'm going to try and shift them at less money.' He paused, calling on every single optimism cell in his body. 'Thing is, you know, that's going to mean . . . your cut will be less.'

Lightweight raised his eyebrows and shook his head – slowly, end-of-storyish.

'Listen,' said Dash, quickly. 'Look at yesterday. Not a nibble, mate. Everyone we stop I tell them how much the speakers cost and they're off like their clothes are on fire. Not very many people have, like, four hundred quid just hanging around in their accounts. And if I can't sell anything there's no cut, is there? I can't hand over your per cent of fuck-all, do you see what I mean? So it just makes sense.' Dash felt his heart heavy at the fundamental stupidity of having to explain it. 'It just makes sense that if I can sell more by selling them for less then your end will be less, but it's still better than nothing. Isn't it?'

Lightweight cranked the window down and spat. 'Just sell some speakers, man,' he said, and Dash wasn't sure what he meant by that. Was he reluctantly agreeing? Or not?

'All right, then,' he said. 'Let's get on down to Holloway Road.'

'For real this time?'

He cast a look over at the shop – his last hope before he crossed the border to Holloway Road. 'Yeah, for real.' Clapping his hands together, trying to gee himself up. 'Let's go.'

They were on Holloway Road. Not actually on it – they'd driven past the tempting campus buildings but the traffic was heavy, wardens everywhere, so they'd hung a left by the cinema ('Turn there, where it says Odeon') and were cruising slowly along. Dash kept an eye on the wing mirror, radar tuned, looking for Also Available in White.

'I saw Roland Gift down here once,' he said. He and Sophie had come to see the new James Bond and had hurried from the tube (the days before the van came into his life, this was; those rose-scented, *Brideshead* days). She'd been moaning because she'd worn the wrong shoes, and was giving it some on the pavement when they both noticed someone looking at them, bemused – at her, really, at her cussing and scolding, 'It doesn't matter if we miss the bleedin' adverts. If I'd known we were doing a marathon I would have worn my trainers . . .' that kind of thing. It was Roland Gift, of the Fine Young Cannibals. Standing there looking just like Roland Gift. Not changed a bit. He gave a little laugh and was suddenly meeting a friend while Dash and Sophie stood there, basking a little in the moment of making Roland Gift laugh. They'd missed the trailers. Dash thought she'd done it on purpose. Suddenly declaring she needed popcorn, that it was all part of the experience. He'd never heard that from her before.

Anyway. Lightweight gave a snort at Dash's Roland Gift gambit. Dash, meanwhile, had the radar going in one direction and was scanning ahead in the other. Looking for a student, one who'd just left his digs perhaps, making his way to college.

Hopefully having switched off his stereo wishing his speakers had a bit more poke.

At last. A kid walking towards them with a denim jacket and a faraway expression. He'd do.

Dash put on his salesman face. As they'd pulled up he'd side-mouthed the instruction to keep an eye out for Also Available in White, but as he went into his script he glanced at the driver, and Lightweight sat smoking and holding the collar of his denim jacket. Not keeping an eye out in other words. Still, the kid had a nothing-to-lose-by-looking expression on his face, which Dash found heartening as he jumped down from the van. He threw open the doors and stepped to one side, letting the boy-juices start flowing.

'They look pretty cool,' said the kid. He hadn't asked how much yet but, 'And expensive . . .'

'Jesus, yeah, they're expensive,' said Dash. 'But to be honest, I'm letting them go for stoopid dosh. Like, all I want is a couple of drinks out of it, you know? It's found money, as far as I'm concerned. I'm late for another job and I don't have room for them in the van. Here . . .' He pulled himself up over the lip of the van and suddenly felt utterly defenceless. The Holloway team could turn up now and he'd never see them arrive. The first thing he'd know would be the slap of baseball bat into palm, a figure at the van doors, trapping him in. He hurried to drag the speakers over, thudding down to the road and casting a nervous look left and right.

'They're fucking heavy, too,' he said, to reinforce his want-rid persona. 'Feel that.' Bricks, bricks, do your work, he thought, as the kid moved forward dutifully and hefted the Auridial.

'Yeah, yeah,' said the kid. And Dash saw that he was getting ready to stage a polite retreat. 'Yeah, they're nice but, really, I don't think I can afford . . .'

'Guess what they're worth,' said Dash, pretending not to notice the kid's leaving signs. 'Go on, have a guess.'

'I dunno. I really . . . dunno. What?'

'Come on, pair of studio speakers like these. Top of the range, professional jobs. Just have a wild guess.'

'Um . . . three thousand quid?'

Dash looked at him. 'Well, no, mate, not *that* much. They're not made of gold. Look, here, I'll show you.' From his pocket he pulled the dog-eared promotional leaflet, and thrust it at the kid. He let him inwardly digest. 'Now guess how much I'm asking for them.'

'I dunno, mate. I really dunno.' Sounding a bit hacked off now.

'Well, you've seen how much they go for. What if I was to say . . .' and here he paused, thinking, Might as well try high. Can't hurt. '. . . six hundred quid.'

The kid laughed, held up his hands. 'No way, mate. I haven't got that kind of money.'

'Three hundred, then.' Bought them for two hundred, a hundred clear profit. What do you call a fire at an estate agent's? A good start.

But the kid was having none of it. He looked longingly up the street. Dash took the opportunity to do a recce of his own. 'Sorry, mate, I really don't have the cash.'

'Look, okay, really, it's just a bit of extra cash. What about two?' Headshake from the kid.

'A hundred?' Now he was running at a loss. A hundred quid lost on the speakers. What the hell? He'd paid for them once, might as well pay for them again.

And now the kid's interest was piqued. He smelt a bargain. 'I've got fifty. It's the most I can afford.'

A savage one-hundred-and-fifty pound loss. Eat that, New Order.

'Okay,' Dash said at last, 'done.' He stuck his hand out to shake.

Half an hour later they were back in Holloway, cruising the streets again. In the back was a new set of Auridial collected from home. He hadn't even bothered taping bricks into the back, just grabbed the box and left, fifty quid richer, only another four hundred and fifty to go. (And if there was something nagging at him, that Lightweight hadn't enquired about the last sale, hadn't asked after his cut, well, he ignored it for the time being. He had this idea he was on a roll.)

'You're keeping an eye out, aren't you,' he urged, 'for the Holloway Road crew?' Lightweight grunted what might have been a yes but didn't shift.

They cruised. ''Scuse me, mate,' said Dash, to the next likely-looking victim. 'I don't suppose you've got a minute.'

He did have a minute, the kid. Stopping (he thought) to give directions, his upbringing had given him insufficient ammo for dealing with the likes of Dash – too polite, too wary of giving offence. Before he knew it he was standing at the back door of the van while Dash, perspiring freely, his eyes darting up and down the road, was showing him a set of speakers.

'A hundred,' said Dash, when it got to the close. What a pushover. Minutes later they were all in the van, delivering a set of Auridial to the kid's pad. Dash could hardly stop his knee shaking, all the nervous energy. Delivery done, they returned to Clarke Street, now reaching the kind of heights Dash hadn't seen since the early days. That morning's quota sold! Now, time to make a dent in Speakers' Corner. (Still no word from Lightweight. He can hear the sales, thought Dash. Like, he must be able to hear what kind of money they're fetching. Not a dickie-bird, though.)

Back to Holloway Road. What did they say when a business was going to the wall? Haemorrhaging cash. That was what he was doing. But all in the aid of raising the capital. He looked at his watch, judging the hours between now and meeting Chick, thinking that if they kept going at this rate they might just make it.

'All right, mate?'

''Scuse me, mate?'

In another hour he'd sold two more sets of speakers. He was half-way to what he owed Chick and he began to dream of pulling this day out of the fire. He stopped reflexively checking for the enemy van every couple of seconds, relaxed into his role. He started to feel like the old Dash again, fast of mouth and full of wit, not the sad loser he'd lately become, wonderer of what-ifs.

Pay Chick off, get home, change into Warren's suit (Versace, very nice), go to see Gary Spencer for seven. It could be done, he thought, watch-checking again.

'All right, mate?'

''Scuse me, mate.'

He sold another set. This time for a hundred. Not bad at all.

It can be done, he thought, as they raced back to Clarke Street for more speakers. It can be done.

8

'Oh, Max, I thought I was never going to hear from you.'

'Hello, Verity.' He forced a sardonic smile. Tried to sound playful. As though his cares were few, not legion.

'Okay. Hello, Max, how are you? Fine, good. But the last time I saw you . . .'

'Ver, can I come in?'

She pursed her lips and decided to let whatever it was wait. 'Come on, then.' Stepping aside to allow him in, she wrinkled her nose as he moved past her. 'Look, Max,' she said, door-closing, 'please don't take this the wrong way, but you smell a bit.'

He checked his internal readings and found that he didn't care. No, sorry, there it was, a tiny chip of shame, somewhere deep and dark, that by allowing himself to get to the stage of public noxiousness he'd somehow failed Verity, the Coleman name. But that was all it was, a tiny twinge, a smidgen. There were more pressing concerns.

Still, he made a play of smelling his armpits. 'Really? I'm sorry. Is it that bad? It's the coat.'

'I know. It's fit for the dump. Even Oxfam'd reject it.' Verity, the kind of person who took her stuff to charity shops.

'I could try Age Concern.'

They'd reached the kitchen, the familiar kitchen, all shiny surfaces, cleanliness, organisation. More than ever he felt as if he didn't belong.

'I think even Age Concern would turn up their noses,' said Verity, smiling. 'Just dump it, Max. It's a nice day, you must be boiling in it.'

'I like the sleeves,' he said. 'It covers the scars.'

She looked at him and frowned. Both of them thinking it was a cheap shot, the way he'd tried to excuse his smelliness.

'The least you could do is get it dry-cleaned.' She harrumphed, then moved to the kettle.

For a moment or so he let himself imagine that once-mundane task, the act of visiting the dry-cleaner. The old him had loved its smell and its almost impossible heat, the doormat that set off the bell, a few words with the friendly Turkish guy, or his wife, who chewed gum and was less friendly but darkly attractive.

'Okay,' he said. 'I'll take it to be cleaned.' Knowing he never would.

'Do you want tea?' she asked, also knowing that he never would take the coat to the dry-cleaner.

'Thank you.'

In a few moments, Verity put a mug, steamy, in front of him and gave his hair a ruffle.

They'd finished their tea before either of them realised they'd drunk it in silence. It struck Verity, who was suddenly embarrassed and wondered what she'd been thinking about all that time. She stood, scooped up her empty mug and raised question-eyebrows at Max: Finished with that? He nodded and watched as she went to the sink, pulled on a pair of yellow Marigold washing-up gloves and ran the hot tap. Squit-squit of the squeegy. He stood up. 'I came, actually, because I wondered if you have the spare keys to my van.'

She dumped the mugs in the hot water, adding a few more bits and pieces she had by the sink.

'They're in the drawer, marked Max V-keys.' She said it in a self-deprecating can't-help-but-be-organised tone.

'Thanks.' He went to the drawer and pulled. The other advantage of being an arty craftsman: he was allowed to be absent-minded, it was practically in the statute books. So he could lose his keys on a regular basis, and had eventually surrendered the spares to his sister for safe-keeping. Inside he saw a plastic document folder. The kind of thing someone like Roger would use to keep his quiz questions in crisp condition. This one was headed 'Mariner Quiz Night (genius edition)' and dated some days hence. Coughing – a cover-up cough – he pulled the folder from the drawer, rolled and roughly sausaged it into his coat. Then he made a play of rooting until he found the white tag, the words 'Max V-keys'. 'You're great, Ver, thanks.'

By rights she should have been admonishing him about losing his set. Instead she peeled off the gloves and turned to him with a serious, suspicious look. 'Why do you want the van keys, Max? You're not taxed or insured, or MOT'd probably. You shouldn't be driving it.' The gloves were in her hand, the way German commandants in films slap them into one palm.

'I need it for a job,' he said. 'Just a quick one.'

She dropped the gloves to the draining-board. 'Oh, God, what kind of job? For the Florence Nightingale from prison?'

Bet Chick's never been described like that before, he thought. 'No, a furniture job, obviously.'

She looked severe. '"Obviously"? Why "obviously"? And, Max, why have you not said anything about the little boy?'

He turned his head so she wouldn't see him lie. 'I was wrong. They don't have him. I was putting two and two together and making five.'

'Well, I think you're right,' she said, 'but it still leaves the nasty matter of . . . whatever it is. Embezzlement – no, extortion. That *you* are a part of. And now you're apparently about to drive your van illegally. You say you're desperate not to go to prison – you could have fooled me.'

'I don't think they send you to prison for driving with no insurance.'

'But what about your record?'

The shock seemed to freeze the room. Verity's eyes appeared to process and contract.

'My record?' He didn't need to repeat it; she knew what she'd just said. 'My *record*?'

'I didn't mean—'

'I haven't *got* a record.'

'I know. You did nothing wrong.'

Suddenly he was flashing back to his mother in a bed, her skin raw and blotchy, breath foul, her body given up trying to process its poisons. Still in custody then, Max had been accompanied and his mother had tried to make light of it. 'Ooh, a man in uniform. I am honoured.' Max had come to say goodbye, they all knew it. She told Max she loved him; that she loved him no matter what. Unable to stop himself his eyes had flicked to the prison guard who stood in the room; Andy Morris had returned his gaze impassively, but had known the pain of those words. Known that mud sticks.

'No matter what, eh, Verity?'

'I didn't mean it like that,' she cried. 'I didn't mean it like that at all.'

'I don't suppose Mum meant it. I don't suppose the guys in prison meant it, or Mrs Larkin's daughter, or the kid who calls me Paedo.'

'No,' she said. 'Don't say that. Please don't say that.' Wet in her eyes now. 'Why do we have to argue? I don't want to argue.'

He stood and went to where she'd retreated against a worktop, one hand absentmindedly brushing it down as she fought back tears. He put soft arms round her and pulled her to him. It broke the hex: she wriggled away, mock-disgusted, 'Urgh.'

'I'm sorry.' He retook his seat, wafting his own smelly-smell about him. 'I'm so sorry I've brought all this into your life. I think if there's one thing I want you to know it's that.'

He knew he could never be truly forgiven, even for something he hadn't done; knew he could never forgive himself. And at that moment he realised that, although she probably despised herself with every atom in her soul, through some combination of genes, upbringing, status and the dear-held beliefs of the marital home, she couldn't help herself: he had become a stain on her life.

For a long time there was silence between them, a silence during which Max fought a wave of loneliness so fierce he thought it might actually engulf him.

Then, at last, he said, 'What did you mean, "I think you're right"?'

'About what?'

'Earlier, you said, "I think you're right," when I told you they don't have Ben.'

'Well . . . I think you're right.'

'Yes, but why?'

'I'll show you,' she said. 'Come with me.'

9

Chargrilled, the big, tough black man of Barnaby Horton's dream-stroke-nightmares, had a thing about palindromic times. Eleven minutes past eleven, loved it. If he caught the clock saying ten minutes past eleven he'd sit and watch until the digits clicked on to make 11:11. The same backwards as it was forwards. A particular favourite was twenty-two minutes past ten in the p.m. You had to have a twenty-four-hour clock but he'd never had any problem with that. 22:22. They had a little plastic clock with sticky feet stuck to the top of the dashboard. Chargrilled had bought it from a petrol station along with a violently strong vanilla-scented Magic Tree. The clock was a little compass-like bubble, so whatever angle you held it, the time always stayed upright. It sort of bobbed about as though it was suspended in liquid. Also Available in White had never been turned on its roof, not so far as Chargrilled knew anyway, but now if the van should ever find itself wheels to the sky he could at least still read the time.

Now he squinted at the bubble clock. It was thirteen minutes past three in the afternoon and would soon be 15:15. Whether that strictly speaking counted as palindromic he wasn't sure: maybe it was just symmetrical. Whatever. Some people waited decades to see planets moving across the sun through telescopes the size of missile silos. Chargrilled waited to see palindromic times.

Kris, beside him, the driver – unlike Lightweight in every way, apart from their respective jobs – sat eating a sandwich three-pack from the M&S along Holloway Road. Long ago they'd decided on a no-fried-chicken-in-the-van rule, out of respect for each other, the environment of the van and a shared feeling that two black men in a white van eating chicken from grease-soaked boxes was one stereotype too far. Same for the no-tabloid-on-the-dashboard rule. Although they sometimes put a copy of the *Daily Telegraph* there, just to be ironic.

Fourteen minutes past three. Something caught Chargrilled's eye to make him look up from scrutiny of the compass clock. A white van drove down Holloway Road, past where they were parked, indicating to turn in by the Odeon. It had 'try slapping the top of this fucker' written in dirt on the back.

'What the fuck?' said Kris. He'd seen it, too – it wasn't like it was being subtle or anything. Gobbets of cheese and spring onion escaped his mouth as his jaw went floorwards.

Chargrilled and Kris watched Try Slapping trundle along their field of vision. The two of them wore expressions like they'd just been violated unexpectedly by a horse. They looked at each other, Chargrilled already reaching to locate the baseball bat he kept beneath the seat, Kris reading his mind, twisting the ignition, the van roaring into life.

'Those two, man . . . Those two. Those fuckin' rubes.' Chargrilled was outraged, indignant. There was such a thing as fair play, and this was an insult to his sense of it. There was also such a thing as respect, or – for Christ's sake – simply a fear of the kicking Chargrilled and Kris would deliver if they caught them. That scene outside the depot was a trailer, not the main attraction.

15:16. He'd missed it. Chargrilled brought the bat to the seat, kneading the handle with twitchy fists as they turned in by the Odeon and bumped noisily over the traffic calming. Ahead – some way in the distance – Try Slapping was rattling along like it owned the place, like it had all the time in the world. Kris winced as the van bumped dangerously fast over the traffic calming – a metal screech, carving silvery dents into the humps behind them.

'Yeah, slow down, man,' said Chargrilled. 'You'll fuck the van up.' Kris relaxed on the gas and Also Available slowed, the other team still up ahead – but reaching a junction now.

And not stopping. Pulling straight out into traffic. Chargrilled and Kris both rearing back in their seats as if some two hundred yards away they might still be affected by the collision. But no collision came. Both of them, Chargrilled and Kris, went, '*Fuu-u-uuck*,' simultaneously as traffic screeched to a halt and drivers reached for their horns, but Try Slapping swung left out into the junction, tipping slightly, righting, wobbling, but speeding off unharmed.

'He's seen us, Char,' said Kris. 'He must have seen us.'

They reached the junction and pulled out with rather more finesse. No sign of the other van in the road ahead.

Chargrilled and Kris frowned at one another; 15:19, said the clock.

Lightweight report: outlook dark. Severe shaking of the outer extremities. In financial news, the Dash index was up. Thanks to that last sale he now had just £150 to earn before he'd raised enough at least to pay Chick. Not that he wanted to get it out and count it – not with Lightweight brooding and strangely silent on the subject of money. He thought, though, totting up in his head, he was pretty certain. The problem was, time was getting on now. These sales, it wasn't like they were quick. Once you'd done the pitch you still had to get to a cash machine, then back to whatever hovel the student lived in, then on to Clarke Street for fresh supplies. He'd thought about just chucking a load into the back, but why risk a winning formula? Still, it ate into the time. The whole process could take up to an hour, maybe more, depending on Lightweight's driving, which fell, at the best of times, below any kind of national standard, and was, as the day wore on, increasingly erratic.

He knew the kid was trouble as soon as he clapped eyes on him. As they pulled to the kerb and before Dash had even opened his mouth he wore an expression that said he was perplexed at being so put-upon. Maybe stoned, Dash thought, or more likely that was his default mode, a kind of woolly befuddlement. 'You're not going to believe this, mate.'

The kid seemed to recoil, as though he'd not been aware of the van at the kerb. He put a shielding hand to his forehead and squinted at Dash. 'Sorry, mate, believe what?'

'What I've got here. You want to take a look at this, you really do.' He was leaning, both hands out of the van, beckoning Befuddled Kid over. Befuddled Kid took a few cautious steps forward, glancing left and right, angling his head to look at the Auridial leaflet Dash was holding out to him. 'Got a set of these in the back. Brand new. How much you reckon?'

Befuddled Kid looked like he was trying to think about it, not seeming to grasp its rhetorical roots.

'Here, look, I'll show you.' Dash interrupted his thinking and pointed out the price on the leaflet.

The kid did a little impressed bounce, nodding enthusiastically. 'Wow,' he said. 'That's a lot of wonga.'

'It's proper Auridial, you see,' said Dash. 'Now, ask me how much I'm asking for them – it's all right, I'll tell you.' As he climbed down from the van and opened the back doors, he went into the familiar story, the whole got-to-get-rid-of-them thing, wanting beer money, 'Well, a night out, at least. What do you reckon a night out's worth, then?'

The speakers stood at the lip of the van.

The kid shrugged. 'Dunno what a night out costs, mate, it's all students' union with me, innit?' He grinned and mimed doing a little dance, arms close to his sides, the approximation, presumably, of a night out down the students' union.

'Well, a hundred quid, I reckon,' said Dash.

'Jesus, your nights out, maybe.'

'I don't mean literally, mate. I mean that's about what I could let these speakers go for.'

Befuddled's mouth turned down. 'To me?'

'If you want 'em. And trust me, I got a set myself – you want 'em.'

'Well, I haven't got a hundred, mate, sorry,' Befuddled Kid looked a cross between confused and genuinely very sorry he didn't have the cash. Something caught his eye and he looked into the back of the van, saying, 'You planning on having a barbecue, then?'

Hopefully not, thought Dash, but ignored the question. 'All right, you've twisted my arm,' he acknowledged the cliché with a grin, 'I'll let you have them for fifty quid.' He gave the speakers a loving pat; not too loud, obviously.

The kid thought about it for far too long, umming and aahing until Dash was beginning to fear Lightweight might spring from the cab in a repeat performance of yesterday. Eventually, they were all in the van and Lightweight was taking them to Holloway Road, where the kid and Dash went to the ATM. Back in the van, the kid was giving them directions.

'Why down here?' said Dash. 'We saw you on the next street up.' He didn't like the way the kid was peering about himself, as though looking for familiar landmarks – the way you would if you didn't know a place very well.

'Oh? Is this not it, then?' he said, mystery solved.

Lightweight hissed loudly. His trembling seemed to have intensified; he was beginning to look like a man in an electric chair. And Dash could sense the irritation pouring off him, the familiar *L'eau de Lightweight* tang.

'Left here,' said the kid, peering.

'This isn't it, either,' said Dash, craning over, trying to see a road sign.

'Yeah, but the street you picked me up on, I don't actually live there. But you get to it this way.'

'I know, but if we go back to where we started you can find your way from there.'

They carried on and reached a junction. A shriek of anguished gears as the van jerked to a stop.

'Left here,' said the kid, seemingly oblivious to Lightweight.

Lightweight over-revved and the van mounted the kerb as they pulled out. Dash looked around him as if he was barely able to believe what he saw. 'This is Holloway Road,' he said, voice suddenly high-pitched. They were on Holloway Road, heading back up, about to describe an almost perfect circle half-way to Camden and back. 'Look, go left here,' he directed, pointing, feeling like the bright one out of the Three Stooges.

'It's not this one,' said Befuddled Kid. Huge *huff* from Lightweight. The kid didn't seem to notice.

'I know it's not this one,' said Dash. He was speaking, really, to both of them, trying to pacify Lightweight at the same time. 'But here's where we started so you can just retrace your steps, can't you, to where you came from?'

They bumped over the traffic humps, each lurch making Dash feel sicker. When he ran a hand across his forehead it came away wet. He tried to take deep breaths.

'Where I came from?' repeated Befuddled Kid, looking confused. 'But I came from a mate's house.'

'*Fuck's sake*,' snarled Lightweight, beside him. The van picked up speed, the three of them jumping out of their seats.

'Right at the junction,' said the kid.

Then, 'No, left.'

Followed by, 'No, it's right.'

'Will you make up your mind?' snapped Dash, then, suddenly, to Lightweight: '*Will you slow down?*'

'Definitely left,' said the kid, banging the dashboard, certain.

And Dash's hands were there too, bracing himself, pushed back in his seat as the van – not slowing, Lightweight's face a picture of pent-up violence – hurtled out of the junction.

For a moment or so Dash felt disorientated as though he was surfing along the tops of cars, the van seeming to drift out into the road, tyres losing their grip. Lightweight grimaced as he roped the wheel round to straighten up. Rubber in pain and blasting horns in their wake.

'Jesus,' managed Dash, the word strangled.

Befuddled Kid was half turned in his seat. 'Fucking hell,' he breathed, awestruck. 'That was some bit of driving, mate.' For the first time he had seemed to register Lightweight's presence, leaning across a still-petrified Dash to deliver his compliment.

'For fuck's sake,' said Dash, recovering the power of whole sentences. 'Will you just. Tell us. Where you live. *And will you*,' to Lightweight, '*slow down?*'

10

The car was delivered that morning. They were due to leave in the afternoon. They used it to go to the Syp, their nearest *super-mercado*, a strange homogenous collection of weird bread, inedible-looking meats, Nescafé and Heinz. And pornography. At least they put it on the top shelf but, Jesus, thought Merle, his eyes drawn upwards as if controlled by wires, some of this stuff. He had a look at the paperback novels for something to read on the way home. All the interesting ones seemed to be in German so he rejoined his wife, who carried a basket. There were some things she wanted to get for the journey back. Little bottles of water for the two of them, some wet wipes, some sweets for the girl who'd looked after the cat and a bottle of something foul and green for a neighbour. Around them the salt of the earth were buying their food. They were mainly English and German and just as Merle remembered them, but wearing fewer clothes this time: loud, obnoxious, seemingly oblivious to everything, even their own children. Soon, he thought darkly, in a matter of hours in fact, he would be forced once again to share airport space with them.

She paused and picked out some strawberry Jaffa Cakes; or, to be strictly accurate, some Jaffa Cake-*style* cakes. The holiday's single bonus as far as Merle could see was that you could get them in a flavour other than orange.

'Do you want to take a packet home?' she said, brandishing it at him.

'Yeah, great, thanks,' he said, touched.

'Well, we haven't got room and they'll get crushed anyway,' she laughed, putting them back on the shelf.

A little boy did some skids past him and he reflected that the supermarkets at home didn't have skiddy tiles like this one; in fact, the last time he'd visited one it had had adverts stuck on the floor. Huge stickers grubby from thousands of pairs of shoes. Jesus, this place. All the dirt was on the shelves.

'Oh, I'm only joking, you can take a pack if you want,' she said, and he did, flashing a mind-where-you-go look at the skidding boy.

They walked on. 'But you have to carry the basket, Gentleman Jim,' she said, and gave it to him. They stopped by the booze.

'By the way,' she said, 'don't think I didn't hear you yesterday, asking after Trisha Campbell.' She looked at him, part smirk, part accusation.

'In a professional capacity. She's Chick's wife.'

'I see,' she said archly. You had to be careful with her when she was like this, he knew. She had this trick of pretending to take something lightly so you got over-confident, and then she'd swoop. It meant that he could never assume she was joking. 'And how was she, Trisha Campbell, the girl you once said I should be more like?'

Almost twenty-five years ago, it had been. Trisha Campbell had had a way of wearing her skirt that he'd liked. He'd thought Trisha was something of a style queen (he hadn't been present when all the other girls called her a slut), so he'd suggested to Karen that she wear her skirt like that. Not that he wished she could be more like Trisha Campbell, just in that one sartorial aspect, that was all. Merle tried to explain this as they passed a display of huge water bottles with plastic handles.

'Well, go on, then, how was she?' said Karen, smiling broadly now.

'Okay, she's okay. She's had a boob job' – *what* did he say that for?

'Has she? Oh, Clive, she's had a boob job. Clive . . . you're going red.'

'I am not.'

'You are. And you're doing that smile, like your lips are dancing.' She shook her head at how disgusting and predictable men were. 'Trisha Campbell,' she said to herself. 'Got a boob job. Her age.' Then, to Clive, 'How big did she go?'

'I don't know, do I?'

'What? Didn't you find out? I'm surprised at you, Clive. I bet she went big. Great big pendulous ones.'

'Thing is,' said Clive, wanting to be the architect of her entertainment, not the butt of it, 'they were a birthday present from Chick.'

'Birthday present?' She laughed. 'Well, don't you go getting any ideas. I'm happy with perfume.'

11

Chargrilled and Kris might have been no fans of the stereotype, but still, there were certain situations that called for it and sitting here now, hunched forward, prowling the streets for Try Slapping, was one of them. At least that's what Chargrilled thought as he simmered, slowly and meaningfully smacking the baseball bat into the palm of his hand, the *spak-spak* of bat on flesh the only sound in the cab as they searched for their nemesis: I'm going to try slapping the top of you, motherfucker, thought Chargrilled, a little bit of him applauding the thought.

They came to a junction: road to Camden off to the right, traffic crawling past, Islington to the left, craning both ways to look for the rival team. There was a flash of red livery as a double-decker went past, then stopped, an illegal van in the bus lane kangarooing to a halt behind it.

It stopped right across the junction, the two vans at angles to each other, a Try Slapping in White shape. Chargrilled and Kris sat there, agape, watching the three occupants of the cab, who seemed to be involved in some kind of fierce disagreement.

The bloke in the middle, the white speakerman, looked their way, then back at whoever he was shouting at, then did a double-take and looked their way again. He squinted, pushing his face forward, like, were his eyes deceiving him?

He stared. Chargrilled and Kris stared back at him. Chargrilled raised the bat into view. The white speakerman jumped like he'd been goosed, then was turning to the driver, shouting something at him.

It was 'Go. Shit-fuck, go, get a move on. It's the Holloway boys.'

They'd come barrelling down the bus lane, a three-headed Shout-a-Tron. Lightweight had finally broken a tetchy silence and the three of them were suddenly all arguing at once, Dash forced into a peacemaker role.

Now Lightweight followed the path of Dash's finger and saw the van, and the bat, and yanked the wheel to the right, dragging the van out of the bus lane and into the traffic. Cars moved for them, just. A path opened up and Lightweight urged the van into it, taking it across the traffic into the far lane, the road clearer here, gunning the engine, gears complaining.

A look in the wing mirror told Dash that Chargrilled and Kris had done the same thing, using the channel created by maniac Lightweight, themselves pulling away from the congestion. Their van: same make, same model, same year probably. It just seemed faster to Dash, sleeker, more graceful. It didn't have Lightweight driving it, that was the thing. Dash was now gripping the dashboard with both hands. Next to him Befuddled Kid did the same. He was aware of Lightweight now – he'd woken up to that particular danger.

'Um, look, mate,' said Befuddled Kid, 'perhaps you should just give me the money back, yeah? Drop me off here. I'll find my own way home.'

'Don't worry, we'll get you home,' said Dash, trying his best to sound like this was nothing more than a wee glitch. Lightweight pulled into another bus lane, shooting past traffic on the outside. *Jesus, they have cameras for this kind of shit! If the police see us we're fucked!* Behind them Also Available in White was doing the same thing. Dash could no longer see the occupants, just the pitiless oncoming cab, the grille like bared teeth, nose to the floor, hunting them down. 'Go left here.' He desperately wanted them off the main drag.

Lightweight hoisted the wheel round and, once again, the van tilted almost dangerously as they rounded the corner.

*　　*　　*

14:39. Soon be 14.41, and that, thought Chargrilled absently, was probably a proper palindromic time. Their little bubble clock had its work cut out staying upright as they, too, hurtled into the side road.

Up ahead Dash's fingers were like claws on the dashboard. He was petrified, half expecting a child to come darting out from between parked cars, a ball bouncing away from him. Or a homeless lady, her pram full of carrier-bags knocked high into the sky by their speeding van as she waved an angry fist. Befuddled Kid was keeping his mouth shut, either judiciously or because he was simply too scared to speak, Dash couldn't tell. All three were now pitched forward, half braced for impact, half willing themselves onwards.

'Go right,' said Dash, trying to think, working out that they couldn't be far from Camden, where they might be able to lose the other van round the back of the market, get rid of the fucking kid, and then . . . Then what? He glanced into the wing mirror – Also Available gaining. He could see their two faces, he could see something red, like an air-freshener, stuck to the top of their dashboard; he could see the tip of the baseball bat in the passenger's hands (and if he'd been able to freeze the image and view it at his leisure he might have laughed at how it looked as though he was grasping his own, huge, unfeasibly bulbous penis). Then they were at the junction and Lightweight was releasing a greatest-hits package of dangerous driving: mounting the pavement, shooting out into the path of oncoming traffic where they were received by a blanket of angry horn-blowing from evasive-action drivers, their faces a mix of fear and outrage.

Still, though, you had to hand it to the grey man. He didn't hit a single vehicle, nothing hit them and, what was more, they were out of the junction, speeding off – and Also Available in White? Dash checked. There it was, nose out at the junction, not attempting anything quite so suicidal, fast becoming just another dot in the mirror.

'I think we've lost them,' said Dash, something you tended to hear only in films. The thought made him laugh. Beside him, Befuddled Kid caught the bug and both of them were laughing nervous, white-boy laughs. Lightweight pursed his lips in silent anger and hawked a greeny out of the window.

Befuddled Kid – maybe it was the excitement of the chase knocking something loose – suddenly got better, and really quickly, at the whole navigation lark. Some minutes later they were pulling up in front of a row of Victorian conversions and Dash and he were jumping out. Dash, a puddle of nervous sweat, head twitching, helped drag a speaker to the front door. The kid waved goodbye. 'That was a blast. I think,' were his parting words.

Dash slammed the rear doors shut and saw the words 'try slapping the top of this fucker' scrawled on the back.

'Idiot.' Angrily he wiped it off with the ball of his hand, leaving a clean band in the dirt.

He climbed in and looked over at Lightweight. 'Well done,' he said. 'That was some good driving.'

Lightweight was into the compliment, but expressed it by sneering a what-a-bitch look at Dash, then, 'Where to now, man?'

'Home, back, to get another set.'

'Then where?'

'Back round here.'

Where there be demons, yes, but he had no choice: time was getting on, he still wasn't there yet. He had just one bat-blind desire: to get the cash.

12

'What am I looking at?' Max sat in front of Verity's computer screen. She stood over him, hand on the mouse.

Verity was pleased with herself. Max's revelation about Ben had lost her sleep so she'd padded to the computer in the early hours to see if she could find anything that might bring her peace of mind. The idea of going to the police was torturing her: loyalty to her brother pulling her one way, ethical, civic, moral duty another. She was looking for something to ease her conscience.

And she'd found it. She'd found something that made her sit upright in her seat and gasp. As she was saying now, to Max, 'They can't have him, because, look,' and she clicked to a story in her cache.

Max read:

LET'S BRING HIM HOME

Extraordinary times call for extraordinary actions. And in these worst of all days, when a six-year-old boy can be kidnapped in a crowded London tube station, we must all play our part.

That is why today we are offering a reward of £150,000 for information leading to the safe return of Ben, or to the identity of his captors.

It's the least we can do.

Editor Griffin Todd, said: 'It is our duty to reflect the desires and wishes of our readers, and at the moment the nation has but one longing.

'To see Ben returned safely to his family.

'We hope that by offering this sum it may prove the final

incentive for someone to come forward. Somebody, somewhere will know where Ben is. Knowing they have financial security may persuade them to do what they know in their heart of hearts is the right thing.'

Head of the hunt to find Ben, Detective Chief Inspector John Strapping, said: 'We firmly believe that Ben is alive but being held against his will, probably by a woman. This may be a woman you know. Perhaps a friend, neighbour or family member who may have been acting out of character recently. If you think you know who this person is I urge you to get in touch. We need your assistance.'

Today, *we* have done what we can do to help.

Will you?

13

'To you, mate, a hundred.'

It was to be the last sale of the day. He didn't know it yet (although he fervently hoped it, for sure) but it was also to be the last time he would ever sell a pair of speakers. The funny thing was, he was on fire today. Building up the cash, which was pushed, a pleasant, reassuring bulge, into the pocket of his jeans, he had also grown in confidence. If he hadn't been in such a hurry, and wasn't panicking about the deadline, he could probably have sold them at the usual price – that was how good he was today.

But that luxury wasn't his to savour. Glancing at his watch he had – what? – an hour to find the rest of the cash and get to the Flat Cap for six. Hand over the money (hopefully avoid the now-traditional bog visit, kissing the floor like the Pope) then back home, change into his smarts and off to the job interview.

So, no, he wasn't going to risk trying to sell them at full price, he just needed the cash.

The stress of the day had taken its toll on the Auridial leaflet. It was exhausted. It kind of hung in the kid's hand like he was trying to read a piece of boiled cabbage. It was on the verge of extinction, disintegration. The kid barely looked at it, entranced instead by the speakers which – bless them – never failed to work their magic. They posed there like sexy mermaids inviting him to his doom. He looked at them, imagining himself sitting in their shadow, their flanges pulsing.

'How come you only want a hundred for them?' he said.

Dash could see a white van coming down the road, maybe a couple of hundred yards away and approaching to the rear – too early to tell whether it contained the Holloway boys. He had a choice to make: cut off the customer and run, or hang fire and hope it wasn't them. He was too close to leave now – he decided to hold firm.

'Oh, mate,' he said, hardly concentrating on his own words, 'I just want rid of them. All I'm after is a drink for me and him,' indicating the cab, one eye on the approaching van. 'To be honest, if it ever got back I was selling them on for a profit I'd be out of a job. It's a once-only kinda deal, you know? Bit of beer money for me, mint pair of speakers for you. We're all happy.'

The van was turning off. Still impossible to say whether or not it was the Holloway Road boys. Relief gave Dash a friendly punch in the stomach.

'Yeah, all right, mate.'

'Sorry, what?' Dash was distracted. His T-shirt was soaked.

'I said, Yeah. I'll take them for a hundred.'

17:15. Chargrilled was watching the clock again when the van formerly known as Try Slapping the Top of this Fucker suddenly came into view.

Apart from aliens or two-headed women, the enemy van was the last thing either of them had expected to see, having delivered what they thought was the final fright. (They hadn't reckoned on the desperation of Dash.)

Kris said what Chargrilled was thinking: 'Those two, man. They are un-fucking-believable.' The white guy was standing at the back doors, clearly mid-sale, talking to a kid, who stood nodding at him. Once again, Chargrilled and Kris stared with naked amazement at the scene in front of them. 'They're either wrong in the head or they got balls of steel. We gonna take 'em, yeah?'

'Nah, man, hang a left here.'

Kris hissed displeasure but did as he was told, Chargrilled explaining tactics: 'Come round in front of them, so they can't drive away. We'll bust 'em up and we'll tax them, too. They must have takings on them, man. Go right here.'

They went right, now coming up a street parallel to Try Slapping. Two right turns away from cutting off the other van . . .

Meanwhile, Dash clambered into the van and helped the kid in. 'Cash machine – what bank is it?'

'Any'll do, Barclays, but any is okay.'

'Okay, go Holloway Road.' Lightweight performed the world's worst three-point turn, stalling, getting angry honks from a crappy Nissan, but eventually pulling off back in the direction they'd come.

Which was away from Also Available in White, which turned proudly, stealthily, into the street, fully expecting to come nose-to-snivelling-nose with Try Slapping.

Once again Chargrilled was self-parodically slapping his baseball bat into the palm of his hand. At the non-sight before them he stopped. 'Where they gone, man?'

There was no sign of Try Slapping on the street. Kris knuckled the steering-wheel in frustration, throwing a pissed-off-your-fault look at his partner.

'Don't sweat it,' said Chargrilled, his eyes ranging the pavements, thinking quickly. There was no sign of Dash's punter.

'Holloway Road,' he commanded. 'Try the cash machines.'

It was 17:18.

The kid was told to make it quick because there was a traffic warden down the street. As he was a bit nervous of the driver (he probably would never have got into the van if he'd known that the driver would (a) smell as bad as he did, and (b) radiate an atmosphere of barely controlled rage), and because he wanted to get it over with, he didn't ask for a receipt or look at his balance or arrange a mortgage or any of the other stuff you can organise on a cash machine. He dialled up the digits, snatched the cash and darted back to the van.

Inside, Dash had been telling Lightweight that this was the last sale of the day; that as soon as they'd finished with the kid they'd settle up the money and go their separate ways, yeah? He watched Lightweight's face for a reaction because he was still wondering how this was going to pan out – how the grey man would react when they divvied up and his share came to not-much. Not good, he didn't think. His throat constricted at the thought.

'Ready.' The kid was back in the van and they were taking off, all scrunched up together in the front, none checking the wing mirrors to see Also Available in White join Holloway Road, its two occupants who saw the kid climb into the van and the van pull off ahead of them.

'More cash for us,' said Chargrilled, pleased he was right, that he hadn't stuffed it up. Pleased also that they could help themselves to an extra five hundred quid or so.

He noticed that the speakermen ahead had wiped 'try slapping the top of this fucker' off their rear doors, a clean strip there instead. He shook his head, smiling. These *clowns*. 'Just keep on them, man,' he said.

They followed as the rival van moved up towards Archway and past the Private Shop, where Chargrilled and Kris instinctively looked to see if anyone they knew was going in or coming out. Ahead, Try Slapping jerked in and out of traffic, cavalier use of the bus lane from Lightweight. Also Available, a smoother, more stylish customer, kept its distance, biding time, not wanting to burst from cover just yet.

Dash, Lightweight and the kid looked instinctively at the Private Shop as they passed. In the wing mirror, Dash caught a flash of white van, which disappeared momentarily behind a bus. Again it was too far away for him to see whether it contained the Holloway Road boys. As he watched, it slowed to let a car pull out of a junction, not in any hurry. Not them, then, and he went back to fretting silently, letting himself believe that everything was going to turn out okay.

They went left at Archway, turned into the kid's road, this one blessedly certain about where he lived. Dash helped him out with the speakers, then took them to his front door and, leaving speakers and kid in the lobby, waved goodbye and scooted back to the van. He threw a look down the road. Back at the junction with Holloway Road there was another white van. The sight stopped him. It was parked up, although he didn't remember it there when they'd driven into the road. But it *was* parked up, and some distance away, too. He squinted hard at it, unable to see whether it had anybody in it and wishing all white vans didn't look the same, that the other crew had some distinguishing feature on theirs – one you could see, anyway. Couldn't be them, though, not just parked up like that. He climbed into the van.

'He's getting back in,' said Chargrilled. They were peeping over the dashboard. They'd crouched there while discussing whether to confront them now or follow them some more, debating the relative merits of here or not here; formulating their plan of attack. Kris, no weapons, just fists honed on the streets of north Finchley, would take the passenger side. Chargrilled wanted the lanky black geezer to whom he had taken a fierce (and, he didn't know it, but suspected, a wholly reciprocated) dislike. Here or not here, though? The decision was made for them as Dash reappeared, cast a look their way, stopped, prairie-dogged to see, then got back into the van. 'Phew,' they went. He didn't know it was them. Kris righted himself in his seat and turned the engine over. Their eyes went to the exhaust of Try Slapping, and they waited for it to fire up.

But it didn't.

Inside, Dash looked into the wing mirror. The other van sat there. *Not them*, he told himself. *Calm down, it's not them.* All the same . . . 'Let's get a move on, shall we?' he said.

Lightweight flicked a fag butt from the window, turned and blew a final lungful of smoke into Dash's face, casting him into a nicotine shroud from which he emerged looking watery-eyed. 'Nah, man,' he said, slowly. Deliberately. His voice like creaking gallows. 'Settle up, you said. Once we'd dropped this guy. How's about we do that now, eh?' He smiled a deathly rictus and held out a trembling hand.

'Yeah, okay, no worries. Here you go.' Dash pushed a hand into his pocket, the denim wet, money sticking to his skin as he rooted, and drew out a balled-up wad of notes. He counted damp money into Lightweight's hand. Moist tenners. Thirty, forty, fifty.

With his other hand Lightweight removed the cash from his outstretched palm and put it on his side of the dashboard, safe-keeping. His other hand stayed where it was. The death's-head smile. The hand still there, outstretched and trembling. They both looked at it, as though it had grown suddenly without either of them noticing.

'Look, mate, it's what you're owed,' said Dash, his eyes not leaving the hand. He said it like he hadn't been half expecting this all along, like yesterday never happened. 'That's the deal.'

'Nah, man,' drawled Lightweight. 'Gimme half.'

Half? 'Come on, mate.' A drop of sweat pinged on to his T-shirt, then another. 'I owe Chick. I can't give you half.'

Lightweight hissed, 'You ent hearing me right, bitch. Gimme half.'

'I could tell Chick about this. It's his money. I owe it to him.' *I'll tell on you.* He knew how utterly beaten he sounded. A younger version of himself, court jester in the kingdom of the hard lads, would have mocked whatever luckless victim had said that. Like, *Ooh, scared.* And those year-below victims, what were they doing now? Settled? Successful? There were evenings when they took the tube home after drinks with mates from work, bit squiffy and their thoughts turning to schooldays. They thought of Dash, the wisecracking commentary to their moment of pain. They hated him more, even, than the owners of the hands that had dug into their blazers, trawling for dinner money, pulling ties so tight they could never be unknotted, slapping and gobbing. They hated him more than they hated the hard lads because he was so nothing without them; they dreamt of it being one-on-one. Them and Dash. And whatever Dash was doing now, they wished him ill with it. They hoped that that big-gobbed, lippy, sarky kid was dead or in prison. And suddenly Dash wished he could find them. Say sorry to Colin Stumple, the Stutterman. Stumple came on to the Dash radar, and no matter how far away he was, even at the opposite end of a long, linking corridor, Dash would cry, 'It's the St-st-st-st-stutterman!' Tracking his shameful journey, casting him a soul-crushing searchlight, hailing him with a stutter-past. He wanted to s-say s-sorry to Colin Stumple. He wanted to say sorry to Gavin Porter, whose mum-prepared bottle of orange juice he'd nicked and pissed in, then sat with evil-faced mates as a lunchtime Gavin Porter opened and sniffed at his packed lunch, its cargo of leaky bottle and Dash-piss. Sorry to Jason-oh-what-was-his name because he'd hung around as Jason manfully (showing more courage and character and resolve than Dash would ever possess) stood up to his tormenters, hung around going, 'I don't think you wanted to do that,' in the catchphrase of the day, as Jason-oh-what-was-his-name curled up outside the school gates and vicious trainers thunked relentlessly into his body, arms pin-wheeling for balance. 'I don't think you wanted to do that.' Two hard-lad groupies – single mothers-in-waiting – laughing it up with him as Jason-oh-what-was-his-name raised his bloodied head and was sick on the pavement, a final kick thudding into his side, fags stolen anyway, Walkman bust for his trouble.

He wanted to apologise and say to them all that it was okay; things had turned out as they should, the world was working fine. Because he had not prospered and was not happy, justice had been done, and that they had been right: he was so nothing without the hard lads.

'Gimme half or I'm taking it all.'

'No.' The word was devoid of any meaning. It was a strangled, pathetic holding pattern, postponement of the inevitable. And then Lightweight was fishing in his jacket, there was a ratchety click and Dash had a box-cutter at his throat. Gasping, he felt the pressure of the blade there, knew it had cut and felt a tiny droplet of warm blood run down his neck. His chin was angled up, his eyebrows gone comically high as though he'd been crudely face-lifted against his will.

'Now,' said Lightweight, with the curled lip of a man who tortures pets for fun. 'I'll tek it now.'

'Uch, uch, okay,' managed Dash, and he raised a holding-nothing hand for Lightweight to see, shifting his weight, Lightweight adjusting the blade against his neck minutely, a warning look, pushing the hand into his jeans pocket and reaching for the rest of the cash. He pulled out a cauliflower-head of notes and tossed them to the dashboard, his body staying rigid as if he was paralysed from the waist up.

'More,' said Lightweight. Press of the blade against neck. 'There's more.'

'Look. Please . . .' said Dash and felt in return the knife dig at his throat. He was pulling up from the blade, his head angling away and seeing in the wing mirror that the van, which had been parked up before, had now moved. At least, he thought it was the same van. It was as though it had crawled forward; was now parked just two cars away.

17:38. Chargrilled and Kris looked at one another, the van ahead not moving.

'Pull forward.' Chargrilled pointed at a space two cars behind Try Slapping.

Also Available in White nosed into the road, growling forward, haunches tensing, Kris ready to gun it if Try Slapping suddenly leapt away.

'Here,' Chargrilled whispered unnecessarily, and they slid into the spot, Try Slapping motionless ahead, nothing from the exhaust. 'Kill the engine, man, kill the engine.' They sat there a moment or so, then Chargrilled looked up the street, craned to see behind, too.

'Okay,' he said, hoisting the bat. His hand was on the doorhandle, finding the give and holding it at the click. 'Ready?'

Kris nodded ready.

'Let's fucking do them.'

*   *   *

And, Dash noticed, the passenger door was open. A delivery, perhaps? Even with the blade at his throat he thought this, weighing the odds: a delivery, the driver darting quick-style to someone's front door, depositing a package, back in a trice. Because there was nothing on the front of Also Available in White to identify it. But then again, that was wrong because (and his neck seemed to tighten, the blade pushing, Lightweight, '*More. There's more*') there *was* something, wasn't there? That red thing like an air-freshener on the dashboard. 17:39.

They must have been waiting a moment or so at the rear of the van, indicating to each other like mercenaries on a final jungle mission. Suddenly, in the wing mirror, Kris – mirror-shaped. Dash's eyes flicked to the driver's mirror and there was Chargrilled, a parody of Man With Bat, hunched and holding the weapon to his chest like a thug in a videogame.

It happened so, so quickly. Wasn't this sort of thing supposed to take place in slow motion? It didn't. He had time for two thoughts: *shit*, followed by *great*. He was already twisting away from the box-cutter, the knife left suspended in thin air. He bashed the lock down just as Kris reached the door and the handle jiggled angrily but didn't open. Lightweight realised – too late – that Chargrilled was at his back, a split-second behind his partner. Chargrilled yanked open the driver's door – *thunk* – and Lightweight was sent off-balance, eyes wide, Chargrilled pulling him from the van and into the road with insouciant ease.

Lightweight hit the tarmac with a sound like rolled carpet dropped off a balcony.

The bat thwacked into his body with a sound like somebody beating that carpet.

He had time for an '*Urgh*'.

Chargrilled saw the box-cutter in one flailing hand (Lightweight was all arms and legs, like an overturned insect) and brought the bat on to Lightweight's wrist smartish. The box-cutter dropped. Lightweight rolled and tried to stand as Chargrilled stood over him, straddling him, raising the bat to make sure he wasn't going to get up, no way. Shiny with effort he swung the bat again, this time with a 'Fucker!' as he brought it down. And again – why not? 'Fucker!' *Thwack*.

'FUCKER!' *Thwack*.

A car that had stopped in the street started to reverse. The driver's face was like he'd intended the whole time to stop and reverse; as if there was nothing untoward happening here, nothing he'd bother reporting. Just a couple of black guys going at it. Probably some kind of drug deal gone wrong.

'FUCKER!' *Thwack*.

Forgetting to be ironic, Chargrilled swung the bat as if he was at a coal face, all the time some dim part of him imagining that Kris was working a similar magic with the passenger.

Dash had locked the door, though, and, even as Lightweight hit the road with the carpet thud, he was propelling himself across the seats and reaching for the driver's door. The last thing he saw of Lightweight before he pulled the door closed was the grey driver assuming foetal – assuming it like a foetus fearing head injury – trying desperately to wriggle away from the bat.

But Dash was on the inside, and so was the money, and the doors were closed and he punched the driver's side locked, already sliding into the seat and thumbing the ignition.

Yanked from his bloodlust by the sound of the door closing, Chargrilled looked up and heard Kris shouting at the same time. He realised that all was not well on the second front. The van started up and Chargrilled swung at the driver's window. Inside, Dash ducked, a hand reflexively protecting the side of his face. The window crunched. A small anus-sized hole appeared but the glass didn't shatter, registering its disapproval with a seemingly unprovoked crack that made its way across the window like an afterthought. *Kur-ruck*.

For a half-second Dash was genuinely bewildered at the way events suddenly favoured him. As though to escape now would be an abuse of Lady Luck's hospitality.

17:41. He got over that quick enough. The van jerked forward. He stalled but started it again. Then he was driving and, eyes on the mirror, saw the two rival speakermen, a van-sized gap apart. Kris was on the pavement, pissed-off, denied; Chargrilled on the road with Lightweight at his feet. Kris was watching Try Slapping speed off, Chargrilled already turning his attention to Dash's partner, the bat coming up and striking again. Dash saw it and winced, almost feeling the blow. He was away now, but not too far away to see that Lightweight had stopped moving.

The road ahead was clear, the Holloway pair not bothering to give chase. They were stick-men in the mirror now, Lightweight a blob on the floor (that didn't move – could be . . . you never knew . . . He could be . . .). Dash came to a halt at the lights. They were on green but he stopped anyway. He ducked his head and peered into the wing mirror at the road behind. Lightweight was motionless. He glanced at his watch, back at the mirror.

17:42. The bat came up and Kris was there. Chargrilled snapped instantly out of it, hardly needing Kris's restraining hand on his. At his feet Lightweight lay blowing a small bubble of dark red, mucusy blood from his nose. He coughed and decorated the road the same colour. He was alive. Chargrilled realised that, for a second, he hadn't been sure, and in that moment he'd seen an entire alternative reality unfold in front of him: tattoos, push-ups, regular customer at the library trolley. A life he felt he could adapt to, if he had to, but in all his heart he didn't want to have to. But, no, the guy was alive, coughing and groaning and rolling slowly, like a drunk, his arms at his ribs, busted, spitting more blood. Alive.

'Jesus.' Kris said the single word and stared around at the houses. He saw curtains twitch into place. Chargrilled raised himself to his full height and Kris thought he looked a bit green around the gills. He was reaching down to Lightweight, grabbing him by his jacket and pulling him to the side of the road.

'Fuck, man, we better go,' said Chargrilled, also looking at the houses, thinking, What should I do with the weapon? Drop it? Keep it? Yes. Keep it and destroy it later. The pair cantered back to the van, Chargrilled feeling like the bat was red hot and lit up in his hand. They climbed in and Kris saw for the first time that Try Slapping was still in view. It was at the lights ahead, stopped there even though they were green. Chargrilled saw it, too. They stared at the van, idling at the lights; could have gone but hadn't.

Dash's hands were shaking on the steering-wheel. He sucked nervous sweat from his top lip as he watched the Holloway two get into their van and knew that, in turn, they sat watching him. Then it pulled into the road, the stand-off broken. Dash's hand went to the gearstick, ready. Their van pulled up to where Lightweight lay in the gutter.

17:43. Dash watched. He watched, saying, 'Oh, no,' because his mind had conjured the image of Also Available in White delivering the *coup de grâce*. That pitiless bonnet seeming to dip and sneer as its rear wheels crunched over his injured driver. And it looked like the *coup de grâce* might happen – he thought he'd be proved right – because the van did go into reverse. But in it Chargrilled and Kris were aware of Try Slapping up ahead and knew it was coulda-but-not-going – and they knew that the passenger had seen what almost happened, the murder that was so nearly committed. Kris threw the van into reverse to escape the shame of that gaze, three-pointing to let the white boy do what he had to do. Rescue his mate. They'd done enough.

Also Available sped off; Lightweight was in the road. He moved, rolling slightly: one arm flopped over like it was made of tin cans and string – broken, probably. Dash threw the gears into reverse, the van screaming as he raced backwards, picking up speed, hurtling towards where Lightweight lay.

For a second he considered it. Let his van finish what the Holloway Road boys had started. He imagined bumping over the body and the thought gave him an evil shudder, one laced with a sudden sense of liberation. How easy it would be, just to keep on going. The problems it would solve . . .

But then he was out of the van, not wanting to think about what he was doing, sure it was foolish, that he'd end up regretting it, but unable to stop himself nevertheless.

'Jesus' he said, echoing Kris. Lightweight was in a bad way. Broken face, parts of it already puffed and bruising; bleeding from nose and mouth. He had been right about that arm: the fingers were twig-like, pointing in odd directions, knuckles and joints already ballooning to twice their normal size. God knows what state his ribs were in. One of his legs moved as if it was pawing at the road; the other lay still.

'Mate?'

Lightweight groaned. Moments earlier the man had held a knife to Dash's throat and Dash touched his neck at the memory. The box-cutter was on the ground. He picked it up, retracted the blade, tweezered it between forefinger and thumb and dropped it into the pocket of his jeans. Leaning down to Lightweight he said, 'Mate? Can you move?' There was a liquid groan, gurgle-like in response.

Now what? Was it okay to move him? By doing so did he risk, dunno, moving a broken rib perhaps, driving it into his heart and piercing him dead? If that happened would it count as manslaughter? If he left him there in the street and he died would that count as manslaughter, even murder? If he called an ambulance but left before they arrived (because he had to leave, couldn't hang around – 'Six p.m. on the dot,' he'd been told), would that be leaving the scene, and if Lightweight died, then leaving the scene of a murder?

'Mate, can you move?' A moist moan. He bent down and wrapped an arm round Lightweight's shoulders, trying to hold his body still, then hoisting up from the knees. A gurgle turned into a wet scream. 'Okay. Okay, mate. We're gonna get you to a hospital.'

Yeah, one of his legs looked broken: it sort of dragged behind, trainer scuffing the road as Dash slowly walked him to the van. Then, with a burst of strength and more screams from Lightweight, he manoeuvred him into the passenger seat. Thankfully, Lightweight was ironically named in only one respect. Dash darted round the van, saw faces at the windows of the houses, half expected to hear a siren.

(But nobody did call, of course: nobody did anything but watch, relieved at least that the body in the road was being moved out of their street, away and nothing to do with them any more.)

Now with his bleeding but breathing passenger (hoarse, ragged breaths he didn't like the sound of, thinking about those broken ribs, like knives in his gizzard), Dash headed back up to the lights, thinking, Hospital, hospital, and dimly remembering seeing a sign for one near by, back towards Archway. He glanced at his watch and gulped.

18:14. He found the hospital after much searching, missed turns, going-the-wrong-way-down-a-one-way street – that kind of thing. Until, finally, he was driving up the ramp, peering at nests of signs looking for Casualty, A&E, whatever they called it. At the entrance he'd checked for people, seen no one, dived out of the van, run round to the passenger side and opened the door. Lightweight fell into his arms like an off-duty ventriloquist's dummy, his rubbish arm swinging, groaning and attracting the attention of two nurses who chose that very moment to step outside the unit.

Dash had Lightweight on the tarmac, his hands under his shoulders. He looked at the nurses, feeling vaguely like a grave robber. They looked at him, conferred wearily, and one moved back into the unit while the other trotted over, the look of not-another-one about her. 'Name?' she said, kneeling to Lightweight.

'His name? I dunno. I don't know the bloke.' Dash was looking at the van, wanting to get back in, the deed done.

'Hello?' she said to Lightweight. 'Can you hear me? Can you tell me your name?' Then to Dash, 'What happened to him?'

'Dunno. I found him by the side of the road.'

She looked at him, like, Pull the other one. 'What was it? The van?' She studied it as if checking for bloodstains and brain matter.

'No, nothing like that. I, um . . . He's been beaten up, I think.'

'He's been beaten up badly, by the look of things. Hello? Can you hear me?' Lightweight groaned. 'Can you talk? Can you tell me where the pain is?'

Lightweight gurgled; his eyes sprang open.

'There we go,' said Dash, happily. 'Looks like he's going to be fine.' He'd been crouching but now he sprang to his feet, ready to make a move for the van.

'Just a minute, please,' said the nurse. 'Can you wait there a moment?'

Lightweight gurgled a second time, trying to say something to the nurse, who bent to hear him make some moist noises. His finger came up like E.T.'s, pointing towards Dash, who was dancing nervously.

'He says you're a dead man,' repeated the nurse to Dash, then, 'Sorry, no . . .' She put her ear back to Lightweight. More wet sounds. 'You're a *fucking* dead man.' She looked accusingly at Dash. 'Now do you want to tell me what's going on?'

'No. I mean, I really don't know him.'

The nurse shook her head in disgust. Lightweight stopped gurgling. She thumbed his eyes. 'Is he a drug-user?'

'Yes, I think so. Crack. He's recovering, supposedly.' Dash felt duty-bound to give this information.

'So you do know him?' She looked at him and noticed something for the first time. 'What's happened to your neck? Do you want to tell me what really happened? And where do you think you're going?'

Going was where he was going. 'I'm sorry, I'm terribly sorry,' he said, over his shoulder, 'but I've got to go. I swear I just found him by the side of the road,' calling now as he wrenched open the driver's door.

'I'm going to take your number-plate, you know,' she shouted back as he started the engine and drove away.

14

18:38. 'Where the fuck have you been?' Heedless of the landlord and the other customers (the two old crones plus two equally
old Lotharios, all drunk), Chick leant across the table and dragged
Dash towards him, his T-shirt bunched in Chick's meat-fist. 'I
told you six o'clock. I told you to be here at six o'clock, *no
fucking later,*' he bawled wetly into Dash's face, his bottom lip
bulbous, veined, and shining like offal. 'And don't you fucking
dare ignore your phone, you fucking little poof.' Angry spit
crowded the sides of his mouth, Dash getting an early bath.
Chick's balloon face was shot a livid red, anger in every single
blocked pore. In all his life, even in films, even during that bit
in *A Few Good Men* where Jack Nicholson starts shouting at
Tom Cruise, Dash had never seen anyone so angry. For a second
the feeling was vaguely surreal as he found a part of him stepping outside himself to stand in awe of this spectacular rage, as
if he wasn't its subject. But there was the fist at his throat, the
gob in his face . . .

'I'm sorry,' he choked. Chick let go and shoved, sending him
sprawling off the stool. The crones and their boyfriends hooted
as he picked himself up, righted the stool, pushed a hand through
his hair and sat down. He watched Chick with cowed head as
Chick sat shaking, his chin angled, a slight wobble around the
chops. The deep red of his face gradually began to diminish.

'You better have my money,' he said at last, almost petulantly.

Hardly daring to take his eyes off Chick, Dash shifted his hips
to reach for it, exactly five hundred pounds, every penny owed
to Chick.

'Vouchers?'

Inside, Dash sighed. The vouchers. The *fucking* vouchers. He had some as well. Oh, the irony – he'd got them with his barbecue lighter fuel. 'I'm sorry, boss, they're at home. I'll bring them next time. I—'

Chick reached over and slapped him. The blow caught him high up by the eyes, which watered. He held the side of his head, more in humiliation than in pain as, behind him, the crones gasped, then giggled. This was better than the telly.

'Best make sure you do. Now, get us a drink in while I count this lot.'

Slight problem. 'Boss, I don't have any money.'

''S all right, the cash machine's over the road.'

'I don't even have any money in the bank. I don't have a thing.'

Chick looked at him for a long moment. He had Dash's takings scrunched in one hand, bookie-style. And he looked like a bookie, or like a money-lender who should be cast out. He looked like scum, which was what he was. He seemed to decide. 'Tell you what, go over the cash machine anyway. Bloke begs there called Kenneth. Tell him Chick wants the week's money. You can get the drinks out of that.'

'Come on, boss, that's not me, not doing something like that. Please, I sell speakers.'

'Not enough, obviously, if you can't afford to buy a mate a drink,' said Chick, with more patience than Dash deserved. 'Maybe you ought to branch out. I got a bit of work I can put your way per'aps? Get some practice in now.'

'*What?* Boss, I can't—'

Chick held up the palm of his hand. The crones and their paramours gasped again, ready for more violence. 'Do you want another one of these?' threatened Chick. 'I'd get moving if I was you. And don't think this is my round either. You're going to owe me for this.'

Kenneth was an old, paper-skinned man, who looked as though he might have spent more prosperous times selling brushes from a barrow. He held out his hand as Dash came towards him. 'Spare change?' he said, his face hopeful.

'I'm sorry, mate, I'm really, really sorry.' Dash couldn't look at the man, couldn't meet his gaze. 'I come from Chick. He says he wants this week's money.'

Kenneth gobbed. 'How'm I supposed to know you're from Chick? Could be anyone. I ent seen you before.' He was more feisty than he looked. Just Dash's luck that the first homeless person he'd ever mugged turned out to be a sprightly OAP.

'Look, mate, please, I'm sorry, but don't make this any more difficult than it already is. I came from just over the road, the Flat Cap. Chick's in there. He says he wants his money.'

Kenneth shook his head emphatically. 'No. Oh, no, no. I'll give it to him meself. He sends people out, then says he ent done it. It's a fiver here, a fiver there. He uses me like one o' them.' He indicated the cash machine at his back.

'Look, just give me the money.'

There was a KFC cup between Kenneth's feet and simultaneously they both realised it was there. Dash scooped up the cup before arthritic Kenneth could shift his old bones towards it. 'You know what you are, dun'cha?' he said, as Dash tipped out the money: there was enough for a pint of Guinness, just. He pocketed the cash.

'I'm sorry,' he said, and turned to cross the road.

'Scum,' said Kenneth. And he shouted it again as Dash crossed the road. Once more as he pushed open the door of the Flat Cap and went inside.

18:55. Chick had counted the money and was looking mollified as Dash planted a pint of Guinness in front of him. He'd watched that Guinness being poured – watched it like a hawk, telling the landlord (Saxon T-shirt today), 'No shamrock,' and watching him smirk as he reached for a glass.

Why did it have to be Guinness? he thought, looking at his watch, the Guinness left to settle on the drip tray as the landlord went to entertain the crones.

Now he had five minutes before he was due to see Gary Spencer, who was, he reckoned, a good five or six minutes' drive away. This was not good. Maybe not fatal, but not good all the same. What was also not good was the favour he had to ask Chick.

'Boss,' he said, as Chick slipped the counted money into the pocket of his tracksuit top, a grotesque satire on tracksuit tops everywhere. 'Boss, there's something I've got to ask you.' He pushed hair out of his face.

Chick's eyes were hooded, making love to the head of his Guinness as he raised the glass to his lips and slurped. 'Fire away.'

'It's, like, business hasn't been all that good lately. Like I say, I've been struggling a bit. I was wondering . . .'

Chick was looking at him with an intense and genuine interest. He was looking at him the way you might plant something and watch it grow: fascinated, and satisfied that nature was doing its job. It was always going to come to this, thought Dash. Since that first meeting in this very pub, Dash crudely carried away by his new hard-lad mates. He'd never stood a chance. It was always going to come to this.

'. . . wondering if tomorrow I could, like, not pick up any speakers from Phil. Just for tomorrow.'

'Well, then, you'd have nothing to sell.' Sip to hide a smile.

'I have, though. I've got some left.'

'Have ya? What? You got a backlog?'

'Yeah, well. A bit.'

'Consider it done, then. Don't pick up no speakers tomorrow.'

Dash felt as though strong, caring hands had gripped him from behind and pulled him to his proper height. 'Oh, really? Oh, boss, that's great—'

'You're still going to need to pay Phil, though.'

A different, less caring pair of hands pushed him back down. 'But . . .'

'Yeah, cos otherwise how is Phil going to pay me?'

'But I can't – I just haven't got the money to pay Phil tomorrow. What you've got there is the last of my cash. I've got nothing else.'

'That's a problem, then, innit? You could ask him for them on account, but I know Phil, he's a tight little bugger, he'll knock you right back.' He frowned as if considering a great and taxing problem. 'Tell you what, I could lend you the cash.'

Dash nodded and felt his shoulders slump more, if it were possible.

'I should be able to manage that,' continued Chick, 'but on one condition.'

'What is it?'

'You do me a little favour tonight.'

15

19:21. He didn't really have time to fetch Warren's suit from home, but it was on the way so he stopped off.

Leaving the van parked none-too-straight at the kerb he thundered up the stairs, and grabbed the suit, whipped off his clothes and plunged into the trousers, pulling on the jacket over his T-shirt. Damn. He'd been hoping the overall effect would be smart-stroke-cool – kind of Eric Claptonesque. Instead he looked like a man who had pulled his suit on over a scruffy T-shirt. The trousers were too long and, of course, he was matching them with trainers. Again, he'd been thinking of the trainers-suit combo – hip young soul singer in this instance; again, he just looked like a jerk who couldn't afford decent shoes.

But it was Versace. And, like most people, he knew that funny-looking, ill-fitting Versace was infinitely preferable to something without a label. At the very least it sent out the right message – that he was making an effort.

So he transferred the contents of his pockets into the jacket and dived out of the flat, pausing at the bottom of the stairs, listening out.

'A favour tonight,' Chick had said. Dash had been surprised, but it was a weary kind of battle-blunted surprise. The old guy downstairs, an 'associate' of Chick's? And there he was, thinking they had nothing in common. Was he home now? And what exactly had he done to upset Chick? There was no sound so he let himself out, jumped into the van and pulled away. He didn't dare look at the time.

19:28. Gary Spencer's office was a door at the side of a Chinese takeaway, a nameplate announcing his tenancy. Now Dash looked at his watch; he was a bollock-shrivelling twenty-eight minutes late. He composed himself, shrugged back his shoulders, feeling them move, not with the jacket but within it, like he was wearing a soggy cardboard box. He pressed the buzzer.

'Yeah?'

'Hello, it's Da – Darren. I've come to see Gary Spencer.'

'This *is* Gary Spencer, and you're late, mate.'

It had been a long time since Dash had attended a job interview. In fact, scratch that, Dash had *never* attended a job interview. The nearest he'd come was careers lessons at school, where the teacher's task had been to teach kids the basics of interviews, and Dash's task had been to wind up the teacher. He didn't think a humorous mock interview where he'd claimed to be a disabled astro-physicist was going to help him much here. Still, though, there were the basics, the common-sense stuff; you had to turn all the negatives into positives. He'd decided on the drive over that he was late because he'd been working hard at his job – that was the kind of professional, conscientious employee he was, and imagine how you, Gary Spencer, might benefit from that same conscientious and professional approach to work. What an asset Dash might be.

'I'm terribly sorry,' he said, into the grille below the name-plate, trying to make himself sound as posh and businesslike as possible. 'I'm afraid I got involved in a work . . .' (*work what?*) '. . . issue,' he cringed, 'that I couldn't get away from. Um, that it wouldn't have been professional to walk away from.'

'All right, all right. I don't want your life story. You alone?'

'Yes, of course.'

'Of course nothing, mate. Wait for the buzz, then push the door. Come up to the first floor. First office on your left.'

Dash went in, looked warily around. What had he expected? Glass lifts, security guards and receptionists with fluttery eyelashes? No, but still. The building was kind of manky, if he was honest. He found himself at the bottom of an echoey stair-well painted public-convenience blue. The stairs themselves were covered with a half-dead carpet, stench of cigarette smoke in the air. Dash realised he had no idea of the nature of Gary Spencer's business as he climbed the stairs. All he'd known was that as long as it wasn't selling speakers he would be happy. Now, for the first time, the thought 'Out of the frying-pan, into the fire' formed in his mind, but he chased it away and climbed up to the first floor. He came to a landing, a door wedged open, which led into Gary Spencer's portion of the building. Rubber plant, small table piled high with ancient copies of celebrity magazines, a wall-mounted coffee machine with a Post-it note announcing 'not working' stuck to it. And, sure enough, three doors.

The first on his left was ajar. He knocked. Gary Spencer said, 'Come,' and Dash briefly thought that if the careers teacher had said, 'Come,' during the mock interview then he would have been severely punished for it. But this wasn't the mock: it was the real thing. So he came.

Gary Spencer sat behind his desk, looking even more shiny and leather-skinned and violently hair-gelled than he had before. In front of him was a glass of what was probably cranberry juice, a smoking fag in the ashtray. He pushed himself back in his seat as Dash came in, stretched expensively, flashed too-white teeth. 'Darren. Sit down, mate.' The gravel-pit voice fitted him like a glove.

Instantly Dash knew that he was hopelessly in awe of Gary Spencer: the suits, the cough-sweets voice, the tan. (And had he stopped to think, even for a second, he would have recognised his in-awe feeling: it was exactly how he had felt when he met Chick, the leisurewear, the baseball cap, the cough-sweets voice . . .)

Gary Spencer appraised Dash. 'Nice suit,' he said. 'Armani, is it?'

'No, it's Versace,' said Dash.

'Course, yeah. Should've recognised the cut.'

Dash instantly made it his life's ambition to 'recognise the cut' of expensive designer suits. Whatever it was Gary Spencer did here, he wanted in.

'Must have cost you a bit,' said Gary Spencer.

Dash nodded, worldly-wise. 'Yeah, a bit.'

'Why din'cha get the right size, then?'

Which threw Dash. Smirking, Gary Spencer leant forward and picked his fag from the ashtray, sucked on it so hard that Dash could hear it burn, then bashed it out. The ashtray was the same thick, jewelled glass as the cranberry-juice beaker.

'Um,' said Dash, thinking, How do I get out of this?

'It's all right, ignore me, I'm just pisser-pulling.' He leant back and shrugged himself into his own, neatly fitting suit. He looked at Dash, but his eyes seemed to flick to the side and Dash realised that there was a mirror on the wall behind him. Gary Spencer put his ring finger to his eyebrow and smoothed it down. Dash had never in his life, not once, smoothed down his own eyebrow but he was already filing the gesture away for his new incarnation.

'Ah.' Dash smiled. In on the joke. The butt of it, yes, but in it on it.

'Well,' Gary Spencer spread his hands, 'now you're here at last—'

'Yes, like I say, I'm really sorry about that, but—'

Gary Spencer silenced him with a Pope-like palm. 'Don't matter, don't matter. Maybe you'll be as dedicated when you work for me, eh?'

Dash, nodding, awarded himself a gold star for good excuses, pulling his lateness out of the fire like that, Of course, of course. Nodding too much and looking a bit silly, so stopping himself.

'Why don't you start by telling me a bit about yourself?'

'I'm afraid I don't have a CV,' said Dash. He'd thought about this on the way, anticipating (or told to anticipate by the exasperated careers teacher, who'd thought at the time, Laugh it up, dole-boy. Laugh it up) that there would be some kind of 'tell me about yourself' question, and that it should be met with a neatly folded CV pulled from the inside pocket of the Versace and a talk through its salient points. Gary Spencer gave him an amused don't-matter look as Dash continued, 'But I can tell you what I do now,' which was the first and only job he'd had, he might have added, but didn't. 'As you know, I'm in the audio-equipment trade.'

'Yeah, yeah,' said Gary Spencer. 'That's right. Tell me a bit about that. How'd you get into that racket?'

Racket? Did he mean racket, as in job? Or racket as in scam? Dash thought the latter but decided to press on as if the former was the case. 'Well,' he said, 'I spotted an opportunity to go into business for myself . . . or, rather, an opportunity for me to branch out and offer myself . . . a new challenge.' Gary Spencer nodding, good, good; Dash thinking, Yeah, 'challenge', nice one, Dash. 'And this opportunity presented itself so I grabbed it with both hands.'

'Excellent, excellent. And what does it involve exactly?'

So maybe he didn't know about it. 'Well,' said Dash, 'it's a street-distribution enterprise. I buy the speakers and sell them to customers at low prices. No overheads, you see.'

'Right, right, yeah. And these speakers, what make are they, then?'

'Auridial.'

'Auridial?'

'Yeah.'

'Well, now.' Gary Spencer leant back to consider. 'I'm a bit of a stereo man myself, wife says it keeps me off the streets. Can't say I've ever heard of Auridial, though.'

Dash felt a mild twinge of disquiet, dismissed it. 'That's because they're professional quality,' he said, his smile suddenly forced.

'B&O, I've heard of. Denon. Nad. Technics – I've heard of them, too. Never heard of . . . what was the name again?'

'Auridial – but that's because they tend to use them in clubs and bars and studios and that. They don't get . . . you know, in the home that much.' Not in most people's homes anyway, he thought, an image of the Clarke Street speaker herd in his mind.

'Well, they don't unless you're around to sell them,' said Gary Spencer, smiling.

'That's right.' Smiling back. Steering the talk into calmer waters. 'So, anyway, I've been in the audio-equipment business now for—'

'They work, though, do they?' interrupted Gary Spencer. 'I mean, they're pukka an' all?'

'Oh, yes. They're blue-chip.' *Blue-chip?* Nice. Cooking on gas here.

'Good bass?'

'The best, yeah. They're famed for their bass. Because of being in clubs and that.'

'I see.'

'So . . . shall I continue?' He was keen to move on because he had a little speech planned about wanting to develop the sales skills he'd acquired in a different arena, one that was less . . . 'van-orientated', shall we say?

'What sort of people buy them, then, these Auridial?'

'Sorry?'

'What I mean is, what sort of people do you stop in your van?'

'Well, discerning people. Blokes like you. You know, people who look like they might know a thing or two about decent audio equipment.'

'Speakers.'

'Yeah.'

'You don't sell any other audio equipment, just speakers?'

'That's right.'

'Just wanted to get that straight. Do you have to do much of a sales job on them, then, these discerning blokes you stop?'

'Ah, right, yeah. Well, of course, since I started the job I've been developing my sales techniques and I think I've managed to reach the point where I can sell pretty much anything to anyone, which is why I'm hoping to—'

'Snow to Eskimos?'

'Bring it on,' laughed Dash.

Gary Spencer didn't laugh back. 'That's what I like to hear, because that's exactly what I sell.'

Dash studied Gary Spencer carefully. He looked serious, not

even the beginnings of a smile. 'Is it?' he said cautiously, trying not to commit himself. Maybe this was an interview technique the careers teacher hadn't known about. Better play it safe.

'And the thing is,' continued Gary Spencer, 'they're mainly women, these Inuits to whom we sell snow. Is that going to be a problem for you?'

'Um, ah, no, I don't think so,' said Dash, thinking, Maybe it's some kind of snow substitute. Oh, God, it's not cocaine, is it? Snow to Eskimos. It could be some sort of code for selling coke to people who take coke.

'You ever sell your speakers to women?' asked Gary Spencer.

'Not really, no. I mean, you know yourself, it's mainly blokes into that kind of thing.'

'Right, right, yeah. So you've never sold a set to a woman?'

Dash thought about it. 'Well, I have, yes. Once.'

The bird in the Merc who had the long, delicious legs. He'd stopped her in more carefree times – those days when he and Warren had been rocking it. She'd just unfolded her long, delicious legs from a soft-top outside the Perfect Fried Chicken along Stoke Newington high street. He'd stopped more for the chat than anything else; ended up selling her a set for *five hundred quid*. 'A very stylish woman,' Dash told Gary Spencer, doing all but winking at his prospective boss. The speakers were a present for her husband, she'd said, but what Dash remembered about that particular encounter was that she was *definitely* coming on to him, and he insinuated as much as he told the tale, adding that she'd said – now he remembered it – how her husband was a bit of a stereo man, which just goes to show the kind of discerning . . .

And as he relayed the story he thought that (come to think of it) Gary Spencer was a bit of a stereo man, and looked like the kind of bloke who'd have a wife with long, delicious legs who drove a soft-top Mercedes. Dash felt an urgent tickle at the back of his neck, that feeling of disquiet again. Gary Spencer was looking hard at him. 'You did well there, then, son,' he said, coldly.

'Well, you know . . .'

'Bit of a cracker, was she? Bit lively?'

'Well, no, not really . . .' Dash was shaking his head.

Gary Spencer sat staring at him, his chin resting on a fist that looked too clenched. Then: 'Tell you what,' he said, standing and holding out a guiding hand to Dash. 'Why don't we go next door and have a look at the snow-selling operation, eh? You've got yourself a job if you want it.'

Suddenly that wasn't such great news. Dash had a bad feeling about this. He stayed seated. He glanced at the doorway. 'Um, well, perhaps . . . maybe you could tell me a little bit more about the job. I mean, selling snow to Eskimos. It sort of – ha-ha – it sort of sounds like a joke, doesn't it?'

'I promise you,' said Gary Spencer, voice hard, 'it ain't no joke. Now, let's go next door, shall we?'

Dash's legs didn't want to let him stand. The chair didn't want to let him go. He stood anyway, releasing the chair slowly and walking to where Gary Spencer stood by the door, edging along his guiding arm. He glanced at the exit door. It was no longer wedged open and he realised he hadn't heard it close. Gary Spencer was pointing at the next door along. 'Through there,' he said, flint-eyed.

'Thing is, Mr Spencer . . .' started Dash.

'Just go through there. We'll talk about it inside.'

Dash grasped the door handle. Maybe his feeling was wrong. Perhaps he'd turn the handle and walk in, and inside there'd be a little team of friendly salespeople welcoming him to their ranks. 'This is George, he's the office joker,' that kind of thing. He'd be shaking their hands and laughing a private laugh at his overactive imagination.

He opened the door and walked in.

There was no team of friendly salespeople.

'Shit,' said Dash.

16

He was the man they call Paedo.

And why would Trish do that, release Little Ben to a man they call Paedo?

The thought, nagging at him.

'I've got to know,' Trish had said, on the bench in front of the Eye.

Why?

Why did she have to know?

'I'll bring him home,' he'd told her.

'I ent letting you take him out of the frying-pan,' she'd said in reply.

Because she had to know, didn't she, what he was going to do with Ben?

For it to work.

'You see?' said Verity. She thought she was bequeathing him peace of mind. 'You see. They can't have the little boy.' She was excited now. 'If they had him, or if they knew where he was, they'd be trying to collect the reward, wouldn't they? You were right, it's a scam.'

'Yes,' he said, frozen, an instant of knowing that was exactly what Trish and Chick were attempting to do – they were trying to collect the reward. Only it's not like they can roll up to the cop shop, Ben in the back seat, and merrily admit keeping him locked up, cheque'll do nicely, thanks. No, they need a fall-guy. A bloke in the book depository. And who better than the man they call Paedo?

A sudden nauseating, vertiginous sensation. The kind people pay to feel on rollercoaster fairground rides. Scream-if-you-wanna-go-faster. The horror-film, cling-to-your-partner proxy thrill. Only real. Your world shifting, nothing significant any more, things that no longer matter, and it's almost funny that they once did. A great, whooshing, elemental contraction. That was the feeling. Like that.

He felt sick.

Thought he might actually be sick: dump it there on the deep-pile. He rode the feeling, refusing to let it show on his face.

Not that it made anything all right, she'd added quickly. 'You should still go to the police.'

Standing – dazed, but trying to hold it together – he promised her that he would give it thought and he let himself go soft as she came to him and put her arms round him, resting her cheek against his chest and hearing his heart beat. She loved him, then and always, but it didn't mean things could ever be right again between them. Each mourned what they once had.

Minutes later Max left, having made an arrangement he knew he would never keep. He went home, sucking a cigarette and letting himself into his flat where he sat in his old sofa and waited for Trish to ring him. She was betraying him, he knew that now. And, really, he had to congratulate her because that had been some kind of BAFTA award-winning performance she'd given; she'd almost got away with it – would have done if it hadn't been for Verity's efforts. Now he knew, though.

And it didn't change a thing.

Because if he obeyed the Verity voice and went to the police – even anonymously – they'd take him down with them. They had enough to do it, too. He'd willingly handed them evidence of his night-time jaunts to Kettering and, as 'Charlie' had said, there'd be CCTV, maybe even fingerprints, enough to place him as an accomplice.

And if he obeyed a voice of self-preservation, if he did nothing at all – blew the whole set-up – then what of Ben, a little boy locked in a warehouse in Walthamstow? Could he live with himself? Would he want to?

No, it didn't change a thing, knowing he was the fall-guy. Or almost nothing . . .

* * *

Later, he heard the sound of a van in the street and peeked out of the curtain. Darren's van, at the kerb, Darren getting out.

He was wearing a suit jacket with no sleeves, raggedy cuts where they'd been hacked off above the elbows. He wore matching trousers, again bearing haphazard slices where the legs had been shorn off, effectively making them shorts. There was something about Darren, though – the ashen face, the look of pure defeat – that suggested his attire was by far the least of his problems.

Max knew how he felt.

17

It had turned out that Gary Spencer didn't sell snow to Eskimos. Or coke to people who took coke. Whatever he sold – if, actually, he sold anything at all – would forever remain a mystery to Dash.

In the office was a chair and a desk. In the chair sat the woman who drove the soft-top Mercedes, her long, delicious legs crossed, one hand fiddling with her hair. She'd been looking out of the window and was now staring at Dash, who sensed rather than saw a second man just inside the door. On the desk was a pair of Auridial speakers. If he wasn't very much mistaken, they were the very speakers he'd sold to the woman with the long, delicious legs.

'Famed for their bass sound, are they?' said Gary Spencer, from behind him.

Dash made to turn round. In his mind were vague thoughts of trying to reason with Gary Spencer. He was a businessman, after all – they both were. Surely he'd understand . . . But before he could voice the pleading words Dash was in a bear-hug. He was lifted, feet dangling and kicking, then thrown wrestler-style to the deck.

Above him loomed man number two, Gary Spencer's muscle, grinning pit-bull down at Dash.

'You recognise my wife, then?' said Gary Spencer, his face a distant tree-top.

'Urgh . . .' groaned Dash, face to the carpet tiles, already massaging a wrist hurt by breaking his fall. And thinking madly.

Thinking: *Shit*.

Thinking: How can I have been so dumb? *Job interview*. He'd borrowed a suit, for God's sake. His parachute had turned out to be a rucksack. A rucksack full of turds.

Thinking: What are they going to do to me? A beating? A bullet in the back of the head? Dash, who had hit the kid who had Tourette's and now he sleeps with the fishes. Let that be a lesson to all you would-be bad lads.

Thinking: *How am I going to get out of this?*

'I'm really, really sorry,' he managed, prone and hurt.

'You'd better be fucking sorry.' Then, to the muscle: 'Get him up.'

The muscle reached down and grabbed Dash under the shoulders, pulled him to his feet.

'Professional speakers, are they?' said Gary Spencer. 'Professional what?'

'Look, please, I'm really sorry—'

The muscle punched Dash hard in the stomach and Dash went down a second time, coughing. 'Urgh.' His hands were at his stomach. He was on his knees – literally as well as metaphorically.

'Gary,' complained the wife, a sort of wheedling tone to her voice that Dash dimly remembered having been disappointed by when he'd first spoken to her (and didn't he now regret *that* particular sale?). 'You din't say nothing about hurting him.' She should have had honeyed, smoky tones. Instead she sounded like a fishwife. Still, you couldn't fault the sentiment.

'Oi, Frank,' said Gary Spencer, to the muscle. 'Don't hit him. Who said you was to hit him?'

'Sorry, Gal.'

'Spence.' Gary Spencer sounded exasperated. 'Just Spence. And if you're gonna call me anything, can you not make it "Gal". It sounds like guys 'n' gals, dunnit? Just stick to Spence.'

The muscle bridled. 'This I don't get, bruv. What's the point in *me* calling you Spence?'

'He's right, Gary. You're both Spencers,' chipped in the wife.

Gary Spencer ignored his delicious-legged, yet fishwife-sounding missus, sighed and commanded his brother: 'Get him up.'

Frank reached down and hefted Dash back to standing. Dash's hands were still wrapped round his stomach, his insides singing agonised madrigals. Frank perched him on the edge of the desk where he half sat, half stood, wincing, bandaging himself with his arms.

'If anyone's going to hit him, it's going to be me.' Gary Spencer took hold of Dash's hair and lifted his head, fist pulled back. Dash looked at the fist, then mashed his eyes closed, whimpering despite himself; ashamed of the sound but unable to prevent it.

'Gary,' warned the wife.

'Open your eyes.'

Dash shook his head no. Gary Spencer's hand scrunched painfully in his hair. 'Open your fuckin' eyes.'

'Gary.' The wife. Voice like Wednesday-morning drizzle.

Dash shook his head again, eyes screwed tight as raisins.

'I tell you what, mate,' said Gary Spencer. 'You've got some fucking neck on you, I'll give you that.' To his wife: 'This is definitely him, then?'

'Yeah, that's him, but leave him alone, would ya? He's only a kid.'

Dash opened his eyes, hoping it wouldn't be a provocative gesture. The fist was still there, wound back. It moved as if to strike. He flinched away, hair still held. Gary Spencer laughed.

'Gary,' warned the wife again.

'What are we going to do with you, eh?' said Gary Spencer, the fist still threatening.

'Please, look, I'm really sorry,' said Dash, a cry-baby break in his voice.

'Go through his pockets.' This to Frank, who thrust his hands into Dash's jacket, immediately finding and retrieving the box-cutter.

'Uh-oh,' said Gary Spencer. 'He's only got himself a knife. What's this for? You planning on building a model aeroplane?'

'It's not mine,' said Dash quickly. His eyes were on the knife, which was now in Frank's hand. The ratchety click as he extended the blade. A smile like he'd enjoy using it.

'What are you doing with it, then?' asked Gary Spencer, reasonably.

'It's a long story.'

They were crowding in on Dash, the pair of them. He heard the wife in the corner, huffing unhappily, and from somewhere far away there was the sound of a police siren, rising and falling. For a moment Dash fondly imagined coppers bursting in wielding truncheons . . .

The blade was held in front of his face, bisecting Frank's evil smile. Frank raised the box-cutter so the tip of the blade was millimetres away from Dash's eye. Dash heard a pathetic mewl and realised it was his own.

'All right, leave it,' said Gary Spencer, after what felt like an age of wet palpitation, Dash staring at the knife in front of his face. 'We don't want him shitting himself in here, do we? We'll never get it out the carpet. What else has he got in there?'

Dash flashed back to his flat, quick-changing to put on the suit and unthinkingly transferring everything from his jeans into Warren's Versace. Everything, including the two hundred quid for which he'd sold the final shards of his soul. All he had. The lot. And he knew as the muscle's fingers found the sheaf of notes that he'd lost it. In that moment he thought he would have preferred the beating, even the single bullet to the back of the head, a kneecapping perhaps. Anything rather than give up that money. Without it he had two hopes, and one of them was Bob. Without that money his choices had been reduced to a single, solitary option.

'Check it out,' said Gary Spencer, as the money came into the public arena. His brother was already counting it.

'How much did you pay for the speakers, darlin'?' said Gary Spencer, to his wife.

'Five hundred quid,' she replied, peevishly. The guilty speakers sat at Dash's back like butter wouldn't melt.

'There's two hundred here,' said the muscle.

'Which means you owe me three hundred quid,' said Gary Spencer. He let go of Dash's hair now. 'See, I'm gonna let you take these worthless pieces of shit back with you. I'm thinking of inserting them, mind, bit by bit, woofer by tweeter, up your arse. But only after I've got my money back.'

Frank tossed the money to the desk. It fluttered to rest.

'What's the suit worth?' demanded Gary Spencer, slapping at the jacket.

Oh, no. 'Please. It's not mine.'

Gary Spencer mimicked Dash: '"*It's not mine.*" Well, nothing's yours, is it? Van, knife, suit. You got anything that's yours, mate?'

'Not really,' admitted Dash.

'Well, I dunno. What do you reck, Frank? How much is a Versace suit, these days? It's in quite good nick. Bit of wear round the knees, like, recent, but fairly good nick all the same. About three hundred quid, I reckon, second-hand.'

'Please,' said Dash, pathetic, lost and defeated.

'Let's have it.' Gary Spencer stood back, motioning with his hand. 'Come on, let's have it.'

Dash looked pleadingly at Mrs Spencer.

'It's all right, she's seen a bloke in his pants before,' said Gary. 'Here, you're not going commando, are you?' Dash shook his head. 'Right then, let's have it.'

Dash slid off the desk and undid the too-big trousers, letting them drop and unleashing the sudden odour of man in crisis. Same with the jacket, forlornly holding them out to Gary Spencer, who indicated for him to put them on the desk. He was left in boxer shorts, trainers and T-shirt. He shot a look at Mrs Spencer, who appraised him, twirling a lock of hair before averting her gaze.

'On second thoughts,' said Gary Spencer, 'I'm all right for suits at the minute. You want this, Frank?'

Frank said no, not his size, too small. He was smiling a Chilean torture-chamber smile as he said it.

'Well, you might as well have it back, then,' said Gary Spencer. 'But, look, it's a bit too big for you.' Dash knew what was coming. 'Why don't we alter it for you, eh?'

'Please, it's not mine,' repeated Dash vainly, impotent as Frank picked up the jacket and used Lightweight's box-cutter to hack off the sleeves.

Not an easy job. The Versace suit was a well-made garment;

there was the lining to slice through. Frank enjoyed the vandalism, giggling as he worked. His brother joined in. Even Mrs Spencer was laughing it up as Frank went to work on the trousers, customising them to just above knee length. The new clothes were held out for Dash to put on and he climbed into them, unsure whether to be happy – the three of them were enjoying themselves, and were therefore less likely to go down the bullet route – or to feel wretched and ashamed. In the event it was a mix of the two feelings as he stood there, reluctantly modelling the slashed Versace.

'Give us a twirl, Anthea,' commanded Gary Spencer, and the three of them were guffawing as Dash slowly, disconsolately, turned round. 'Arms out, come on, let's see it proper.' Obedient, he held his arms scarecrow-like so they could admire Frank's handiwork.

'Good job, Frank.'

'All right, Gary,' piped up Mrs Spencer. 'That's enough now, okay?'

'Yeah, you might be right,' conceded Gary Spencer. 'One more thing, though.' He brought his face close to Dash. Frank mirrored his brother, the box-cutter held up. A tiny thread of Versace dangled from the blade. 'I want you to apologise to the missus.'

'I'm really sorry,' said Dash quickly.

'No, you fuckin' numpty. Not like that. On your knees.'

On my knees? I'm already there. Dash looked at him, like, Come on. Gary Spencer indicated to Frank, who moved forward threateningly.

'Okay, okay,' said Dash, holding up a stop hand. He turned to where Mrs Spencer sat at the window, suddenly, disgustedly aware that there was something quite arousing about what he was doing. Hating himself for feeling that way as he did as he was told. He bent to one knee, a proposal stance.

'Properly, come on.'

Then the other. On his knees now. Skin chafing on the worn carpet tiles. Ridiculous in his cut-off suit.

'They was a present,' justified Mrs Spencer, almost apologetic, 'for his birthday.' On her face was a mix of sympathy and superiority.

'I'm very sorry,' said Dash, 'for selling you the speakers.'

'That's okay,' she said primly. 'Apology accepted.' She looked above him at her husband frowning, like, Show's over.

'Right,' said Gary Spencer. 'We're finished with you, mate. Now take your fucking speakers and fuck off, and if I ever see you again, it won't be your suit we're slashing. Do I make myself clear?' As if to take the piss, he clicked the box-cutter closed and popped it back into the breast pocket of the jacket, patting it almost affectionately. 'Might need this,' he winked, 'in case you meet the guy the suit *really* belongs to.'

And as Dash, in his oversized, cut-off suit, like some kind of tramp-Scout-Versace hybrid, loaded the speakers into his van, with Gary Spencer and Muscle watching him (the occupants of the Chinese takeaway watching him; passers-by, just people who happened to be walking along the street, watching him), as the shame and humiliation hung over him like the smell of vomit, which once it's in your nostrils seems to inform all your olfactory data from then on, he knew one thing.

He was going to have to set fire to the depot.

Part Four

YELLOW SUBMARINE

1

As well as the noises he heard, Ben had discovered something else about his surroundings. First, that Auntie was telling what his dad called a great stinking whopper about this being her spare room. Not to mention the one about her toilet being decorated.

He was constantly being told that there were people in this world who weren't as lucky as him, so maybe those people had horrible spare rooms, not like his parents, or where he slept when they went to Nanny Snape's. Even so, he was now certain of a number of things. First, a spare room is a part of a house where guests are kept, and houses have toilets that guests are allowed, even encouraged, to use. They're not asked to use buckets, which they then have to cover with a piece of old kitchen worktop that the hostess removes for a few minutes before returning it, smelling slightly bleachy, with a queasy smile. Second, spare rooms where guests are kept have beds. And proper beds. Not this metal thing with scrapy legs that he had to sleep on that had once felt very comfy (courtesy of the white grit) and now was not so.

And, third, who kept metal shelves full of paint pots in their spare room? Up against a wall, they were, a long set of screw-together shelves, like the ones they had in their garage at home in Cowley Close, except older and flaking and not bearing neatly arranged toolboxes, coils of garden hose and various bits of barbecue equipment and watering-cans. These just had paint pots, used ones, it looked like. Most, if not all, had paint caked round the lid and they were stacked, shoved into the shelves, three deep and two or three high, effectively bricking up that wall. It meant you had to go right up and stare through the gaps to see that there was a window there.

But there was. Behind the shelves at what you'd say was normal window height, there was a window.

He'd got into a habit now. In the morning Auntie (or the mystery man) would come with his flask of baked beans and sausages and a bottle of Sunny Delight, which he'd mentioned one day that he really liked. (And he didn't mention to Auntie that he wasn't allowed it at home, only when he went to friends' houses for tea and birthday parties. A guilty thrill whenever he drank that Sunny Delight. 'Muck,' his mother called it. She even tutted when the adverts came on the TV.)

Once he'd finished breakfast under the watchful Auntie eye (becoming suddenly wordless, communicating through smiles and nods as he kept the grit in his mouth ready for spitting it into the bucket), Auntie would leave as he pretended to flake out on the bed. The door would close. He'd open one comedy eye. Before now she'd opened the door again, to check on him, he thought, so these days he was extra specially careful. He'd count to at least fifty, and do it the proper way, 'one-one-thousand, two-one-thousand, three-one-thousand,' until he was sure she'd gone. After that he'd swing himself off the bed and do the spitting thing, then he'd wait until the noises started. How long they went on he wasn't sure, but after some time they'd stop, then there would be a long gap and then he'd have to pretend to be asleep for the second visit, the Chicken McNuggets and the Coke, the drink, smile, wait, spit process again.

There was time, in what he began to think of as his 'day', that he had to himself. Safe time. Between Auntie leaving and the noises starting, for example. And he used it to start looking more closely at the windows behind the shelves. It was like a big game of Jenga. He could drag out tins of paint to see the windows behind. For the most part what lay behind was like turning on the TV hoping it would be cartoons and finding out it was the news – boring and disappointing. The windows were not the opening sort and, worse, even if they were the opening sort they opened out on to nothing. Against them were stacked boxes, completely obscuring them, blocking out light and any hope of an exit. The boxes said 'Auridial' on them.

And then, and then . . . he discovered something else. Two things, really, in fairly short succession. First, there was one window that wasn't quite as secure as the others. A window that could be persuaded to open, in other words; next, like Dash, Ben had cause to marvel at just how little there was inside your average Auridial speaker. This was because, having worked his way into one of the Auridial boxes (surely the boxes he heard being moved around in the day?) he found speakers inside, yet another obstacle in his way. But, hey, like Dash he found that the back of the speaker clipped off easily, and instead of an inside bristling with electronic components ready to deliver superior bass, Ben saw . . . nothing. (Actually, a woofer, tweeter and crossover network, but compared to the space inside the speaker cabinet, nothing.)

He regarded the ever-growing tunnel he was creating, thinking, What if . . . ?

What if he could crawl through the speakers and their boxes until he reached the end? Could he escape? Did he want to?

2

Merle and Karen were waiting in the departure lounge when she said it. Merle had been sitting there attempting to make small-talk, trying not to hate the whole experience. Or, rather, trying not to show Karen how much he hated the whole experience.

'Wonder what the weather's like back home,' he said.

'Mm,' replied Karen, who was trying to read a magazine but was distracted by her husband's leg, which bounced nervily up and down, jogging the plastic seats on which they sat.

'Hope they come round with drinks more than once this time,' he said. 'On the flight, I mean. They only came round once on the way out. You want more than that. Don't you?'

'You do,' she muttered. (Bounce-bounce. Jog-jog.) She was beginning to feel seasick.

Beside her, making comments like, 'Hope the taxi's there for us when we get back,' and 'You know, I've had a lovely time this holiday', Merle was twitchy with distaste for his fellow man. Everywhere he looked people in leisurewear were smoking and filling their faces with food and drink, and in the tiny gaps between face-filling they bawled instructions at their young, who were either slumped with an electronic game, or shouting at one another, or trying to look like football thugs or porn stars, the mini-pops versions, or doing a combination of all three.

And the worst thing was, nobody could see it. Nobody else in the whole place thought this experience was anything worse than mildly boring; most of them seemed to be having the time of their lives. Not only was he in his own personal hell, there was no one around to marvel at the flames. Karen could have done, he knew, but chose not to indulge him; pretended immunity to the constant, profane riot around them.

Until, at last, she cracked.

She put down her magazine, staring at Merle's fidgety legs with open exasperation. 'Will you just calm down?' she hissed.

'I'm sorry, I can't. I'm a bit wound up. These people are winding me up. Why can't they just behave—'

'Stop it,' she whispered angrily. 'They're just people on holiday, doing what people on holiday do.'

'Are they?'

'Yes, they bloody are.' She paused. 'Look, I tell you what,' she said.

'What?'

'You hate everybody so much, think everybody's some sort of scumbag waiting to happen, do me a favour and picture Patrick and Deborah Snape sitting over there with Ben.'

Merle started. 'You what?'

'Go on. Imagine they're sitting over there, in that corner, the three of them.'

Merle looked over to the corner as she said. He did with his imagination what he'd been unable to do in real life: he put Ben, Pat and Deborah back together.

'And what are they doing?' asked Karen. 'Are they sitting there like you, scowling at everyone else like they're from another planet? Or are they just sitting there, perfectly happy, getting on with their own lives and letting other people get on with theirs?'

'They're just sitting there, yes.'

'They are, aren't they? Like everybody else, they're not hurting anybody—' Merle started to say something but she shushed him. 'Not *really* hurting anybody – nobody *sane*, anyway. They're just minding their own business and getting on with their lives. Now, Clive, please, before I start screaming, just get on with *yours*.'

'Okay, okay, I'm sorry.' She'd made him slightly ashamed of himself. She returned to her magazine. His leg continued shaking. She placed the palm of her hand to stop it. 'Sorry,' he repeated, unaware he'd even been doing it.

'Just relax,' she said, more softly.

He looked enviously at her magazine and wished once again

that the Syp had stocked some good books in English. 'What are you reading?' he asked.

'I'm reading about celebrity boob jobs before and after,' she said, smiling. 'Right up your street, really.'

'Yeah, great, let's get a read of it after you, then.' He said it in his best teenage-voice-breaking impression and it cracked her up. He craned over to see.

One of the pictures on the page was of a celebrity leaving a nightclub. She was wearing a baseball cap and had her head down. All you could see was a great split dune of cleavage in a plunging top. It was reminiscent, he thought, looking at it. Like a porno version of the Holloway Road CCTV footage, only with a spangly handbag instead of Ben.

Karen was looking at the picture, too.

She looked at him. She was tapping her lips with her finger, looking very thoughtful indeed. 'When was it then?' she said.

He waited for her to explain herself, at last prompting: 'When was what, Kaz?'

'Sorry,' she said. 'Trisha Campbell's birthday. When was it?'

3

'The front door you can crowbar,' Trish had told him on the phone. Mrs Judas. 'You've got to make it look like a break-in so Charlie won't suspect.' He'd had to stop himself snorting a derisive 'Really?' 'There's a reception they use as an office, but you go through that and into the main warehouse. It's full of speakers but if you go right to the back you'll see another door. There's a corridor full of junk and at the end is another office, one that's never used. It's more like a storeroom – poky little place, it is. That's where he is. You'll make it look like a break-in, won't you?'

'Yes,' he'd responded, blank.

'When you've got the boy, call me to let me know he's safe,' she urged, and he could imagine the wheels such a call might set in motion. If he ever made it.

He didn't have a crowbar, but he did have a hammer and a strong chisel; and it was these he went looking for in the cupboard beneath the stairs.

It was a walk-in cupboard, a good bit of storage for a flat so small, and not the kind of space you'd neglect unless you were Max. In it were painful, material reminders of a life less horrific. He realised it was the first time he'd gone in there since prison, since clearing out the shop and emptying his tools from the van to stow them in the flat for safe-keeping. The cupboard smelt of wood, and his fabric bag of tools was covered in a fine layer of plaster dust, dislodged by his upstairs neighbours thumping up and down the stairs. It was the same in the van. It had been parked at the pavement for so long that litter, mulch and other urban debris had become packed into the gap between its tyres and the kerb – as though the van was forming a symbiosis with the street. A while ago somebody had written 'fucker' in dirt on the side. That was faded now, itself dirty. Inside, though, there was the smell. Sawdust and polish and beeswax. Painfully nostalgic. He'd loved it once and loved it still, but he'd lost its companionship for ever; lost it the day he opened the door to a girl who called herself Feather.

He keyed the ignition and for a sticky moment thought the van might not start. It wheezed and turned over but didn't catch. Max took a deep breath then twisted the ignition key a second time, a third, until the van coughed and he was dipping the accelerator to get it warmed up, realising he could barely see through the windscreen and getting busy with the wash-wipe, a film of disuse gradually cleaned away, a rainbow-shaped hole to peer through. He reached to put the heater on, thinking it should be warm for Ben; thinking how familiar the actions were. As if it was only yesterday. Down in the passenger-side footwell was a coffee mug, and he dimly remembered putting it there, diving out of the flat late one morning, drinking the last dregs of his coffee on the move. At the traffic-lights a girl in one of those new Minis had looked at him, smiled. In return he'd raised his mug in a toast. She'd smiled some more and they'd gone on their way, and whatever she was doing now he hoped she was a damn sight happier than he was.

Now the mug rolled around in the footwell and it annoyed him as he drove. It annoyed him so much that he pulled over on Seven Sisters Road, leant down and deposited it on the pavement, leaving it behind as he carried on to Tottenham Hale, then Walthamstow, bound for the depot.

Once there he parked the van, looked up and down the darkened road and saw . . . nothing. Nothing unless you counted a skip, a lorry trailer (rusting, no sign of the cab), a burnt-out car of indeterminate make, a mattress, the odd vehicle parked here and there.

He stepped out of the van and walked into the yard, only the sound of his footsteps and the hum of distant traffic from a far-off road.

The depot was as Trish described it. An office entrance adjacent to huge roller doors. Perhaps there was a security system, normally. If so, it had been turned off, especially, he had no doubt, for his visit. Everything from here on in was a formality: he was sticking to a script that had been written for him. Doing it obediently. Pulling an old pair of woollen gloves from his pocket he put them on. There would be no fingerprints – not this time. Next he fitted the chisel into the doorframe, half surprised they hadn't left the door open for him, and was about to swing when he stopped, removed the chisel, reached into his back pocket and produced a bank card. Thought so. The card slid past the doorframe to the Yale lock. He pushed the card which bent without seeming to bother the Yale. With the heel of his hand he gave it a hearty shove and the lock clicked back. The door opened and he replaced card, chisel and hammer in his pocket, then stepped inside.

Like he'd been told, a reception area. Only it wasn't the kind of reception area that received guests. Once upon a time, yes, but not any more. There were two desks in the room and, perhaps a long time ago, tidy secretaries had sat at them transcribing dictation and taking calls. Now they cowered beneath piles of rubbish. White plastic coffee cups, ancient tabloids, takeaway boxes, delivery dockets, a sheaf of leaflets rubberbanded together. He picked one up. 'Superior Bass Response!' it said, and Max recognised the name Auridial from the boxes he had seen ferried to the flat upstairs at home. He wondered about that; whether his neighbour knew of this place. Then he put the leaflet back on the desk and looked around some more, searching for the door through to the main warehouse.

The silence of the place made him itch. He could feel his scrotum crawl as he went to the rear of the room. Here there was a hallway. Long, dark and smelling of cardboard and the insides of metal toolboxes. He found a light-switch; a striplight seemed to wait until he was sure it wasn't working before it flickered reluctantly into life. As she'd said; as well as the men's toilets, and the ladies, and what looked like a tiny kitchen area, was a door.

He tried it. It opened and he walked through, senses sharp.

Almost complete silence. Dark, too. Inside the door he tried a row of light-switches and a corresponding line of fluorescent tubes flick-flicked into action. It was the sound, the hum the lights made – the way it seemed endless – that told him how big the space was.

He was in the main warehouse. To his right were the roller doors. He knew about them even though he couldn't see them, thanks to boxes of Auridial, pallets of them everywhere, stacked two high to just over head height. A maze of Auridial. He wove his way through them, heading for the back of the warehouse and looking for the second office.

Silence. Just the hum of the lights. His own footsteps. And, he realised, his breathing.

At the back of the warehouse an L-shape had been cut into the room by what he assumed was the office. It had a flat roof, on top of which were rolls of thick, black hose, provenance unknown. Just as Trish said, pallets of Auridial had been stacked along the office wall, obscuring any windows. The fork-lift was in place. And there it was, the door. It looked never-used. Deliberately so. He could see that a pallet of boxes had been pulled in front of it to half block, half disguise the door and guessed that if it wasn't for his scheduled visit they'd have been placed with even more care, completely obscuring it. He wondered – if he hadn't known, if Verity hadn't had something to show him (her busy-bee-beavering at the computer), whether he would have guessed now anyway, his prairie senses telling him, *This is all too easy.*

There were padlocks, as Trish'd said there would be.

He leant and pulled at the pallet, already, conveniently, at an angle to the door.

On the phone she'd told him where to find the keys, and running his hand along the top of the doorframe it was obvious they were never usually stored there (of course not) because they came away thick with dust. The contrivance disgusted him. The fact that he had obeyed disgusted him. Because there's no other choice. A mantra running through his head. There's no other choice. *If I take the child, I go to prison.*

So far he'd done exactly what they wanted of him.

But if I don't take the child, and I go to the police – I go to prison anyway.

But even knowing that he felt compelled to do it, because *if I don't take the child and don't go to the police . . . then what happens to Little Ben?*

The keys slid smoothly into the locks, probably oiled in honour of the occasion. CHUNK. He pulled them from the catches, pushed open the door.

There was a corridor, which he guessed would have made a useful decompression chamber as far as Ben's kidnappers were concerned. The walls were lined with brooms and mops in buckets, factory debris. The floor was that knobbly lino, and the corridor had a smell, which he couldn't place at first, and didn't until he'd walked the short distance to the next door where there was a black bin-liner. In it were empty McDonald's boxes, remnants of the Chicken McNuggets they brought Ben, and now, for the first time, the actual physical fact of *Ben* came to Max. He was no longer a wraith in Max's head. When he opened that door the child would be behind it, and he'd be sleeping, drugged, having eaten his Chicken McNuggets and drunk his Coke. And Max was to save him.

He felt along the top of the second doorframe, found the key (and another thick coating of dust), brought it down and fitted it into the padlock.

The first thing he saw was a poster of Roy Keane; it had been stuck to the wall.

Which was sort of rude and thoughtless, bearing in mind that the whole world knew Little Ben supported Arsenal, and Arsenal supporters are no great fans of Roy Keane. Still, at least it indicated a willingness to make things homely for the boy, he thought.

Someone, probably Trish, had made an effort to see that he was comfortable – as comfortable as possible, given that he'd been separated from his family and locked in a warehouse in east London. There was that, at least.

In the corner of the room was a camp bed. On it there should have been a little boy.

4

Dash was at home when his mobile rang. He was sitting on the sofa, morose and deflated – like a bean-bag drained of its contents. In the moment between the phone ringing and him reaching for it his heart leapt. It could be Sophie. It could be Sophie saying she was on her way home tonight, and how about that Chinese? And . . . what was that, hon? My toothbrush gone? Bless you, no, it was a bit manky and that so I chucked it away. Bought myself a new one at lunch.

'That Dash?'

It wasn't Sophie. Of course. The phone's window told him exactly who was at the other end. *It wasn't Sophie*, and he had no choice but to take the call.

'It's Dash, yeah,' he replied, eyes finding the ceiling.

'*Boss.*'

'Yes, boss, it's Dash.'

'Right.' Chick cleared his sinuses with a noise like a dinosaur's final breath, received the contents into his mouth. Dash held the phone away from his ear. 'Whatchoo got to tell me, then?' added Chick.

Dash screwed up his eyes, forcing the answer from himself, squeezing it out like he had electrodes attached to his testicles, hot oil in his eyes. 'The bloke downstairs has left, boss. I saw him go.' He said a silent sorry to the comrade he betrayed. 'Just like you said he would. He's gone out in his van.'

Chick made a moist sound with his mouth, a satisfied noise. 'Right,' he said, in the manner of a man whose plans were coming together. 'Good. Stick there. By my reckoning he should be about three-quarters of an hour. I want to know exactly when he arrives back. Got it? If he's not back in an hour give me a call anyway. If you see anybody or anything going in or out of his flat, call me. You got that, Dashus?'

'Yes, boss.'

'You watch that flat.'

'Will do, boss.'

'And you're looking for what?'

'A bloke, boss. The bloke who lives here coming home.'

''Sright. And probably – what?'

'A kid. He's likely to have a kid with him – a kid in a hat.'

''Sright. Bit of a domestic issue I've been asked to help out with. Nothing that concerns you, understand?'

'Boss.'

'You watch it carefully, Dashus, got it?'

'Yes, boss.'

'Talk later, then.'

Dash threw the phone away from himself, disgusted with it. Even more disgusted with himself for ever thinking that a mobile phone was a cool, aspirational product and just the sort of thing he should own, rather than what it really was – a piece of shit. And yet, and yet. Whatever was going on – whatever trouble the guy downstairs was in with Chick – he still had to burn down the depot. Because tomorrow was beginning to make its presence felt, and even with Lightweight in hospital he had to pick up the speakers. And, yes, he could go to Phil with a sob story, driver disabled, that kind of thing. You never know, Phil might punch him a matey blow to the jaw and give him the day off on compassionate, man-down grounds. But so what if he did? There was always the next day, a new driver. He'd still have to pick up speakers the morning after, or the morning after that. The thing was, it would never stop unless he managed to put a stop to it himself. Chick would carry on squeezing.

He'd been standing – when the phone rang he'd taken to his feet to talk to Chick, as though to do so might somehow benefit him. But now he sighed and dropped to the sofa. As he did so, something on the floor caught his eye and he recognised Sophie's handwriting even as he reached down to pick it up, knowing instantly – *that very second* – what it was, and dreading it.

A single piece of paper, folded once, only not creased down – just enough for it to stand up. So why it had been on the floor, he had no idea. Funny – he'd been doing so well on the speakers today. A few more cleared and he would have seen it.

He opened it, read it. 'Dear Darren,' it said. 'I am so, so sorry, but I have decided to leave . . .'

He read it with a feeling of detachment, as though what he read wasn't actually his Dear John note but somebody else's; some other poor guy given the boot for a set of non-existent crimes. At least it explained the missing toiletries. It was with the same feeling of detachment that he saw himself toss the note to the top of one of the Auridial boxes, lean forward from the waist, bury his head in his hands and weep, as though he was having some out-of-body experience, hovering above himself and watching his body racked with sobs, wondering, if you broke it down, how much of it was real, and how much performance, how much of it was for lost love and how much for a life sent down the wrong chute by a playground punch many years ago, how much of it was sheer self-pity.

He watched himself cry and wondered how long he would continue, because there weren't *that* many tears, surely. There must only be a finite supply before the body parched itself . . . Until he saw himself raise his head from his hands and, with that same measure of performance, decisively wipe the wet from his face. He stood up. Suddenly. A surprise thought, like sunlight through bomb dust.

He had an alibi.

Or, rather, an alibi was waiting for collection, his name on it.

Because if he could get to the depot and back before the guy downstairs returned, he had a cast-iron, tight-as-a-nun's-chuff story prepared. Because as far as Chick was concerned he was at home. ('My money's on young Dash,' says Phil, surveying the still-smouldering ashes of the depot, weary firemen damping it down, Phil thinking they might have to pay Young Dash a visit, like – get him to say where he was last night, know what I mean? But . . . 'Nah,' says Chick, 'he couldn't have done it. He was at home, I can vouch for that.')

And another thought, coming up on the inside. With the depot cremated there would be no speakers to sell. Only he had a flat full of them and everybody knew he did, because he was sad, laughable Dash with the Stoke Newington beat where the punters were worried that nasty, horrid things like speakers might damage little Crispian's hearing. With clients like that it stood to reason that he had a house rammed full of the fuckers. Which he could sell on. Not to people in the street, no, but to *other speakermen*.

If he could get to the depot and back in time.

And . . . if Chick wasn't there – at the depot, that is. Which he had been the other night.

He picked up his phone and dialled Warren, who answered nervily. Dog Years was still on his mind. 'Yeah?'

'Woz?' Dash tried to sound as upbeat as he could. 'Woz, it's Dash.'

'All right, bro. Where's my suit? You said you'd have it back tonight . . .'

Dash cringed at the thought. 'I was going to get it dry-cleaned for you, mate. You know, just as a thanks.'

In fact, the mutilated two-piece was in a pile in the bathroom where Dash had peeled it off – pulling the shame from his body but unable to erase it from his mind. As he did so he mused that when he'd put the suit on it had been in mint condition with a life-saving wad of money in it. Now it was barely more than a bikini and all it contained was Lightweight's box-cutter. I could try slashing my wrists with it, but I'd probably just fuck that up, too, he'd thought, pushing it into the jeans he changed into.

'Yeah?' said Warren now. 'Well, don't take it to no pikey cleaners, right? Tek it somewhere they know what they doing. It's my best suit, man.'

'Okay, Woz, no worries. Listen, I wondered – you wouldn't do me a favour, would you?'

'What kind of favour?' said Warren, wary. By lending Dash

the suit he felt he'd exorcised his guilt demon; he wasn't keen on doing the guy any more favours.

'Just . . . could you go to your balcony, see if Chick's car's there?'

Warren paused. 'That all?'

'Yeah.'

Dash heard somebody (LaDonna, clearly) in the background: 'Warren? *War-ren?* Who is *that?*' Even over the phone Dash could discern a threatening emphasis.

''S Dash,' he heard Warren reply, muffled and weary. Then, to Dash: 'Just wait a minute, man, yeah?'

A click as Warren's flat door opened. Now Dash pictured his erstwhile driver on the concrete landing. Craning his head, looking out over the estate.

A moment later: 'Yeah, it's there. Why do you wanna know?'

Chick's Saab was there. And maybe a little bit of Dash – some angel in his head – had been hoping Warren would say, 'No. Sorry, mate, no, it ent there,' meaning Dash couldn't risk a trip to the depot, relieving him of that burden.

But Warren didn't say that. He said, 'Yeah, it's there,' and asked why Dash would want to know.

'Nothing,' sighed Dash. 'No reason. But cheers, mate, yeah?'

Dash ended the call and wiped his face, still wet from crying.

Okay, he told himself. We've crashed. Now it's time to burn.

How long? Half an hour? He flew down the stairs and to the van, throwing open the rear doors, wanting to check that the barbecue lighter fuel was still there. Sure was. Keeping it company was an Auridial box, and he had a sudden thought. A thought, like, okay, he was going to the depot. So maybe if he was quick he could load up the van with Auridial before he torched the place, have even more of them to flog to the speakermen. The thought went through him and tickled the back of his neck. He imagined them all turning up for work in the morning. (The blackened husk of the depot. The sweet smell of charred speakers in the air. Firemen damping down, etc. They're shrugging their shoulders: 'What are we going to do now?' Dash there, too, innocent as a newborn, alibi intact: 'Well, as it happens, guys, I've got a few at home I could let you have.')

For the first time in for ever he imagined himself getting out of this situation – maybe getting out of it for good. And smelling of roses, too. Get a new suit for Warren – that was the first thing to do – perhaps have some left over for himself into the bargain. He hoisted himself up, scuttled into the back of the van and reached for the box. Get this one in the flat, he thought, make more room in the van – *fucking fill it* with boxes from the depot. He lifted it, turned – and saw a figure standing in the doorway.

Lightweight, it seemed, was not a man who made empty threats.

5

'Ben?' said Max, softly; stupidly, really, considering he was in a small office – perhaps where a put-upon warehouse manager had once toiled – and it was clear that the room did not contain a six-year-old child.

It had done, though: it smelt slightly of urine – Max saw a bucket in the corner of the room, loo roll beside it, a piece of laminated wood on top. And on the floor at the foot of the camp bed was Ben's football album, creased and thumbed from hours of reading; a porno car magazine, too. Nothing else to read, though, nothing else to do. His woolly Arsenal hat lay next to the football album. Max knew he would recognise Ben at once, of course – it wasn't like he'd have grown a beard or anything – but those items, the album and cap, were as good as finger-prints. They hadn't been taken away from him: they had been left here because to remove them would have been an act of inhu-manity surpassing all before it. They *were* Ben. They were all he had in this place that made him Ben.

Then he noticed the shelves, that gap in the paint pots; and behind the shelves the window, the hole in it. From outside he'd noted the pallets stacked up and the fork-lift presumably disabled so it couldn't be moved. It kept the pallets firm against the windows, a barrier blocking out light and possible escape. But now Max saw that one of the windows had been broken, once, probably a long time ago – maybe some workers playing an impromptu game of cricket one afternoon, ball into the window, emergence of the put-upon warehouse manager: 'Which one of you dick-slaps did that?' One of the dick-slaps had fixed the window with packing tape, and it had stayed that way for years – you could tell, the marks the tape had left, it had been there for ages – until recently, when somebody had picked it off and removed the glass from the frame.

He went closer, thinking that, even with the glass gone, how could you . . . but then seeing close-up exactly how. The boy had gone through the window, and – it seemed incredible – actually *got into* one of the boxes stacked against the window. Peering at the window he could see the cardboard had been torn, a portal formed. Next, it seemed, an attempt had been made to drag it back into place from the inside.

Max darted out of the room, through the corridor and into the warehouse. If Ben had got into the box he could have climbed out of the top, might have hurt himself. Max tiptoed to study the top of the box, looking for signs of an exit. As though Ben might have sprung from it like a jack-in-the-box. But it was intact: the flaps were down, and taped down, too. He was still inside, had to be.

Returning to the office, Max put his face to the window. 'Ben,' he said. Feeling slightly foolish, he reached out and knocked politely on the box. 'Ben,' he repeated. In return there was a sound that might have been a whimper, a frightened noise. Max felt something like shame slithering in his gut. The poor kid was terrified. More frightened of him, a stranger, than of Chick or Trish.

'Ben,' he said gently, 'my name is Max. I'm here to help you. I've come to take you back to your mum and dad. Back home, mate. You want to go home, don't you?'

Silence from inside the box. No, not quite. A shift. Perhaps he was trying to get out, but couldn't. How on earth could he fit inside the box anyway? Max knocked again.

'Ben, mate?' As if calling him 'mate' would make everything okay. Not that it had any effect – and it wasn't like he could reach in and physically drag the boy out, not the best way to get his trust. Because that was it, wasn't it? He had to get Ben's trust. He looked around him, then turned back to the box. 'How do you think Arsenal are going to do this season, mate?' he asked, a man talking to cardboard.

The cardboard was silent. Time passed.

'Come on, mate. I've come to take you home. I can't do that if you're going to stay in there the whole time, can I? You've got to trust me, Ben. I promise you, I've come to take you home.'

Still no reply from the Auridial. Max felt the beginnings of panic. What if he couldn't entice Ben out of the box? What was he supposed to do then? And how come he was awake anyway? Trish had promised him a near-comatose Ben, not a wide-awake potential escapee.

There was a wheedling tone in his voice when he next said, 'Ben? Mate?' And, frankly, he would have ignored himself if he'd heard it. Frowning, he looked around for inspiration. There was just the bed, the hat, the sticker album and porno car magazine.

So Max began to sing.

He sang, 'In the town, where I was born, lived a ma-a-n, who sailed to sea. And he told us of his life . . .' and here Max forgot the words, mumbling them until he got to 'And we lived beneath the waves in our ye-llow submarine.

'We all live in a yellow submarine, a yellow submarine, a yellow submarine.'

'We all live in a yellow submarine,' sang Ben, from inside the box.

'A yellow submarine,' sang Max.

'A yellow submarine,' they sang together.

There was a movement, then Little Ben's face appeared, and Max could have hugged him.

Perhaps he might have done, had there not been a sound from outside. The atmosphere in the warehouse seemed to shift to accommodate it. An engine, tyres fat on tarmac. A van. It pulled up outside – almost, it seemed to Max, right up to the roller doors. His own van was parked in the road behind a skip. This one had driven all the way into the courtyard and was parked directly outside the depot.

Ben's eyes found his. Already jittery they widened with fear, probably sensing the tension in Max.

'Tell you what, mate,' said Max, as calmly as he could manage, 'why don't you just pop back inside there for a moment or so? Just to be on the safe side.' Madly, he found himself wondering how you spoke to six-year-old boys. He realised that he very much wanted to be Ben's friend. 'Don't worry, everything'll be all right, promise. I'll say the code word when the coast is clear, okay? What do you want the code word to be?'

There was a clunk from outside the roller doors. The van door opening.

'Quick, Ben, a code word.'

'Stegosaurus,' said Ben.

'Okay,' said Max, impressed. 'Okay, stegosaurus it is. In you go, then.' Ben disappeared back into the Auridial box.

'You okay in there?' asked Max, already whispering.

'Yes,' replied Ben, his voice an echoey version of itself.

'Not scared?'

'No.'

'Okay, good. Just hold tight, then.' He hurried out of the office, into the corridor.

Now he stood with the door at his back, just the towers of Auridial for company. Looking up at the striplights he cursed himself for leaving them on, but reasoned that if someone saw them, what was the worst thing they might do? Turn them off? They wouldn't see Max in the shadows. And if they came back here, well, if that was the case they were coming for Ben, or for Max, and they had to be met. Max had a hammer and chisel in his pocket, the weight of them reassuring. Perhaps he could sculpt them into submission.

He strained to hear. There was a sound like the rear doors of the van opening, then footsteps. He tensed, thinking that if the roller doors went up he could retreat into the corridor, but the footsteps continued, going – yes – to the front-office door. Whoever it was entered the office but after that it was difficult to decipher their movements.

Then, a new sound: the door between the office and the ware-house opening. It was only a matter of yards away, but with the boxes of Auridial in the way he could see nothing. Still, he pushed himself back, made himself small, holding his breath. If they came to the back they might see him. What he heard then made his soul sing. It was the sound of a box being lifted, a small grunt of exertion from whoever was doing it. Now they were going back out to the van, loading the box into the rear. A pickup, that was all it was. He rejoiced silently. They were collecting boxes of Auridial. The footsteps returned, another box of Auridial lifted and taken. Each time it happened he felt a little calmer, listening to the journey of the feet, through the reception office to outside, a second more distant grunt as the box was loaded into a van.

They returned, another box was lifted, and Max waited until he heard the feet crunch on the tarmac outside before withdrawing into the corridor and pulling the door closed behind him. He strode quickly but quietly back to the office and to the Ben portal, where he knocked and said, 'Ben,' then remembered: 'Stegosaurus.'

Ben's head appeared from the hole in the Auridial box. Max had a shushing finger to his own lips. 'It's okay,' he whispered. 'It's someone come to pick something up. They won't be much longer. We'll just wait here a moment or so, okay?'

Ben nodded vigorously. 'Then,' added Max, 'we'll get you home.' Another enthusiastic nod from Ben.

In the room he could no longer hear the footsteps. 'Wait there a sec,' he whispered, and went back up the corridor, opening the door to the warehouse to find it pitch black. Whoever it was had concluded their business and switched off the lights on the way out. Returning to the office he found Ben had retreated into the box and he said the code word again, helping the boy out of the box and back into the room. Now, for the first time, he saw Ben properly, a Dickens-urchin look about him. Trish was right, he needed a bath; his hair was greasy, his clothes – his first-football-match outfit – filthy and reeking. His eyes were bright sparks in a face coated with three weeks' grime.

'Okay, mate,' said Max. 'Let's go, shall we?' He looked around the room. 'Here, do you want your hat on?' Ben shook his head.

'We'll keep it for later, eh? Let's not forget the football book, shall we?'

When he offered his hand Ben took it, and Max's heart filled as they left the room. Ben blinked at the corridor, looking behind him, connecting the one place that was so familiar with the other, just a door between them. He spotted the bin-liner with the empty takeaway bags. Max let him acclimatise, feeling a strange, protective tranquillity, the child's hand in his.

The feeling didn't last long, though. It was replaced by another more urgent emotion, as they reached the corridor and opened the door to the warehouse

They looked at one another as if each might have the answer as to why the warehouse suddenly smelt of smoke.

6

Lightweight was standing at the rear doors of the van. The last time Dash had seen Lightweight the grey man had been using a nurse to threaten Dash with extreme violence. Death, in fact, if Dash remembered correctly.

He was hunched over, one arm wrapped round his ribs. Dash could see his head rise and fall as he breathed hard and ragged. Then he was grimacing as he pulled himself into the van, behind him darkness and streetlamps. Now, like Dash, he stood in the van, bent over. The two of them facing each other like polite Japanese gents.

Lightweight held out a hand and, for a second, Dash had to fight an urge to laugh, because hunched over, with his hand held out like that, his arm wrapped round himself he looked like – like a zombie. An unstoppable, you-cannot-kill-what-does-not-live, flesh-eating member of the living dead. And he was coming to get Dash. And he wouldn't stop. Ever.

The zombie hawked and spat a green, which slapped to the floor of the van like Dash's brains would when the zombie ate them. He took a step back.

Lightweight gave context to his outstretched hand. 'I'll take that money now, bitch,' he said.

Dash held out his own hands. Some outraged part of his brain was thinking how unfair all this was. For God's sake, he'd taken the guy to hospital. He probably would have died on the pavement if Dash hadn't gone back for him. And how does Lightweight repay him? Turning up here, looking like the living dead, demanding money and threatening him with violence. Well, this is a *fine* way to say thank you.

'Look, mate,' he faltered, 'stop a minute, yeah? I haven't got any money.' He was thinking madly. 'After I dropped you off at the hospital – because I did, you know, like, you weren't fully conscious, I guess, but it was me who picked you up and got you to Casualty, all right, just . . . you do *know* that, yeah?'

Lightweight kept coming. His leg – obviously not broken, wounded, though – dragging behind him as he approached.

'But the thing is,' continued Dash, 'after I left you, I fucking ran into the Holloway Road boys again. They did me in the van . . .' and the school-Dash wouldn't have let that one go, either '. . . and took all of the cash. *All* of it. *Cunts.*'

He was now glued to the back of the van. Lightweight stopped moving forward a second to grin, revealing lips still grimy with blood, mouth a ragged Manhattan skyline of teeth. 'You ran into the Holloway Road boys,' he snarled.

'Yeah,' nodded Dash, for a second believing he'd fooled Lightweight, who hawked again and spat – some of it red, Dash saw.

'But they din't touch you, yeah? They just let you go on your way?' he hissed. 'It's bullshit, bitch. Now give me the money.'

Dash edged to his left. 'There isn't any money, mate.' Now he was thinking, Come on. Sure, Lightweight had a psychological advantage, but he'd just been beaten half to death with a baseball bat; had probably been given horse-strength drugs in the hospital before he no doubt discharged himself, probably at further risk to his health, and was a crack addict (recovering). Clearly he, Dash, had the physical advantage here. Plus he still had Lightweight's knife. The thought gave him a shot of confidence and he pushed himself off the back wall of the van, raising himself as far as he could, which wasn't far.

'Look,' he said, voice firm. The thought of the knife in his pocket settled him but he didn't want to use it. Not yet. 'I don't have the money, mate, all right? It's all gone. And, I know I owe you a bit, and I'm going to pay you back, but – sorry – it's not going to be tonight. I think the best thing for you to do is get back to the hospital.' And with the balance of power in the van shifted in his favour, he began to think he should offer Lightweight a lift, but he couldn't do it now, not enough time. He could call a cab maybe. But who was going to pay for that?

Lightweight slapped him.

It was the shock as much as the power of the blow that flung Dash backwards. Immediately he felt his face redden. He'd been slapped. The kind of blow he felt sure Lightweight would call a bitch-slap. (Twice he'd been slapped today. First Chick, now Lightweight. Factor in the Gary Spencer encounter and anybody'd think it was some kind of National Hit Dash Day. Slap Dash, even.)

'Give me my money,' said Lightweight.

'I can't.' Dash, bent over, had a hand to his cheek. The knife was in his top pocket.

Lightweight slapped him again. Dash heard the smack sound and felt the firework of pain at his cheek. The whole time Lightweight hadn't taken the other arm away from his stomach.

'Look, mate—' Dash began.

Lightweight slapped him again.

Only, this time Dash lost it. Because the world wasn't working if he got slapped by a half-dead, doped-up junkie. Because, yes, in the car-boot sale of his soul, pride was mostly long gone, but not all of it.

He put both hands to Lightweight's chest and shoved. Lightweight screamed in a manner that suggested Dash had, quite literally, found a sore point. And because he was bent over, he sort of fell backwards, arse first, his arms – both of them now – reaching for Dash as he did so. Dash, already pushing forward, was pulled back, the two of them thumping to the floor, Lightweight's head catching the side of the Auridial, arms and legs tangled like a game of Twister ending.

Dash was first off, pulling himself from the tangle, making for the doorway. His legs were caught and he was kicking them even as he reached into the pocket of his jeans and pulled out the box-cutter. Twisting, he brandished it in front of him, down to where Lightweight held his legs.

Except when he kicked his legs the arms fell away, and

325

Lightweight was lying on his back, more or less exactly as he fell, and leaking from the back of his head on to the van floor was a dark coat button of blood. The blade wasn't extended, Dash realised, and he click-clicked it open, holding it there while his mind processed the available data.

He's not moving. He's dead. Or – he's knocked himself unconscious, which would explain the blood. Or – he's blacked out from the pain in his chest. Or – some combination of the two. Either way.

Dash pulled himself to his feet and glanced out of the doorway behind him. The scuffle had lasted barely a second, but there was nobody there, nobody in the street whom he could see. He pulled the doors closed anyway and scuttled back to where Lightweight lay. Hand to his heart Dash felt a beat, so he wasn't dead. Thank God for that. (Or not thank God for that, depending on how you looked at it, because at least if he was dead he couldn't come alive again.) Now he glanced at his watch and saw that he'd lost five minutes he could never get back. He scooped up the two bottles of barbecue lighter fuel, jumped from the back of the van, slammed the doors on near-dead Lightweight and threw himself into the cab. Still time. That was what he told himself.

It was on the way down that the idea occurred to him to leave Lightweight in the blazing building. It was an act, really, of self-defence (he told himself). If he didn't kill Lightweight now, Lightweight would rise and come after Dash, and he'd never stop; Lightweight was half dead anyway; plus he'd most likely be the prime suspect, putting Dash even further in the clear. Plus he'd no longer owe him money.

Plus; he really, really hated Lightweight.

(This was what he told himself.)

He knew he was being reckless when he pulled into the courtyard rather than parking in the road. But he had no time. Throwing open the doors to the van he checked on Lightweight again, then shoved him as close to the side of the van as possible to make room for more speakers. Then he was scooting up to the office door, reaching into his back pocket for the tube pass where he kept his cards, pulling out his bank card.

Which wasn't his bank card at all, he realised. It was Sophie's.

He stopped. He didn't have to burn down the depot. He had Sophie's card, and she had money in her account – he'd seen it. All this time. All this time he'd had the means to get the money. Whirling around, he held the card out in front of him like a playing card he was about to make burst into flames. He didn't have to do this, he could leave now, a day's grace at least. Whirled back. But that was all, wasn't it? A day's grace. One more day and he'd be right back in the same position, only he'd never get an opportunity like this again. Never.

Decided, he pushed Sophie's card into the lock, tripped it and stood back as the door swung open. He half feared a burglar alarm would start clanging, or that an enraged pit bull would come bounding out of the gloom.

Inside, the main office was dark but the lights were on at the back. He stepped through, looking around him. Nothing. 'Hello,' he whispered, suddenly respectful of the silence. His skin prickled. Never seen the office this way before. This was its secret life and he was like some seedy interloper. 'Hello.' Again, barely more than a whisper. He held the bottles of barbecue lighter fuel behind his back just in case a late-night Phil should come bustling from the bogs, doing up his flies. Nothing, and what were the chances anyway? He moved inside now, placing the bottles on the floor while he continued to check the office. There was a strip of light beneath the door to the warehouse and he went to it, opened the door. All was silent. That prickly feeling intensified. Why had the lights been left on? 'Anyone there?'

The boxes of Auridial stayed silent. Now he moved back into the corridor and checked the toilets. Nobody. He had the place to himself, he was certain of it. The lights on – what? They'd just been left on, maybe they always were. He went back into the warehouse and helped himself to a box of Auridial, then hefted it out to the van where he checked Lightweight was spark-out on the floor. Back at the depot he took three more boxes of Auridial, about all he could fit into the back if Lightweight was in there, too.

Except Lightweight wasn't going to be in there for much longer. He made two more trips to the depot, leaving these boxes on the tarmac, ready to load into the van once he'd disposed of Lightweight.

Now he stood at the back of the van and checked his watch. Shit. He was out of breath, his eyes on Lightweight. All he had to do was carry the body into the office, douse it with barbecue lighter fuel, douse the office and the boxes in the warehouse, and he'd be free. He pictured himself dousing the body, tried to paint it as a joyous, triumphant scene – Dash finally pissing on his enemies – but couldn't. He tried to picture himself dousing the office then leaving Lightweight inside it, but this time, crucial to his conscience, not actually soaking Lightweight in barbecue lighter fuel.

But he couldn't picture that either.

At last he'd found his place to stop. Still pretty south of his normal place to stop, true, but there it was. Murder was up ahead, but I'm going to stick here at Arson, thanks. It meant he hadn't completely lost it. For that, he had reason to be thankful.

For the second time that day he was going to take Lightweight to hospital – that was what he was going to do. So instead of picking him up and leaving him to a fiery death, he snatched up one of the two boxes of Auridial at his feet, quick-marched it back into the depot and returned it to the warehouse. Back again and Lightweight still out cold he picked up the second box and returned. Then he grabbed a bottle of barbecue lighter fuel and yanked off the top. The squirty bottle was like the washing-up liquid bottles young Darren had used for water fights – except filled with highly flammable fluid. Standing just inside the warehouse door he soaked as many Auridial boxes as he could, then moved backwards, starting a line of fluid leading back into the office, swinging to squirt it across the breadth of the office, hardly registering Lightweight from the corner of his eye.

Thinking about it later, Dash imagined Lightweight slowly regaining consciousness and pulling himself – his hate, his rage, his barely functioning limbs and dangerously loose ribs – out of the van. The injured grey zombie looked around himself and no doubt recognised the depot from his daytime visits. Then, seeing the open office door, the light on there, hearing, maybe, the sound of Dash, he dragged himself towards it. Dash imagined Lightweight's trailing foot dragging along the tarmac of the fore-court. In his mind's eye he saw one of Lightweight's hands held in front of him, the other clasping his stomach. He imagined Lightweight making a sound like a dead man recently awoken.

Then Lightweight reaching the office, his eyes scanning the room, looking for possible weapons, spotting something on a desk.

Which was where he was when Dash next saw him. Not seeing him until it was too late . . .

He'd been backing out of the warehouse; Lightweight had been standing hunched at a desk where he'd found a Stanley knife, the handle wrapped in brown tape. As Dash backed into the room Lightweight stood upright and brandished the knife. On his face was a twisted, nasty smile.

Which disappeared as droplets of barbecue fuel from Dash's wild swing reached him. The smile seemed to melt away from his mouth, suddenly relaxing round the cigarette he was smoking, which fell from his lips. And as he realised exactly what was about to happen – that no good can ever come of a lit cigarette making contact with barbecue lighter fuel – he tried to catch it, unsuccessfully. So instead of catching he seemed to juggle it, unwittingly batting bright orange embers into the air.

Dash thought it a good time to beat a hasty retreat. So he did, pulling the office door closed behind him on his way out and running for the van, tuning out the *whump* of fire at his back. Ignoring the sudden heat on his neck.

He was racing home when a mist of fear and panic at last parted and sense raised a tremulous hand. His head was violent with what-to-do. In the end he had to say the thought out loud, make it the victorious voice. Because if he hadn't, he might have kept on driving. 'What am I doing?' he enquired of himself. 'What the fuck am I doing?'

And there it was, out in the open. What. The fuck. Was he doing?

The windows of the van were open; he hadn't fixed the top properly to the top of the barbecue lighter fuel and it had spilt in the cab, filling it with the benign fumes of Sunday afternoon. Except they weren't so benign. (Those same fumes in the office. Dash slopping fluid into the warehouse, turning, Lightweight there, the Stanley knife held. His fag. A sound, like, *woof* . . . then, *UH-WOOF*.)

He had to go back. He was Dash. He'd hit the kid with Tourette's, yes; he'd stood by with the single-mothers-in-waiting and said, 'I don't think you wanted to do that,' as the hard lads taught Jason-oh-what-was-his-name a lesson. He'd made Colin Stumple's school life a m-m-misery. But he didn't leave people in burning buildings. Not even people like Lightweight.

He pulled to the side of the road, ignoring people at a bus stop, taking deep breaths and dragging his hair out of his eyes. He'd waited until he saw smoke before leaving – the fire was good and started. But maybe if he got back in time . . .

He cut across traffic, heading back towards the depot, muttering to himself as he drove. 'Jesus. Please. Jesus. Please.' Back through Tottenham Hale and past the dog track where he'd once seen Vinnie Jones. Past that and into the industrial estate and the 'Jesus. Please' died in his throat at what he saw. Smoke. A huge blanket of it, dense and black enough to shame the night. Still he drove up to the entrance and there he stopped. The heat, even this far back, was terrific, and he could taste the smoke. But it was the flames that prevented him getting out of the van. They were fire-monster arms embracing the office door, the window already broken with heat and coughing smoke into the courtyard. Flames were licking around the bottom of the roller doors, at the sides, the corrugated metal already black.

A little bit of him couldn't help but admire the efficiency of the fire.

Another little bit of him thought, *Oh. Oh, dear God*.

Then there was the howl of sirens and he could see the sky announcing spinning blue lights. He pulled away from the courtyard entrance, still stunned, drove a short way up the street and stopped again, watching the apocalypse smoke above the depot, the fire engines pulling into the estate behind him, one turning into the courtyard, another remaining in the road outside. He watched as firemen ran for hoses, two of them in consultation, pointing towards the burning building. Dimly he thought that, once upon a time, years ago, he'd wanted to be a fireman. And even more dimly he remembered hearing somewhere that most arsonists were frustrated firemen, which was clearly true, since he was a newly minted arsonist. And even more dimly than that, he remembered – probably from the same source – that police catch arsonists by hunting for them near to the scene of the crime because firebugs can never resist sticking around to watch their fire at work.

There was a tap at the driver's window.

The policeman was holding a large torch, like a baton, the kind of torch that cops in American films carry. They double up as a club, which is why the cops always carry them over-arm. Dash recalled telling Sophie that particular bit of information. She'd asked why Tommy Lee Jones was carrying his torch that way and that was what he told her. But she didn't believe him because Tommy Lee Jones was alone at the time: there was no way he was going to need to use his as a club. Well, it's just force of habit, he'd told her and she'd laughed at him like he was bull-shitting, which he wasn't, but he had to agree: it did sort of sound like he was.

At the passenger side was another policeman, and when Dash turned to look at him he shone the torch in his face.

Dash sighed. It was a long, long sigh.

'Do you want to exit the vehicle, please, sir?' said the cop at the driver's door, like he was giving him a choice.

'No thanks,' Dash wanted to say. 'I'll just pop off home if you don't mind.'

The cop stood away from the door to let Dash open it. Behind him the second cop was opening the passenger side. The first was doing an exaggerated usher's motion with his oversized torch. 'Nice view, is it?' he said, indicating the fire behind them, a third fire engine was arriving.

'It's terrible, isn't it?' said Dash, thinking suddenly that, Okay, sure, it looked bad (it looked very bad) him being there, the fire raging. But it didn't mean he'd done it, did it? He was innocent until proven guilty.

'You having a barbecue?' said the second policeman from behind him. Dash turned to see him emerging from the van holding a bottle of barbecue lighter fuel.

His colleague looked first at the bottle, then at Dash. He rolled his eyes. 'All right,' he said wearily. 'Come on, mate.'

For some reason, as if he'd gone into Hollywood autopilot, Dash turned and spread his arms, assuming the position against the side of the van and expecting arms to start patting him down. When nothing happened he looked behind himself to see the two policemen guffawing at him. Perhaps his expression was heartrending enough to stop them, and one of them put him out of his misery. Dash was frisked. They coughed to get serious again.

Now he heard his rights being read. 'You do not have to say anything.' All that. As though they should be different in real life somehow – so you knew it was real.

The second policeman had stepped away and was talking on his radio, now coming back, and whispering something to the first. Dash heard one word: 'Body'.

'My, we are in trouble, aren't we?' said the first policeman.

7

Not long after, when Dash was sitting in the police car being ferried to the station, he would suddenly think about child abduction. He was, despite everything – unbelievably – fretting about not ringing Chick. Then he was wondering why – why did he have to ring Chick about a man with a little boy? What was a little boy doing with the man downstairs who lived by himself? A loner like that, black coat, a bit creepy, him and Sophie had always thought, forever peeking out of his windows and scuffing about in the hallway.

It had taken a selfishly long time to occur to him, but when it did he leant forward between the seats of the car, hands behind him, handcuffed there, about to say something of great import. The policeman in the passenger seat placed a hand to his forehead and gently – but the kind of gently that brooks no argument – pushed him back to the seat.

'Just stay there, son,' he said, bored.

Dash wriggled to get comfortable again. 'No,' he argued. 'Look. I've got something I want to say.'

The passenger cop didn't bother turning round, because, like all cops, he'd seen and heard it all. 'Save it, yeah? We're not interested.' He yawned.

'Please,' insisted Dash. 'Just let me say this one thing.'

Now he sat in a small room. Everything had that ring now, that edge of being something he'd done by proxy thousands of times before, watching the process of being booked in, led to a cell, then out to another room – they probably called them 'suites', 'interrogation suites' – this one with a table, tape-recorder, two plastic chairs and the inevitable tin ashtray.

The door to the room opened and two officers entered, one of them a PC who stood by the door. The second man, this one wearing a suit, was tanned, smoothing his tie as he sat and began to peel the wrapping from a cassette tape.

He smiled at Dash, who smiled back, tentatively, wondering if it was some kind of policeman's trick.

The tanned policeman kept smiling. 'Hello, Darren,' he said at last.

'Hello,' said Dash.

'And it is Darren, is it? Not Daz, some other nickname?'

'Dash, actually,' said Dash, relaxing slightly.

'Really? Okay, still – I'll just call you Darren, if it's all the same.'

Dash nodded.

'I'm Detective Inspector Merle,' he said. 'And you've been brought here on suspicion of . . . arson, is it?' He tapped a file he'd brought into the room with him, 'They're still pouring water on it, but I gather someone's been pulled out of there.'

Dash looked at him. 'Is he dead?'

'Is who dead?'

'The person they've pulled out.'

Merle studied Dash carefully. 'I haven't got an up-to-date report on his condition. I can get one in a moment or so. But in the meantime I understand you told the arresting officer you've got some urgent information, possibly involving the abduction of a child.'

Dash nodded vigorously, his hair falling in front of his face.

'Specifically, you gave the officer a couple of names you believe may be involved in the abduction of a child.'

Dash nodded again.

'One of them a, uh, Maxwell Coleman of sixty-four Clarke Street, your downstairs neighbour, and the other . . .' Merle sighed a big sigh '. . . is why I'm here to talk to you.'

Merle finished unwrapping the second of the two tapes and slotted them into the machine, clicking the doors of the tape machine closed. He found himself biting his lip. 'Okay,' he said.

'Before we start, let me say that I get a lot of people coming in here telling me they know something about this . . . about kids going missing or being abused. And they're usually doing it because they've got a score to settle, because they want a reward, because they're just stupid, or sick, or because they think their wholly fabricated bit of so-called information somehow means they're going to get off.

'And, looking at you, I'm guessing that since you're sitting there facing an arson, which may turn out to be an unlawful killing, maybe even murder, you might be trying for that last one. And if you are, you'd better say now before I press that button, because I'm telling you, if you're wasting even one second of my time on this case, I'll be all over you like the chicken-pox.'

Dash nodded.

'And bear this in mind,' continued Merle. 'A couple of hours ago I was on a plane back from Majorca, and they only came round with the drinks trolley once.' He said this more for the benefit of the uniformed officer in the room, who shook his head in disgust. 'Plus, instead of going directly home to face whatever minor household crisis will have occurred during our absence, I've come straight here. And I've done that not because I was desperate to get back to work or because I really wanted a major dust-up with my missus,' again, this was half directed to the PC, who sympathy-frowned in response, 'but because of what you've told the arresting officers. So you see, don't you, how vital it is that what you've got to tell me turns out not to be wasting my time?' Dash nodded. 'You want to go on?' Nodded again. 'Sure?' Nod. Merle reached and pressed on the recorder. He waited out a long bleep before he did the introductions. 'Okay,' he said to Dash. 'You say you have information involving a possible child abduction.' Dash nodded again. 'For the tape, please.' Dash said yes. 'Okay, then, let's hear it.'

Dash took a deep breath. 'I work for a man, his name is Chick.'

Merle leant forward. 'Right, yes,' he said.

Something about the way he said it made Dash say, 'You know him?'

'I know his work, yes. But what about him?'

So Dash told him.

Trish's mobile rang. Or, rather, it buzzed. Set to vibrate, it hover-crafted across the kitchen table, drifting away from her hand as she reached to pick it up. She'd been biting her fingernails. Opposite her at the table, Chick was smoking. He'd pulled the peak of his cap low over his face and was hunched down in his seat. Each dealing with their nerves in different ways. At the phone's buzz he jumped, looking at it wide-eyed. From the front room he could hear the television. MTV. Carl cussing along with some R&B duet, adding his own swearwords – like it needed them.

'It's not him, it's Patsy,' said Trish, looking at the window of her phone.

'Fuck's sake, your mates. Cut her off,' growled Chick. The two of them stared at each other. 'Go on then,' he insisted. 'Fucking cut her off, will ya?'

He'd had his own mobile in his hand, already flash-forwarding to a speech he'd been running through his vile head: 'Here, Merlin, you know you said to keep me ear to the ground for news on that little boy who's missing? Yeah, well, I might have something for ya. Before I do, though, yeah, this reward they're offering . . .'

She threw her mobile back on to the table and stood up.

'Paedo ent rung, Trish,' said Chick, warningly. 'Why ent he rung? You said you was going to tell him.'

'I did,' she snapped. 'He said he would. But your mate ent rung either, so he can't have done it yet.'

'It's been hours.'

'Well, maybe he waited after I spoke to him, I don't know,' she bawled at him.

'Dash called to say he'd left,' bawled Chick back.

'Well, I don't know, maybe he went for a drink first,' she double-bawled in return.

He gave her a withering look from the table.

'And anyway, what's your little mate up to?' she added, spitting poison.

Chick tried Dash's mobile again. Nothing. Not switched on. That little poof was dead when he got his hands on him. Proper dead. 'This ent playing out how it should,' he said, thinking.

'Where is he, Charlie?' said Trish, hands in her hair.

'Fuck should I know?'

'Well, what's going on?' Voice rising, panicking.

He rounded on her. 'FUCK SHOULD I KNOW?'

'Then what are we going to do? You think he's taken the kid somewhere else?'

'God give me strength, Trish. Fuck. Should. I. Know.'

She ignored him. 'Charlie, look, as long as he's got the kid we can still ring Merle. It don't matter if Paedo hasn't taken him home.'

They were both standing now, Trish reaching shakily for the Rothmans.

'Let me think,' said Chick. 'Let me think a minute.' He took a seat and readjusted his cap. Then, 'Right.' He went to the side and scooped up the keys to the Saab. 'You get down the depot. Take the four-by-four. See if the kid's there. If he ent, clean up as planned. If he is, I dunno, hold tight.'

'And where are you going?' she demanded.

'I'm going to find Paedo,' he said darkly. He pulled a small kitchen knife from the block and wrapped it in a tea-towel. Trish stood staring at him. 'Well, go on then,' he said. 'Get a fucking move on.'

At that moment. From the front door: *RAT-A-TAT-TAT*.

Before either of them could stop him, Carl was scampering from the front room to answer. Chick slid the kitchen door closed and the two looked at each other, mouths wide and questioning, hearing Carl open the door.

DI Merle returned to the office and took a seat beside Dash, who sat bowed, his face framed by hair. Merle seemed jazzed by what Dash had told him but he kept a police-face, smoothing his tie and sitting down as before. 'All right,' he said. 'And this somehow fits in with tonight, does it, what you've told me so far?'

Dash nodded wearily. 'Like I said, he'd told me to wait for the man downstairs . . .'

'Max Coleman.'

'Yes. I'd see him with a boy, then I had to call him.'

'Yeah, okay. And?'

'It meant . . . it gave me an alibi. It meant I could I burn down the depot without him thinking it was me.'

Merle leant back from the table and crossed his arms fiercely. 'So instead of reporting your fears of a possible child abduction to the police, you used the opportunity to set fire to a building?'

Dash's head dropped. 'Yes,' he said, his voice wet with shame.

'Ah, well, that's okay, then. Case dropped, mate. You might as well go home,' said Merle, harshly. He left a pause, hearing Dash sniffle behind his hair. Saying, more softly now, 'Look – as we policeman say, you're not doing yourself any favours here.'

'You don't understand,' said Dash, quietly. 'You don't understand what he's like.'

Merle laughed, but not unkindly; fondly, at the naïvety of youth. 'I do, mate. I understand perfectly what he's like.'

'He would have kept on squeezing,' said Dash, more to himself.

'Well, you'll choose your friends more carefully in the future, then, won't you?'

Dash raised his head and nodded, sniffed.

'Although your social opportunities are likely to be a bit on the narrow side in the near future.'

Sniffles from Dash. 'What I'm saying is,' he said, 'I had no choice.'

'That's what they all say, mate,' replied Merle.

The door opened and someone called him out a second time. Thirty seconds later he was back. 'Right,' he said. 'For you, I've got some good news and some interesting news.'

Dash looked at him.

'First, the good news. This body at the depot isn't a body at all. In fact, he's very much alive and kicking. So much so that he's discharged himself from hospital.'

With every cell of his intelligent, thinking mind, Dash knew that Lightweight being alive was good news for him. Somehow, though, he couldn't bring himself to feel it. It meant he was out there, and if he was out there he was coming to get Dash.

'And the interesting bit of news is that this Duracell bunny isn't your friend Lightweight. This guy's white.'

8

Chick and Trish were listening at the kitchen door. 'What's he doing up there?' spat Chick.

'I don't know, I don't know.' His wife was shoving him.' Get out there and find out. Get the fuck out there.'

'All right, all right.' He slapped at her bothering hands. 'I'm going.' And he pulled open the kitchen door and took a step into the corridor. He adopted a terrace pose, legs apart, hands come-on-then at his side, stomach out.

'All right, Paedo,' he said. Carl was disappearing back into the front room.

'Just been hearing his latest battle rhyme,' said Max, who stepped into the hallway.

Merle had said the man they found wasn't black, but Max had been. Until about twenty minutes ago, his face was tanned a charcoal colour, occasional glimpses of the old skin beneath, in the lines around the eyes, in the trackmarks down the cheeks. But in between the hospital and here, Max had gone home, and he'd washed away the evidence of the fire from his cheeks, even quickly washed his hair, and when he arrived at Neesmith House he had left his smoke-smelling black coat in the cab of the van. It was the first time Chick had seen him without it.

'What are you doing here, then?' said Chick, trying to strike the right note.

Saying nothing, Max moved down the hall towards him. Then, 'Can I come in?' he said, reaching the kitchen door. Chick moved and the two of them took their seats at the kitchen table, Trish at the side. She fired querying looks at Chick, who sat with his eyes fixed on Max, trying to work out how this one was going to go.

'Thought I'd come and find out where you want me doing the bags tonight,' said Max at last. He'd sat with his legs outstretched, his hands in his jeans pockets. Now he leant forward amiably. Chick was blank confusion.

'You know,' added Max. 'Where I'm working tonight?'

Inside he was hurricanes. Sick-off-the-side storms. His hands were in his pockets and one of them clenched his Stanley knife so hard the pain was almost exquisite. Everything behind his skin was knotted hard and screaming.

Because he'd lost the boy.

In the depot the towers of Auridial had gone up as well – better – than Dash could ever have hoped. Pillars of fire with superior bass. They belched smoke and Max was suddenly, horribly, disoriented as he moved through the warehouse with Ben. Flames seemed to materialise from the suffocating, dense blackness; smoke refused to budge as he pushed his way through. He held the child to him, trying to create some kind of filter for his mouth. His own he couldn't even clamp a hand over. Then he was going through the door into the office corridor and here, suddenly, everything was light.

The first thing he saw was fire; the next thing Lightweight, who half sat, half lay at the opening to the corridor, almost foetal, coughing. Max had time to recognise him as Dash's companion, the grey-coloured man he'd seen standing by and watching Dash load speakers into the back of his van.

To Max's left the flames had touched everything, right up to the office door, and they were slithering towards the corridor, where the toilets and kitchen politely awaited their turn to be consumed – and where, at the end, there was a fire escape. It had mops in buckets, and brooms, and a fallen-down sign blocking it, but it opened when he pushed it and he found himself in a tiny backyard where he laid Ben down, then crouched and went back into the corridor, filled with smoke now, feeling his lungs in his chest, feeling them hot there; hearing the breath in his throat, a cardiac wheeze. His hands were heavy and floppy as he reached Lightweight, grabbed him by the shoulders, and dragged him backwards, Lightweight still, incredibly, remaining in the same position – like it was a plaster cast of Lightweight he was dragging, a body found at the foot of a spent volcano.

Then they were collapsing out of the fire door and Max was thinking how he should close it to keep the blaze on the other side. He was thinking it and willing his legs to move and wheezing, grabbing breath at the same time. His eyes were stinging, wet and useless, streaming from the effort of trying to breathe. He stretched out a hand to the door but that hand fell, and the last thing he saw before he lost consciousness was Lightweight lying fighting for breath himself, his leg kicking strangely as he did so, and beyond Lightweight, Ben, and Ben was coughing, but short bursts only, nothing to worry about, which was good, Max thought. At least the boy's okay . . .

At last Chick spoke, having delivered what he felt was a suitably appraising look. One that seemed to say, 'I've got the measure of you,' but could also be interpreted another way, if there wasn't a measure to get. 'There ent no bins to do tonight, Paedo,' he said. 'And, by the looks of you, what you need is to get home and get yourself a good night's sleep. What the fuck you been up to?'

'That was the other thing I wanted to see you about,' said Max. Now he produced the Stanley knife, introduced it into view, clicking the blade out as he did so. Chick didn't flinch; Max would have to stand to reach him anyway. Still, the room's aura crackled at the presentation of the knife; all felt it. Now Chick was thinking of his own knife, still wrapped in the tea-towel on the top, a well-timed leap away. His eyes went to it. Max's eyes followed his and saw nothing, a tea-towel.

'You wanted to show me your new knife?' said Chick, smiling. 'Was that it? It's very nice, mate, yeah. Now put it away, there's a good Paedo, eh? I could get the wrong idea about it, like you're coming into my home and threatening me with it. Threatening me in my own kitchen with my missus standing there and my little boy in the other room. Because if I did think you were doing that I might get very upset indeed.' He jutted his chin and flexed slightly, part of him still thinking about that knife, thinking what he was going to do with it when he got hold of it.

The Stanley knife stayed. Max held it, his elbow on the table. 'You were trying to set me up,' he said.

Chick let out a big breath and pushed himself back in his chair. 'I don't know what you're talking about, mate.'

'You do. You were going to wait until you knew I had Ben, then tell the police, knowing that I'm *Paedo*, so they're bound to go for it, leaving you to collect the reward. I would have told them, you know that. I would have told them it was you.'

Chick laughed, no longer bothering to deny it. 'Course you would. And they'd look into it, only there's no evidence.'

'Apart from the fact that I know you.'

'You work for me, so what? You been round here loads of times and you said a few things that got me worried, so I reported my worries to the authorities, and if they come knocking when you've got the boy in your flat,' he leant forward, face twisting, '*probably about to pull his trousers down*, then what do you expect them to think? You suddenly blaming me ent going to help.'

'The boy, then.'

'Boy ent never seen me.'

Trish said suddenly, 'You what?'

'Just stay out of this a minute, Trish,' warned Chick.

'What do you mean he's never seen you? You been down there with his dinner. How come he's never seen you?'

'Just fucking stay out of it,' snapped Chick, his eyes not leaving Max.

'The depot,' insisted Max, squeezing the handle of the Stanley knife, his hand white around it.

'The kid don't know where he's been kept. The depot was going to be cleaned tonight, and I mean really cleaned.' He mimed striking a match.

Max laughed drily. 'Somebody got there before you.'

'What?' The confident look fell from Chick's face and his eyes flicked to Trish who shook her head, confused, in return.

'The depot was on fire. It was burning. I was inside it. So was the boy.'

'Where is he?' barked Trish.

'Trish,' warned Chick, eyes on the blade. (Thinking about that knife on the side.)

But she ignored him. 'Where is he? What have you done with him?'

She nauseated him. 'He's still in there,' Max said nastily, pointlessly. Just to hurt her at that moment. 'He's dead.'

She sobbed. A hand went to her mouth and she grabbed the side for support.

'It's bullshit,' snapped Chick, pushing himself away from the table as he did so. 'He's fuckin' lyin', Trish.'

Max ignored him. 'There was someone else there, a black guy.'

Chick was shaking his head, though, genuinely confused. 'I don't know what you're talking about. No fucker should have been there tonight.' A harsh sob leapt from behind Trish's hand. 'Shut it, Trish. He ent dead. Paedo's trying to shit us up.'

'You've killed him, Trish,' said Max, evenly.

'No,' she sobbed.

'Sorry, Trish. You've killed him, and you know what's really going to crack you up? You would have gone down, too. Chick knows that. Because it was a woman who took Ben. And that woman was you, and the police are going to know that because I'll tell them and they'll come straight back here, only this time they'll be coming for you. And he knows that's what'll happen. He's trying to give you up just the same as me. Why do you think Ben never saw him? You were going to go down, too.'

'You better shut your mouth, Paedo,' said Chick, controlled. 'And you,' to Trish, 'don't you listen to a fuckin' word.'

Trish had stopped sobbing. She stood with both hands over her face.

Chick looked away from her. 'Nice try, Paedo. Now, I tell you what, I'm getting pretty fucking tired of this. You better put that knife away before I lose my temper.'

'You try and send me to jail for the rest of my life, and it's your temper we should be worried about?' said Max.

Chick's face darkened. 'Listen here, you noncy cunt, you're forgetting who you're talking to. You put that thing away now.' He leant forward. 'Because you ent going to do anything with it anyway, are you, mate?'

He dropped back again. Prove-me-wrong look. Go on, prove me wrong. And Max realised that he was a man who had come armed with a knife he had no intention of using, hoping its mere presence would be enough to get information on who the black man was, knowing now that he was wrong. Still he held the Stanley knife.

Chick crossed his arms, satisfied he was right. 'Well, I'll tell you one thing, Paedo. You're fired.'

'My name is Max,' said Max, 'not Paedo.' He lay in wait for his own anger to come, wanting to climb on to its back and ride into battle, slice at the fat face in front of him.

'Sorry, Paedo, you'll always be Paedo to me. Know you from prison, don't I? Terrible business as well. You seen his wrists, Trish?' She sniffled. 'Churned up they are, not a pretty sight. Could be worse, though, eh, Paedo?' (Chick was thinking of that knife now. A leap to the side, unroll the tea-towel before Max had time to react.) 'It could be worse, couldn't it? Because you could be dead, couldn'tcha? Left up there to bleed to death on hooks, like at the meat-packer's. Only you wasn't, was you? Because someone got you off them hooks.' Max felt his hand shaking, the blade seeming to judder like a faulty speedometer in front of him. 'And who was that who got you off the hooks, Paedo? Do tell.' The Stanley knife shook, Chick thinking, The knife on the side. 'WHO WAS IT?' he bawled, pressing himself forward.

'You,' Max was shocked into saying.

Chick stretched backwards and locked his hands behind his head, saying, 'No, actually, it wasn't.'

'What?' Max was hearing a rushing sound in his head. 'What did you say?'

'Yeah – no. I mean I know I've been kind of taking credit for that one, but I gotta admit I was nothing to do with it. Matter of fact, mate, if I'm totally honest with you, I was one of the blokes getting you on them hooks. And I gotta tell ya, at the risk of upsetting your feelings, like, I was hoping you were going to bleed to death like the other one.' He smiled at Max. 'Like a fuckin' pig.'

There never had been a debt. There was no debt to pay.

'And you know why I wanted you to bleed up there?' said Chick. As Max's face had registered shock he'd minutely edged the chair further away from the table. 'Because you're a dirty pervert and you deserve to die.'

Max looked at him. 'Say that again.'

'By all means. You're a dirty pervert, and you deserve to die.'

The exact wording. 'It was you,' breathed Max. 'You were sending me the letters.'

Why don't you do the world a favour and kill yourself? That was another.

'Yeah,' smiled Chick proudly. 'It was me.'

The Stanley knife shook. 'Why?'

Chick shrugged, smiling. 'Geezer's got to remember his roots. Thought you should remember yours.'

'I didn't . . .' Max's voice was shaking. 'I didn't . . . do anything.'

Chick's mouth was twisted. 'Says you, *Paedo*.'

Those letters, like flames licking round his coffin . . .

And then he was flying forward, the knife swishing in the air. Chick was ready, more than ready. He was up, pushing the kitchen table towards the oncoming figure of Max, reaching the side and grabbing at the knife wrapped in the tea-towel.

Trish got there first.

Perhaps she'd been thinking, Yes, how come Charlie had never revealed himself to Ben? And how was her husband planning on explaining away the woman – her – in the CCTV pictures? Perhaps she was thinking that Max was dead right – she was going to go down, too.

So in one stride she reached the side where Chick's fingers reached for the tea-towel.

And swiped it away so he grabbed at nothing.

An instant of shock, of realisation. Chick reached for her but she backed away and he lunged after her, raising a hand as Max came at him from the side, the knife slashing.

Then Chick was skittering backwards, his hands held in front of him. One was trying to stop the bleeding from the other, but he was going to have to do better than that. The slash was from elbow to wrist. Blood sheeted down his forearm, already a smart spattering sound as it met the kitchen tiles below.

'Fuck,' snarled Chick.

Rancid with hate, Max moved towards him, the Stanley knife held out. Chick backed away. I can do it, thought Max. He could step forward, and slash at that big, fat, self-serving face until it was ragged and bloody and, most of all, ashamed. Cut at the face to obliterate a debt that never was. Slash at the hands that had thrust his on to hooks; that had written letters calling him a pervert. And keep on slashing. Keep on until Chick was burst open and his insides slopped to the kitchen floor and, for just a second, the all-too-brief blink of an eye, there'd be something right with the world.

There was the sound of the Stanley knife ratcheting closed. Max pushed it back into his jeans pocket.

Warily, Chick watched him, still holding his bleeding arm, whimpering. From behind Max, Trish threw him a tea-towel and he picked it up, applied it to the cut. 'Have you got another one, love?' Another tea-towel came sailing over.

Max turned. 'I'm going,' he said.

Trish stood, face streaked with tears, watching her Judas husband trying to stem the bleeding. 'He ent really dead, is he?' she said. 'Please say. He isn't, is he?'

Max looked at her, a woman who'd been on a tube train one day, who, unlike her fellow passengers, had not chosen to ignore the frightened little boy on his own, who had probably, Max thought – at least in the beginning – wanted to do the right thing.

He went to the door. 'No, he's not dead,' he replied. 'No thanks to you.'

9

Lightweight, who could read perfectly, recognised Ben Snape at once. After he'd finished coughing and spitting a red-flecked greeny, and looking dispassionately at the unconscious Max – a man who had just saved his life, and who now lay dangerously close to the fire – he hobbled over to Ben, wearing what he hoped was a friendly, trustworthy smile, and in strangulated tones reassured Ben that he was going to look after him.

Which he did by taking Ben to a drug-dealer and trading him for some rocks of crack, to help with the pain.

'What *the fuck* do you think you're doing?' screeched LaDonna, who, as far as Warren was concerned, was 'with her girls'; not that he would have cared either way. On Lightweight's arrival she'd escaped to another room. Now Lightweight sat in the front room being comforted by a glass pipe, a Clipper and the DVD that, until five minutes ago, LaDonna had been watching with her man Dog Years. She bet the sofa was still warm; her cup of tea was there as well – not that she had any intention of going to fetch it with that animal in there.

'What *the fuck* do you think you're doing?' she repeated. She was standing at the bedroom door, ready for action. 'Whatchoo letting him stay for? Get him out of here.'

LaDonna suddenly clapped a hand to her mouth, only just noticing Ben, who stood beside Dog Years, his eyes wide, otherwise miraculously unperturbed. He was just glad, really, not to have to spend any more time with the thin man who kept patting his head.

'Who are you, darling?' said LaDonna, hard heart softening at the sight of the little boy.

'He's your new best mate,' said Dog Years, palming his mobile.

Indicating the bedroom he commanded, 'Get him in there and play some Xbox till I get my shit together.'

'What?' bridled LaDonna. 'I ent no fuckin' babysitter.'

'Keep it down,' urged Dog Years, a look down the hall to the front room where Lightweight sat. 'I think . . . I think . . .' Over Ben's head, as if the boy wouldn't hear him, he was mouthing, '*It's that kid*,' but LaDonna either didn't understand or chose not to, screwing up her face. In the end Dog Years gave up. 'Look, I just need to get some shit sorted, man, and I'll be back. I just need you to take care of him for a bit.'

'I don't even know how to *work* the fuckin' Xbox,' she spat.

'I do,' said Ben. She pursed her lips and looked down at him.

'That settles it, then,' said Dog Years, and for a moment the three of them were a little family unit.

'Here y'go,' said LaDonna at last, holding out a terrifyingly garish hand. Ben took it and regarded her nails. She regarded his. Together they went into the bedroom, where Ben showed LaDonna the finer points of Halo – she turned out to be very good at it.

Meanwhile, out in the flat, Lightweight continued relaxing with his pipe as two of Dog Years's young friends arrived, their BMX bikes parked in the forecourt downstairs. They said hello to Lightweight, who regarded them with distaste, coughing, flicking the Clipper. Then the young mates did as Dog Years asked, which was to receive a holdall full of drugs paraphernalia. A confused Lightweight gave up his pipe to one of the youngsters who insinuated it was to be refreshed, then took it away, added it to the contents of the bag, then left. Dog Years watched them go, then made another phone call. He went back to the bedroom.

A question from Lightweight followed him as he went: 'Whass going on, man?' He sounded hoarse, his teeth set.

'Relax, man,' Dog Years called back. 'Be back in a sec, yeah?'

'Where you been?' accused LaDonna as he entered the bedroom, not taking her eyes off the TV screen.

He ignored her, bending down to Ben who sat in awe of

LaDonna's vicious joypad skills. 'Hey, little man,' he said. 'Let's just get it clear how things panned out here, yeah? Cos the police are going to arrive in a minute . . .'

'*The police.*' This from LaDonna.

'Just shut up a minute.' He turned back to Ben. 'And they're gonna ask you some questions, and I just want to make sure you're going to tell them the truth about how me and my girl looked after you here, okay?'

There was a knock at the front door. A pounding, really.

'That'll be them now,' said Dog Years, standing.

It was quite some battle.

After opening the door to four uniformed officers, and leading one into the bedroom, Dog Years joined Ben, LaDonna and the WPC as her colleagues attempted to arrest Lightweight. 'Best just wait here,' the WPC had said, so all four sat on the bed listening to the sounds of struggle from the front room. Dog Years marvelled at how the policemen stoically stuck to their lines; how they continued to refer to Lightweight as 'sir', even though he was high on crack and had kicked one of them in the bollocks, spat at another.

'They better be careful of my TV,' said Dog Years to the WPC, who grimaced sympathetically. 'You're paying for my stuff if you break it, man,' he warned.

Abruptly the noise of strife ceased.

'Perhaps you should just wait here,' said the WPC, but almost as soon as she had left the room Dog Years followed her up the corridor and entered his front room to see the cops gathered round, staring down at the body of Lightweight. There was a kind of hush, like little boys just broken Mum's favourite ornament. The WPC was kneeling and, as Dog Years entered the room, she was shaking her head, saying, 'He's dead.'

The policemen all looked at one another. They didn't know it yet, but in the struggle one of Lightweight's ribs had broken free of its moorings, puncturing his heart and killing him. All four of the officers in attendance were about to get a long holiday as Lightweight's death was investigated.

Dog Years, meanwhile, was staring at his TV, dirty great footmark on the screen, thinking, Someone's gonna pay if that's damaged.

But Max left Chick's home knowing none of this. He pulled the door closed behind him and went quickly down the stairs, away from the estate, trying one, two, three phone boxes before he found one that worked, and made a call that was relayed to a car already on its way to Neesmith House. The occupants, one of them Detective Sergeant Simon 'Cy' Cyston, were told that in light of this new information they'd be wanting backup, and when that backup arrived one of the officers was Detective Inspector Merle, who accompanied Cy to the door.

They knocked and immediately there was the sound of running feet and a shout, 'Carl!' from Trish. 'Get in there!'

But no one came to the door. They knocked again. Cy and Merle looked at each other, sighing. Leaning down, Merle thumbed up the letterbox. 'Trish,' he called. 'Trish, it's DI Merle. We know you're in there, love, why don't you come and answer the door?' He felt himself flex a little. Trisha Campbell. She's had a boob job.

'It's Charlie,' she called from the kitchen, voice echoey. 'He's had an accident.'

'Dad!' yelled Carl.

'No, just stay in there, love,' from Trish.

Merle tutted. 'Just open the door, Trish.'

'He needs the hospital.'

'All right. Well, let's have a look at him. We'll get him an ambulance.'

Through the letterbox Merle saw Trish at the kitchen door, Chick with her, a huge, blood-sodden sleeve of tea-towels round his arm.

'Cut yourself shaving, have you?' said Merle.

Chick peered down to where the letterbox was being held open. 'I need the hospital, Merlin. I require urgent medical treatment.'

Merle frowned and straightened as the door opened. The two of them were already trying to move out into the walkway, like a pair of old soldiers returning from battle. For a second or so he was diverted by Trisha Campbell, and thought of how Karen would ask him later: 'How did she look, then, the girl you wanted me to be more like at school?' And how he'd answer, truthfully, 'Not a patch on you, Kaz,' and how she'd accuse him of fibbing anyway.

Then, 'Wait a second, wait a second,' he said, holding up his hands and stopping them. 'We're acting on some information here. No one's going anywhere. We'll wait *here* for the ambulance, all right? *Inside.*'

'What are you talking about?' managed Chick. Merle thought he was probably playing up the poorly soldier bit.

'I'm talking about information we've had regarding your involvement with the disappearance of Ben Snape. An allegation that you have important evidence pertaining to the investigation actually in your flat. So we'd like to take a look round, and we can wait for the ambulance while we're doing it, okay?'

Chick looked shocked for the second time that evening, genuinely so. One thing he knew, there wasn't a single thing in that flat connecting him with Ben Snape. Anything now was circumstantial.

Beside Merle, Cy started, his eye caught by something behind Trish and Chick. Merle craned around. MC Carl was standing behind his parents, just appeared from the front room, unable to contain his curiosity any longer.

Merle and Cy looked at one another. Cy said, 'All right, Carl? Do you want to tell me where you got the hat and the sticker album from?'

'I'm sorry, but I haven't brought you a cake with a file in it or anything,' said Sophie, looking around the visitors' room then back at Dash. She was only his second visitor. First, Mum and Dad, counting as one, had crowded on the other side of the desk, leaning into each other for support, desperately trying to be as upbeat as possible. 'Well, it's not *too* bad,' they said, inspecting the room as if they were about to say the place could do with a lick of paint. All three decided to ignore the knocking sound coming from the table next to them, the low urging of the prisoner, the resigned industry of his female visitor.

Dash studied Sophie now. Despite the joke, he could tell that the experience – the queuing, the search, the constant threat, whine and hate of the other prisoners' girlfriends or wives – had shaken her. Beneath pints of fake tan she was strangely pale. Still, though, she was here. Good of her to come. He laughed. 'That's all right, Soph. Thanks for coming anyway.'

She looked at him. 'Well, you still owe me a load of cash.'

He looked ashamed. 'Sorry.'

'That's okay,' she replied, mollified, then wagged a pretend-angry finger at him. 'But I *do* want it back. So you better start sewing mailbags or whatever it is you do in here.'

The court had laughed when, in his defence, it was revealed that the depot was due to be burnt down anyway. Perhaps the judge took pity on him. It was a custodial sentence, but short; the solicitor seemed to think it was a great success as they were dragging Dash to the back of the room in handcuffs. If he was honest with himself, it could have been worse, and at least Sophie had been contacting him. (She was preparing something on how she couldn't get enough of her bad-lad boyfriend, the diary of her break-up having been well liked but not quite the door-opener she had thought it would be – not until she mentioned how Dash had been sent to prison.)

She leant forward. 'Here,' she said. 'Are you anybody's *bitch* yet?'

He tutted and shook his head. 'It's not like that. People don't go around having bitches. Not my category anyway.'

She looked a mix of impressed and scandalised. 'Ooh, are you a "category" prisoner, then?'

'Everybody has a category.' He sighed.

'Oh.' She sounded disappointed. 'But your category is one that doesn't have bitches?'

'Well, I don't know about everyone else, all I can tell you is about me.'

'And you're not anyone's bitch?'

'Soph,' he leant forward, pointing at himself, 'perhaps *I* have a bitch.'

'Oh. Well . . . do you?'

'No.'

'Oh. Why did you say that, then?'

'Nothing. Doesn't matter.'

'Well, what do bitches do, anyway?'

He looked around to check that no one was listening. 'Favours and stuff.'

'Sex stuff?'

Motioning with his hands for her to keep it down, he whispered, 'Not always, no. Look, can we stop talking about bitches now, please?' Funny, this subject had never cropped up when his parents had visited.

'Okay, okay. It's just that there's a bloke over there who keeps staring at you. I wondered if you were his bitch, that was all.'

Dash turned to look behind him and returned the man's wave as their eyes met. 'No,' he said, turning back to Sophie. 'No, he's just a bloke, that's all.'

'Who is he?'

'Never you mind, all right? He's a bad bloke, that's all you need to know.'

'Ooh, is he? Really? What's he in for?'

For Dash, some habits would never die. He leant forward conspiratorially. 'You know the kid who was in the warehouse?' he said.

'Yeah.'

'To do with that.' He lowered his voice even more. 'In for a long stretch.'

'Really? Long?'

'Oh, yuh. *Long*.'

'Life?'

'Might as well be.'

'And he's a mate of yours?'

Dash nodded sagely. 'We look out for each other, yeah.'

'Really?'

'Yeah. Look, Soph, keep your voice down, okay?'

'Okay, okay,' she said, casting a look at the man across the way, thinking, despite herself, Cool. 'Listen,' she said. 'I was thinking, maybe, after you get out of here – perhaps we could give it another go.'

It was his turn to say, too loudly, '*Really?*' There was a high note in his voice he didn't want misinterpreted. 'Really?' he corrected, more deeply.

She softened her eyes. 'Yes,' she said gently. 'I think I'd like to.'

'I'd like that too,' he said, the pair of them like two amateur actors saying their lines. For a moment or so they looked dreamily into each other's eyes and Dash imagined things getting back to the way they'd once been. He wanted to ask about Peter. He knew there'd been some kind of fall-out over money, but other than that, the details he'd been given were hazy.

'But I tell you one thing,' she added. 'You're going to have to seriously make it up to me, okay?' He nodded. She smiled and looked around the visitors' room, thinking about those Gucci sunglasses she'd had her eye on.

A bell rang to signal the end of the period and Sophie stood up, her confidence draining a little. She was already dreading the return journey. Dash stood, too, and they gave each other a kiss that Dash wanted to be all mouths and tongues and restrained passion, but Sophie made into a little peck by turning her cheek and stretching her mouth out of the way.

'You'll come back, then?' he said, after the messy kiss.

'Of course,' she replied.

He smiled at her, said mawkishly, 'I think we deserve each other,' a desperate attempt at romance in the visitors' room, predominant scent of smoke, body odour, and maybe something even worse.

Lust for my Bad-Lad Boyfriend? she was thinking. No. *Jailbird Boyfriend Won't Let Go.* That was much better.

'Yeah,' she replied dreamily. 'We deserve each other.'

As they went their separate ways, Dash was filled with a warm, fuzzy feeling that things were going to be all right. After all that, they were going to be all right. The feeling lasted until he was approached by his mate, the bloke Sophie had seen looking their way.

'All right, Dashus?' said Chick.

'All right,' sighed Dash.

'All right, what?'

'All right, boss.'

'Much better. That your girlfriend, was it?'

'Yeah, that was her.'

'Very nice. Strange colour but very nice. Wouldn't mind a go on that myself. Now, whatchoo got planned for later?'

Dash pushed his hands into his pockets. 'Cinema. Nightclub. Maybe a round of golf earlier on.'

'You what?'

'Nothing, boss. I ent got anything on is what I meant.'

'Good,' smiled Chick. 'Cos there's a couple of errands I want running – all right?'

'Yes,' said Dash, suddenly very, very tired. 'Yes, boss.'

*   *   *

Ben thought often of the man who had sung 'Yellow Submarine' to him. As rescue attempts went, his had not been without its flaws, seeing as how Ben had ended up in the clutches of Lightweight, then in the home of Dog Years, who, thankfully, had alerted the police. Nevertheless, Max was often in Ben's thoughts.

The house on Cowley Close had been different when he returned to it, and he knew instinctively that his absence was why. When he had been reunited with his father, the two had hugged each other and when Ben had tried to break away from the hug, Pat had continued it. At last Ben became aware of a snuffling sound above his head and he realised his father was crying, which made him cry, too, because he'd never known his dad to cry before. It was scary.

'I'm sorry,' he said, the crying somehow his fault.

Pat dropped to his knees and held his son's face. 'No,' he said, 'don't be sorry. I'm crying because I'm so pleased to see you, Ben. We've . . . missed you.'

We've missed you. Shorthand for, We feared the worst, and worse than the worst. In the darkest of moments we feared for sick visitations on your little body and we would find ourselves shaking, uncontrollably, in the heart of midnight. We feared you might be dead. We even hoped you might be dead rather than suffer badly. We thought we might never see you again. We blamed ourselves, and in even darker moments we blamed each other.

'I missed you, too,' he replied.

He bore the weight of his parents' relief. There were times when, if he could have vocalised how he felt, he would have exclaimed, exasperated, 'I'm here now. Stop *staring* at me!' For ages they seemed always-present. One or other of them was always touching him, grooming him as an excuse to touch him. For around six months after his release from the Auridial depot in Walthamstow, Ben never had a hair out of place, was never shirt-untucked, no stray crumbs or chocolate smears on him. He was Kettering's own Dandy Dan.

Chicken McNuggets were never spoken of at Cowley Close.

Ben had gone off them. He announced it one morning shortly after his release, saying, primly, 'I don't like Chicken McNuggets any more.' Pat and Deborah looked at each other across the kitchen table, Deborah stroking her son's arm. The same for beans and sausages.

Neither was Max ever spoken of. Not after the first time, when Ben came down for breakfast and met the same daily expectant gaze of his parents, felt the gratitude and love there.

'Morning, darling,' Deborah instantly up, fussing about Ben, 'here,' wiping the sleep from his eyes, pulling out a chair and reaching for the cereal. (His favourite cereal – everything now was his favourite. Ben found himself pining for the days when he was forced to do things he didn't want to do.) 'Did you sleep well?'

He sipped his juice and looked up at his parents, who stared down at him as though they expected him to disappear in a puff of smoke. It could be wearing, sometimes, the constant, grateful scrutiny.

'I saw the man last night,' he said.

They looked at each other. 'What man?' they chimed.

'The man who sang "Yellow Submarine",' he replied evenly.

'Was it in a dream?' said Pat.

'No, in real life.'

They looked at each other again. 'Whereabouts, Ben?' said Pat, voice loaded with worry. 'Whereabouts did you see the man?'

Ten minutes later Pat was on the phone, ringing Merle who told him that, no, Max had not been picked up. He was wanted for questioning, but there were no charges pending; he wasn't considered to be a danger.

'Why do you ask, Pat?' said Merle.

'Is it possible he could have made his way here?' said Pat.

'Well, yes, he's been there before. But, again, why do you ask?'

Because Ben had been in his bedroom the previous night. He'd been up late playing a new Mario game on his new Game Boy. Peering between a gap in his curtains he had looked out into the recreation ground behind his house and seen the climbing frame there. On the climbing frame he saw the 'Yellow Submarine' man. He knew it was the 'Yellow Submarine' man because of the big coat he wore, and because, when he waved, shyly, before closing his curtains and going back to sleep, feeling safe and warm and – that word – loved, the 'Yellow Submarine' man had waved back.

ACKNOWLEDGEMENTS

Thank you so much to Jaime Smith, who saved my iBook and its contents, which I hadn't backed up, and some of which you've just finished reading. Relief doesn't even cover it. Thank you also to those who helped with the writing of this book. They are: my agent, Antony Topping, my editor, Amber Burlinson, Lucy Fawcett, Dave Taylor, Andrew Gordon and Rob Waugh, who gave it early read-throughs, Hannah Markham for telling me about the hooks, and Neil Wileman for procedural pointers. I'd also like to thank, for other and assorted reasons, Henry Jeffreys and Jocasta Brownlee at Hodder, Louise Sherwin-Stark and everybody in Hodder sales, Ellie Glason at Greene & Heaton, Katy Follain, Toby, Sarah and Daniel, Mum and Dad, Granny, Dave, Nat and Georgina, Joanna Anderson, David Roberts, Sam Baker and Kate Monument, David and Maria Granger, Alex Simmons, Steve O'Hagan, Nick Taylor, John Dilley, Julia Gasiorowska, Gerald Mowles, Eddie Lloyd-Williams, Neil Mason at War Child, and, most of all, Claire.

ANDREW HOLMES

Sleb

Here's a top tip for the heavy drinker: never get drunk and force your way into the home of the country's biggest pop star, wielding a gun. It's bound to go off, big time.

Christopher Sewell is famous. He used to be an advertising sales executive with a wife, a drink problem and not much more. Now he's serving life for the murder of Felix Carter, who used to be a famous pop star with an acting career, a drink problem and the world at his feet. Only he's dead now. How and why Chris killed Felix is a mystery. Until, that is, he agrees to give a single interview from prison. Just the one interview, mind. You know what these celebrities are like . . .

'A thoughtful study, as well as a gripping psychological thriller'
Independent on Sunday

'Ingenious twist . . . Holmes has a great line in drunken, rage-filled monologues that collapse into pathos. Very funny'
Literary Review

'Holmes is a very funny storyteller'
The Times

'Tragic, funny, touching . . . [*Sleb*] succeeds through brilliant characterisation and a cunningly devised plot. A talent to watch'
Big Issue in the North

'Deliciously sharp celebrity satire'
Heat

'A fascinating insight into the nature of celebrity and obsession'
Red

'[*Sleb*] is not only a brilliant satire on the shallow times we live in, but also a moving portrait of the disintegration of one man's life'
Hello!

'A funny and enjoyable book . . . Holmes's caustic perspective manages to hit the mark'
Express on Sunday

SCEPTRE

ANDREW HOLMES

All Fur Coat

What happens when two men become dangerously obsessed with the same woman?

One, the ex-pop star with his glory days a distant memory. The other, an artist with a dark past and an even darker future. And the girl? She's a lap dancer at All Fur Coat, but she desperately wants to be a model. She doesn't know it yet, but she's playing a very risky game. By the end of the week, nothing will ever be the same again.

A dazzling, pacy and darkly comic novel about addiction, ambition and obsession, by the acclaimed author of *Sleb*.

'I am very jealous of Andrew Holmes. This is
mean, twisted and hilarious'
Jenny Éclair

'Andrew Holmes is one of very few writers whose
characters truly leap off the page. His novels are so spot-on
it's scary. You don't read his prose . . . you live it'
Matt Thorne

'[Holmes] showcases a genius for the sort of venomous one-
liners mere mortals can only dream of'
Mirror

'Holmes's second novel is a slick, seedy affair that bears
comparison with Martin Amis's *London Fields* . . .
exceptionally visceral writing'
Scotland on Sunday

'Fun and punchy'
Big Issue

'A compelling page-turner with a twisted
sense of humour'
Star

SCEPTRE